Your Beautiful Lies

Louise Douglas

TRANSWORLD PUBLISHERS
61–63 Uxbridge Road, London W5 5SA
A Random House Group Company
www.transworldbooks.co.uk

YOUR BEAUTIFUL LIES
A BLACK SWAN BOOK: 9780552779265

First publication in Great Britain
Black Swan edition published 2014

A CIP catalogue record for this book is available from the British Library.

Addresses for Random House Group Ltd companies outside the UK can be found at: www.randomhouse.co.uk
The Random House Group Ltd Reg. No. 954009

The Random House Group Limited supports the Forest Stewardship Council® (FSC®), the leading international forest-certification organisation. Our books carrying the FSC label are printed on FSC®-certified paper. FSC is the only forest-certification scheme supported by the leading environmental organisations, including Greenpeace. Our paper procurement policy can be found at www.randomhouse.co.uk/environment

Typeset in 11/14.5pt Giovanni Book by Falcon Oast Graphic Art Ltd.
Printed and bound by CPI Group (UK) Ltd, Croydon, CR0 4YY.

2 4 6 8 10 9 7 5 3 1

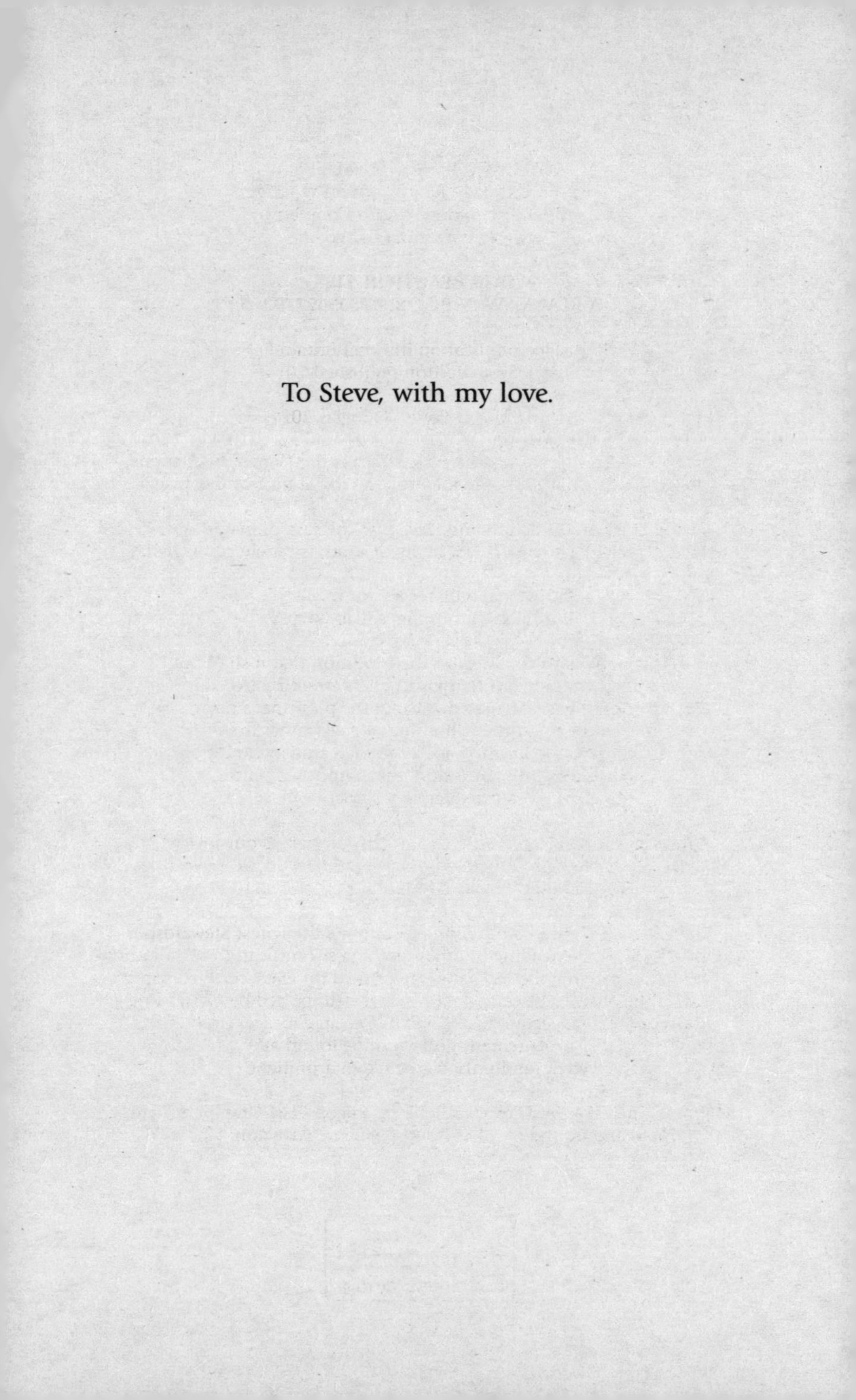

To Steve, with my love.

CHAPTER ONE

Matlow, South Yorkshire, March 1984

Annie Howarth woke with a feeling of absolute dread.

She did not know what had disturbed her. She opened her eyes slowly and looked around. She was at home in the master bedroom at Everwell and everything seemed to be as normal.

It must have been a bad dream, she thought, *that's all.*

She climbed out of the bed and went over to the window, pulling back the curtains and gazing out at the moors. Then she turned to look at the photograph on the wall. It was of her wedding day in April 1975, nine years earlier. Annie and William were standing together outside the church with his colleagues from the South Yorkshire police forming a guard of honour behind. William looked grand in his formal police regalia. Beside him stood his best man, Paul

Fleming, smiling broadly. Annie, on William's other side, looked young and anxious, clutching her flowers.

She was dressing when William came into the room, wearing one of the trademark suits he favoured because the colour matched both his hair and his eyes. He put her coffee on the bedside table, rested his hand on her shoulder, at the base of her neck. She pressed her cheek into his hand.

'Do you have to go now?' she asked. 'It's so early.'

'Yes, I do. I'm meeting the Chief Constable of Nottinghamshire.'

'And he's more interesting than me?'

'Of course not, but needs must, Annie.'

'I know, I know.' Annie moved away. She opened the wardrobe door and looked inside. 'What is it today that's so important? The miners' strike again?'

'What else? I suspect it's going to be a long, tiresome day.' He sighed but Annie could already sense an eagerness in him to be away and to be attending to his job. 'Would you pick up my shirt from the dry cleaner's?' he went on. 'I'll need it for the dinner dance tomorrow.'

'Yes, of course. I'm going into town to see Mum today anyway.'

'I'll see you later, then.'

'OK.' She held up her face to him and he kissed her forehead.

'You won't forget the shirt?'

'I won't.'

Annie listened to William's footsteps on the stairs, and mentally followed his progress as he turned off the music in his study and locked the door, put his coffee cup in the sink in the kitchen, picked up his briefcase, walked across the hall, checked his appearance in the mirror, then opened and closed the front door. Outside, she heard his footsteps on the gravel and then a pause as he climbed into his car, fastened the seatbelt and checked that he had everything he needed for the day, as he always did. After enough time had elapsed for William to finish this routine, she heard the Jaguar's engine breathe into life and its quiet crackle over the gravel and down the drive. She listened until the car had turned into the lane and driven away. Then she finished dressing and went to wake her seven-year-old daughter.

Elizabeth's room was along the landing, close to her grandmother Ethel's. Annie pushed open the door and went inside, stepping over toys and books to reach the bed. She leaned over the child, smoothing the fair hair from her forehead.

'Hey, sleepyhead,' she whispered. 'Wake up.'

Elizabeth wriggled further down the bed. 'No,' she said, her voice muffled. 'I don't want to.'

'You have to, chicken, or you'll be late for school.'

'I don't want to go to school today.'

'Tough. You have to.'

Annie picked up Scooby, the toy dog that went

everywhere with Elizabeth, and made him nuzzle at her neck. The child giggled and sat up. Then she cocked her head, listening to a sound in the distance.

'What's that?'

'What's what?'

'It's a motorbike! It's Johnnie, Mummy! Why has Johnnie come so early?'

Mother and daughter scrambled to the window and peered out. A motorbike was bumping up the drive, a young man hunched over the handlebars. Elizabeth waved frantically and Annie watched as her younger brother pulled his Yamaha up outside the house, kicked down the stand and took off his helmet. He crunched towards the front door.

'I'll go down and see what he wants,' said Annie. 'You get yourself dressed, Lizzie.'

'But I want to see Johnnie!'

'Dress first.'

Annie ran down the staircase and into the hall, which was large, light and airy with an ornate Indian rug in the centre. She opened the front door and there was her younger brother standing on the doorstep with his helmet tucked underneath his arm, swinging the key fob in the shape of the A-Team van on one finger. Behind him, the sun was already high over the moors, colouring last year's bracken a red so bright that it seemed as if the hills were alight.

Annie crossed her arms and looked her brother up and down.

'You've grown taller even since last week,' she said.

'Oh, get off,' said Johnnie.

'But no better-looking. What are you doing here so early? Do you want to come in for a bit? I can make you a cup of tea.'

He shook his head. 'I have to get to the colliery,' he said. 'I just wanted to tell you that—'

'Johnnie!' Elizabeth came galloping down the stairs, the buttons on her blouse undone, her school tunic unzipped and her socks in her hand. She threw herself at her uncle and he picked her up. She wrapped her arms and legs around him and clung to him. 'You've got to come in and have some breakfast,' she said. 'It's the law.'

'Says who?'

'Me. And I'm the boss!'

Johnnie grinned. 'Well, if Miss Elizabeth Howarth says so, who am I to argue?'

They followed each other into the kitchen. Elizabeth wore her uncle's helmet while she gulped down her cereal, and Annie made tea and toast. She put a mug down in front of Johnnie.

'Well,' she said, 'go on then. What is it? What did you come here to tell me?'

Johnnie took a deep breath. He glanced at Elizabeth and said quietly, 'Tom Greenaway's back.'

'I thought he was still in prison,' Annie said.

'No, he's out. I was talking to him not ten minutes

ago. I stopped off for petrol and he was there in front of me, filling up his truck.'

Annie spread honey on the toast, making a mess of it. She pushed the plate towards Johnnie.

'I wasn't sure who he was at first. He came over to me, all friendly-like, and he said: "It's Johnnie Jackson, isn't it?", I said it was and he said: "Well, you won't remember me – you were only a kid when I went away, but I used to go out with your sister." And then it clicked.' Johnnie picked up the toast and pushed the whole slice into his mouth. Annie put another on the plate.

'Who's Tom Greenaway?' asked Lizzie.

'No one,' Annie and Johnnie said together. Lizzie shrugged. She pretended to be making the key fob drive around the kitchen table but Annie could tell she was listening.

Johnnie went on: 'He asked what I was doing and why I wasn't on strike, and I told him I was working in the kitchens at the colliery – that it were only the miners that were out, not the support workers.'

'You'd have thought he'd have known that.'

'Mmm.' Johnnie took a drink of tea. 'Then he asked if I wanted to see his truck.' He said to his niece: 'Pass me the sugar, Lizzie. Ta. It's a good 'un – a Ford pick-up. Writing on the side an' all. I said: "You're doing all right for yourself," and he said, "Yes, I am." Apparently he's been out of prison for a while now and has started up his own business – laying hedges and tree-felling and the like. Greenaway Garden Services, it's called.'

'He was always one for the outdoors,' Annie said quietly.

'He asked about you – how you were, what you were doing, if you were all right.'

'Did you tell him anything?'

'I didn't think you'd want me to.'

'No.'

'I'm not daft, Annie.'

'I know you're not.'

'You *are* daft,' Lizzie whispered.

'And you're a cheeky bugger,' Johnnie whispered back.

'Go upstairs and brush your teeth, love,' Annie told her.

Johnnie waited until the child had gone, then he pushed back his chair and stood up.

'Tom asked me to give you this,' he said. He took a folded piece of paper from the pocket of his jacket. 'I was going to throw it away, but he said it were important. He made me promise.'

Annie took the paper. She wrapped it in her fingers, pressed it into the palm of her hand.

'I told him you wouldn't read it. I told him you wouldn't have owt to do with him ever again. Was that right, Annie?'

'Yes,' she said. 'That was exactly right.' She smiled at her brother, reached up to kiss his cheek. And then, while he was watching, she opened the door to the old coal-fired stove and dropped the paper, still folded, into the flames.

CHAPTER TWO

Annie made up a tray for William's mother, as she did every morning. She was scooping the boiled egg out of the pan with a spoon when Mrs Miller, the private nurse, came in through the back door.

'Morning!' she said cheerfully. 'And what a lovely one, too. It feels like spring out there.' She shrugged off her coat. Annie slipped the egg into the egg cup on the tray.

'About time it picked up a bit,' she replied. 'Right – this is all ready for you to take up, Mrs M. The tea's fresh in the pot and there's toast and a bit of that apricot jam that Ethel likes.'

'That's grand,' said Mrs Miller. She put her voluminous handbag down on the kitchen table, opened it, and rummaged inside. Elizabeth, who was ready for school, sidled over. 'Ooh – look what I've found,' Mrs Miller said. 'A Finger of Fudge. Do you know anyone who might like that, Lizzie?'

Elizabeth smiled shyly. 'Me?' she suggested.

'Oh! You? Well, I never would have thought. You'd best take it then.' Mrs Miller passed the chocolate to the child. 'Save it for your elevenses,' she advised.

'Thank you, Mrs Miller.'

'You're welcome, pet.'

'Come on now, Lizzie, we're going to be late,' Annie said. She opened the back door, Elizabeth ran through and Annie called goodbye to Mrs Miller.

They followed the path round to the front garden and Elizabeth skipped to the spot on the lawn where she always stood to wave goodbye to her grandmother. Ethel Howarth liked to look out from the little square window of her bedroom in the gable end of the house. Sometimes she forgot she had a granddaughter and did not come to the window at all. That morning though, when Annie and Elizabeth looked up, Ethel was there, her face a pale shadow behind the glass.

'I'm going to do a cartwheel for Grandma,' Elizabeth announced, throwing her satchel onto the lawn.

'Quick then,' said Annie.

She shielded her eyes from the sun and looked at the house. Everwell had been built a century earlier for the family who originally owned the Matlow colliery. The house had been named after the well in the back garden and had changed hands twice before William bought it back in 1971 with money he'd inherited from his father. He'd had the building sympathetically refurbished and modernised before he married Annie. From the outside,

Everwell was still as beautiful as it had been when it was first built. An old wisteria was draping its new spring leaves around the faces of the mullioned windows. The garden sloped downhill, daffodils bobbing at the edges of the lawn, lines of 100-year-old beech on either side of the gravel drive. The derelict gamekeeper's cottage that William would, one day, either renovate or knock down stood beside the wall of the home meadow, and beyond was the sweep of the moor, rising 400 yards away beneath a perfect blue sky.

It was a beautiful place to live. Sometimes, even now, Annie could not quite believe her luck, how far she had come.

After dropping Elizabeth off at her private school, she drove her Volkswagen Golf down towards the town. The colliery had been built on the side of the hill, its buildings, slagheaps, wheels and towers looming over the town. Annie had to slow and stop the car because a crowd of men had gathered around the gates and were blocking the road. An older man in a jacket and trilby was addressing the men through a megaphone; she couldn't hear what he was saying, only the boom and echo of his voice. Some of the men were standing or sitting on the boundary wall; others were grouped on the road, smoking and laughing into their collars. A couple of police officers were talking with them, sharing jokes and cigarettes. The older men were muscular and stringy, their faces beneath flat caps hollowed out from years of working underground. The younger ones had longish hair. A few were still wearing flared jeans. Matlow was always a couple of years behind the rest of Yorkshire when it came to fashion. Annie looked at the faces and recognised a few of them. She had been at school with some of these men, back when they were boys.

As she inched the car forward a few feet, she heard a burst of crude laughter. Were the men laughing at her? Mocking her? She knew the townspeople still called her names behind her back – her mother, Marie, had told her they did. Perhaps the men sitting on the wall recalled the days when she lived in Matlow and worked in the typing pool at the Town Hall. Perhaps they remembered that she had once been Tom Greenaway's girlfriend.

Annie exhaled shakily. She was moving very slowly, just a few feet at a time. Then suddenly a shout went up somewhere in the crowd and those around her dropped their cigarettes and moved away, huddling closer together. Fumbling with the gearstick, she put the car into second and accelerated away.

Annie drove on past the new housing estate and into the older part of town, past the Salvation Army hostel and the shell of the 1960s shopping centre with its graffiti and broken glass. She turned by the municipal baths, stopped at the dry cleaner's to pick up William's shirt, and then headed back towards the lines of residential streets that tottered down the side of the hill, the terraced houses built for the miners and their families.

Both Annie and Johnnie had been born in the front bedroom of number 122 Rotherham Road, in the bed their parents still shared. As Annie pulled up outside the house, Marie Jackson opened the door. Annie stepped into the gloom of the narrow hall and allowed herself to be hugged by her mother in the small space between the stairs and the coats and jackets hung on the hooks by the door. Marie's arms were strong and sinewed, her bleached hair tied in a bun, hoops through her ears and her face made up as it always was, her eyes outlined in black beneath plucked arches of eyebrows.

In the kitchen, the kettle was already on the boil and slices of home-made parkin, black and sticky as tar, had been sliced and buttered. Beyond the window was the yard – the dustbins, last year's Christmas tree, parts of a push-bike that someone had given Johnnie, and a rabbit hutch. Annie's father's two whippets were lying on an old blanket in a patch of sunlight.

'Where's Dad?' Annie asked. 'I thought he was off today.'

'He's gone up the pit to hear what the Union has to say. They want to get everyone out.'

'I saw a crowd up there. They all looked in a good mood.'

'Aye well, this is one battle they can't lose. The whole country's behind them.'

On the hob, the kettle began to jump and whistle.

'Go and have a seat in the front room, Annie. I'll bring the tea.'

Annie went into the living room and perched on the seat of her father's chair by the window that overlooked the street. The brown fabric of the armrests had been worn shiny by his elbows and hands, and the springs had gone in the seat cushion. The room smelled of coal, and a brown sheen of cigarette smoke had been laid down over the years, giving everything an ochre tint.

Marie came in with the tray and put it on the table.

'Everything all right with you, Annie?' she asked. 'You're looking a bit peaky.'

'I'm all right.'

'Go on, spit it out. What's mithering you?'

'Nothing. I just . . . Oh, Mum – did you know that Tom Greenaway's back in town?'

'Oh,' Marie said. 'It didn't take long for word to reach you.' She sat down heavily and reached down the side of the couch for her cigarettes and ashtray.

'You knew?'

'I ran into Sadie Wallace the other day. She told me.'

'What did she say?'

'Not much. Not to me. She still gives me the cold shoulder after what your Tom did to her grandma.'

'If Sadie had paid a bit more attention to her grandma in the first place instead of leaving her in that awful bungalow all on her own, then . . .'

'All right, all right,' said Marie. 'Let's not start all that again.'

She offered a cigarette to Annie, who shook her head.

'Does Dad know he's back?'

'Don't be soft. Do you think your Tom—'

'He's not *my* Tom.'

'Do you think he'd still be in one piece if your dad got wind of it? Best thing for everyone would be if Tom Greenaway went back to whatever hole he's crawled out from.'

'Yes. That would be best.'

Marie lit the end of her Embassy. Then she said: 'Anyroad, you'd best watch yourself, Annie. Be careful. Mind what you say.'

'Oh, let people talk if they want. It doesn't bother me.'

'It's not the talk I'm worried about.'

'What then?'

'I mean, what's Tom Greenaway come back for if he's not come back for you?'

'Matlow was his home. He doesn't know anywhere else.'

'He knows he's not welcome here. His family are long gone. He's been saying he wants to clear his name, but nobody's interested. There's nothing for him here that I can think of.'

'There might be a perfectly good reason.'

'Aye, and he might be after finishing what he started with you.'

Annie looked down at her hands clutching the mug in her lap. She looked at her wedding ring and the dainty engagement ring, the sapphire surrounded by diamonds. The rings had once belonged to William's grandmother and they were like protective talismans.

'If that's what he thinks, he's got another think coming. Do you really believe I'd have anything to do with him now?'

Marie rested her cigarette on the lip of the ashtray and worked with a fingernail at a bit of parkin that had glued itself to the back of a tooth.

'You didn't show a lot of sense last time you had dealings with that lad.'

'That was a long time ago. Anyway,' Annie straightened her spine, 'let's not waste any more breath on Tom Greenaway. I need a new dress. I thought I'd go and have a look in town. Are you coming with me?'

'What do you want another new dress for? Haven't you enough already?'

'There's a dinner dance at the Haddington Hotel tomorrow night. It's a top-level police do. Anyone who's anyone will be there.'

Marie pulled a face. '"Anyone who's anyone",' she said in a hoity-toity voice. 'And they'll all be looking for fashion tips from Mrs Annie Howarth, will they?'

'William likes me to look nice.'

Marie laughed her throaty laugh. 'William doesn't care what you wear. You've got him wrapped around your finger. You'd think he'd have more sense, him being old enough to be your father and all.'

The disparity between Annie's age and her husband's was a topic Marie was fond of raising. Annie ignored her and finished her tea. 'I'll be off now,' she said. 'And I'd appreciate it, Mum, if you'd have a little more faith that

I'll do the right thing with regard to Tom Greenaway this time.'

'Aye well,' said Marie gruffly. 'I'll believe it when I see it.'

CHAPTER THREE

Annie was back at Everwell unpacking her shopping when Mrs Miller came downstairs.

'Mrs Howarth's sleeping like a baby,' she said. 'Are you all right to sit with her if I pop out for an hour?'

Annie nodded and went up to her mother-in-law's room. She tapped gently on the door, and when there was no response, she opened it and went in.

William had had two bedrooms knocked through into one large room for Ethel when she came to live with them. This had created a pleasant, sunny space, with the bed, commode, washbasin and wardrobe at one end and a couple of easy chairs, a small settee, a television and a table at the other. The old lady was asleep in her armchair. Mrs Miller had tucked a cushion behind her head and covered her over with a crocheted blanket. Ethel's mouth was open and she was snoring quietly. She looked as vulnerable as a baby bird, the skin that covered her skull powder-puff pink beneath her sparse white hair. One bar of the electric fire was burning and the room was very warm. Annie moved over to the window and looked down. She could see the spot where Elizabeth always waved goodbye in the mornings, the grass worn away by her shoes, and the first hint of blossom in the purple-leaved cherry tree beside the derelict cottage. Up on the moor, two brown deer were grazing, taking turns to stand guard. In the distance, Annie could see the glint of metal from the cars in the car park at the mine and the dark silhouettes of the works and their sprawl.

She sat by the window, picked up a magazine that the nurse had left, and flicked through the pages. There was an article about an American pop star called Madonna. Annie looked at the photographs. She liked the way the girl was dressed, with her swept-over hair, her heavily made-up eyes and hooped earrings like Marie's. Annie wondered if she could find some long, lace gloves to go with the dress she'd bought. Madonna wore bracelets and bangles over her gloves and a dozen necklaces were strung around her throat. It would not be a difficult look to copy – only William probably wouldn't like it. He preferred it if Annie was not 'blown about by the winds of fashion'. He liked her to look classic. On the next page were pictures of Princess Diana, but then there were always pictures of Diana; it was as if the world would never have enough images of her. Sometimes, Annie compared herself to Diana. Diana was younger than Annie, of course, but they'd both married older, wealthier men, both had had to endure a great deal of public attention and comment, and Diana, like Annie, sometimes seemed to struggle a bit with her role.

Annie closed her eyes, leaned back in the chair. She would never admit to anyone else that she thought she was like Diana. They'd only think she was getting above herself again. She thought about what her mother had said and tried not to be upset by her constant nippy little criticisms. Marie was, after all, stuck in a tiny, smelly house with a husband who had all the refinement of a wild boar. Of course she was jealous of Annie.

Annie was warm and sleepy, and she must have dozed off because she did not hear a vehicle come up the drive, or a knock at the door. She only found the flowers on the doorstep after Mrs Miller had returned and she was leaving to pick Elizabeth up from school. They were not shop flowers, but spring wildflowers, moor flowers in delicate shades of yellow and blue, forget-me-nots, celandine, thrift, yellow oxlips, primroses and violets. Annie took the small envelope that lay beside the jar and prised open the flap. Inside was a piece of card. On the back was a pencil sketch of a wren and six words.

When can I see you? Tom.

'Oh no,' Annie whispered. 'No, you won't get to me that way.'

She picked up the flowers by the stalks – they drooped in her hand, shedding petals like confetti –

and went outside, across the lawn to the gate that separated the garden from the home meadow, where Jim Friel's small herd of dairy cattle was grazing. She whistled to the cows, and as they wandered over, she tossed the flowers over the gate and dropped the card after them. The lead cow sniffed the flowers, and then picked one delicate, ragged stem of blossom and began to chew, slime drooling from its big soft lips.

'Thank you, cow,' said Annie, and she brushed the pollen from her hands before turning and marching back to the house.

CHAPTER FOUR

The next evening, while William was changing for the dinner dance, Annie poured herself a glass of wine and took it upstairs. She met Ethel on the landing, the old woman leaning on Mrs Miller's arm, shuffling towards the bathroom.

'Who's that?' Ethel asked the nurse. 'What's she doing in my house?'

'That's your daughter-in-law.'

'I've never seen her before. What's she doing here? Who is she?'

Mrs Miller smiled apologetically. 'Come along, Mrs Howarth,' she said.

'I don't like the look of her!' Ethel said. 'She's not a Howarth.' She cowered from Annie. 'I don't trust you,' she said. 'You're going to bring trouble to this house.'

Annie was used to Ethel's forgetfulness and to the hurtful things she sometimes said. Still she wished her mother-in-law would realise that she would never deliberately do her any harm.

'Now, now, Mrs Howarth, don't take on so,' said Mrs Miller, and she winked at Annie and coaxed the old woman away.

Annie went into the bedroom and stood by the window, sipping her wine and pressing her fingers against her temple.

Behind her, William was knotting his tie at the mirror and looking at her reflection in the glass.

'Is something wrong?' he asked.

'I've got a terrible headache.'

William came across the room and stood with his hands on her shoulders. He kissed the back of her head. 'Have you taken an aspirin?'

She nodded.

'Then you'll feel better soon.'

'Yes.'

She wished he'd go away. She wanted to be on her own for a few minutes. She wanted time to stand and gaze out at the sunset over the moor. Beneath the elegant scent of William's eau de cologne, Annie could smell the medicated soap he always used to wash his hands at the end of each working day. He used it to kill all the germs, scrub away the grime of the people he'd met, the crimes they'd committed, the ugliness, the poverty and misery and sheer messiness of life in a South Yorkshire mining town. William ran every aspect of his own life in a neat and ordered way and would never understand why other people could not do the same. According to him, it was simple: all people had to do was follow society's rules.

Annie moved away from her husband, away from his soaped hands and his minty breath and his clean smell. 'I'll be all right in a minute,' she said. 'I'd better start to get ready now, William.'

'Of course,' he said. 'I'll wait downstairs.'

He left, and Annie changed into her new dress and sat at the dressing table to do her hair. Elizabeth wandered in trailing her dressing gown and lay across the bed so that she could watch as Annie pinned heated rollers in her hair. The little girl pulled faces along with her mother as Annie applied eyeshadow, mascara, lipstick.

'Why do pretty women wear make-up and ugly men don't?' Elizabeth asked.

'I don't know.'

'Ruthie Thorogood says it's because the ones with most make-up get the richest men.'

Annie sighed. 'It might be something like that. But that doesn't apply to you, does it, because you're going to . . .'

'Have an education and a career!' Elizabeth finished the sentence for her. 'Although I might be a pop star instead.'

'I'll leave you to break that news to your daddy.'

Annie stood up, picked a pair of shoes that she knew would hurt her feet from the bottom of the wardrobe, and slipped them on. She sat on the bed for a moment, smoothing the child's hair.

'I wish I could stay in with you tonight,' she said quietly.

'Why? I thought you liked dancing?'

'I used to like it.' Annie closed her eyes and remembered hot nights in the Locarno in Matlow a decade earlier and afterwards, always, Tom walking her home; how she had been giddy, crazy with love for him. 'Tonight the music will be old-fashioned and I'll probably have to dance with lots of boring men,' she said.

'Daddy's not boring.'

'Daddy doesn't like dancing.'

'Why do you *have* to dance with the boring men? Why can't you just say you don't want to?'

'It's called etiquette,' said Annie. 'It's what you have to do if you want to carry on being invited to police dinner dances. Get under the covers now, you can sleep in our bed while we're gone. Mrs Miller is staying here tonight to look after you.'

She bent down and kissed Elizabeth.

'Be good.'

'I'm always good.'

'And I'm the monkey's uncle.'

Downstairs, William was waiting in the living room. He had not troubled to light the fire that evening, and it was cold in the room. He stood up when Annie came in and there was no denying he looked the part in his dinner suit. He had a presence that was a combination of severe but classical good looks and a strong character. It was very attractive.

'Is it the strike?' Annie asked.

'Is what the strike?'

'The reason why you're frowning.' She reached up to brush a few pieces of fluff from the shoulder of his jacket.

'It's not looking good,' he said. 'The consensus is that it might drag on until the summer.'

'As long as that? Bloody hell.' Annie did a twirl. 'Do I look all right?' she asked. 'It's a new dress. And I borrowed the gloves from your mother. She said she didn't mind.'

He held out his hand to her. 'You look perfect,' he said. 'I like your hair like that. It's very . . .'

'It's called fashionable,' Annie said.

She passed him her wrap and he slipped it around her shoulders. Then he put his hand in the small of her back and escorted her out to the waiting car. He opened the door for his wife and sat beside her in the back, giving instructions to the driver. Annie enjoyed the luxury of the big car, of being driven to the prestigious function. She had done well for herself, nobody could say otherwise. Who would ever have thought it? Annie Jackson from Rotherham Road – the girl who, not so long ago, had been the black sheep of the entire town after her boyfriend was found guilty of manslaughter – riding in the back of a limousine with a husband who was one of the most important police officers in the

South Yorkshire force, a man who was universally respected and admired.

Her mother didn't have to worry, Annie thought. Nobody was going to change *her* world. Nobody was going to bring *her* down to the place she'd come from. Most of all, no man was ever going to come between her and William, and certainly not Tom Greenaway – not even if he were the last person left alive on this earth.

CHAPTER FIVE

The ballroom at the Haddington Hotel was full of women dressed in bright colours and men who were suited and booted or dressed in formal police regalia. A clamour of voices echoed around the room with the fancy pelmets and chandeliers, the flower arrangements, the dome in the centre of the ceiling. Annie drifted amongst the guests on William's arm.

'You're very good at this,' she said.

'At what? Making small talk? Complimenting the wives of my colleagues when none of them comes anywhere remotely close to you?'

'You're good at being dignified,' Annie whispered. 'And you have an authority. The men are afraid of you and the women fancy you.'

William pretended to be unaffected by this observation but she knew he was pleased because he puffed himself out a little and held her close.

The guests were eventually seated at long tables,

arranged around three sides of the dance floor, with the band setting up on the stage at the far end. There were dozens of bottles of wine on tables already laid with napkins and baskets of bread and china crockery. Annie was seated next to William and she was glad to see Paul Fleming on her other side. He smiled broadly when he saw her and gave a little mock bow.

'How are you, Mrs Howarth?' he asked.

'I'm fine, thank you, Mr Fleming. And you?'

'Mustn't grumble,' said Paul. 'Although a policeman's lot is not a happy one.'

'So I've been told.'

'The job would be much easier if it weren't for the criminals. They're an inconsiderate bunch.'

'Always breaking the law, apparently.'

'Ha!' said Paul. 'You wouldn't believe the things they get up to.'

'Still, it keeps you off the streets.'

'Which is no bad thing.' Paul politely offered Annie the bread basket. She took a roll, broke it onto her side plate and buttered it. To her right, William was talking to the Lady Mayoress. His back was half-turned to Annie.

'Where's Janine?' she asked Paul.

'At home with the baby. The little lass got a cold and Jan didn't want to leave her with a sitter. Here.' He took out his wallet and showed Annie a snap. His young wife was smiling proudly. In her skinny arms was a chubby baby wearing a pink dress.

Annie passed the picture back. 'Chloe is one bonny baby,' she said.

'Takes after her father, don't you think?'

At that moment the lights were dimmed and a spotlight picked out the Chief Constable standing on the stage. He was a solid, imposing man, square-shouldered and meat-headed with his hair shaved uncompromisingly. He tapped the microphone and it screeched a couple of times before he made it work. He went on to praise the efforts of the force over the last twelve months and to give a summary of the highs and lows.

'There are many challenges ahead,' he warned. 'Our first, and most important, task is to keep the mines open so that the law-abiding minority, those decent men who want to get to work, can do so, without being intimidated or threatened. It's also important to reassure the general public that the police are in control of a situation which is in danger of escalating into violence at any moment.'

There was a murmur of assent.

'Over the coming weeks, this strike is likely to take hold and spread, like an infectious disease,' he continued. 'The longer it goes on, the more difficult our job will become. We've been planning for this situation for months, but our opponents are determined men. They want to cause maximum disruption. They want to bring the government to its knees. The leaders are the real enemy, but they're hiding behind the ignorant hordes who, like sheep, will do whatever they're told to do.'

'Ignorant hordes?' Annie muttered. 'Sheep? That's my father he's talking about!'

Paul leaned his head towards her. 'Don't take any notice,' he murmured. 'The man's an idiot.'

Annie held back her anger. The Chief Constable continued.

'We're expecting flying pickets from South Wales and other regions. These thugs,' he paused so the word could make an impact, 'are coming to bolster the numbers disrupting the Yorkshire pits. They're dangerous men, professional agitators. They're looking for trouble and we're prepared for the worst.'

The speaker then bowed his head to show that he was finished and was enthusiastically applauded by almost everyone in the room. A representative from the Coal Board was up next. He talked unconvincingly about the likely social effects of the industrial action and the importance of being united in the face of such entrenched opposition, and finished with a joke about an Englishman, an Irishman and a Scotsman.

During the meal, William was in demand; people wanted to talk to him and in between courses he was rarely in his chair. Paul was attentive to Annie, but he was popular too, often distracted. Annie picked at her food, sipped her wine. Waiters refilled her glass until she lost count of how much she'd had and eventually she reached a point where she seemed to exist in a little bubble of isolation. In the bubble, everything happened very slowly, while around her, the world had speeded up. People talked so quickly that she couldn't understand what they were saying. Different faces came into focus in front of her and their mouths moved and then they disappeared again. She smiled in a dazed way at a hundred people whose names she instantly forgot. It was an odd kind of loneliness.

After the meal was finished, as the waiters were clearing away and people were standing in little groups smoking, the band came onto the stage and began to play. Annie danced with William, and then she was passed into the arms of an old man with silver hair who smelled of cigars, and then with a large-bellied sergeant who held her so close she could smell the sourness of his breath. After that, the Chief Constable asked if he could have the pleasure and Annie told him no, he could not. She walked out of the ballroom through the double doors that opened into the hotel's marble foyer, washed the smell of the men from her hands at the basin in the cloakroom, and followed little metal finger signs stuck to the walls that pointed towards the bar. Her head was spinning. She bumped into the wall once or twice and had to hold out her arms to steady herself. She planned to ask for a large glass of iced water and find a dark corner somewhere where she could sit quietly for a few minutes until the noise and clutter in her mind calmed a little.

The bar was at the very back of the hotel. It was a square room, far darker than the ballroom, with a bar running along the near wall. A young barman leaned on the counter on his elbows, cupping his face in his hands. Opposite, French doors opened onto a balcony that was lit by hundreds of small bulbs; it looked over the gardens in the valley at the foot of the moors. The bar was full of tables and chairs, and balloons were tied to the chair-backs. Because the French doors were open, it was cool, and although there were perhaps forty people there, they were quiet, listening to the singer – a young girl with Afro hair, wearing jeans and a cheese-cloth shirt, who curled over her guitar on the tiny stage.

Annie stood at the doorway and listened to the girl sing a song about love. She felt tired, so tired that she wished she could just fall to the floor in a bundle and sleep where she fell. She leaned against the wall and closed her eyes for a moment – it couldn't have been more than a moment. When she opened them, she found herself looking into the face of Tom Greenaway.

'Annie,' Tom said, and he had a look of shock on his face that mirrored hers.

'You!' she said, and she raised her arm as if to slap him but she was too slow and he took hold of her wrist.

'Don't be daft,' he said. 'Don't make a scene.'

'Don't tell *me* what to do!' she replied, and the people sitting at the table closest to them looked up.

'Please, Annie, I—'

'And don't you ever dream of sending me flowers or letters or playing any kind of tricks like that again!'

'Let's sit down,' Tom said. 'Let's talk.'

'I don't want to talk. I don't want to be anywhere near you. Get your hands off me!' She tried to back away but she stumbled on her heels, and if he had not held her, she would have fallen.

'If you carry on like this they'll throw us out,' Tom said.

'They bloody well ought to throw you out! I'm surprised they let you in. Do they know who you are?'

'Annie, just calm down, just—'

'I said *get away from me*!' she cried.

'Are you all right, miss?' A young waiter was at her side.

Annie opened her mouth to ask him to eject Tom, but at exactly the same moment the anger and hurt and frustration that had been rattling around inside her came together in a nauseating wave of emotion that she could not contain.

She covered her mouth with her hands.

She looked up at Tom, panic in her eyes, and he realised what was wrong.

'I'll look after her,' Tom said to the waiter, and the young man moved away.

Tom put his arm around Annie – she was too desperate to resist – and he half-dragged, half-carried her through the bar, out of the tall French doors onto the balcony. The night air was so cold, it was shocking. She gripped the icy balcony railing with both hands, leaned over and vomited painfully. She heard the splatter of liquid on the shrubs below.

'Oh God!' she whimpered.

'It's all right,' said Tom. He was holding back her hair. He was holding on to her.

She was still retching, so he helped her down a wrought-iron staircase that wound its way into the hotel gardens. At the bottom of the steps she leaned over and threw up again into the flowerbeds. Tom rubbed her back, but she pushed his hand away. The retching seemed to last forever, and after that came the weakness and the desire to cry like a child. Annie would not give in to that.

'All right now?' Tom asked.

Annie nodded. She spat out the last of it and then wiped her mouth with the paper napkin he gave her. He put his jacket over her shoulders and helped her upright.

'Take your time,' he said. 'Breathe the fresh air.'

'Don't patronise me.'

'I was trying to help.'

'Well, don't.' She looked back to the hotel. 'Did anyone see?'

'I don't think so. Come away from the light while you get your breath back.'

'I don't want to talk to you.'

'You don't have to. But if you don't want anyone to see you like this, you need to come into the gardens.'

She allowed him to lead her away from the flowerbed and along the path which led between rhododendron bushes that were taller than she was. Their leaves quivered in the breeze. Annie's breath was a cloud in front of her. She held the jacket around her. It was soft, worn and it smelled of woodsmoke and of the outdoors. It smelled of Tom.

They came to an ornamental metal bench, and she sat down. He stood beside her.

'Are you following me?' she asked.

'Of course I'm not.'

'Then how did you know I was here?'

'I didn't. You walked into me, remember? I'm here because I know the girl who's singing in the bar. I gave her a lift. She lives in the flat below mine on Occupation Road.'

'Oh.' Annie exhaled. 'Does she know who you are? What you did?'

'She knows the truth.'

'That you killed an old lady?'

'I never did anything to hurt anyone. I know it's hard for you to believe, Annie, but—'

'Every word that comes out of your mouth is hard for me to believe, Tom Greenaway, because every word is a lie!'

Annie's voice was rising. She shuddered and sank back into herself.

'Go away,' she said. 'Leave me alone.'

'I can't leave you on your own like this.'

'I've managed perfectly well without you for the past ten years.'

'Didn't you read my letters?'

'What letters?'

'The letters I wrote to you from prison.'

'I never received any letters.'

'Annie, you must have.'

'I didn't.'

Annie stood up again and began to walk. He went with her. She could not see his face. He was walking beside her hunch-shouldered, with his hands in his trouser pockets.

'While you were in prison writing me imaginary letters, I got married,' she said. 'But you know that, don't you, Tom? Not that a man like you would ever let something like that get in your way.'

'I didn't come back to ruin your life, I—'

'I have a husband, Tom, a husband who cares for me.'

'You don't know what he—'

'And I live in a beautiful house and I have a beautiful child. I have a better life than you could ever even imagine. A better life than you could ever have given me.'

'Do you *really* know him, this husband of yours? Do you *really* know what he's like?'

'I know he has integrity. I know he's honest. I know I can trust him.'

They stood and stared at one another. She tried to compose herself but she was out of breath and dangerously close to crying.

After a few moments, Tom said, 'I didn't kill Edna Wallace, Annie. I didn't.'

'Just shut up, Tom,' she said. 'Shut up.' She took off the jacket and let it fall behind her onto the path. 'Leave me alone,' she told him. 'Stay away from me.'

'Why won't you listen to me?'

'Because you're a liar!'

'No! *No*. Annie, I've waited all these years to come back to you and tell you what happened, and the least you can do is give me five minutes to make you understand.'

'But I *do* understand! I understand that you're bad, through and through. I understand that I never want to see you again!'

'Listen to me, Annie!'

'No, I won't listen. Not now, not ever. Go away – leave me alone. If I see you again I'll tell my husband you've been following me and he'll have you locked up.'

Tom stared at Annie for a moment. Then he said, 'All right. All right, if that's what you want.'

'It is what I want.'

'OK,' he said. 'I'm going.' He turned and began to walk away from her, and away from the hotel.

'Where are you going?' she called.

He did not answer. He did not look back. He quickened his pace to a run.

'Tom!' she called, but the word disappeared into the darkness. Annie stood and watched the space where Tom had been. For a few moments she caught glimpses of him in the moonlight, as he ran away from her, and then he reached the woodland that marked the boundary between the hotel gardens and the moor. He disappeared altogether then, into the darker shadows of the hillside.

'Good riddance,' Annie muttered to herself. She leaned down to take off her shoes and she hooked the straps over her fingers and ran barefoot across the gardens back to the hotel. A young man was standing at the bottom of the spiral staircase that led up to the balcony. He was smoking a cigarette. Annie didn't realise it was Paul Fleming until she reached the steps.

'Are you all right?' he asked. 'I noticed you'd gone and I got a bit worried.'

'Yes, yes, I'm fine.'

'Annie, what's wrong?'

'Nothing's wrong. I needed some fresh air, that's all.'

She pushed past him and went back into the hotel. In the Ladies, she washed her hands and face, rinsed her mouth and sprayed herself with perfume. She was perfectly composed when she went back into the ballroom and resumed her place at her husband's side; she even managed to be pleasant to the Chief Constable when he offered her another glass of champagne.

CHAPTER SIX

That night, a woman was murdered and her body left on the moors above Matlow town.

She was found by a young couple, honeymooners who were hiking across the Peak District. They had stayed in a bed and breakfast just outside the town the night before and made an early start, so early that the mist still hung over the moor and the dawn light was weak and hazy. They could only see a few yards in front of them, but they had proper walking boots, waterproofs and an Ordnance Survey map in a plastic sleeve; they knew they would not get lost as long as they followed the path. They noticed the scarf caught on the branch of a tree like a flag but might have missed the body if the young man, a doctor, had not stopped to tie his shoelace. He sat on a rock and looked down and saw a woman lying on a slab of rock below, one arm outstretched as if she were reaching out for help. The young man scrambled down and quickly established that the woman was dead.

The honeymooners were sensible people; they did not panic, but it took them a while to decide what to do. It seemed wrong to leave the body alone, but the young wife did not want to stay with it on her own in case whoever had put it there returned; nor did she want to retrace her footsteps without her new husband at her side. The pair could see no obvious signs of nearby habitation through the mist, but both Everwell, and the farm beside it, were marked on their map. The farmhouse buildings were closest and they thought the best thing to do would be to make for there, and hope there was a telephone. Before they left, the young man took off his jacket and laid it carefully over the body.

The couple then walked as fast as they could downhill, tripping and stumbling in their haste to find help. It took them the best part of forty minutes to come down off the moor. They cut across one of farmer Jim Friel's fields, and Jim spotted them scrambling through the meadow when he was bringing the cows back from milking. They waved and shouted to attract his attention and he went over with his dogs – and when they told him what they had found, he took them back to his cottage, where there was indeed a telephone. From there, the young man called the local police, who instructed the couple to stay where they were until the squad car arrived. Jim put the kettle on because the young woman, in particular, seemed pale and was possibly showing signs of shock.

He took the tea through to his guests.

'Drink this,' he said to the woman. 'It'll put hairs on your chest.'

'Thank you,' she said weakly.

'While you're doing that, I'm going to call my neighbour, Mr Howarth. He's a big cheese in the police.'

'Oh yes?' The young doctor raised his eyebrows over the rim of his cup.

'A top man and a good man an' all. My lad, Seth, he went off the rails a while back – right off the rails. His mum had gone and left us, see, and he got hisself in all sorts of trouble. Drugs, the lot. But Mr Howarth sorted it out. He said what Seth needed were a helping hand, not a prison sentence. Me and the lad'll always be grateful to him for that. Always.'

'Good,' said the doctor. 'Very good.'

'Anyroad,' said Jim, 'I don't expect as you want to know my life story. I'll go and telephone Mr Howarth. He'll know what to do about the poor dead lass on the moor.'

Unfortunately, that morning William had risen early and taken his shotgun from its padlocked case in the lobby to go hunting. It was Annie who came downstairs to answer the telephone. She was tired and sore-headed after the dinner dance and in the wake of her encounter with Tom Greenaway. She found it difficult to take in what Jim was saying.

'Are you sure, Jim?' she asked. 'Are you sure there's a woman dead on the moor?'

'Aye,' said Jim. 'Left on t'rocks like a piece of rubbish.'

'Perhaps she fell.'

'The people who found her reckon she was put there.'

'Oh God. That's terrible.'

'You'll be sure to tell Mr Howarth when he comes back?'

'Yes, I promise.'

'He'll want to know what's going on.'

'Yes, of course, Jim. Thank you.'

She had barely put the telephone down before she heard the siren of a police car going past on the lane that led up to the farm. Soon after that, William returned with a brace of rabbits. Annie told him what had happened as best she could without alarming Elizabeth, who was eating cereal at the kitchen table. William immediately telephoned the local police station; after that he called Paul Fleming and Annie heard him having a long, urgent discussion. Then he raced upstairs. A short while later, he came back down with his hair damp from the shower, wearing a pair of police-issue overalls on top of his clothes. The skin was stretched tightly over his face and he was pale with tension.

'Jim's going to give me a lift up the moor in his tractor,' he said. 'Reinforcements are on their way to block the footpath, but I want to see the site while it's still relatively undisturbed.'

Annie turned to him, 'But William, it's Saturday. I've hardly seen you all week. It's supposed to be your day off. You said we would do something together as a family. You promised.'

'Darling, I can't ignore a suspicious death on our doorstep.'

'There are other police officers available.'

'It's less than half a mile from Everwell. How would it look if I didn't show my face?'

She burst out: 'You say it's your duty, but the truth is you'd rather be there. You're happier at work than you are with me and . . .' Annie glanced at Elizabeth and tailed off.

'That's not true,' William said. 'You mean the world to me, Annie – you and Lizzie. You know you do.' He kissed her sulky face and said gently: 'I'll be back as soon as I can. Lock up after me. If you see anyone acting suspiciously – if you see anyone at all – call the station.'

Annie nodded. She followed William into the hall and fastened the deadbolt on the front door after he'd left. She leaned her forehead against the wood for a moment and felt a pang of loneliness. She had nothing to do.

Mrs Miller had brought Ethel down to the conservatory and was reading aloud to her from the weekend newspaper supplements. Elizabeth had finished breakfast and was lying on her stomach on the living-room floor watching *Scooby Doo* videos on television. Nobody needed Annie. There was nobody nearby she could telephone and ask to come over, nobody she could speak to about what had happened the previous evening at the Haddington Hotel, nobody she could talk to about Tom, nobody she could tell about the woman on the moor.

She busied herself checking that all the doors and windows were closed and locked, then made herself a mug of coffee and took it upstairs. She filled the bath and lay in it for a while, watching the steam dancing up from the surface and thinking about the poor woman on the moor. She wondered how the woman had come to be there and who she was and why somebody had left her in that cold, lonely place.

She slid down into the water until it covered most of her face, and only her nose and her forehead were dry. Life was fragile and unreliable and everything could change in a heartbeat. Annie knew that.

CHAPTER SEVEN

Annie did not see her husband for the rest of that day. He came home in the evening, looking tired, but she knew from his face that he was happy, in the way that work of this kind always made William happy.

He kissed Annie's cheek when he came in, and took the tea she offered him, but he said hardly anything and went straight upstairs to shower. Annie took a bottle of Chardonnay from the fridge and poured herself a glass, then she uncorked a bottle of Cabernet Sauvignon and filled a glass for William. She took both glasses into the living room. She had already laid and lit the fire, drawn the curtains, made a salad and boiled new potatoes to go with the quiche she had defrosted for their supper.

When William came down again, he went into his study and, moments later, Annie heard the opening chords of Beethoven's Ninth Symphony. This was the music he preferred after a particularly difficult day. He found it soothing and would listen to the whole record before he did anything else.

Annie picked up the two glasses and took them into the study.

'I brought you some wine,' she said.

William snapped open the locks of the briefcase on his desk. He took out a sheaf of papers, pushed his glasses up to the bridge of his nose and stared down at the paperwork.

'I know you'd prefer to be left alone with your work,' Annie said, 'but I've been on my own, not counting the company of a child and the very elderly, all day. Can I sit with you for a bit?'

This time he took the glass she offered him although he did not drink but put it back down on the desk. His face was etched with fatigue and there was a distance in his eyes. Annie perched on the arm of his chair and waited for him to speak.

'I have a lot to do,' he said at last.

'I know.'

'I'll come and sit with you when I'm finished.'

'But William, that might not be for hours.'

He looked up from his papers, glanced at her over the top of his reading glasses, and then looked down again.

'All right,' he said as he studied the documents. 'What is it you want, exactly?'

'To talk,' Annie said. He did not respond. He was so deep in thought that she might as well not have been there. 'I'll tell you about my day,' she said. 'It was quiet. Nothing much happened. Your mother was on good form, she remembered who we were, and Elizabeth painted a picture of a pirate ship. That was the highlight. They've both been in bed for ages.'

'Good,' said William. 'Good.'

'I looked at the moor through your father's old bird-watching binoculars, but I didn't spot any murderers. Apart from that, I've been waiting for my husband to come home and spend some time with me.'

William sighed. He pincered the flesh between his eyes with a thumb and a forefinger.

'Annie – you know how it is. When something like this happens . . .'

'It takes priority over everything else, family included. Of course. Silly me.'

'Don't turn into a harpy. I thought you were better than that.'

'I only want a little of your time.'

'And you will have it – but not now. Right now I need to read through these papers. The first twenty-four hours–'

'– in a case of unlawful killing are the most crucial. I know. So tell me about it. That way, you can work and I can be with you.'

'I can't do that. You know I can't. It would be unethical.'

'Do you know who she is yet, the woman?'

'No.'

'Nobody's gone missing?'

'Not from Matlow.'

'Or maybe nobody's noticed that someone's missing yet.'

'Annie, please, stop.'

'What does she look like?'

This time, William looked up. He stared hard at Annie for a moment, and he frowned.

'What?' she prompted.

He shook his head. 'Nothing. It's nothing.'

'Tell me.' When he did not reply, she persisted. 'What is it, William? What were you going to say?'

'It doesn't matter.'

Annie took a drink of her wine. She waited for a few moments, but he did not move, or say anything else.

'Do you have a suspect?'

'Yes,' said William.

He was staring at his papers in a deliberate manner.

'Tom Greenaway's back,' Annie said quietly.

'I know,' William said. 'We've already pulled him in for questioning.'

'You think he's responsible for the woman's death?'

'It's a possibility.'

'Dear God.' Annie stood up. She wrapped her arms about herself. 'I saw Tom last night, at the hotel,' she said. 'I talked to him.'

'I know,' said William. 'Paul told me.'

He made a fist of his left hand on the desk. He held the fist for a moment, and then stretched out his fingers. The golden wedding band shone against the wrinkled skin of his fingers, the curly grey hairs on the back of his hand.

'It was strange to see him again,' Annie said. 'But you

don't really think Tom would have deliberately killed someone do you?'

'I don't know what to think yet. That's why I need to sit here and read the reports. That's why I need the time and space to work out what to think. So for the last time, Annie, please will you leave me alone.'

Annie stood up. She crossed to the door where she paused, considering saying something else – then decided against it. She left the room closing the door quietly behind her.

CHAPTER EIGHT

Annie did not sleep well that night. Several times she woke with the same sensation of dread she'd felt before; several times she dreamed she was up, looking out of the window and watching a dead woman walking through the mist. She lay in the bed, cold with anxiety and shaky from the wine she'd drunk, imagining she could hear the dead woman's footsteps as she walked away, imagining she could see her waving to her from the moor. And then she realised it was not the woman who was waving, but Tom Greenaway.

It was impossible for her to lie in, so she was up early on Sunday morning – but still not as early as William. Either he had left the bed while it was still dark outside, or he had not come to bed at all. This had happened before.

Annie took two paracetamol from the packet in the bathroom cabinet and swallowed them with a glass of water. Then she sat on the bed and put heated rollers in her hair, fastening them with metal grips that scratched her scalp. The weather had taken a turn for the worse. Squally clouds were racing over the moors, and drifts of soft grey rain trailed from the sky. The ancient clamour of rooks that for centuries had nested in the trees on the moor's lower slopes was tossing and turning over the meadows of the farm; hundreds of birds thrown about like black handkerchiefs in the air.

She wondered as she wound a piece of hair around a roller what was happening to Tom that morning. It would be hard for him. The Matlow police would not treat him kindly, not after what he'd done before. They were bound to blame him, a murder happening soon after he returned, and it wouldn't just be the police; everyone would blame him. He was the obvious suspect and people would be glad if he was guilty because then the matter would be sorted. Only it couldn't have been him who killed the woman; it couldn't have been. He wouldn't do that. He just wouldn't.

She thought of him locked up in the police cell, he who hated enclosed places, who used to pale with panic at the thought of stepping into a lift, or even going through a turnstile. How was he coping? Or had he come to terms with his claustrophobia since he'd been in prison? Would it be easier for him now?

Stop it! Annie told herself as her thoughts drifted again to Tom. *Stop dwelling on him.*

Mrs Miller did not come on Sundays so, with the

rollers in her hair, Annie went into Ethel's room, helped her to wash and dress and they went slowly down the stairs together, Ethel leaning on Annie. William was in his study. The door was closed and no music was playing. Annie settled Ethel in the conservatory, fetched her tea and toast, and then she made a start on the lunch for later. The Flemings were coming over as well as the vicar, an old schoolfriend of William, and the vicar's family. There was a lot to do.

Annie peeled the root vegetables and put them in a pan with water. She made a cheese and mustard sauce to go with the cauliflower, then prepared the stuffing and the apple sauce. She set the oven to low, laid the pork shoulder in a roasting pan half-filled with onions and leeks, rubbed salt into the cut skin of the meat, and put it on to cook. When she'd done as much as she could towards the dinner, she went upstairs to fetch Elizabeth. She found her in her bedroom, half-dressed.

Annie looked at the child, then put her hands on her hips and said, 'Sorry, Lizzie, but you'll have to take off the legwarmers.'

'Why?'

'You know why. Daddy likes you to look smart when we're out.'

'Everyone else wears them.'

'Not to church they don't.' Annie took a pair of white socks from Elizabeth's underwear drawer and threw them gently at her daughter.

Elizabeth batted away the socks with her hand. 'I'll

look like a baby,' she grumbled. 'Everyone will laugh at me. Why are you so horrible to me?'

'Because I'm your mother, it's my job.'

Elizabeth picked up the socks and glared at them. 'I am *never* going to make my children wear such stupid clothes,' she snapped. 'Never! My children will be able to wear exactly what they want.'

'Good for your future children,' Annie said.

They heard the chime of the doorbell. Elizabeth stood on her bed and looked out of the window.

'Who is it, Lizzie?'

'Uncle Paul.'

Annie went and stood beside her daughter. She could see the top of Paul's head, his shoulders rain-spattered. Then William stepped outside and pulled the front door shut behind him. The two men stood talking, oblivious to the rain, their two heads close together. Paul was animated, agitated. He gesticulated with his hands, he looked up to the sky and blinked away the raindrops. William put his hand on Paul's back and patted it. The shoulders of their jackets were soaked through, darkened by the wet. Eventually William pointed to the car, and the two men got inside. Annie watched them talking until the car windows steamed up, and it was as if they had faded away.

'Come on,' she said to Elizabeth. She helped her finish dressing and then the two of them went downstairs.

'Why did Paul need to see you so urgently that it

couldn't wait until after church?' Annie asked her husband, when he came back in.

William frowned and brushed at the raindrops on his jacket. 'We had to let Greenaway go. He had an alibi for the early hours of Saturday.'

'Oh,' Annie said. And she didn't mean to, but her heart gave a little skip of relief that Tom had apparently had nothing to do with the dead woman on the moor.

CHAPTER NINE

At Holy Communion that morning, prayers were said asking God to bring a speedy conclusion to the miners' strike. The congregation also prayed for the souls of the dead. Although the woman on the moor was not specifically mentioned, everyone knew that it was her they were praying for.

Annie sat next to Janine Fleming and did her best to entertain baby Chloe during the parts of the service when it was best that she kept quiet. Chloe didn't make a peep during the hymns, when it wouldn't have mattered if she had, but was inclined to screech unpredictably during the sermon and moments of reflection. Janine looked half-dead with tiredness.

After the service, the Howarth family drove home in silence. Annie gazed up at the moor, its colours muted by the rain.

Reverend Thorogood, his wife, who came from a land-owning family, and children, two skinny girls who were older than Elizabeth but went to the same school, arrived at Everwell soon after the Howarths, and the Flemings pulled up behind them. Elizabeth ran to Paul and he hefted her onto his shoulders. Janine followed with Chloe, now swaddled in several layers of pink.

'Let me take her,' Annie said when they were inside. 'You're such a bonny girl, Chloe, aren't you? Eh? Such a pretty little thing!' She wriggled the baby's arms out of her snowsuit and took off her knitted hat. Beneath it, Chloe's wispy hair was stuck to her head with sweat. Her scalp was covered in a crusty layer of cradle-cap and she smelled yeasty.

Annie bounced the baby on her hip. 'You look done in,' she said to Janine.

'She doesn't sleep well,' Janine replied. 'She has me up every hour or so and then she won't settle.' She glanced at her husband. 'He doesn't even seem to notice.'

'It'll get easier,' Annie said. 'Honestly it will. Now come on into the living room and relax.'

In the living room, the adults sipped sweet sherry while the children lay on the floor and looked at a comic. The vicar's wife, Julia Thorogood, liked to take centre stage.

'Isn't the news all too dreadful?' she began self-importantly. 'They're fighting at the mines, shooting one another in Northern Ireland, and to top it all off we have a murder on the moors. I wonder if this is the beginning of the end for society.'

'I'm sure it's not that bad,' Paul said, and he treated Julia to one of his most charming, boyish smiles. 'They say the threat of nuclear war is receding and Liverpool looks set to sweep the board this year.'

'I'm glad football cheers you up,' Mrs Thorogood said tartly. 'I can hardly bear to listen to the news any more.'

'I'm sure it's all part of God's plan,' said her husband. 'You'll see.'

'Is it time for *Bergerac*?' Ethel interrupted.

'Not yet,' said Annie.

'Oh.' The old lady looked disheartened. 'I enjoy *Bergerac*. I do like that Charlie Hungerford. He reminds me of my husband.'

She put her trembling hand on Paul Fleming's arm. 'My husband is going to take me to Jersey for our anniversary, dear,' she said. 'I shall have to be careful I don't muddle them up and come home with Charlie by mistake.'

She laughed at her own joke. Paul laughed too. Annie glanced at her watch and said: 'Excuse me, but I must see to the dinner.' She propped baby Chloe up amongst the settee cushions and left her to chew her fist.

Elizabeth and the vicar's two daughters followed Annie out of the room.

'Can we go and play upstairs?' Elizabeth asked.

Annie nodded, but she took hold of her daughter's arm, leaned down and whispered: 'Only no legwarmers, and no Murder in the Dark. The Thorogood girls had nightmares after last time.'

'OK,' Elizabeth said cheerily. 'Come on, let's go!' She clattered up the stairs with the two older children following timidly behind.

Annie went into the dining room. It was a grand room, with oil paintings on the walls; an ornate chandelier hung over the table. She spread an antique linen cloth, and on top of that she put the table mats with hunting scenes and the silver cutlery from the family canteen. She could hear the rain spattering against the window and the sound of Julia Thorogood's voice holding forth from across the hall. She turned on the light because the room had become gloomy, opened the sideboard and took out the serving dishes. Then she heard footsteps on the stairs and went out to find one of the Thorogood children coming down, sniffing.

'Oh Ruthie, love, what's the matter?'

'Elizabeth said the killer man is going to come and get us all.' Her pale eyes were wet with tears and her lower lip was trembling.

Annie sucked in her breath. 'What a load of rubbish,' she said. 'Elizabeth knows perfectly well that her Uncle Paul and her daddy are going to catch that man and send him to prison. Now why don't you come in the kitchen with me and help with the dinner?'

The child looked dubious.

'I need someone to decorate the trifle,' Annie explained. 'With sweeties. You look like just the right person for the job.'

The kitchen was pleasantly steamy and smelled of roast meat and boiled vegetables. Annie set Ruthie up at the table with the trifle, a tub of glacé cherries and a packet of Jelly Tots. She went to the stove, took the lid off the vegetable pan and stuck a fork into the flesh of the potatoes. As she did so, there was a knock at the back door.

'Oh, who can that be now?'

Annie put down the fork, crossed the room and opened the door. The air was cold, as cold as it had been that year. Standing outside, wrapped up against the rain, were Jim Friel and Tom Greenaway.

'How do, Mrs Howarth,' said Jim.

'Hello, Annie,' said Tom.

Annie held on to the doorframe. Her heart was beating so hard she thought it would break through her ribcage and come out of her chest.

'What do you want?' she asked in a quiet voice. 'We're just about to have our dinner.'

'Mr Howarth wanted some grout. We've brought it up for him,' Jim said, shaking out his arms to dislodge the rain. 'He said he wanted us to make a start on the repointing as soon as.' He glanced at Annie, who was staring at Tom. 'The tractor's broken down. Tom here gave me a lift up in his truck.'

Tom showed Annie the sack in his arms, as if to persuade her that no harm was meant, but the harm was already done. Annie could not take her eyes off his face. In daylight she could see how it had changed. Oh, it was still Tom, but the years in prison had taken their toll. His face was less handsome now, with the beard and the weathering, but it was more interesting. A scar beneath his left eye made Annie feel a pang of tenderness. His skin was wet; a drip ran down his cheek to his jaw, and she had to hold herself back from reaching out to wipe it away.

Jim shifted from foot to foot. 'We'd better put the sacks undercover, Mrs Howarth, else they'll be ruined.'

'Yes, of course.'

'Where do you want them?'

'Here. In the lobby.'

'Right.'

Tom stepped forward, and Annie moved back to give him more room, but when he had placed the sack on the floor and he stood back up, his eyes were level with hers. She could see the flecks of green and brown in his irises, the darkness of his lashes, the new tiny wrinkles in the skin and the shadows around them. He used to kiss her eyelids. He used to kiss them so gently. He used to press his thumbs against her temples and make little circles that relaxed her and soothed her and turned her on . . .

'Annie,' he said, quiet as breath. 'I need to talk to you. Come and see me.'

'No. No, I won't.'

'Annie? Is everything all right?'

She turned and there was William standing behind her. His hands were at his sides, his fists loosely clenched. He had taken off his tie and his throat flared red beneath the open collar of his shirt. He took hold of her shoulder. His fingers held on to her tightly.

'Go back to the others, Annie,' he said, but she did not move.

Tom pulled himself up to his full height. His face was pale. He swayed on his feet.

'Superintendent Howarth!' he said. 'It's been a long time. Last time I saw you was in the courtroom. You were giving evidence against me.'

'Go, Annie,' repeated William.

'No, stay,' said Tom. 'There's things I want to say to Mr Howarth that I'd like you to hear.'

Jim nudged Tom to shut him up. 'We brought your grout, Mr Howarth,' he said. 'I'm sorry about this. Tom promised me he wouldn't say owt about—'

'That courtroom, that trial, was the best part of ten years ago,' Tom went on. 'Does it seem like ten years to you, Mr Howarth? Because it does to me.'

'Get off my property, Greenaway.'

'I expect time passed quickly for you. You've been busy, haven't you, what with courting our Annie here, having a kid, furthering your career.'

William pulled Annie's shoulder so hard that she had to step behind him. She stumbled and bumped into the chair on which the vicar's daughter was kneeling, to decorate the trifle. The child gave a gasp of surprise.

'Get away from my family,' William said. His voice was low, and calm, and deathly.

'Those ten years didn't pass quickly for me,' Tom said. His voice was strong too. It had an undercurrent of threat to it. 'They went very, very slowly. I had a lot of time to kill. And do you know how I used that time?'

Annie took hold of Ruthie's hand.

'Tom,' she said, 'please. There are children here.'

'I'm not after causing any trouble,' Tom said. 'I'm after clearing my name.'

'Come along, Ruthie,' Annie said.

'And I will!' Tom called after her. 'You'll see, Annie, you'll see that I will.'

William moved suddenly forward – and at the same time Annie pushed the little girl out of the room, shutting the door behind her. She took her straight into the cloakroom, where she turned on the taps and spoke calmly to the child as she washed the cherry syrup from her hands with a flannel.

'Why are they shouting?' Ruthie asked.

'I don't know,' Annie said.

'Are they going to have a fight?' Ruthie's face was wan. Her eyes were round and large. 'Are they going to kill each other?'

'No, of course they're not,' said Annie.

She splashed water down the drain as noisily as she could but it still did not completely mask the sound of angry voices coming from the kitchen. Her heart was beating so hard it hurt. She waited until she heard the kitchen door slam, then she turned off the taps and dried Ruthie's hands and sent her back into the living room to find her mother.

Annie darted over to the hall window. She watched Tom and Jim Friel go back to the truck. Tom banged his fist on the side of the vehicle. Jim said something to him and Tom looked back towards the house. Annie stepped away from the window. A few moments later, the two men climbed into the truck and drove away.

Annie was hot with fear and confusion. Outside, the world had turned the colour of water. The sky and the ground were grey and the moor had all but faded into the weather and disappeared. Puddles were forming on the drive. The wheels of the truck had left lines in the gravel leading away from the house towards the lane.

William came out of the kitchen and picked up the telephone. He did not notice his wife, alone by the window alcove as he dialled. After a moment or two, when somebody answered, he said: 'Greenaway's been here. He's been up to my house. I thought I told you . . .'

He listened intently for a few moments.

'It's not acceptable,' he said. 'I won't have the safety of my family compromised.'

He listened again, then snapped, 'I don't care about resources. Whatever it takes, you make sure this doesn't happen again.'

William put the receiver back on the handset. He stood in front of the mirror, adjusting the knot of his tie, composing himself. Then he walked towards the living room and opened the door. Annie heard the rise of voices as he went into the room and the fade as he pulled it shut behind him. She could hear children's footsteps on the landing upstairs. She leaned against the wall and pressed her hands into her eyes.

'Annie?'

She jumped up, found a smile. 'Hi, Janine.'

'I need to change Chloe. I think she's – you know.' Janine wafted her fingers in front of her nose.

'Yes, of course, you can use the bathroom.'

'Is everything all right?'

'Yes,' Annie nodded. 'Yes, everything's perfect. Our dinner'll be ready in a minute.'

CHAPTER TEN

Annie came down from her bath in her nightshirt, with her hair wrapped in a towel. The study door was closed, and there was no rim of light beneath it.

'Hello?' she called. 'William?'

'In here.'

She followed the sound of his voice into the living room. He had pulled the easy chairs close to the fire, and poured them both a generous tumbler of Laphroaig over ice. Annie tucked herself into the empty chair. She sipped at her whisky and looked into the flames.

'I thought Lizzie would never go to bed,' she said. 'Sometimes that child really tests my patience.'

'It's time you started being firmer with her.'

'What do you mean?'

'Let's face it, Annie, her manners are appalling.'

Annie felt her hackles twitching. 'You mean I'm not doing a good enough job with her?'

'I didn't say that.'

It's what you meant though.

William rattled the ice in his glass. 'Julia Thorogood commented today . . .'

'And Julia Thorogood's opinion is what counts, is it?'

'Annie, please. She wasn't being critical. She merely suggested—'

'I can imagine.'

'How can we have an adult conversation if you won't listen to me?'

'I don't want to have this conversation. I don't care what Julia Thorogood thinks of me. She's a sanctimonious cow and I can't stand her.'

William blinked slowly. 'Whatever your opinion of Julia, you have to admit her children are well-behaved.'

'They're timid little mice, that's why. She's bullied all the spirit out of them.' And when William sighed, pointedly: 'Go ahead, sigh all you like. You should see how she behaves at the well-dressing meetings, William. If anyone has a different opinion to her she just ridicules them or shouts them down. It's not a committee, it's a bloody dictatorship.'

'Perhaps you could be more cooperative.'

'And perhaps *you* could be on my side instead of hers.'

'I am on your side,' William said. 'Always.'

Neither of them spoke for a moment, then William cleared his throat. 'What happened today – Greenaway turning up like that here – it won't happen again.'

'No.'

'I've warned him that if he approaches you, if he tries

to talk to you – if he so much as *looks* at you – I'll have him arrested for harassment.'

'All right.'

'I won't have him bothering you.'

'He doesn't bother me. I have no feelings for him at all.'

'I'm not taking any risks. Not with you or Lizzie.'

Annie picked up her glass and looked at the flames in the fireplace through the ice. 'William,' she said, 'there wasn't any doubt at all, was there, about Tom being responsible for Mrs Wallace's death?'

'No,' said William. 'None whatsoever.'

'He seems determined to persuade me that he's innocent.'

'He is a determined and persuasive man. You know that.'

'I know.' She sipped her drink. 'And you really think he might have had something to do with the woman on the moor?'

'He has an alibi.'

'You don't believe the alibi. I can tell.'

William rubbed his chin. 'It might be a coincidence that a few weeks after he returns to Matlow we have our first unlawful killing in a decade.'

'But?'

'I have never believed in coincidence,' said William. 'Never.'

CHAPTER ELEVEN

The next Thursday, Annie drove down to Matlow as usual. The town was littered with the aftermath of a protest march. She had watched clips on the news – had seen the miners holding their banners high as they marched through streets lined with cheering crowds and the police all bunched together, a mass of black coats and helmets forming a human barrier behind them. The trouble had not broken out until later. Windows had been broken in some of the buildings, placards lay abandoned on the pavements, and police tape fluttered from lamp posts. Every inch of wall-space was plastered with posters and flyers.

Rotherham Road looked pretty much as it had always looked. The front door to number 122 was open. 'Ooh-ooh!' Annie called. 'Is anyone home?'

'I'm out here!' her father called back.

Annie walked through the kitchen and out into the rear yard. Denis was crouched down, fastening muzzles onto the snouts of the whippets. A stub of a cigarette burned between his lips.

'Where's Mum?'

'She was offered an extra cleaning shift. She couldn't turn it down. Not now.'

'No.' Annie reached out to see if the clothes pegged to the rotary drier were still damp. Then she looked at her father, the moles on his neck, the pale skin behind his ear, the freckles on his scalp and the breeze lifting his thinning hair. When he was with his dogs, gentle like this, it was hard to remember what he was like when he was in a temper, how people were scared of him. 'Shall I put the kettle on?' she asked.

'Leave it. Come for a walk with me. I haven't seen you for weeks.'

They took the dogs down to the canal and walked along the towpath until they were out of the town boundaries, no longer flanked by walls but by barbed-wire fences and grass and fields. Denis unmuzzled the dogs and let them off the leads. 'G'on then, lads,' he said. 'Get us a rabbit or two for us tea.' The dogs streamed off into the fields. 'Look at that,' he said. 'I love to watch them go.'

Father and daughter walked side by side. Annie picked a switch of willow and swung at the new branches and the budding leaves. She tickled the catkins, and yellow pollen rained down on her hand. Denis stopped every now and then to talk to a fisherman or look at what he had in his holding net. Father and daughter had never had much to say to one another, and since the scandal of Tom Greenaway, what few words they used to have had dried up.

'How long do you reckon the strikers'll hold out for?' Annie asked at last.

'As long as it takes.'

'Thatcher says the miners can't win.'

'What does she know about owt?'

Annie looked at the sky reflected in the water and watched a duck paddling about in the weed.

'But if nobody's getting paid and there's no Social, how will people manage?'

'We'll get by. The Union'll see us right.'

They came to a place where the road crossed over the canal. The footpath beneath the bridge was narrow and slippery, and water dripped from the brick archway into the blackness below.

'Johnnie never used to like coming through here,' Annie recalled. She trailed her switch along the bricks. 'He thought every bridge had a troll living beneath it.'

Denis chuckled. 'It were because of that story, the goat one.'

'*The Billy Goats Gruff*. He used to hold his breath and run through as fast as he could.'

'Too soft, that's his trouble. Always was, always will be.'

Annie smiled. 'Remember that time you brought Johnnie fishing up here and he fell in trying to rescue a bee from the canal?'

Denis nodded. 'A bloody bee!'

'And the time he ate the maggots 'cos he'd seen you warming them in your mouth.' Annie shuddered.

'And we were all too scared to tell your mother why none of us wanted our tea!'

They both laughed. 'The good old days,' Annie said.

Denis frowned. 'They were all good before you took up with that Greenaway lad.'

'Oh, Dad.'

'I never liked him from the start.'

'You didn't like him because he didn't want to go down the mine, that was all,' said Annie.

'I said not going down the mine was a sign of bad character, and I was right, wasn't I?'

'He was claustrophobic. He couldn't help it.'

'It's not natural, a Matlow lad being afraid of the mine.'

Annie shrugged. She crossed her arms, and walked ahead. This was an old argument, one that neither of them would win.

'I know he's back in town,' said Denis. 'He's been going round telling folk how he's innocent.'

'I know.'

'I'd have more respect for him if he'd come clean; if he put his hands up and said he was sorry for what he did to that poor old bint and that he wanted to make amends.'

Annie kicked a stone.

'You'd think he'd have got the message last time.'

'What message, Dad?'

'That he's not welcome here. I was all for going round and teaching him a lesson but your mother was set against it.'

'Please don't do anything, Dad. There's been enough trouble.'

'That's what your mother said. "Ignore him, Den," she said, "and then the bugger will go away." '

'She's right,' said Annie.

Denis looked at his daughter.

'I reckon he'll pack his bags and go,' said Den, 'once he realises there's nothing for him here.'

'I reckon you're right,' said Annie.

'There isn't anything for him here, is there, Annie?'

'No,' she told her father. 'There's nothing at all.'

CHAPTER TWELVE

It was a warm Saturday morning. Annie came into the hall. William was leaning over his briefcase, checking its contents.

Annie sighed and crossed her arms. 'Do you realise that three days have gone by and we haven't had a single conversation with each other?'

'I'm busy.'

'I think that should be your epitaph, William.'

He did not laugh. He did not react at all.

'It's Saturday,' Annie said. 'You've been working round the clock again. I've been on my own. I—'

William snapped the case shut, picked it up and left through the front door, closing it behind him.

Annie pulled a face at the door. She didn't watch him drive away but picked up the telephone and dialled the Flemings' number. Janine answered.

'Hi, Janine, it's Annie. I'm guessing you're on your own too. I was just wondering if you'd like to go out and do something with me. I could pick you up – and Chloe, obviously – and maybe we could drive to the coast or something.'

'The coast?' Janine's voice was drowsy.

'Oh God, did I wake you?' Annie asked.

'No, no,' said Janine. 'I wasn't really sleeping.' She yawned. 'I was just having a little nap.'

'I'm so sorry. I didn't think.'

'You weren't to know. Chloe's teething and I'd just got her off.'

'Please, Jan, go straight back to bed,' said Annie, 'and take the phone off the hook. Pretend I never disturbed you.'

'But you want to go out.'

'We can do it another day. I'll call you.'

'Thank you,' Janine said croakily. She sounded terrible.

Annie went into the kitchen and stared out at the moor.

Mrs Miller looked up from the sink. 'Why don't you go and have a poke round the shops, love,' she said. 'I'll watch your Lizzie if you like.'

'Oh, thank you, that's kind. But it's not the same any more. Half the shops are closed and there's not much left in those that are open. Besides . . .'

'Besides what?'

'It doesn't feel right, me spending money when most people don't have two pennies to rub together.'

'I should think the shopkeepers would be glad of your custom.'

Annie picked at a nail. 'The woman in the off licence down Colliery Hill wouldn't serve me the other day. She said she wouldn't take money that's come from police wages.'

Mrs Miller sniffed. 'Some people are too proud for their own good. Don't let it get to you. You didn't start the war.'

'No.'

Lizzie looked up. 'Can we go up the moor?' she asked. 'Can we have a picnic?'

'Daddy said not to.'

'Because of the lady who was killed?'

'He thinks we should stay close to home just until the bad man is caught,' said Mrs Miller.

Lizzie looked at her from under her fringe. 'Maybe it was a bad woman.'

'Maybe.'

'Maybe she was jealous of the dead lady so she put her hands round her throat – like this – and strangled her until she stopped breathing.'

'Lizzie, please, it's not nice to talk about things like that.'

'Why not?'

'It just isn't. And anyway, Daddy says it must have been a man who killed her.'

'Why?'

Mrs Miller rolled her eyes. 'Oh, don't you ever go on, Lizzie Howarth. Why don't you both go for a walk just up to the woods? There's plenty of people still takes their dogs up there so you'll be safe enough. Don't wander too far, and if you're not back at teatime I'll send out a search party.'

So Annie and Lizzie walked in the woods where the buds were unfurling bright green and the new leaves were tender and soft. Spring was rolling on and the wildflowers up on the moor were becoming more abundant by the day, scattering colour on the mid-slopes, pink and blue and yellow that would only last for a few days before the flowers were battered by the wind, or a storm.

Lizzie swung on her mother's hand and chattered about this and that, while Annie let her mind wander. She imagined herself up on the moor. She remembered moments from her youth, moments with Tom. She wondered if he was still in Matlow, or if he had left. She had heard nothing of him for days now. It was likely that he was gone. But if he was gone, where was he? Would he come back again? He wouldn't have given up trying to clear his name, not that easily, not if he was innocent. And what if he *was* innocent? What if he had spent almost ten years in prison, he with his claustrophobia, for nothing? *Don't think of him, Annie,* she told herself. *Stop your wondering.*

'Boo!' Elizabeth jumped out at her from behind a tree and Annie was so lost in thought that she was startled.

'Oh you!' she laughed, although her hand was over her heart, trying to calm it. 'You made me jump.'

'Did you think I was the murderer?'

'No,' said Annie. 'I thought you were an annoying

little girl who I'm going to chase, and when I catch you I'm going to . . .'

'You're going to what?'

'I'm going to tickle you until you beg for mercy!'

Many hours later, Annie saw the Jaguar lights coming up the drive. She met William at the door. When she kissed him, he did not exactly push her away, but her greeting slipped from him like water from a stone.

'It's been a bloody day,' he said.

'Was there trouble?'

'We've got to close the motorways to stop the pickets moving around.'

'If you shut the motorways, won't they just go a different way?'

'We're blockading all the major roads.'

'God,' said Annie, 'what next. Do you want some tea?'

'I'm going straight back out,' he told her. 'I need to clear my head.'

He unlocked the door to his study, put his briefcase inside, then went upstairs to change. He came down again a few minutes later, fetched his gun from the case in the lobby and left the house without another word.

Annie stared at the door for a moment or two.

'Nice to see you too,' she murmured. Turning, she noticed that the study door was ajar. Without pausing to think twice, she went inside.

The late-evening sunlight came through the study window and lit the papers neatly arranged on William's desk. On the wall were watercolours – a small, original Thomas Girtin and prints of the Yorkshire countryside. A framed photograph of Annie holding a two-year-old Lizzie in her arms had pride of place on the desk. Annie pulled out the desk chair and sat down. She spun herself around a couple of times. She felt nervous and excited to be in the office, which was normally out of bounds.

She tried the handles to the desk drawers but they were all locked, and although she searched, she could not find the key. There was a small filing cabinet in the corner, but that was locked too. Annie knelt beside William's briefcase. She pressed the catches to release them, but they didn't give either.

'Bollocks,' said Annie. She sat back on her heels. Then she returned to the desk.

A single buff envelope lay on top.

Annie opened it. Inside were a dozen black and white photographic prints and a newspaper cutting. She looked at the cutting first. It was dated 15 January 1975 and the headline was: *MATLOW MAN GUILTY OF MANSLAUGHTER*.

A gardener from Matlow was today found guilty of the manslaughter of the elderly widow who had regarded him as a surrogate son.

Thomas Logan Greenaway, 22, stood impassive as the verdict was announced in Sheffield Crown Court.

Over the course of the week-long trial, the jury heard how

Greenaway had worked his way into the affections of Edna Wallace, 83, a widow who lived alone.

Mrs Wallace had confided in Greenaway that she had considerable amounts of cash and jewellery hidden about her bungalow in Salford Avenue, Matlow.

Greenaway admitted that he had taken more than £500 of Mrs Wallace's money, although he insisted it had been given to him by Mrs Wallace who, he said, had told him she did not want her family to inherit her savings.

He told the court that he had let himself into Mrs Wallace's bungalow on the afternoon of 28 September last year, to find the old lady lying on the floor in the dining room with a severe wound to the back of her head. Mrs Wallace died in hospital later that day.

A subsequent police investigation concluded that Mrs Wallace had come home and disturbed a burglary in progress. She had been pushed over in the ensuing scuffle.

The police arrested Greenaway after a ring belonging to Mrs Wallace was found hidden in his room. The ring had sentimental value for Mrs Wallace and several witnesses testified that she would never be parted from it voluntarily. There was no evidence to suggest anybody else had been in the bungalow.

Judge Mr Justice Cooper said Greenaway was a 'dangerous and manipulative liar and a fantasist' who had abused the trust placed in him by Mrs Wallace. He said Greenaway seemed to have convinced himself of his own innocence. 'Fortunately,' he said, 'it was not so easy to pull the wool over the eyes of the jury.'

Somebody had circled the words *dangerous and manipulative* and beside the words, in the margin of the newspaper, was the word *psychopath?* It was not William's handwriting.

Annie put the cutting down on the table. She had seen it before. She'd seen the headlines in all the papers. She knew exactly what had happened in that courtroom; she'd been there. She'd stood in the witness box and told the court the intimate details of her relationship with Tom. She'd been shamed in front of the whole town. It had been one of the worst experiences of her life; everyone looking at her like she was some kind of whore. And God, the names she'd been called afterwards. The things people had said. The humiliation that had followed her round like a bad smell until William had swept her away from Matlow and its nasty-minded people.

She shook her head to chase away the memories. Then she picked up the envelope, carefully took out the photographs, and carried them to the window, to look at them in the light.

Each one depicted the dead woman on the moor, some taken close up, others from a distance. Annie could see that the victim was a young woman, slender and pale, with longish, darkish hair strewn about her face and her shoulders as if it had been blown in the wind. She had been photographed *in situ*, with one arm raised above her head as if she were reaching out for something. She did not seem solid enough to be made of flesh and blood, but rather something natural and ephemeral, belonging to the weather or the moor. Annie held up a close-up picture of the young woman's face. She was fair-skinned, freckles dotted on the bridge of her nose and on her cheeks. She wore a small stud in the lobe of one ear. Her eyes were open and she seemed to be gazing at something in the distance. Mascara had run around her eyes, giving her a clownish appearance that made the awfulness of her death even worse. It was impossible to tell if she had been crying before she died and her tears had smudged the make-up, or if the rain had done that to her after her death.

Annie was almost certain she recognised the woman, although she could not place her. She looked at the picture again and tried to imagine the face as it would have looked when the woman was alive, when the make-up was fresh. She thought back to the time when she'd asked William what the woman looked like, and remembered how he had almost told her something – the troubled expression that had crossed his face. And then it came to her.

The reason the dead woman seemed familiar was that she looked like Annie. The two of them could almost have been sisters.

CHAPTER THIRTEEN

Annie stopped off at the newsagent's to buy a paper and found Johnnie there, swinging his A-Team key fob and deliberating between the choice of chocolate bars. When he caught sight of his sister, he ducked around the counter. Annie went the other way and cornered him.

'What's up?' she asked. 'Why are you avoiding me?'

'Nothing's up and I'm not avoiding you. I've got 15p and I can't decide between a Mars Bar or a Yorkie.'

'What's that on your face?'

'It's nowt, Annie.'

'Show me.' She took hold of his chin and tilted it downwards. The skin around his left eye was swollen and faintly purple. She reached up and touched his cheek with her fingers. He winced.

'What happened?' She kept her voice low so the shopkeeper would not hear.

'It was an accident,' Johnnie mumbled.

'That's no accident – someone's given you a shiner. Who was it?'

Johnnie looked at the floor. He wiped his nose with his wrist.

'Who did it?' she repeated.

'Some lads jumped me.'

'Why?'

'They said I was a scab.'

'Had you crossed the picket line?'

'I had to. I'm in NACOD, aren't I? All the canteen workers and chefs are. We're not on strike.'

A flicker of anger ignited in Annie and took hold at once. 'Are they beating up everyone who crosses the picket line or just the kids?'

'I'm not a kid.'

'Intimidation's their idea of democracy, is it?'

'It was only a few lads.' Johnnie frowned. 'It wasn't that bad. Please, Annie, don't take on. And don't say owt to Mr Howarth. Nobody wants the coppers involved.'

'I won't say anything. But they can't get away with that, Johnnie, it's not right.'

'Nothing's right these days,' her brother replied.

Back at Everwell, William was packing an overnight bag. He had rules for packing, just as he had rules for the rest of life. Everything he needed was laid out on the bed in the order in which it was to go in the small case. Annie sat down on the edge of the bed, accidentally rumpling a shirt. William immediately reached out to smooth it.

She heard him give a small tut of frustration at her carelessness.

'You're not going away again, are you?' Annie asked.

William looked up at her. The expression on his face implied that he was hardly packing the bag for fun.

'I'm afraid so. The government's called a crisis meeting in London.'

'You're always at meetings these days. What is it this time?'

'Strategy planning.'

'More wargames.'

'You could call it that.'

'And whose side are you on?'

'I'm not on anyone's side. I'm just doing my job. Did you get the newspaper for me?'

She passed it to him. On the front page was a photograph of a small group of old women throwing tomatoes at a police convoy. They were surrounded by a larger gang of onlookers, all of them laughing, cheering the old women and mocking the police. William looked at the picture for a moment and then put the newspaper down.

'It's that kind of thing that makes us look ridiculous,' he said. 'What do they think we should do? Lock up the pensioners?'

He breathed out slowly, then balled the underwear he'd laid out on the bed and put it inside his shoes to make the most of the available space. Annie tried not to be irritated by his precision.

'How long will you be away?'

'A few days. Three or four at most.'

He laid his towel flat on top of everything else and then zipped up the case. Annie noticed how the bright spring sunlight picked out the lines in his face, and the grey in his eyebrows and hair. She noticed how his jaw-line was softening, and the redness in the skin of his neck. She noticed how his eyelids were folding over his eyes.

'You look tired,' she said.

'I haven't been sleeping well. I'm worried about the murder. We're not doing enough. We don't have the resources. I feel we're letting the victim down.'

'She's dead, William. What you do or don't do won't make any difference to her now.'

'What if it happens again?'

'Do you think it will happen again?'

'I don't think anything. I don't know.'

He took a pair of cufflinks from a little tray on the chest of drawers.

'Let me help you with those,' said Annie. He held out his wrists and she inserted the cufflinks for him. This close, she could smell his cologne and the mints he used to freshen his breath. 'You worry too much,' she said gently. 'You can't carry the responsibility for the world on your shoulders. You can only do as much as you can do.'

'We don't even know her name. The only thing we do know about her is that she had a child,' William said.

'The post mortem showed she'd given birth at least once. Somewhere in this world is a little boy or girl without a mother.'

Annie smoothed his sleeves and then wandered over to the window. She looked out at the moor, at the cloud shadows racing across the slopes. William came to stand behind her.

'Annie?'

'Yes?'

'Be careful while I'm away,' he said. 'Make sure you lock the doors. Promise me you won't go up on the moor, not on your own.'

'I'm not afraid.'

'I know you're not.' He kissed the back of her head and he said: 'But perhaps you should be.'

CHAPTER FOURTEEN

The next morning, Annie went to Matlow. The railings outside the colliery were strung with National Union of Mineworkers banners, home-made posters that said SAVE OUR JOBS and others that mocked the Prime Minister and Ian MacGregor, the head of the National Coal Board. The entrance to the mine was lined with a double row of policemen wearing long dark coats and helmets. The miners were more loosely grouped behind them. They had lit a brazier although it was a bright, blustery day and the smoke was blowing this way and that. Annie looked for her father amongst the men but could not see him.

She drove to Rotherham Road, parked outside her parents' house, walked up to the front door and knocked.

After a moment or two, Marie opened the door a crack. It was dark inside the house but Annie could see that her mother's hair was a mess; her face was blotchy and had the wan puffiness it always had when she was upset.

'What are you doing here?' she hissed. 'It's not Thursday.'

'I want to talk to Dad.'

'Go away, Annie, not now.'

'Mum, let me see him.'

Marie tried to close the door. Annie pushed back, panting, 'Have you seen what's happened to our Johnnie?'

'Of course I bloody have.'

'They can't do that to him!'

'They can and they did – and you charging in here like the bloody cavalry won't change anything. It won't happen again.'

'And what if it does, eh? What then? What if next time they kill him?'

'It's over now. He's agreed not to break the picket.'

'Oh, so that's all right, then. Our Johnnie's been bullied into doing what the Union wants him to do – and never mind what *he* wants.'

Marie leaned forward. 'Listen, Annie,' she said. 'There's things going on that you don't understand. You don't know what it's like for us.'

'I know what's right and what's wrong. You taught me!'

Annie heard her father's footsteps on the landing. He leaned over the banister. 'Who is it, Marie?' he called.

Marie opened the door wide. 'It's Miss Always-Bloody-Knows-Best.'

Annie stared up at her father. Denis Jackson was

wearing darned socks, old trousers belted at the waist, and a sweater with a diamond pattern on the front over a shirt. There were pillow-crease marks on the skin of his left cheek and he had the bleary look of a man who has just woken.

'What's all this then?' he asked.

'Nice to see you too,' said Annie.

'She's seen Johnnie,' Marie informed him.

'Oh.' Denis came down the stairs in his stockinged feet. He was not a tall man, but he was broad-shouldered and muscular. He had been a boxer when he was younger and he still trained the boys at the club in town. Annie had to step back to make room for him in the hall.

'You're not going to tell me it's all right what they did to Johnnie, are you, Dad?'

'It's sorted.'

'Are you going to report those who did it to the Union?'

'Of course I'm bloody not.'

'So you condone what they did? Is that what you're saying?'

Her father sighed. 'If we're going to have a long discussion about the rights and wrongs of this strike then you'd best put the kettle on.'

Annie squeezed past Marie, who was still frowning, and went into the kitchen. Her father followed. She filled the kettle from the tap, lit the gas, and banged it on the stove.

Denis emptied the ashtray into the pedal bin, put it back on the table, pulled out a chair and sat down. Annie picked up some cups from the drainer on the sink and placed them on the table. She took a half-empty milk bottle from the fridge, and the sugar bowl from the windowledge, then sat down opposite her father.

'Go on then,' she said. 'Explain it to me, Dad, how what happened to our Johnnie is all right by you.'

He lit the cigarette, closed his eyes as he inhaled, and then smoke gushed from his nostrils.

'Thatcher wants to close the pits,' he said. 'All of them. If that happens, what's left for people like us? What's left for Johnnie and Johnnie's children? Nowt, that's what.'

'Yes, but—'

Denis held up his hand. 'We're in for the long haul this time, pet. The only way, the *only* way we'll get through it is if we stick together. All of us. Not just the NUM boys, but everyone – steelworkers, railworkers, support workers.'

Behind Annie the kettle whistled. She took it off the hob, filled the teapot and covered it with the knitted cosy.

'Fifteen hundred men work in Matlow Pit,' Denis went on. 'How are they going to feed their families if it closes? Where are they going to find work? Mining's all we've ever done – we don't know how to do owt else. I don't want your mother spending the rest of her life cleaning bloody offices while I'm sat on my backside doing nowt.'

'But beating up Johnnie doesn't make it right! That just makes the miners bullies, same as the government. What's he supposed to do, and those like him, if their democratic ballot was not to strike?'

'You can't be loyal to both sides. You have to nail your colours to the mast. He's done that now.' Denis tapped the ash off the end of his cigarette.

'He's been forced to do it.'

'He'll understand in time. So will you.'

Annie stood up. 'No,' she said. 'No, Dad. I understand that the Union's important, and the mine and the jobs. I understand all that. But family is *more* important, you know it is.'

Annie picked up her bag and went out through the back door, banging it shut behind her.

CHAPTER FIFTEEN

She needed to be alone. She needed to walk off her anger. William had told her to stay off the moor but she was not afraid, she was angry, burning with it. If any murderer came close to Annie while she was in this frame of mind, he'd best watch himself. She felt a kind of relief as she walked. Going against William's will, putting herself at risk, was gratifying. It was a small rebellion but a good one.

She took the lower path, the one that climbed more gradually up the hill, passing through Jim Friel's farmland. The way across the field was stony and wet. The cows tugged at pale, scrubby grass still not recovered from the winter. At the field edge the new growth of wild daffodils bowed their heads and the blossom buds were tight little knots of green on the blackthorn. Tiny flies hovered in the air and the birds were busy in the hedgerows. Annie climbed over the stile and took the path through the woods, cool and dark. The call of a cuckoo echoed amongst the trees and the ground beneath the branches was greening as bluebell leaves fingered their way through the winter's mulch. She walked on and she saw a figure up ahead, a woman. A large dog bounded around her. As Annie came close, she recognised the woman.

'Janine!' she called.

Janine turned. She was wearing jeans and a long, green waxed jacket that had seen better days. Baby Chloe was hooked into a sling carried beneath the jacket.

Janine raised her hand and waved, and then waited while Annie caught up with her.

'Paul hasn't banned you from coming up here then?' she asked.

Janine tucked her hair behind her ear. 'He says we're all right if we've got Souness with us.' She nodded towards the dog. 'He's a failed police dog but Paul keeps him up to scratch on the commands. He'll attack if I tell him to.'

'Is it OK if I walk with you then?'

Janine smiled. 'Yes, of course it is. It'd be nice to have some company.'

The dog came over and sniffed at Annie. He was a huge German Shepherd. His head came up to her waist. 'It's all right, you can pat him,' said Janine. 'He's friendly enough when he's not working.'

'Don't you worry about him with the baby at home?'

'Oh, he stays outside. In a kennel.'

They walked on uphill, together. They chatted for a while about this and that, and then, as the walking became more arduous, they fell silent. As the two women went higher, the woodland thinned and soon Annie could see the roof of Jim Friel's cottage over the brow of the hill, and beyond that, stark against the dun-coloured moor-side were the sprawling mineworks, the police vehicles grouped together beside the slurry pond. The sound of a voice projected through a megaphone, strident and dogmatic, occasionally drifted close on the breeze. Still further away, and lower down, the town was a maze of streets and buildings covering the basin of the valley and climbing up its sides.

Annie and Janine avoided the path that most walkers took, the wide path that went around the side of the hill, the one the honeymooning couple had taken the day they found the body. The higher they went, the smaller and less significant the farm buildings and Everwell and the mineworks and Matlow town became. They reached a rocky piece of land, and sat down in the sunlight, dangling their legs over the side of a small overhang. Chloe was asleep in the sling, her head lolling to one side. The dog lay down in the shade with its chin between its paws.

Annie leaned back on her hands.

'From here, it doesn't look far from the town to the big houses set back from the lane, does it?' she said.

'No, it doesn't. It can't be more than a couple of miles.'

Annie pointed. 'See that house there? The one with the grey roof with the little cottage beside it? That's Everwell. When I was growing up, that house seemed as distant to me as the moon.'

'But you knew it?'

'Oh yes, I knew it. All the town children went up there once a year for the well-dressing – they still do. I always used to sneak a look through the windows.'

'And you liked what you saw?'

'I thought it looked like heaven.'

Chloe had woken. She was squirming and whining. Janine pulled her out of the harness and wiped her nose. The baby rubbed at her eyes with her fists. 'Do you mind if I feed her?'

'Of course not.'

Annie made a pillow of her jumper and lay back on the rock. The warmth of the sun was making her sleepy. She closed her eyes and listened to Chloe's whimpering as Janine unbuttoned her dungarees and settled her at the breast.

'Is your Paul working every hour God sends?' Annie asked.

'Mmm. I hardly see him. He's always promising he'll do more to help with the baby but he's so tired when he comes home these days that I don't like to ask him to do anything.'

'And I don't suppose he notices how tired you are.'

'No.'

'William never noticed either when Lizzie was small. The men reckon looking after babies is easy.'

They were silent for a while.

'Paul thinks the world of William, you know,' Janine said at last.

'It's mutual.'

'Paul aspires to be just like him. He says he's never met anyone with so much integrity.'

Annie laughed. 'William has that, all right. But it's not easy being married to someone who's so righteous all the time.'

'No. I don't suppose it would be.'

Annie listened to the contented sounds of the baby feeding.

'You used to know Tom Greenaway, didn't you?' Janine asked.

'Yes. We grew up together. Why?'

'Oh, I just wondered.'

'Paul's asked you to interrogate me, hasn't he?'

Janine laughed. 'No, not at all. He told me that Tom had had a difficult childhood and I was interested. I trained to be a teacher, you know, before I got married. Tom's mother died when he was a baby, didn't she? And his father treated him badly.'

'That's about the sum of it.' Annie picked at little stems of grass beside her. 'His dad expected Tom to follow the traditional career route for Matlow lads: leave school at the earliest opportunity and go straight up the hill and down the mine, but Tom couldn't do that. Just the thought of going underground was enough to turn him white as a sheet.'

'Oh. That must have been difficult.'

'Tom's father was a horrible man. He thought Tom's problem reflected on him. He used to call him his pansy-boy – and worse.'

'Poor kid.'

'A lot of people tried to help.'

'Yes, but children who are told all their life that they're useless build walls around themselves. They'll say what they think people want them to say. They often have trouble with the truth, even when they're grown up. Does that sound like Tom Greenaway?'

'I don't know.'

Janine unhooked Chloe from her breast with her little finger and a dribble of milk ran down the baby's chin. 'You greedy little pig,' she said with affection.

Annie wrapped her arms around herself. The sun had gone in and she could feel a chill in the air. She looked back across the moor.

'We ought to get moving,' she said. 'The mist's coming in.' She stood up and helped Janine to her feet. Behind them, the dog stretched and yawned.

Annie looked down once more at Matlow town, fading now into the fog, and she wondered if Janine was right about Tom. She remembered the things he had said to her when they were going out together, the promises he'd made to her. Had he just been telling her what he thought she wanted to hear?

Such lovely words he'd said to her. Had every one been a lie?

CHAPTER SIXTEEN

The next day was blowy, and by late afternoon the wind was picking up, pushing through the trees and rattling the gutters. Annie was startled when Paul Fleming's face appeared at the kitchen window. He smiled and waved and she rushed to open the back door.

'I did ring the bell at the front,' he said, 'but there was no answer.'

'I didn't hear it,' said Annie. 'The wind's making such a racket. Are you looking for William?'

'No, no, I know he's in London. I was looking for you.'

'Well, you've found me. Do you fancy a brew?'

'All right, go on then,' said Paul, 'if you twist my arm.'

He put his briefcase and a heavy-duty plastic bag down on the flagstoned floor and pulled out a chair.

'I saw Janine yesterday,' Annie said as she made the tea.

'Yes, she told me you had a good chat.'

'She's tired – with the baby and everything. I remember how she feels. It can all be a bit overwhelming.'

'I'm going to take some time off as soon as I can; we'll have a week with Jan's mum in Southport. Only nobody's allowed any leave at the moment. There's too much going on.'

'Is there any news about the murder?'

'Not yet. But what do you reckon to this?'

He took a sheet of paper out of the plastic bag and laid it on the table. Annie picked it up. It was a poster. On the top it said: *Do you recognise this woman?* and beneath the words was an artist's impression of a woman's face. The woman was staring straight out of the image, her face expressionless. It looked like a badly drawn picture of Annie.

'It's our lady of the moors,' Paul explained. 'We're stepping up our efforts to identify her.'

'Wouldn't someone have come forward by now if she was local?'

'She might have been passing through. We hope someone will recognise her.'

Annie shook some digestives onto a small plate. Then she poured the tea into cups and stirred milk into them. She sat down opposite Paul.

He took a biscuit and dipped it into his tea.

'So what did you want me for?' she asked.

'Hmm?'

'You said you came here to see me?'

'Oh, nothing really. I promised William I'd keep an eye on you while he was away. He worries about you.'

'I know he does. But he doesn't need to. I'm fine.'

'You're remote out here though, in this big house, on your own. You're vulnerable.'

'I suppose.' Annie looked about her. She had always felt safe in the big old house, but then she'd never had a reason not to feel secure before. 'There is an alarm. We don't use it very often but William says it's a good deterrent.'

'Is it linked to the station?'

'Probably. You know how efficient William is.'

'I'll check. It shouldn't be difficult.'

'Honestly, Paul, I'm sure there's no need. We're fine here. If the worst came to the worst, there's always William's gun.'

'Do you know how to use it?'

'I could hit someone over the head with it.'

Paul smiled. 'I'll have a squad car drive past once or twice a day, just to be on the safe side. And if you're worried about anything, call the station.'

'OK,' Annie said. 'I will.'

When Paul had left, Annie went into the lobby. She rattled the handle to the gun cabinet but it was locked. She had a quick search around the lobby for the key, but it wasn't in any of the obvious places. She thought she would ask William how to open the cabinet when he came back, just in case – just to be on the safe side, like Paul had said.

She took a bag of potatoes from the store cupboard back into the kitchen to peel them, and was almost done when Johnnie arrived. He took off his motorbike gloves and helmet and put them on the table, and Annie went to greet him. His cheek, when she kissed it, was icy cold.

'It's rough out there,' he said, rubbing his hands together.

'You shouldn't be out on your bike in this weather.'

'I'm all right. Is there one in the pot for me?'

'There should be. Help yourself to a biscuit. Oh, you already have.'

Johnnie grinned at her through a mouthful of crumbs. 'Who's this?' he asked. He was looking at the poster Paul had left on the table.

'It's the woman who was murdered.'

'She looks like you. That's a bit weird, isn't it?'

'It's a coincidence,' Annie said, 'that's all. There must be a million women in the world who look like me. How's your eye?'

'Better now.' He leaned over the table so she could look closely at his face.

'You're still a bit yellow round the edges.'

'That's just dirt. Have you got any more biscuits?'

'Johnnie Jackson, you've got hollow legs. Shall I make you a sandwich?'

'You can, but that's not what I came for.'

Annie paused and looked at her brother. His cheeks were flushed with colour.

'What did you come for then?' she asked.

'I wanted to give you this.'

He put his hand inside his jacket pocket and took out a plastic carrier bag wrapped round something the size of a small brick. He put it on the table.

'What's in there?'

'Look inside. You'll see.'

Annie unwrapped the plastic. She reached into the bag and took out a bundle of letters, secured by an elastic band. The letters were addressed to Miss Annie Jackson at the Rotherham Road address and she recognised the writing; it was as familiar to her as her own.

'My God,' she said.

She sat down, unsnapped the elastic band and spread the letters about the table top. Each letter had the same HMP stamp. The oldest had been sent in January 1975, the same month Tom had been sent to prison.

'Do you know who these are from, Johnnie?' Annie asked.

He nodded.

'Where did you find them?'

'In the back of Mum's cupboard, behind all her knitting stuff. She must've forgotten they were there.'

'Mum had hidden them?'

'Yes.'

'She kept these from me all this time? Why would she

do that?' Annie stood up and paced around the kitchen. 'God!' she cried and she banged her hand flat on the table and then pulled out the chair and sat down again. 'If she'd given them to me when I was meant to get them everything would have been different.' She put her head in her hands. 'How could she?' she cried. 'How could she do that?'

Johnnie frowned. 'I wasn't going to say owt,' he said. 'I thought Mum knew best. Then I heard you sticking up for me the other day and I thought I should do the same for you. Besides, it was wrong, wasn't it, keeping them from you.'

'Yes, it was wrong.'

Annie pushed back her hair. 'Tom told me he'd written to me and I didn't believe him. I wouldn't listen. I thought he was lying.'

Johnnie looked anxious.

'Did I do right, Annie? Was it right to bring them to you?'

She reached across the table and laid her hand on Johnnie's forearm.

'Yes,' she said. 'Oh yes, you did right.'

Annie waited until evening, until Ethel and Lizzie were in bed, and then she read the letters.

The first ones were long and rambling. They were a combination of expressions of love and devotion, followed by angry sections in which Tom claimed, time and again, that he was innocent of killing Mrs Wallace, that he would never have harmed a hair on her head, that she was the only person, Annie aside, whom he had loved.

> *I thought at first I wouldn't be able to bear it. I told them I couldn't cope with being locked up but they didn't listen, they wouldn't believe me. They don't know what it's like when you feel the walls closing in on you, when you can't breathe. Why don't you write to me, Annie? Just a postcard would do. Anything. Just let me know that you're still thinking of me. Just a word.*

As the months rolled by, the letters became shorter.

> *I tell the others about you, Annie. I tell them how lovely you are, how strong you are, how funny, how you fight with your mum. I don't think they believe me. I think they reckon I'm making you up. I'm beginning to wonder if that's true. Did I just imagine you, Annie? Are you all in my mind?*

And then:

> *One of the warders here, he told me you're going to marry the Detective Superintendent. That's not true, is it, Annie? You wouldn't do that, would you?*

Annie put the letters down. She poked at the fire until a flame caught. She didn't know what was true, and what was not true. All she knew for sure was that her own mother had kept Tom's letters from her.

Annie did not know if she would ever be able to forgive her.

CHAPTER SEVENTEEN

The next day, the winds strengthened and there was thunder and lightning in the sky. Annie was glad to get back home from school with Elizabeth, glad to lock the doors and settle the family in for the evening.

They sat in the conservatory at the back of the house, Ethel, Mrs Miller, Annie and Elizabeth. The radio was tuned to a comedy quiz and Ethel was listening, laughing along with the audience. Annie was reading a novel, Mrs Miller was knitting and Elizabeth was sitting on the rug drawing. The storm was building outside but inside was cosy, and when the telephone rang in the hall, Annie did not want to move.

'You go and answer,' she said to Elizabeth. The child stood up and ran through the living room into the hall.

'Who is it?' Ethel asked. 'Is it my husband calling? Is it Gerry?'

'I don't think so,' said Annie.

'Where is he then?' Ethel asked. 'He said he'd be

here an hour ago. He's going to take me out to dinner.'

'I'm sure there's nothing to worry about.'

'I need to get changed. I need to do my face. I must look such a state.'

Annie smiled at her mother-in-law. 'You don't need to do anything,' she said. 'You look lovely as you are.'

Elizabeth returned and dropped down onto the floor.

'It was Daddy,' she said. 'He couldn't talk for long. He's got to go and have dinner with some people and tonight they're staying in a hotel in Kensington. He sends his love.'

'Oh,' Annie said. 'That's nice for Daddy.'

'It's not fair,' said Elizabeth. 'We never stay in hotels.'

'He's not on holiday, Lizzie, he's working,' said Mrs Miller. 'It won't be any fun for him. I bet he wishes he was home with you.'

I wouldn't be so sure, Annie thought.

'Do you remember that hotel on the Riviera where we went for our honeymoon?' Ethel asked. 'Do you remember the terrace where we used to eat our breakfast? Honey and figs. Oh, it was lovely there. I was so happy.'

'You've had a good life, Mrs Howarth dear, haven't you?' said Mrs Miller.

'I have,' said Ethel. 'I've been very happy.'

'I think we'll all be blessed if we can say the same when we get to your age.'

The four of them ate their evening meal at the kitchen table. The windows were shaking in their frames, and there was a howling from outside as the wind wound around the chimney stacks. Annie was clearing away the plates when the phone rang again. Elizabeth answered but the call was for Mrs Miller. She came back into the kitchen looking flustered.

'My father's been and gone and done his knee in again,' she said. 'I'm going to have to go home.' She looked at Annie. 'I'm so sorry, dear. Will you be able to manage to put Mrs Howarth to bed on your own?'

'Yes, of course,' said Annie. 'Don't worry, we'll be fine.'

After Mrs Miller had left, Annie drew the living-room curtains and tried to turn on the television so they could watch *Coronation Street*, but it wasn't working. She suspected the wind had dislodged the aerial. Ethel didn't want to sit in the living room without the television so they all went back into the conservatory. Annie picked up her book and tried to re-immerse herself in the story, but she was unsettled. She looked at her watch. It was gone eight.

'You go up to bed now,' she said to Elizabeth. 'It's past your bedtime.'

Elizabeth pulled a face.

'What?' said Annie.

'I don't want to go up on my own. I'm scared.'

'Oh, Lizzie, it's only a bit of wind. It won't hurt you.'

'But what if a tree falls on the house and kills us?'

'It won't.'

'What if lightning strikes and there's a fire and we get trapped upstairs and die?' Elizabeth bit her lip and blinked. 'What if all the lights go out when I'm halfway up the stairs and a murderer comes and grabs me and—'

'All right,' Annie said. 'That's enough.'

She glanced at Ethel. The old lady was relaxed in her chair and seemed lost in thought. She was smiling peacefully and her head was nodding. Annie went over to her, crouched down so their eyes were level and touched her hand. Ethel opened her eyes wide.

'Will you be all right for five minutes, Ethel, while I take Elizabeth to bed?'

'I'm waiting for my husband.'

'I know, but will you be all right waiting on your own?'

'He's going to take me out to dinner.'

'I know, I know. So you wait here. I'll be back before you know it. Is that OK?'

'It's OK,' Ethel said.

Annie checked the French doors that opened into the garden. They were locked. She took the key out of the lock and hid it behind the vase on the windowledge. She could not see much beyond, only the light that fell from the windows onto the lawn. She realised, uncomfortably, that anyone who was outside, in the garden or on that side of the moor, would be able to see in. In the darkness of the night, the conservatory with its lights and glass windows would be blazing like a beacon.

'Come on,' she said. She took hold of Elizabeth's

hands and pulled her to her feet. 'We'll have to be quick.'

They went upstairs and began the bedtime rituals. Annie usually enjoyed this time with her daughter. She liked giving her pyjamas that were warm from the airing cupboard, turning back sheets that were soft and clean, reading to her – all luxuries that Marie, with her collection of part-time jobs, could never afford while Annie was growing up. She tried to hurry things up that night, but Elizabeth was fractious and whiny. At last she was in bed, snuggled up under her mother's arm with her toy dog tucked beneath her chin. Her eyelids were heavy.

'Read to me, Mummy,' she asked.

'I ought to check that Grandmother Ethel is all right.'

'Just a few pages, then I promise I'll go to sleep.'

'Lizzie . . .'

'Please, Mummy!'

'All right. One chapter and then I must go down.'

They were reading a book called *Clever Polly and the Stupid Wolf* about a little girl who, in each chapter, outwitted the wolf who was trying to eat her. Annie thought it was quite a scary book but Elizabeth loved it. Annie read a short chapter. Her daughter yawned.

'Snuggle down now,' Annie said, and Elizabeth wriggled down the bed until her head lay on her mother's lap. Annie stroked her forehead gently, moving the hair back behind her ear.

'Would you like me to leave the light on?'

The child nodded. Then: 'Mummy?'

'What?'

'Stay with me until I'm asleep. Just in case.'

'I need to get back to Grandmother.'

'I'll be asleep in a minute.'

So Annie stayed. She waited until Elizabeth was asleep, and it was so warm and cosy in the bedroom that she dropped off too. It was a noise from downstairs – a loud bang – that woke her. She jumped to her feet.

'Ethel!' she called. 'Ethel, are you all right?'

There was no answer. She scrambled from the room and ran down the stairs as fast as she could go, still a little disorientated. For a moment she could not remember where she had left Ethel. A draught slithered around her legs in the hallway. She could hear the banging of a door beyond.

'Oh God, no,' she whispered, and she ran through to the conservatory.

The blanket that had been wrapped around Ethel's legs was bundled on the floor. Her chair was empty and the door out into the garden was wide open and swinging in the wind, banging on its hinges. A pane of glass had fallen out of the door and lay in shards on the floor.

There was no sign of the old woman. She was gone.

CHAPTER EIGHTEEN

Annie ran out into the garden. There was a half-moon and clouds were racing across the sky. The wind was strong and chilly, roaring through the trees.

'Ethel!' she cried. '*Eth-el!* Where are you?'

She thought the old woman might have gone to the gamekeeper's cottage, but when she reached it the door was locked. Ethel was not there. Annie turned this way and that, too panicked to make a coherent search plan in her mind. She did not think the old lady would have the strength to climb the stile that led into the home meadow, so she concentrated on the garden, first checking the well to make sure her mother-in-law had not fallen into the water, then skirting the garden's circumference, following the border hedge. When the first raindrops spattered onto her skin, she began to panic. She ran all around the perimeter of the house, screaming Ethel's name. And then she remembered the murdered woman on the moor, and she thought if the murderer was out there, watching, he would hear her calling and that might bring him to her. But that was stupid, panic distorting her thoughts. Why would a murderer be out on the moor in a storm? He might be, though. He might be out there watching. William had told her she should be afraid. He believed the danger was real. And Paul Fleming had warned her, too. Was it he who had mentioned the Yorkshire Ripper, or was it someone on television? A killer who attacked the women he came across at random. An unselective murderer. Ethel was out there, on her own, Ethel who could no more tell the difference between a murderer and an honest man than she could climb a mountain.

Annie went back into the house. She called the Flemings' home number and Janine answered. Annie asked to speak to Paul.

'Paul's not back,' Janine said. 'Do you want me to give him a message when he comes in?'

'No,' Annie said. 'No, it's all right.'

She put the receiver down. Should she call the police station and ask for help? Perhaps she should – but if she did, then word would spread like wildfire through the ranks of the force and William would be mortified if all his colleagues, even the most junior ones, were to find out that his fragile mother had been allowed to wander from home on a stormy night. He would be humiliated and embarrassed, he would become the butt of jokes and he would not be able to bear it. Annie did not know where William was staying, she had no way of contacting him, and even if she did, what could he do from London? She thought frantically. Who else could she ask for help? Jim Friel, that was it! Jim would know what to do.

The telephone number for the farm was written on the cover of the telephone directory on the stand in the hall. Annie dialled it with shaky fingers. Jim answered, and she could tell by his voice that she had woken him. He always went to bed early because he had to be up before dawn for the cows.

'Jim, I need your help,' she gabbled. 'Mr Howarth is away for the night and Mrs Howarth, William's mother, has wandered outside and she's only wearing a day dress and she has no shoes and it's raining and I can't find her!'

'Oh dear. Oh flamin' Nora,' said Jim.

'What should I do, Jim? I don't know what to do! I've looked round the garden but I can't see her. What if she's gone out onto the lane? What if she's on the moor?'

'Like as not, she's in the garden somewhere. Are the gates shut at the bottom of the drive?'

'I don't know. I don't think so.'

'You run down and have a look. I'm on my way. I'll check this end of the lane and I'll see if I can get someone to drive up the other way.'

'Thank you, Jim. Thank you so much.'

With shaky hands, Annie put on her coat and boots. She found the torch in the lobby and set off down the drive. She called Ethel, but the storm was roaring; it sucked her voice away. She swung the torch, but all its beam found were leaves and branches, the swaying shrubs, the orange brush of a fox tail disappearing through a hedge.

As she ran down the drive, pictures of Ethel flashed through her head. Ethel fallen somewhere, Ethel cold, bleeding; Ethel reaching the end of the lane and turning onto the main road, picked out in the glare of the headlights of an oncoming lorry; Ethel cowering beside a rock, half-perished in the cold, her thin white hair plastered to her pale pink skull and her dress draped to her body; Ethel talking to the murderer; Ethel confused when he put his hands around her throat; Ethel pushed down onto the rocks; Ethel frail as fishbone.

'Please God,' Annie begged, 'oh please God, let her be all right.'

Normally the drive did not seem so long but that night, with the wind pushing her backwards and the darkness roaring around her, it seemed a hundred miles to the end. And when Annie reached it, the gates were open, as she had known they would be, rattling like chains on their hinges. She turned left, downhill, in the opposite direction to the farm, and began to run down the narrow lane, swinging the torch, calling all the time.

She must have gone 100 yards when a pair of headlights came round the corner, driving up the hill from the direction of the town. Annie stepped into the middle of the lane and frantically waved her arms.

The vehicle slowed and then stopped a few yards in front of her, so close that she was blinded by its headlights. She ran round to the driver's side and already the door was open and there was Tom, climbing out – and for a moment she did not recognise him but then she did and she forgot to be cold to him. She ran to him, she took his hand.

'Oh Tom,' she cried, 'thank God you're here, you have to help me! Did you see anyone? Did you see an old lady? She's got dementia, she . . .'

'Shhh,' Tom said. 'It's all right, Annie. I found her. She's safe – she's here, look.'

Annie stood on the step to look up inside the pick-up truck and there was Ethel, wrapped in a thick old blanket with Tom's woolly hat pulled over her ears, buckled into the passenger seat.

'Oh Ethel! Oh thank God!' she almost sobbed.

'Jim called me,' Tom said. 'He told me to drive slowly up the lane and sure enough, there was Mrs Howarth walking down towards the town without a care in the world. You were going out for dinner, weren't you, Mrs Howarth?'

Ethel smiled. 'It was very nice,' she said. 'I had the chicken.'

Annie was trying to stay calm. She was trying not to fall apart.

'Don't you fret, Annie,' Tom said quietly. 'She's all right, there's no harm done.'

Annie's arms were crossed about her body and her

face stung with cold, and the rain was pelting down, coming down in sheets; the night was growing rougher and wilder. She was weak with relief.

'Hop in the van,' Tom said. 'There's room for a little one, isn't there, Mrs Howarth? I'll take both you ladies back to the house.'

'I left Lizzie on her own,' Annie wept. 'I left the French doors open.'

'It's OK. We'll be back in no time.'

'Anyone could have got in!'

'Annie, love, it'll be fine.'

Tom took her hand and helped her climb across the driver's seat, and she sat in the middle of the row, in between Ethel and Tom. The van's heater was blasting hot air. She reached under the blankets to take hold of her mother-in-law's hand. Ethel had some colour in her cheeks and a brightness to her eye.

'You didn't half give me a fright, Ethel,' Annie said. The old lady's hand trembled between hers; it was light and frail, soft as parchment, cold as ice.

'What did I have for dessert?' Ethel said. 'Did I have the orange sorbet, dear, or did I share Gerry's gâteau?'

'You had a little nip of brandy when you got in the van,' Tom said.

Ethel leaned forward to smile at Tom around Annie. 'And it was very good. You're a very good driver too,' she said. 'We will use you again.'

'Mrs Howarth,' Tom replied, 'flattery will get you everywhere.'

'Although you could do with a decent haircut. If it weren't for the beard, people wouldn't know if you were a laddie or a lassie.'

'That's what my dad used to say.'

'You should have listened to him,' said Ethel, 'because he was right.'

CHAPTER NINETEEN

Jim Friel had been as good as his word. He was waiting outside Everwell with his son, Seth, when the truck drew up. The men were both huddled against the weather, pacing the garden, rain slicing through the yellow beams of their torches.

Tom opened the door and jumped out. 'It's all right!' he called. 'We've got her.'

'Thank the Lord,' said Jim.

Annie climbed out of the van. 'Jim, the conservatory door's broken.'

'We'll soon sort that out, missus,' he said. 'Me and Seth will sort it out.'

Tom carried Ethel into the house and up the stairs while the Friels went into the conservatory to look at the broken pane. Annie put her head round the door to Elizabeth's room, satisfied herself that the child was safely asleep in bed, and then showed Tom into Ethel's room and watched as he set her gently down on her bed.

'Thank you, young man,' said Ethel flirtatiously.

'You're welcome,' said Tom. 'You want to get into some warm clothes, Mrs Howarth.'

'I'll see to that,' said Annie. 'Will you wait downstairs with the others, Tom?'

'Do you want me to wait?'

'Yes,' Annie said. 'Yes, I do.'

She washed Ethel, dried her hair and changed her into her nightclothes and cosy bedsocks. She could hear the men's voices downstairs, gruff and cheerful; she heard hammering; she felt helplessly grateful to them all. She turned on Ethel's electric blanket and put an extra cover on the bed. When she was absolutely certain that her mother-in-law was settled, Annie crept out of the room and came downstairs with a bundle of wet clothes in her arms and a towel wrapped around her hair. The men had made a rough repair to the broken door in the conservatory and cleaned up the broken glass. They were standing, all three of them, in the kitchen looking awkward and out of place.

'I don't know what I would have done without you,' Annie said. 'Will you have a cup of tea? Or whisky?'

'I don't know about these two,' said Jim, 'but whisky sounds good to me.'

Annie fetched the decanter from the living room and poured them all a generous serving. They sat around the kitchen table, clinked their glasses and said: 'Cheers.' The conversation turned to other storms, to people lost and found, to the murder. Annie sat with her legs curled under her. She was worried that the patrol car might pass by and see Tom's truck parked outside the house. She sipped at her whisky and tried to act normally, but she was anxious. Also, she was acutely aware of Tom; it was as if his body was calling out to hers. Now she'd read his letters, she saw him in a different light. He'd written to her so many times and she'd never replied. He had professed his innocence a thousand times. She had given up on him when the court had found him guilty of the manslaughter of Edna Wallace – and yet he had never stopped believing in her.

She remembered how it had been when they were girl and boyfriend. Six whole years she was with him, the best years of her life. They did everything, *almost* everything; he'd pull her close to him and she loved being pressed up against his body, she loved feeling his heartbeat beneath her ear, the sensation of being his, and he hers, and thinking that was how it was supposed to be. He used to lie on top of her and kiss her and she used to ache to have him inside her, but he didn't, he wouldn't, she didn't dare. Her father would have killed them both if she'd ended up in the family way. She had wanted him so badly for so many years – it had been a terrible thing how much she had wanted him – but it had been all right because she'd known the day would come. Tom had told her it would. He had promised and she had looked forward to that day for as long as she could remember.

And now he was back, he was here in her kitchen,

less than an arm's length away. William was away and she was on the Pill. If she wanted to, she could have Tom. She could take him into her big, soft bed and she could love him all night long; she could have him any way she wanted and nobody would ever know and there would be no repercussions. She could say sorry; *sorry for letting go so quickly, sorry for not giving you a chance, sorry I didn't believe you when you told me about the letters, sorry for everything*. There was nothing to stop her, nothing at all – nothing but the thought of William.

Jim Friel put his glass down on the table. He cleared his throat and he said: 'Mrs Howarth, this is a bit difficult.'

Annie wondered if he was about to ask for money. He hesitated a moment.

'Go on, Jim,' said Tom. 'Spit it out.'

'Well,' said Jim, 'you remember last time we were here, me and Tom, when it was raining and we brought the grout up for Mr Howarth.'

'Yes.'

'After you'd left the room, your husband – well, he got quite angry. And he said as how he didn't want Tom anywhere near his house again.'

'Oh.' Annie glanced from one to the other.

'He was quite specific about it. In fact, he went as far as to say that he would have Tom locked up if he so much as put a foot on his land.'

'And he'd throw away the key,' added Seth.

'Aye, that's right. He'd throw away the key.'

Tom nodded. Annie nodded too. 'I can imagine,' she murmured.

'I wouldn't normally go against owt Mr Howarth said,' Jim continued, 'but when you called on the telephone tonight I couldn't think of anyone else I could ask to come and look for old Mrs Howarth, her out in the storm and all. I knew Tom had his truck and I knew he wouldn't mind helping out, and so I gave him a ring, like.'

'It's all right, Jim,' said Annie. 'Don't worry, I'll tell William what happened. He'll understand if I explain.'

Jim looked doubtful. 'You could always just *not* tell him. Least said soonest mended.'

Annie glanced from Jim to Tom and back again.

'It's not like old Mrs Howarth will say owt,' Jim went on. 'Seems a shame to rock the boat when he need never know about any of it.'

'I know, but . . .'

'Seems to me, not telling him will save us all a whole heap of trouble. And knowing about his mother being left on her own and allowed to get out in that rain and her in the state she is will only upset your husband, won't it?'

'I don't keep secrets from William,' Annie said stiffly, 'even if they put me in a bad light.'

Tom finished his drink. 'I'll come and talk to him, if you like.'

'No,' Annie said. 'That's not a good idea. And there's no need.'

'Well, you know best,' Jim said. He heaved himself to his feet and patted Seth's shoulder. 'Come on, lad, time's knocking on. Thank you for the drink, Mrs H.'

'You're very welcome,' said Annie.

'Bring the little 'un up to the farm sometime. We've a couple of orphan calves in the stable. She can give 'em a bottle.'

'Thank you. She'd like that.'

Tom stood too, but he hesitated. He was holding the keys to the truck in his hand, jiggling them from one hand to the other.

'Thanks, Tom,' Annie said.

'Any time you want anything, Annie, anything at all . . .'

She nodded. She could hear her own heartbeat in her ears. All she had to do was give him some tiny signal, say: *Stay*, or reach out her hand.

Tom picked up the hat that Ethel had been wearing and pulled it over his own head.

'Make sure you lock up after us,' said Jim.

'I will.'

'I'll shut the gates at the end of the drive on the way out.'

'Thank you, Jim.'

Still Tom hesitated.

'Are you coming?' Jim asked him.

'Aye,' said Tom. He turned to Annie. 'I never hurt Mrs Wallace,' he said quietly. 'I never laid a finger on her. Do you believe me, Annie?'

'I think so.'

'Well then,' he said, 'that's better than nowt. I'll see you around, Annie Jackson.'

'Yes,' she said. 'See you around.'

CHAPTER TWENTY

Annie did not know what she would do if Tom did return that night, but she thought he might, she hoped he would, she knew he would not. She imagined him waiting until he was certain Jim and Seth Friel were safely back in their own cottage and then driving slowly back up the lane. She imagined him knocking gently at the door, and her opening it and him pushing through, picking her up, not taking no for an answer. She listened to the sound of the rain hammering against the windowpanes. Every now and then she pulled back the curtain, but nobody was outside, no vehicles went by.

She almost jumped out of her skin when the telephone rang.

'Hello?' she cried, breathless. The line was terrible, crackling with static.

'Annie? It's Paul. Janine said you were trying to get hold of me.'

'I'm sorry,' she said. 'It was nothing. I just . . . I just wondered if you'd spoken to William.'

'Why?'

'Only so that I knew when he was coming home. That's all.'

'I don't know. I can get a message to him if you like.'

'No, no. There's no need. I'll see him when I see him.'

'So nothing's wrong? Nobody's been up to the house? Nothing's frightened you?'

'No, nobody, nothing, I'm fine. Honestly. Everything's OK.'

She put the telephone down and looked out through the curtain. All she could see were raindrops chasing down the windowpane. She wandered through the house.

An hour passed, and another. She reread Tom's letters. Each time she read them, she believed his version a little more. She believed that he had not hurt Mrs Wallace, but had found her already lying with her head against the hearth. She believed that he had not stolen the money, but had been given it. She believed that he did not know how Mrs Wallace's ring had found its way into his room. She believed everything except that he had been framed for the crime by William, because William would not do such a thing. He would not. He was incapable of such dishonesty. He would never, ever, in a million years break the rules in such a way.

But why would anyone else have hidden the ring in

Tom's room? What did anyone have to gain from doing such a thing?

When the clock on the landing struck 3 a.m. Annie looked out for the last time. She saw the headlights of the police patrol car creep slowly down along the lane and knew that Tom wasn't coming back that night.

She went upstairs, checked that Elizabeth was sound asleep, and then returned to Ethel's room, where she made herself a nest in the chair beside Ethel's bed. The old woman slept very quietly, and it was peaceful in the room with its scents of talcum powder and soap, the dim lighting, the pillows and cushions and easy chairs. Annie made sure the old lady was neither too cold nor too hot, then she snuggled down. She folded one of Ethel's cardigans beneath her own cheek, and pulled a blanket around her shoulders.

If Tom was telling the truth, then he had spent almost ten years in prison for nothing. To lose so much of his life, if he was innocent, was a terrible thing. Annie wanted to believe Tom, but then she'd always wanted to believe Tom. That was the whole trouble.

That night, Annie dreamed she was on a barge. It was floating down a canal, one of the industrial canals that ran like ribbons between the factories and mills of Yorkshire, built to carry coal from the pits to the furnaces. In the dream, the sun was warm on her skin and it was reflecting on the broken factory windows, the graffiti on the brickwork. There were ducks on the water, fish beneath it and birds in the sky – and everything moved at the same slow pace.

Annie was lying on the roof of the barge, looking up at the tall buildings, the plants growing from the guttering and an aeroplane drifting across the sky like a fish weaving in and out of the clouds. A shadow came over her. It was Tom. He looked down at her, and then, moving very slowly, like chocolate poured from a pan, he reached down to her mouth and he kissed her.

'I know you,' he said. 'I know you inside and out, Annie Jackson, and you know me too.' And as he said that, she felt desire run through her stronger than the sun.

She woke breathless, blinking into the morning gloom. Her neck ached from the way she had been sleeping, and she was cold. Ethel was lying on the bed staring at Annie with cloudy, pale grey eyes.

'Who are you?' Ethel asked.

'I'm Annie, your daughter-in-law.'

'I don't know you. I've never seen you before. Why are you here? Where's my husband?'

'The nurse will be here soon to help you up,' Annie replied. 'Would you like a cup of tea while you're waiting, Ethel?'

'I want my husband. I want you out of here. Get out!'

'All right,' Annie said. 'All right, don't take on.'

She left the room and went back to her own bedroom. She drew the curtains and looked down at the drive below. The storm had brought down twigs and branches, and the gravel was wet and dark. Annie wondered if it would be the same for her as it was for Ethel, whether she would spend her last years slowly forgetting. It would be better, at least, she thought, than growing old regretting what she had not done, grieving for the opportunities she had let slip through her fingers.

CHAPTER TWENTY-ONE

The morning after the storm, Annie took Elizabeth to school as usual. She said nothing about Ethel's wandering to Mrs Miller. She could not settle to anything. It was a cold, gusty day, with more rain in the air. Branches were swaying like dancers shaking their skirts. Annie wrapped herself in her coat, hid beneath the hood then went outside and kicked an old tennis ball about the lawn. She wanted rid of this restlessness. She wanted to feel calm.

She went over to the gamekeeper's cottage and pushed the front door with her shoulder to check if the lock would hold; it did not. The screws that held the lock-hinge pulled out of the wood on the frame and the door swung open. Inside, it was dark and there was a strong smell of rot. Annie stepped forward. The room to her right was just a shell with the timber lathes exposed on the walls and ceiling where the plaster had crumbled away; the room to the left had once been the kitchen, but now it was only a jumble of collapsing cupboards and timbers. She climbed the staircase, which creaked and moved beneath her feet. There was no bathroom and only two small rooms upstairs. Annie went into the larger one and sat on a damp windowseat. Although the windowpane was cracked, the sun was coming through and the room was almost warm. There was a stink of mice. Dead leaves were piled in one corner, floorboards were missing and strips of paper bleached of their pattern hung in peels from the walls. Annie sat and looked out of the window. She stared at the black and white cows in the home meadow; watched the cloud shadows on the moor. She did not know what to do with herself. She did not know how to turn off this thirst that had been switched on, this longing for Tom.

She remembered one of their last days together. It had been summer, a hot spell – Matlow had been dusty and dry. Tom had arrived unexpectedly at the door of the house on Rotherham Road. She was sitting on the doorstep, reading in the sunshine. Tom stood in front of her and smiled. Even back then, his hair was long enough to provoke Denis's disapproval. 'Come on,' he said, holding out a hand to pull her to her feet. 'We're going for a swim.'

He put his arm round her shoulders, his fingers resting on her bare skin. They walked together the whole length of Occupation Road, up to the bridge, and then he helped her over the wall and they scrambled together down the bank. She had tied her cardigan around her waist by the arms. They took off their shoes and left them in the long grass and the lacy cow-parsley that lined the river. She had a nettle-sting on her knee and he insisted on finding a dock leaf and rubbing its green juice on the little bumps. Then he kissed her knee and Annie pushed him away. They tussled for a while. And then the two of them moved on again, jumping from stone to stone downriver, as they used to when they were children, holding on to willow fronds, splashing one another, laughing. The water was icy cold; it looked so clean and pure.

Annie had gone ahead, Tom had followed. The green cardigan bounced behind her as she jumped. Her legs were pale, her ankles and feet white beneath the glassy water. She held out her hands to balance herself. Laughed when she slipped and her hair came loose from its clip and was tangled about her neck and shoulders.

That day, the day she was remembering, they had gone as far as the place where they used to swim; a man-made pool at the side of the river held back by a weir. It used to seem such a long way away, a million miles from Matlow town, but it was probably only a mile or so. Annie and Tom sat on the riverbank, watching the flies dance on the surface of the water. The sun was low in the sky and everything was coloured golden; the light was in her hair and she stretched out her legs and the skin was honey-brown.

'I've nearly saved enough money to buy a car,' Tom

said, 'and once I've got a car, we can drive away from here.'

Annie shielded her eyes from the sun and turned to look at him. 'How come you've saved so much so quick?'

He had a stalk of grass in his mouth. He shrugged. 'It doesn't matter how,' he said. 'What matters is that it's for us, Annie Jackson, you and me. It's our escape fund.'

'Tell me where the money's come from,' she persisted.

She remembered the conversation because of Tom's reaction. He had looked – what? Awkward? Ashamed? At any rate, he had lost his composure.

'Mrs Wallace gave it to me.'

'You can't take money off an old woman, Tom!'

'I told her that. I tried not to take it, but she insisted. She says she'd rather give it to me than it go to her good-for-nothing granddaughter. Sadie never does anything for her. She never visits.'

'Even so . . .'

'Even so what? It's Mrs Wallace's money. She's got all her marbles. She can do what she likes with it.'

'I suppose,' Annie said doubtfully. Then she added: 'I'm not going anywhere with you unless we're engaged.'

'All right,' said Tom. 'Let's get engaged.'

'We'll need a ring.'

'We don't need a ring.'

'We do. It's not official without a ring.'

'Christ, you're never satisfied,' Tom said, and he'd

rolled her over in the grass and kissed her neck and they'd laughed.

They swam that day, that summer's day, and afterwards she, shivery and damp-haired, put on her cardigan and they walked back up the riverbank. Tom held her close to him and she leaned against him and he kissed her head and told her that he loved her. 'We'll get ourselves a Ford Capri and a ring,' he promised, 'and we'll drive away. We'll keep driving until we get to wherever it is we want to be, and when we get there we'll raise a glass to Mrs Wallace.'

'Will we invite her to the wedding?'

'Of course we will.' Then Tom had stopped and looked serious. 'Don't tell anyone about the money, will you, Annie? Sadie would kick up a right stink if she found out. She could cause all kinds of trouble for us.'

Annie had promised that she would not say a word. And she hadn't – not until she'd been forced to, in the courtroom.

In the gamekeeper's cottage, ten years later, Annie sat in the sunshine and she closed her eyes. The day she and Tom had gone swimming had been one of their last days together. One of the last days before poor Mrs Wallace was found dying in her bungalow. One of the last days when Annie had been completely happy.

CHAPTER TWENTY-TWO

After a while, Annie stood up and stretched and left the cottage. Her keys were in her coat pocket. She unlocked her car and drove into Matlow, going the long way round to avoid the colliery. She drove down Occupation Road, all the way down to the roundabout at the bottom of the hill, then back up. The houses that lined the street were high and narrow, built for the Edwardian middle classes with long windows and iron railings around the steps that had once gone down to the servants' quarters and now led to basement flats.

It seemed as if every wall in Matlow had been fly-posted. *Coal not dole* said the slogans. *Closed minds close mines.* Amongst the strike-flyers were the posters that Paul had shown her, appealing for information about the dead woman on the moor. Everywhere Annie looked, the face that looked like hers stared back from walls and lamp posts, from the insides of the front windows of Matlow's houses. Loose posters drifted in the residual wind; they danced along the streets and alleyways of the grubby little town, they settled on the rubbish bags heaped at the street corners, they twisted above the washing that flapped and swung on the lines in the backyards.

Annie could not see Tom's truck anywhere. She parked her car outside the flower shop on Occupation Road and sat there for a while, watching the doors of the houses opposite. When the centre door opened, her heart jumped, but it was a woman in a sari who backed out, struggling to manoeuvre a push-chair down the front steps.

She waited a while longer but when nothing happened, she got out of the car. There were a few flowers in the buckets outside the florist's – skinny-stalked tulips and dull, papery carnations – nothing with any colour or scent. Annie picked a bunch of yellow tulips held together by an elastic band and went into the shop. The woman behind the counter took the flowers. She was overweight, florid-faced and her hair was frizzy. The skin of her hands was red with eczema.

'It's Annie Jackson as was, isn't it?' she said. 'Remember me? Sally Smith. I was in the year above you at school.'

'I remember,' said Annie. 'How are things with you?'

Sally wrapped the flowers in a sheet of paper. 'Not so good,' she sighed. 'Nobody's buying flowers any more. The only thing that's keeping us in business is funeral wreaths. Thank God people keep dying even during a strike.'

Annie felt the eyes of the dead woman look down at her from the pinboard on the wall of the shop.

'I expect things will pick up again soon,' she said.

'Let's hope it is sooner rather than later. That'll be 40p, please.' Sally passed the flowers to Annie. 'I haven't seen you down this way for a long while,' she said. She put the money in the till and looked at Annie from the corner of her eye. 'Have you come to Occupation Road for any particular reason?'

'No,' Annie said brightly. 'No, I was just passing.'

CHAPTER TWENTY-THREE

When Elizabeth came home from school, Annie said: 'Change into your outdoor clothes, we're going to the farm.'

'Why?'

'It's a surprise. A treat.'

'I don't want to go to the farm. The cows smell and Seth is a weirdo.'

'There are some baby calves. You might be allowed to feed them.'

Elizabeth looked at her mother with suspicion.

'All right,' said Annie. 'I'll go on my own then.'

'No! Wait!' Elizabeth ran upstairs and came back almost at once in her jeans and a sweatshirt. They put on coats and boots, left the house and went hand-in-hand across the garden, past the well, over the stile, through the home meadow and into the farmyard. Jim Friel raised a hand when he saw them from across the yard, and Elizabeth ran over to him, awkward in her boots.

'We've come to see the calves,' she called out. 'Mummy said I could feed them!'

'I said *maybe*.'

'As luck would have it,' said Jim, 'it's about time for a feed now. Do you remember how to feed the orphans, young lady? Remember how I showed you last year?'

Elizabeth nodded vigorously.

'Good,' said Jim. 'Come on then, hop to.'

From the darkness of the open barn, Annie saw Seth look up. He was hunched over the engine of the tractor, an open tool-kit beside him. He looked long and hard at Annie and Elizabeth, and then he turned back to his work.

Elizabeth skipped after Jim, through the muddy yard into the milking shed, and returned with a feeding bottle clutched between the palms of her hands. Jim led them to the stable block, and slid back the heavy metal bolt that held the door to. A pair of swallows darted out, so close to Annie that she felt the movement of the air they displaced against her cheek. Inside, the stable was musty and dark; there was a smell of animal and hay. Black cobwebs hung from the rafters. The orphans were nestling together at the back of the stable, but when they smelled the milk they moved towards the visitors on their spindly legs, butting at the farmer in his filthy overalls.

'Go on then,' said Jim. Elizabeth tentatively showed the teat of the bottle to the smaller of the calves. It took it at once, tugging at the bottle; it slurped and sucked, spilling drool and milk, and Elizabeth held on to her bottle and laughed. Jim offered the other bottle to Annie but she shook her head.

She leaned back against the stable door and watched the calves.

'It's nice up here,' she said to Jim. 'Animals are uncomplicated.'

He snorted. 'Don't you believe it.'

'At least you'll never be out of a job.'

'Are you talking about the miners? I've no sympathy for them. Lazy bastards.' Elizabeth looked up at the farmer. 'Beg pardon for the language, Mrs Howarth,' said Jim. 'Beg pardon, Lizzie, but most of those men don't know what a hard day's work is. They ought to try doing what I do, then they'd know what it's like to struggle.'

The calf tugged at the bottle in his hands and Jim scratched the tuft between its ears. His hands were huge and red, his wrists the size of Annie's thighs.

'It's the unions that's the problem. Look at British Leyland,' he said, 'look what the workforce did to that company. Their greed sent it down the pan. If you ask me, Mrs Thatcher's got the right idea.'

Elizabeth looked up at her mother. Annie winked at her.

'They ought to line the strikers up against the wall and shoot 'em. Give the jobs to people who want to work.'

'They're striking to save their jobs, Jim,' Annie said.

'Aye, well. If they'd worked a bit harder in the

first place maybe they wouldn't be in this mess now.'

Annie took a deep breath.

'I didn't come up here to talk politics,' she said. 'I came to thank you for your help with finding old Mrs Howarth.' She took an envelope from her jacket pocket and held it out in her hand. 'This is for you. It's not much, just some beer money for you and Seth. I hope you'll take it.'

Jim rubbed his jaw.

'I don't want your money,' he said. 'What are neighbours for, if not to help?'

'Please,' said Annie. 'It will make me feel better. And there's an envelope for Tom Greenaway too. Will you see him?'

'He's down the Black Horse most nights, playing pool.'

'Then give it to him, will you?' She dropped both envelopes into the pocket of Jim's overalls, and she smiled at him.

He looked at her for a moment.

'All right,' he said. 'Much obliged, Mrs H.'

'And another thing, Jim. I've been thinking, perhaps you were right. There's no point going over what happened the other night with Mr Howarth. No point upsetting him. Best just to forget it.'

He nodded. 'Aye. I think that's right.'

Elizabeth squealed when the calf she had been feeding butted her.

'I've run out of milk and he's still hungry! Can we get him some more? Please – can we?'

'He's had more than enough,' said Jim. 'He'll be round as a barrel if you give him any more.'

'Come on, Lizzie,' said Annie. 'It's time we were getting back. Thanks, Jim.'

She reached out for her daughter's hand. She wanted to be out of there, away from the farm. She had stepped over an invisible line, and knew that there was no going back now. She had set something in motion. What happened next was out of her hands.

CHAPTER TWENTY-FOUR

William telephoned to say he would be back in time for dinner that evening. Annie prepared a beef and ale hotpot that would keep warm in the oven, and while it was cooking she went upstairs to change. She bathed to get rid of the smell of garlic and onion and to soak the day from her face.

In the bedroom she put on a dove-grey dress she knew William liked and a pearl-blue cardigan. She brushed out her hair at the dressing table and put on a little make-up. She still felt itchy and unsettled, as if she had a virus in her blood, as if she were coming down with something.

She heard the taxi draw up outside, saw the beam of its headlights swing across the ceiling. She drew back the curtain to watch William, lit by the interior light of the cab, pay the driver cash from his wallet and take a receipt in return. He must have sensed her eyes upon him because he looked up at the window.

Annie raised a hand, and he waved back to her.

She heard him greet Ethel and Elizabeth and then his footsteps on the stairs. She returned to the dressing table and sat on the stool. She watched his reflection approach hers in the dressing-table mirror. She felt his hand on her shoulder, his kiss on the top of her head.

'You look exhausted,' she said.

'It's been a long few days.' He sat down on the bed and put one ankle on the other knee so he could unlace his shoes. 'Did I miss anything here in Matlow?'

'No,' Annie lied. 'It's all been quiet.'

He was watching her, and she knew she must be reflected three times in the oval dressing-table mirrors with the bevelled edges that were each tilted towards one another.

'Paul Fleming called by,' she said. 'He's been keeping a good eye on us.'

'I'm very glad to hear it.'

Annie leaned forward, closer to the mirror, made fish-lips and brushed on a little gloss. William stood slowly, as if his back were aching. He took off his jacket and hung it on a hanger. In the mirror she saw him take off his belt, and then step out of his trousers. She tried not to look at the wrinkles around his knees, the grey hairs on his chest, the sag of his breasts or the soft little belly that was forming despite his best efforts to keep age at bay. She tried not to look at his old man's underpants.

At dinner, Annie and William sat at opposite ends of

the dining-room table. Ethel and Elizabeth were facing each other between them. They ate the casserole with mashed potato and beans from the freezer. Annie glanced at her husband through the candlelight. She watched the way he cut up his food, how carefully he ate, how slowly. He chewed his food meticulously because he had read that mastication was the best way to avoid indigestion and he was prone to heartburn. After every mouthful he picked up his serviette and dabbed his lips. He sipped his wine. Every now and then he made a little burp, and held his fingers to his lips.

The room was so quiet that Annie imagined she could hear the sound of her husband chewing. He had always eaten slowly and carefully; when they had first married it was one of the things that had made her feel tender towards him, but that evening she had to fight the urge to throw a plate at him, to tell him to hurry up.

'We went for a drive, didn't we, Annie?' Ethel announced suddenly. Having made this pronouncement she carried on eating her food, making little tapping noises as she pecked at her plate with a teaspoon.

'We're going for a drive tomorrow,' Annie said. 'I'm taking you to the hospital to see the doctor.'

'No, no, not that. I'm talking about our drive the other night with that personable young man. We were in a truck. He lent me his hat, you know, William.'

William put his fork down and looked at Annie. Now her mouth was dry.

'What's this?'

'It was entirely my fault, William,' said Ethel. 'I'd gone out to meet my husband, hadn't I, Annie, and . . .' she looked about as if she would find the remnants of the story hiding in the folds of the curtain or beneath the sideboard '. . . and it was raining, I think. I didn't have an umbrella and there was a problem with the bill – we'd been charged twice for the coffee. Was that right, Annie?'

'Yes,' Annie said faintly. 'It was something like that.'

William glanced at his wife and his mother, and then dabbed at his lips.

'I was cold,' Ethel said suddenly, and her mood had changed. 'I was so cold out there in the dark and—'

'Shhh, shhh, Ethel, it's all right,' Annie said. She reached across the table and took hold of her mother-in-law's hand. 'You're all right now,' she said. 'You're safe and warm. You're with us.'

Ethel nodded. 'Where is my husband?' she asked.

'I don't know.'

'Where's Gerry? Where's he gone? Why didn't he come for me?'

Now William intervened. 'Perhaps you should take Mother up to bed,' he said to Annie.

Later, in the living room, Annie knelt beside the fire. She put a log onto the grate and poked at the ashes until a flame broke free and caught hold of the wood. Then she leaned back on her heels and watched the fire.

Behind her, William was silent. Annie looked down at her lap. She picked at the hem of her dress. After a while, when he had still said nothing, she turned to look at him. She had not heard him move, but he was standing at the window with his back to her, staring out into the night.

'What are you thinking about?' she asked.

'A young woman matching the description of our victim went missing from Doncaster last month. Her name is Kate Willis.'

'You think it's her?'

'It could be. The local police faxed over a photograph, but it's not a good likeness. It might be her, it might not be.'

'So how will you find out?'

'I'm going to talk to Kate's husband.'

'Why didn't he come forward sooner?'

William sighed. 'Kate was having an affair. The husband assumed she'd left him. A friend of his was in Matlow and saw the posters. Now he's assuming the worst.'

'Oh dear.'

William walked back across the room. He stood beside Annie, next to the fire, and rattled the ice in his whisky glass.

'It's such a mess,' he said. 'If people would live more ordered lives, so much unhappiness could be avoided.'

'Not everyone can be as organised as you,' said Annie. 'Not everyone has your advantages.'

'It's not a question of social advantage. It's a matter of living by the rules. Don't steal. Tell the truth. Honour your marriage vows.' Annie nodded briefly. She did not look up at her husband. She'd heard this speech a thousand times before. 'People don't realise that rules are for the benefit of everyone. If people would only live by them, there'd be no need for the police or the courts or the prisons. There'd be no broken homes, no tragedies, no heartbreak. Everyone would be so much happier, so much more content.'

'And what if Kate Willis was really unhappy in her marriage? What if the husband was a wife-beater or a gambler or a drunk? What then, eh?'

William looked at her quizzically. 'I'm sure he's not,' he said. 'On the telephone he sounded like a perfectly decent man.'

Annie sighed. 'Sticking to the rules comes naturally to you, William. Everything is black and white for you. It's not so easy for the rest of us.'

'Has something happened?' William asked. 'Has Elizabeth been misbehaving at school again?'

'No, no,' said Annie. 'Nothing like that. I'm tired, that's all. I've been shut up in this house on my own for too long. I'm going up to bed.'

That night, William turned to Annie as she lay awake beneath the covers and his hand lifted the hem of her nightdress and then he was on top of her. She moved a little, to help him, and he came quickly, quietly, politely. He thanked her and he kissed her and then he went back to his side of the bed. He switched on the bedside light and passed her a tissue from the box he kept on his bedside table.

A very short while afterwards, William fell asleep. He snored in his polite, irritating way. Annie turned away from him and pulled the covers over her head.

CHAPTER TWENTY-FIVE

Paul Fleming came to pick William up in a squad car to drive him to Doncaster. They were going to interview Kate Willis's husband together. William wanted to use the time in the car to catch up with what he'd missed while he was in London. Annie stood at the door and waved them off. They sat together, William serene and organised, Paul enthusiastic and eager as a schoolboy going on a trip with his favourite teacher. It was a beautiful morning and Annie could see a faint purple haze hovering over the moor that meant the bluebells were beginning to flower.

She took the bundle of letters from the bottom of her wardrobe, put them in an empty biscuit tin and hid the tin in the gamekeeper's cottage, in the bedroom that she had come to regard as her hideaway. She walked around the gardens, stopped at the well to gaze at her reflection in the little pool of black water. The moor was reflected behind her. Annie turned. She climbed over the stile, walked across the home meadow, and began to climb the moor. She walked through the dappled shade of the woods, the leafy ground beneath the canopy sharply scented by the wild garlic spikes. Annie could not have enough of the new green on the trees and the birdsong, the warmth of the sun on her skin and the freshness of the air.

She stopped in the shade to watch the squirrels chasing one another on the forest floor. She thought of the letter she had given to Jim to give to Tom. Tomorrow. She had asked him to come to Everwell in the morning. What would she say to him? What did she want from him? Was she going to send him away, or start an affair? She didn't know.

She smelled the bluebells before she saw them, and then she saw them spread out before her, thousands of the little flowers, making a purple carpet of the forest floor, and they took her breath away. They filled her with the kind of happiness she had forgotten lately, the kind that comes with knowing that everything changes and that nothing – no sorrow, no love, no fear, no desire, no passion – lasts forever.

Annie sat on a patch of grass in the sunshine and she picked bluebells, just a handful of the flowers. Then she walked uphill until she found the path that wound around the moor and she followed it. She didn't know what she was looking for, but hoped she would recognise the place when she found it, and she did.

The police had taken away all their paraphernalia, the

tape and the tent and the temporary fencing they had used to close off the place where the body had been found, but it was obvious where they had been. The grass at the side of the path had been churned up by vehicle tyres, and a pile of cut brambles had been thrown, untidily, down the side of the hill.

Annie laid her bluebells in a small pile on the rocks. Then she stood up and looked out over the countryside. She could not see the town from here, nor the mine, only green fields and drystone walls, cows and sheep and sky.

Whoever had brought the woman here must have stood in this exact same spot, where Annie stood now. She wrapped her arms around herself. It gave her the shivers to think she was seeing the same view the murderer had seen. It was a beautiful view, but it was a lonely one. Annie was filled with a heavy feeling, a kind of melancholy.

Pull yourself together, she told herself firmly, and as she did so, she heard a noise behind her. She turned, expecting to see someone on the path, and caught sight of a movement, something darting behind a rocky outcrop.

'Who's there?' she called. 'Who is it?' Her voice sounded faint, a tiny noise in all that open air.

It was probably just a bird I heard and its shadow I saw, she thought, but it had not been a bird or a shadow. She didn't know what it had been. She willed herself to walk over to the outcrop, to see if anyone was there, but she couldn't do that. Instead, she turned and began to run down the side of the hill, following the route the honeymooning couple had taken after they found the body. She scrambled over rocks and through undergrowth, she cut her hands and scraped her knees, looking over her shoulder every now and then but not stopping until she had reached the farm. She saw Seth, in the distance, attending to a calf in the field. He looked up at her and stared. She did not catch his eye, but walked quickly along the footpath back towards Everwell.

Annie spent ages scrubbing the first of the season's new potatoes for dinner that evening. She took a packet of last year's runner beans out of the freezer, made a mushroom and butter sauce and grilled a dozen baby lamb chops. At seven o'clock, Paul Fleming dropped William at the door.

'Won't you come in and join us for dinner?' William asked.

'No, thanks. I need to get back. Janine will be going stir crazy with the baby.'

'You both look done in,' said Annie. 'Was it terrible? Did the husband confirm that it was Kate Willis?'

William shook his head. 'No,' he said. 'It definitely wasn't her. Kate has never had children – she couldn't. So we're back to square one.'

CHAPTER TWENTY-SIX

The next morning, William left early for work. Annie took Elizabeth to school and when she came back she found Mrs Miller in the kitchen baking. She wiped her hands on a tea towel when Annie came in and said: 'Your mother called.'

'Oh yes?'

'She wanted to know if you were going down Thursday. She said she missed you last week.'

'It's her own fault.'

'Have you had a falling-out?' Mrs Miller asked.

'My brother Johnnie was beaten up for breaching the picket line,' said Annie, 'and Mum and Dad didn't do anything about it. I gave them a piece of my mind.'

Mrs Miller put the tea towel down. She said sorrowfully, 'Strikes always cause trouble. There's a man down our street who broke the picket line back in 1924 and they still call him Scab Harry today.'

'Yorkshire folk certainly know how to bear a grudge.'

'They do that. But I thought you were better than that, Annie Howarth.'

'Oh, it's not just that. My mother's a devious cow. She's been keeping things from me. Letters that were addressed to me.'

Mrs Miller opened the fridge and took out a block of butter.

'I expect she had her reasons.'

'That's not the point.'

'You should go and see your mother,' Mrs Miller said. 'Talk to her. Sort it out.'

'I don't want to see her,' Annie said. 'Not yet.' She didn't tell Mrs Miller that she had other plans for the day.

She put on her coat and left the house, without saying where she was going. She walked the short distance across the lawn to the gamekeeper's cottage and stood behind it, out of the wind, watching the moor and practising what she would say to Tom when he came – *if* he came.

Perhaps he wouldn't come. He might be tied up somewhere. He might have work to do. Jim might not have given him the letter.

She waited. And waited. She should have specified a time, she thought. Then: she shouldn't have sent a note at all. If he came, she should send him away. Then: if he didn't come, what would she do?

There was a light rain in the air; the top of the moor was hidden by fog. Annie was cold. She went into the cottage and wandered from room to room, peeling strips of damp paper from the walls, jumping over holes in the floorboards, kicking aside the leaves. A dead blackbird lay on the landing; it seemed like an omen and she dared not move it. In the bigger bedroom, she sat on the windowseat and rested her cheek on the pane of cracked glass. She lit matches, for something to do, and threw the spent ones into the old fireplace where the ashy remains of the last fire that had burned there were still clogged in the grate. It seemed that she waited for hours, but at last she saw a figure walking up the grass at the side of the drive. She dusted her hands on her coat, climbed down the creaking staircase and waited at the door. Tom walked towards the cottage. The collar of his jacket was up around his chin. His hands were in his pockets, his shoulders hunched against the rain.

'Hello, Annie,' he said, and although she'd planned in her mind everything she was going to say, now that he was here she found she could not even look him in the eye. She ignored the hand he was holding out to her.

'I left the truck in the layby on the lane, like you asked,' he said.

'Thank you. It's just – the police are patrolling, keeping an eye on the house. If they saw your truck on the drive there'd be questions.'

'It's all right,' he said. 'I understand.'

'Come in,' she said, and stepped backwards to make room for him. He had taken off his hat and was holding it in his hands. 'I wanted to thank you for what you did the other night,' she went on.

'Annie,' Tom said, 'I—'

'This used to be the gamekeeper's cottage,' Annie interrupted. 'William was going to restore it so his mother could move in here after his father died, but when she got dementia, obviously that wasn't practical. So she lives in Everwell with us and—'

'Annie . . .'

'This cottage has been empty for years. It should never have been allowed to fall apart like this. Somebody should have done something. It should at least have been made weatherproof.'

'It's no good talking over the things that really need to be said,' Tom said.

'I've seen photographs. Originally the windows were diamond-leaded, and the roof was thatched. It was very pretty, like a fairy-tale cottage.'

'Why did you ask me here?'

'It's sad really that it's come to this.'

'Annie, please!'

She stopped. She looked at him.

'I asked you to come so that I could tell you something.'

'What?'

'Tell you that . . .'

'What, Annie? What are you trying to say?'

'I don't know,' she said. 'I honestly don't know where to start.' Her voice was quiet and low. She had used that voice with Tom before. It was an invitation.

'I didn't hurt Mrs Wallace,' he said now. 'I never touched her. I came into the bungalow that day and I found her lying on the floor. I didn't steal the ring from her. I was going to find a ring for you, a ring that hadn't belonged to anyone else.'

'I know,' said Annie. 'I believe you.'

'Really?'

'Yes.'

She made no move towards him but she did not step away when Tom came towards her, nor did she tell him to stop when he touched her. She did not resist or cry out when he kissed her; she had not realised how much she had missed him, but when he kissed her the missing overwhelmed her and all she wanted was him – more of him, all of him. His mouth was on hers, his hand holding the back of her head, pressing her against him, and he kissed her as if he hadn't kissed anyone in all the years they had been apart – and it was the same for her. He kissed her until her lips were sore, and his fingers were all tangled in her hair, the palm of his hand on her cheek, and she thought he must be sating a hunger, as she was, and that no matter how much this hunger was fed, it would never be satisfied.

They went upstairs, the staircase creaking and rocking, loose on its nails. They stepped over the dead bird and went into the bedroom, and although it was cold and damp and smelled of mice, Annie did not care. She leaned against the wall and looked up at the dark grey clouds through the hole in the roof and she tried to regret what she was doing, but she could not. There was no regret, only relief, such relief, such happiness.

They came together quickly. She had never in her life felt so out of control, so dizzy, so joyful. There was a rush of heat between her legs and Tom leaned against her, pinning her to the wall with his weight, his gasps, and she clung to him like a starfish clings to a rock.

'Don't let me go,' she whispered. 'Don't stop, don't leave me!'

'I won't,' he said. 'Oh Annie, I won't.' And he pressed his face into her neck and laughed, and she could feel that his face was wet with tears.

At last he moved away and lifted her off him, and down. He stroked the hair from her eyes gently. 'God,' he said. 'Oh God, Annie, I've missed you.'

She looked down, neither ashamed nor embarrassed but thinking she should be. In the last minutes she had become an adulteress. She had already lied to her husband by omission, and now there would be more lies, lies to cover up her infidelity. She had done something that could not be undone, she was no longer playing by the rules.

'Annie, talk to me. Are you all right?' Tom asked, and what she really wanted was for him to lay her down and run his hands all over her. She wanted to be engulfed in him, to drown in him, to be made senseless by sex so no decisions or words or plans would be necessary, or possible. That was what she wanted.

'I'm OK,' she said.

'You're so beautiful.' He caressed her face. He kissed her. 'Annie, Annie, Annie.'

'That was the first time, Tom, for you and me.'

'I know.'

'I've only ever . . .' She could not finish the sentence. She could not bring her marriage and her husband into whatever it was that they had just started.

'You're cold,' Tom said. 'Come and sit in the truck. We can go for a drive. Where do you want to go?'

'I can't go anywhere with you. Someone might see us. I need to get back inside the house. Mrs Miller will be wondering where I am. And the patrol car sometimes stops to see if everything's OK. I've been gone too long. I have to go back.'

He put the palm of his hand against her cheek.

'Can I see you again?'

'If you want.'

'Of course I want. I want it more than anything. Should I meet you back here? In the cottage?'

'Yes. It's safe here. Nobody can see. Nobody ever comes here. Only hide the truck. Leave it somewhere where nobody can see it.'

'You did want that to happen, didn't you, Annie? This was what you wanted, wasn't it?'

'Yes,' she said. 'Yes it was.'

CHAPTER TWENTY-SEVEN

She was changed. Annie was different. She was wide awake. She was alive. She sang around the house, she ordered some new clothes for herself from Mrs Miller's catalogue, she spent ages in front of the dressing-table mirrors making herself up to look like Madonna. She walked taller, felt healthier and better and happier. Johnnie came up to Everwell and his black eye had healed and he was in good spirits too. He was working in the kitchen at the Miners' Club, preparing food for the women to take to the picket line. He wasn't alone; two of the lads he used to work with in the colliery canteen had packed in their jobs too in the name of solidarity. It was almost like being back at work, but they were allowed the radio on while they prepared the food and the women teased them mercilessly. True, they had to find ways to make fewer supplies stretch further but it was good work – it was fun.

Marie called from the phone box at the end of

Rotherham Road but Annie refused to speak to her.

William was still busy. Reinforcements were being bussed into Yorkshire, police officers from all over the country and specialists trained to deal with riots in the aftermath of Toxteth and Brixton. Both sides were gearing up for further confrontation although nobody knew, yet, where it would be. The woman on the moor lay in her drawer in the freezer cabinet of the morgue that was tucked away behind the coroner's office. Nobody came forward to claim her.

Annie filled her days with Tom, seeing him as often as she could, manipulating her time so that she could be with him. She left Elizabeth with Mrs Miller, picked her up late from school, was never home. She invented appointments she had to attend, lonely friends she had to visit, urgent errands she had to run, and they were all lies – lies that made her free. She could not have enough of Tom, and he could not have enough of her, and there was no guilt, no regret. They met in the cottage, they met on the moor and in the woods. Annie had never had so much energy. She felt as if she had been filled with sunshine and was thrilled by the aftershocks of the sex that surprised and delighted her on the occasions she was least expecting them. She had never felt like this before, never. Her honeymoon had been dry as dust compared to this; it was all new and it was heady and glorious and completely addictive.

She and Tom had to be careful. They had to creep around like criminals; hiding at the side of the lane while the police patrol passed by, telephoning one another secretly, using codes and signals, making the most of every second they were together. It was wonderful and exciting and it made her happy – happier than she'd ever been before. She didn't think about what she was doing. She went along with it. She would not stop.

William was exhausted by worry about his dual burdens, the strike and the murder, but he could not sleep. Annie lay beside him invigorated by love as he lay enervated by worry. He took to rising early to go shooting on the moor. The freezer in the garage was full of rabbits and pigeons that Annie knew she would never cook. While William was gone, Annie lay alone in bed and thought of her lover; while he was there she lay with her back to him and she went over every precious word Tom had said to her that day, every delicious moment they had shared, and she did not let herself think beyond that, to what might lie ahead of them or to what was already behind.

One night as she lay awake reliving the day's happiness in her mind, the door opened and light spilled in from the landing. Annie turned and there was Elizabeth, her bare feet sticking out from beneath the hem of her nightie. She was holding her toy dog by one leg.

'What's the matter?' Annie whispered.

'I feel sick.'

Annie slipped out of bed and and put her wrist on

Elizabeth's forehead; it was burning hot. The child suddenly leaned forward and vomited over the landing carpet. Annie wrapped her arms around her daughter.

'Poor little tyke,' she murmured into her hair. She wiped a string of saliva from the child's mouth and held her until the retching stopped and the child fell into her arms. Annie kissed Elizabeth's head. 'Come on, back to bed while I clear this up.'

'I don't want to go back to bed. There's a ghost in my bedroom.'

'Lizzie, there's no such thing.'

'There is!' the girl replied more urgently. 'It's the ghost of the dead lady on the moor.'

'You shouldn't even be thinking about the lady, Lizzie. She's not for children to worry about.'

'Ruthie Thorogood said you would be killed next.'

'She said *what*?'

'She said the murderer was after you!'

'No, no, of course he's not after me. What a horrible thing to say.'

'But the dead lady looks like you, Mummy – I know she does! And Ruthie said that man that's come back has already killed an old lady. She said he's the murderer and he came to our house looking for you and—'

'No, Ruthie's wrong, she's got that all wrong.'

'But what if it *was* him? What if he meant to kill you but he got her by mistake?'

Annie sighed. The bedroom door opened and William's face appeared. He screwed up his eyes against the light.

'What's going on?'

'Lizzie's not well.'

'What's the matter, Lizzie? Why are you crying?'

'It's nothing,' Annie said. 'Go back to bed, William. I'll sort this out.'

She helped Elizabeth change into a clean nightdress and clean her teeth. Then Elizabeth sat beside her, hugging her knees and watching while she cleared up the mess. There were two red circles of fever in the middle of the child's cheeks and her eyes were glittery hot.

'I don't want to go back in my room,' she whined. 'I want to come in your bed.'

'But what if you're sick again? You'd better not. I'll come in with you.'

'I want to be with Daddy.'

'Daddy's tired. You mustn't disturb him.'

'He'll look after me.'

'*I'll* look after you!'

'I want Daddy!'

Annie took hold of Elizabeth's hand and pulled. 'Come on, Lizzie, that's enough, back to bed now.'

'But what if the murderer—'

'Stop it. *Stop it*, Lizzie. Everwell is a big, strong house and all the doors are locked. Police cars are patrolling outside. Nothing can hurt you in here, all right? Nothing can hurt any of us.'

'Do you promise?'

'Yes,' said Annie. 'I promise.'

'Do you cross your heart and hope to die?'

'Yes,' said Annie, 'I do.'

CHAPTER TWENTY-EIGHT

Elizabeth's fever turned into a bad cold. She was prone to tonsillitis, so Annie kept her off school.

She left the child in the living room and waited until Mrs Miller was bathing Ethel before she picked up the telephone in the hall and dialled Tom's number. He answered and said: 'Hello,' and at the exact same moment there was a knocking at the front door and all she had time to say was: 'I can't see you today, I'm sorry,' before replacing the handset in its cradle.

She opened the front door and there was Marie on the doorstep, her face fully made up, a headscarf around her head and a baking tin in her hands.

'I made you a bread pudding,' she said, pushing the tin towards Annie. Annie took it.

'You'd better come in.' She stepped aside to let Marie enter in a cloud of scent and good intentions.

'I caught the bus up to the colliery and walked from

there,' Marie said. 'I wasn't going to go another day without talking to you.'

Elizabeth came out into the hall. 'Hello, Grandma.'

'Hello, chicken! Why aren't you at school?'

Elizabeth coughed theatrically. 'I'm poorly. I was sick on the landing.'

'Were you? Well, I never did.'

'I'll put the kettle on,' said Annie.

Marie went into the living room with Lizzie, and Annie stood in the kitchen, taking deep breaths. She heard her mother's footsteps behind her and turned. Marie had taken off her scarf. Her hair had been dyed again and she'd had a bubble perm which made her seem taller than normal.

'Gillian Up-the-road did it for me,' Marie said. She patted her hair. 'Your father says if I stood next to Olivia Newton-John he wouldn't be able to tell us apart.'

Annie would not smile.

Marie pulled out a chair and sat down. She put her bag on the table. 'Johnnie told me about the letters,' she said.

'Oh.'

'It's no wonder you're cross with me.'

'Cross? Mum, I'm bloody furious! Those letters were *mine*. They were written to *me*. You had no right to . . .' She bit her lip as words, accusations, piled up in her mind. 'If you'd given me those letters when they came, then everything might have been different.'

'You might not have married William, you mean? You

might have continued to hanker after that waste of space you'd set your heart on? Tom Greenaway might have continued to ruin your life even from prison?'

'But he was innocent, Mum. He didn't hurt Mrs Wallace. He didn't steal the money or the ring. He didn't do anything wrong!'

Marie shook her head. 'He's got to you again, hasn't he? Somehow or other he's got to you.'

'No, no, it's the truth.'

'It's not the truth! How can it be the truth? He was found guilty.'

'He was innocent!' Annie shouted.

They both stopped and stared at one another. Marie spoke first.

'How did he do it, that's what I'd like to know?' Marie grumbled. 'How did he persuade you that he was innocent after all this time?'

Annie turned her back on her mother.

'You must have talked to him. And there were you, saying you wouldn't go near him.' Marie was silent for a moment. Then she said, 'Oh Annie, you haven't.'

'Haven't what?'

Marie dropped her voice to a loud whisper. 'You haven't picked up with Tom Greenaway again.'

'Don't be daft.'

'Oh Annie, no. Oh please God, no. I thought you had more sense than that.'

'Mum . . .'

'I knew it. I knew you wouldn't be able to help

yourself. I told you! Didn't I tell you not to have owt to do with him? Didn't I?'

'Mum, you don't have to worry.'

'Don't have to worry? *Don't have to worry!* How could you, Annie Jackson, how could you?'

Marie paced again. The huge hooped earrings swung beneath her perm. 'Thirty-one years I've been married to your dad and I've never opened my legs to another man once. Not once. I never even thought about it.'

'Mum, please, stop it, be quiet! You don't understand.'

'What don't I understand? That I've raised a daughter with no more morals than an alley cat? You're a common slut, Annie Howarth. A whore.'

'No! You know I'm not like that!'

'Oh, don't start with the "poor little me" act. Don't start feeling sorry for yourself. Do you *realise* what you're doing, Annie? Your husband finds out you've been screwing Tom Greenaway and you can kiss goodbye to this nice life of yours – this house, the car, the holidays, the private school. He'll like as not take that little lass away from you too – and what will you do then?'

'He couldn't!'

'Oh yes, he could. You're the one committing the adultery, you're the guilty party. And with a convicted murderer too.'

'It was manslaughter and he didn't do it, and you always said William was too old for me!'

'It's not about me, is it? It's about you. You're the one

who married him. That was your choice – you wanted to put on the white dress and stand in the church and make those holy vows. Nobody made you do it.' Marie came up close to her daughter and leaned down so they were at eye-level. 'Where's it going to end, Annie? Think about it. Do you really believe that Tom Greenaway is going to give you a happy ending? Do you really think he's going to make you happy?'

'He *does* make me happy.'

'Oh, sweet Jesus, holy Mary Mother of God – I wish I could knock some sense into you. Did he make you happy last time? Were you happy when you found out he was a liar and a thief and—'

The door opened and Mrs Miller came into the room. 'What's going on?'

'Nothing,' said Marie and Annie together.

'I came downstairs and found Lizzie crying,' the nurse said reproachfully.

'Sorry,' Annie said. 'Mum's just going.' She pushed past Mrs Miller and found Lizzie cowering in the hallway. She picked up the child and carried her upstairs.

'What's the matter?' Lizzie sobbed. 'Why are you and Grandma shouting at one another? Why is Daddy going to take me away from you?'

'He's not,' said Annie. 'Shhh, poppet, it's all right. Nothing bad's going to happen and nobody's going to take you anywhere.'

A few seconds later she heard the front door slam.

CHAPTER TWENTY-NINE

William was sitting in an armchair reading the Sunday newspapers. Annie supposed she should be grateful that he had decided to sit with his family for once, rather than closeting himself in the study with his work and his music, but she was not grateful. He was with her, Ethel and Elizabeth physically, but not in his mind. He was reading about the strike. Annie would have thought he'd be glad to have a day when he didn't have to think about the strike, but that wasn't the case. He turned a page and cleared his throat. It was the last straw. She wanted to scream at him, she wanted to say: *Stop doing that! You do it all the time! Don't you realise you're driving me mad?* but she didn't. Instead she stretched and said: 'Shall we go for a little walk around the garden, Ethel? The cherry blossom's so pretty.'

Ethel looked up from her chair. 'That would be nice, dear.'

William put down his paper and took off his reading glasses. 'I'll come too,' he said.

'We'll be fine, William. You stay here. You can have a little peace and quiet.'

'I could do with stretching my legs.'

'All right then.' *If you must.*

Annie wrapped Ethel up warm, and then they went outside together, Ethel in between Annie and William, and Elizabeth running around behind. They circled the house very slowly, Annie pointing out the new growth, the birds' nests and the flowers. When they reached the gamekeeper's cottage, William let go of his mother's arm and signalled for Annie to stay where she was.

'The door's been opened,' he said.

Annie held her breath.

'The lock's broken. It's been forced.'

William looked back at Annie and she saw real anxiety in his eyes; she knew he was thinking of the body on the moor and was wondering if something had happened in the cottage, and she could not help but reflect back his panic, because she knew exactly what had happened there.

'Don't go inside, William.'

'I'll have a quick look. I need to know if someone's been inside.'

He was thinking he might find blood, clothing, evidence. He was probably wondering how it would reflect on him professionally, if it turned out that a murderer had been lying low on his property. Annie could not remember what she and Tom had left in the cottage. The biscuit tin that contained his letters was still in the upstairs room. She'd taken other bits and pieces into the room too, to make their liaisons more comfortable.

'It might be dangerous,' she cried. 'William, please don't go in.'

William smiled at her. He had heard the panic in her voice. Perhaps he was touched to think she cared so much about him. 'I'll be all right,' he said. 'I'll only be a moment.'

He disappeared into the cottage. Annie stood on the path with Ethel. Her heart was pounding and she felt light-headed and nauseous. She patted Ethel's hand to reassure herself. A sparrow hopped on the path at their feet. The buzzard pair were hunting over the fields.

'What's happened?' Ethel asked.

'Somebody's been in the cottage.'

'Oh.'

'It's nothing to worry about. It's probably just kids.'

'It's not kids,' said Ethel. 'You go in there, don't you, Annie? You and the driver.'

Annie gasped. 'What do you mean, Ethel?'

'I've seen you. I've looked through my window while Mrs Miller is making the bed and wants me out of her way, and I've seen you meet him. He comes sometimes in the mornings and sometimes in the afternoons. I watch out for him. He still hasn't had his hair cut.'

'You're mistaken,' Annie said weakly.

'No, I'm not. I watch you. I watch you every day. What else is there for me to do?'

'Ethel, please don't say anything, don't . . .'

William came out of the cottage, cleaning his hands on a white handkerchief. He was frowning.

'Somebody's been using it as a base,' he said. 'There are blankets and cushions, empty wine bottles. There's even a jar of wildflowers on the windowledge. It's a right little home from home.'

Ethel gave Annie a meaningful look. Annie squeezed her hand.

'Squatters?' she suggested.

William shook his head. 'I'll need to get it checked out. I need to make sure,' he glanced at his mother, 'that our friend from the moor was never there.'

Annie laughed. 'Oh, surely you don't think that, William. It's more likely kids. It's—'

William was already striding away back to the house.

'Look after Mother,' he called. 'And tell Elizabeth that she must not go near the cottage, no matter what. I'll get the forensics guys over here.'

Ethel looked at Annie. 'Shouldn't we tell him about the driver?' she asked in a quiet voice.

'No, it's all right, Ethel. The driver is a friend.'

'Oh yes.' The old lady nodded, satisfied.

Annie waited until William had gone back into Everwell, then she called Lizzie over.

'Wait here with Grandmother, pet.'

'Why?'

'I just need to get something out of the cottage.'

She ran inside, up the stairs, into the bedroom. She grabbed the biscuit tin, and quickly checked there was nothing else that would obviously give her away. Then she ran back down and outside again.

'What's that?' her daughter asked.

'It's a secret.'

'Will you tell me about it?'

'One day I will.'

'Are we going back now, dear?' Ethel asked. 'I'm ready for a little lie-down.'

CHAPTER THIRTY

William had left a message that he was working late. Ethel and Elizabeth were both asleep and Mrs Miller was staying over because Ethel had caught Elizabeth's cold and she wanted to be nearby in case her condition deteriorated. Annie telephoned Tom and arranged to meet him at the bridge.

She put her head around the living-room door.

'I'm just nipping out for a breath of air,' she said. 'Will you be all right, Mrs Miller?'

Mrs Miller looked at Annie over the top of her reading glasses.

'Is that a good idea? It's so dark out.'

'I've got a headache and I want to walk it off. I won't be too long.'

She pulled the door shut, put on her coat and ran down the lane, cutting across the moor. She didn't want to have to drive past the colliery and risk being spotted by her father or any of his friends; nor did she want to risk meeting the patrol car on the lane and having to explain herself, and it would take too long to drive the long way around. She shortcutted across the scrubby land, jumping the stones, the side of the moor silvery-green in the moonlight. She could hear her own breath, the in-and-out pant; the ground beneath her feet was spongy; fronds of desiccated bracken brushed against her legs and snapped underfoot. She listened out for other footsteps, a sign that someone else was out on the moor, watching, but there was nothing. The only sounds were the hoot of a hunting owl and the distant call of police sirens.

She slowed as she approached the town, to steady herself and to check that nobody was about. Sweat stuck her clothes to her skin. She saw Tom from a way away, lit by the yellow light of a street lamp.

He was waiting, leaning over the parapet of the bridge, gazing down at the water that tumbled frothy-white and glassy over the rocks below. He had walked too – there was no sign of his truck.

He looked up and smiled when he saw her.

'Hi,' he said.

'Hi.'

They stood so close that she could feel the warmth of his exhaled breath and the air between their two bodies seemed magnetised; she would have liked to press herself against him, and be absorbed into him so they were no longer two people, but one.

'Come on,' said Tom.

They turned and walked up the road. The bridge marked the end of the town and the beginning of the moorland. They walked uphill a few hundred yards to the concrete bus shelter that overlooked the town, where they used to come as teenagers, and they sat down. Tom lit a cigarette and then his fingers found their way across the wooden bench and linked with Annie's, and the next moment they were kissing, his hands in her hair, hers slipped inside his jacket. Tom's cigarette rolled away, out into the road, the smoke drifting into the night air.

Annie knew nobody would be out on the moor this late, that there was nobody to hear them or see them, but still she felt exposed and afraid. She wanted to be behind a door, somewhere safe and private, not in the cold bus shelter with its graffiti and fag ends, she and Tom acting like teenagers looking down on the twinkling lights of the town below.

'We have to be more careful,' she said. 'William knows someone's been in the cottage and Ethel has seen us going in and out.'

'Has she said anything to William?'

'No, not yet, but she might.'

'She's hardly a reliable witness.'

'But I can't say she's lying when she's not, and William's no fool. I'm worried I might say something in my sleep or give myself away somehow. I don't know what to do. I've forgotten how to be normal. I don't feel safe anywhere. I've a feeling that something bad is going to happen.'

'That's just your imagination, Annie. It doesn't mean anything.'

'My mother knows.'

'Your mother? How?'

'She guessed.'

'Oh Christ. Will she do anything?'

'I don't know. I don't think so – not at the moment. She won't want to upset the applecart.'

Tom held up his hand and rested the palm gently against Annie's cheek. She covered his hand with hers and they sat still.

The night settled heavy around them. Annie felt cool now; the cold was beginning to work its way through her clothes. She shivered.

She looked at the lights in the windows of the houses in the town below and thought of all the people in those houses. If they looked up to the moor, they would see the colliery lights in the distance and the brazier flames, but they wouldn't see Annie and Tom. They wouldn't know the lovers were there, in the bus shelter hiding in the dark like outcasts.

'I don't think I can carry on like this,' Annie said.

'You want us to end it?'

'No. That's the last thing I want.'

'Then what?'

'I'm afraid, Tom. You say it's all in my mind, this feeling that something will go wrong, but it's not. Sooner or later, something will happen and we won't be able to do anything about it. Mum will let slip to Dad and he'll come after you, or somebody will see us, or you'll get sick of the situation and go away and I . . . I don't know what will happen to me. I don't know what will become of me.'

Tom turned Annie's hand over and traced the lengths of her fingers with his.

'Why don't you leave him?'

'What?'

'Leave William. Come and live with me. We'll go away somewhere, anywhere, wherever you like.'

'And what about my daughter? What about Elizabeth?'

'She can come too. People get divorced all the time. Children survive.'

'He would keep her from me.'

'He couldn't.'

'Tom, someone like William can do whatever he wants. He has money, he has the law on his side, he has a whole police force at his beck and call. He knows the lawyers, he even knows the judges. If I leave him for you he'll take my child and stop me from seeing her. That's what will happen. He wouldn't be able to bear the thought of Lizzie being the child of a broken home, of her living with me and you. He wouldn't be able to bear the stigma.' She sighed. She felt heart-weary. 'I've thought about it so many times, Tom. I've turned it over and over in my mind and it doesn't get me anywhere. I can't leave him, not while Elizabeth is so young. I can't.'

'Then I'll have to wait.'

Tom let go of her hand. She pulled down her sleeves and held her wrists between her knees. She dropped her head so her hair curtained her face.

'Can you imagine what it's like for me,' he asked, 'lying alone at night, knowing you're sharing a bed with him? Can you imagine what it's like to lie there in the dark thinking of you, and knowing that he only has to reach out to you and you'll be there? That you're miles from me and just inches from him? That I'm so cold and he can feel your warmth?'

'He's my husband, Tom.'

'It's like grief, Annie. I've had ten years of it. Ten years to think of him touching you and—'

'Don't. Please don't say any more.'

'But I *do* think about it. Every night I wonder what he's doing to you. It goes round and round in my head, his hands on you, his mouth.'

'Stop it! Stop.' He groaned and she spoke more softly. 'If it helps, we don't have sex, William and I, hardly ever. I think it – it disgusts him. He finds it base.'

'Oh Christ.' Tom stood up. He walked away from her, along the road a little, then he looked at his watch and turned back.

'I have to go,' he said. 'I promised the girl in the downstairs flat that I'd meet her from the cinema.'

'Then go. I'll sit here a little while longer.'

'I can't leave you here in the dark on your own.'

'I want to be on my own.'

'Annie, don't be stupid. You're upset—'

'Tom, please, just go.'

He shuffled from foot to foot, blowing into his hands.

'Please,' she repeated.

'Call me on the phone to let me know you're back safe.'

'How can I?'

'Let it ring twice.'

'OK.'

He leaned down to kiss her, but she turned her face so his lips only touched the top of her head.

'When can I see you again?'

'I don't know.'

'Annie, please.'

'Tuesday. William is going to Sheffield.'

'All right. Tuesday. Where?'

'I don't know. You can't come to the cottage.'

'Come to my flat.'

'Someone might see me.'

'Annie.'

'OK,' she said. 'I'll come.'

She listened to his footsteps as he walked away and she watched her own breath floating in the cold air. She imagined what it would be like to be with Tom always. To know he was coming home to her, to eat her supper with him, to talk with him, not in a rush or quietly or secretly, always scared of being overheard, but openly and always; to spend every night with him; to sleep together, properly, without fear; to walk with him, shop with him, have his children; to grow old with him, to wear his ring.

She could have him. All she had to do was sacrifice her daughter, her husband, her family, her life.

After a while, she stood and stretched, and then walked back down to the bridge. She leaned on the parapet, as Tom had done earlier, and she looked down into the rushing water. The air was cold on her face and the sound of the river was fresh and cleansing. There was something lovely about the darkness, and the depth, and the water below.

But it was a long way to fall, she thought; it was a long way down.

CHAPTER THIRTY-ONE

A forensics team turned up in a white van which they left on the drive at Everwell before trooping across the lawn to the gamekeeper's cottage. Annie stood at the window and watched them. She bit her thumbnail. Paul Fleming was with them and William stood supervising, chatting to his men. He was making an effort to appear relaxed but Annie could tell he was stressed. Paul was doing his best to keep William calm. He was liaising between his boss and the team, smoothing things over. Annie tried not to panic and let her mind run away with worst-case scenarios, but it was difficult when strangers were picking apart her love nest, looking for clues to the identity of the people who had been there, not knowing that one of them was watching from the back window of the big house that overlooked the cottage with her heart beating like a bell and her knees weak with guilt.

The back door opened and Annie jumped.

'Sorry,' said William, 'did I startle you?'

'It's OK, I'm just a bit on edge.'

William put his hand on her shoulder and squeezed. 'I know, it's awful to think we've been violated.'

'Violated?'

'By whoever's been in the cottage.'

'Oh, yes.'

'One of our blankets is inside. The tartan one that was on the sofa in the conservatory. Whoever it was must have been in the house.'

'No.' Annie shook her head. 'No, I noticed that one had gone missing from the line. The washing line. They must have taken it from there.' She smiled a brittle smile.

'Why didn't you tell me if things were going missing?'

Annie laughed. 'Oh William, it's only a tatty old blanket. I didn't think it was important.'

He frowned. 'I've asked you to let me know if anything happens that's out of the ordinary. Why didn't you say anything?'

'So much fuss over a manky old blanket. If it happens again, I'll say.'

She laughed again and her laugh sounded false and she wondered if William could tell that she was lying. She had never lied to him before Tom came back. She'd never had cause to.

On Tuesday, William left early to catch the Sheffield train. When she was sure he had gone Annie hurried Elizabeth into the car to take her to school. Johnnie was coming towards her on his bike as she drove along the lane and he signalled her to stop. She wound down the window and he pulled up alongside and lifted the visor on his helmet.

'There's trouble outside the colliery,' he said. He had to shout over the noise of the motorbike's engine. 'Don't go that way. There's thousands of men up there. They're burning things.'

'What things?'

'Like Guy Fawkes but Mrs Thatcher. And I never saw so many coppers in my life. It feels like it's all going to kick off any minute.'

'Is Dad there?'

'Yep. He was in a lather this morning.'

'Oh God.'

'Don't worry, Annie. Mum says he knows how to handle himself.'

'Until somebody winds him up the wrong way. You're not going up there, are you?'

'No, no. Mum wants me down the Miners' Club peeling spuds.'

Annie kissed the tips of her fingers, reached out of the car window and planted the kiss on his cheek. 'You take care, Johnnie-boy Jackson. And do up the straps on your helmet!'

He pushed her hand away and grinned. 'Can't,' he said. 'The buckle's broken,' and he opened the throttle and rattled away.

Annie dropped Elizabeth at school and then took a

diversion via the supermarket to load up on shopping and get to the town. Matlow seemed different that morning. The air was crackling with expectation – Annie could almost taste it. She drove slowly along Occupation Road, parked the car in the car park behind the little rank of shops and hurried back to Tom's house with her head down, her shoulders hunched up, letting her hair fall across her face to shield it. She could not wait to be safe, inside, with him. He was watching for her from the window and when he saw her he ran downstairs to open the door. She fell into his arms.

'Thank God,' he said, and she almost wept because they were together again.

That day they made love and then they drank tea. Annie sat cross-legged on the futon wearing one of Tom's T-shirts while he played his guitar. They made toasted sandwiches for lunch and ate them in front of the television. Then they went back to bed. They slept for a while, and then they woke and made love for the second time. Annie had her eyes open because she wanted to see, she wanted to remember. Tom said: 'Oh God, Annie,' and then his body relaxed and his head dropped forward and she stroked his hair, waiting for his heartbeat to calm and his breath to slow.

After a moment he lowered his body back onto hers and propped himself on his elbows to take his weight from her. He smiled. Tenderly, he moved the hair from her eyes.

'Thank you,' he said softly and he kissed her.

She slid her feet down the bed, her legs on either side of his. There was nothing of herself that she would hide from him, nothing she would hold back. Her heart beat for him. She tried to ignore the cold little fingers of guilt and shame that tapped at her shoulder and tugged at her heart. She tried to forget her mother's words. She tried not to think of the men at the mine and the women cooking together to feed their families with what little they had. She tried not to think of her husband trying to solve a murder and keep the mines open; she tried not to think that perhaps William was thinking of her.

Tom's eyes studied her face. She could see his pupils moving, and the shape of herself reflected.

'Annie,' he said, 'I love you. Leave him and come and live with me. We'll go away – anywhere you like.'

'Don't, Tom. Don't say things like that.'

'Anywhere.'

She sighed.

'It was your husband who sent me to prison you know,' Tom said.

'Please, Tom, not now. Don't let's talk about it now.'

'If I can prove he's corrupt, would you leave him then?'

She kissed him. 'Shhh,' she said. 'Be quiet.'

He lay beside her, his right arm resting on her ribcage, rising and falling as she breathed, his hand between her legs, and after a while, he fell asleep. The window was open and the afternoon air cooled her. It was like a melancholy creeping over her skin, staining the day. Annie watched the horizontal shadows of the blinds move across the bed, the sheets and blankets tangled and piled like driftwood. She felt the sweat on Tom's chest, his damp breath against her cheek. He snored gently and even his snores, to Annie, were beautiful.

Outside, the traffic murmured and in the distance a siren began to wail, an ambulance or a police car. Annie took no notice. Police cars had been calling out their warnings all day.

Annie closed her eyes. She knew she would have to be up and away soon, showered and dressed and hair tied back, ready to meet Elizabeth from school and to exchange small talk with the other day-girl mothers with a polite, interested smile on her face as if she hadn't just spent the afternoon in bed with her lover. She'd have to put on her underwear and her tights, button up her blouse, zip her skirt, slip her feet into her shoes and her arms into her coat. She would have to tidy up, make up, lipstick a smile onto her slutty mouth, make herself respectable. She'd have to become Mrs William Howarth again.

She turned towards Tom, breathed in the smell of him, sweat and sex, the salty perfume of a man well loved, and tried to make herself believe that everything was fine. But everything *wasn't* fine. It was a mess, and she was hopelessly lost in this tangle of love and sex and deceit and lies and she could see no way out.

The siren was calling; it was coming closer, growing louder – *na-na na-na* – a sound like a banshee wailing, insinuating its way through the afternoon. Just as the sound became so loud that it almost hurt her head, a second siren joined it and there were two of them screaming through the streets.

Annie couldn't bear it. She slipped out of bed, covered herself with Tom's T-shirt and crossed to the window, climbing over his guitar lying on the floor. The sash was open. She looked out. The sparse traffic was pressed up tight to the edges of Occupation Road; some of the cars had two wheels on the pavement. A motor-cyclist looked backwards, over his shoulder, and a woman came out of the general store holding tight to her toddler's harness reins. A little girl in a blue dress was walking along the pavement collecting yellow flowers that had been strewn along it. Annie leaned out and looked to the left, down towards the town centre, and she saw the neon blue of lights as an ambulance rushed up the hill and flashed past below the window, followed by another. Both vehicles sped over the bridge that crossed the gorge, heading towards the mine.

'Tom!' Annie called. 'Tom, something's wrong. Something's happened.'

He jumped out of bed and came over to the window.

'Somebody must be hurt,' Annie said. 'Something's gone wrong at the mine. My dad's up there. What if—'

'Shhh, there are two thousand men up there all told.

The chances are that whatever's happened, it's nothing to do with your dad.'

'But he has a temper on him. When he gets wound up, there's no stopping him.'

Tom pulled the window shut. She turned to him and he put his arms around her and held her tight.

'It'll be all right,' he said. 'Everything will be all right. I promise.'

CHAPTER THIRTY-TWO

On her way back, Annie called in to Rotherham Road, hoping to reassure herself that her father was safe. Nobody was home so she put a note through the door asking Marie to give her a ring when she got back. Then she drove to the school trying to swallow the feeling of dread that was like a bad taste in her mouth. She had the radio turned on in the car and when the news came on, the newsreader made reference to skirmishes at the Matlow colliery, and arrests. There was an interview with a miner who said the police had used unnecessary force, and an interview with a police officer who described the miners as an out-of-control mob. The report claimed that the miners had now been dispersed.

At the school gates, the women were clustered together. They were talking of the fighting at the pit. The mothers held their children tighter these days, they hurried them into their cars and took them home as quickly as they could.

Elizabeth's teacher came out with Lizzie and walked over to the school gates.

'Is everything all right?' Annie asked.

The teacher had her hand on the child's shoulder. 'That's what I wanted to ask you, Mrs Howarth. Are things all right at home?'

Annie blushed at once. 'They're fine,' she said.

'Only Lizzie wrote a poem today and illustrated it.' The teacher handed over a piece of paper. The poem was called *Murder in Matlow* and the picture showed a bloody fight between a male figure holding a spade, and another wearing a helmet. Annie could tell at once that it was a miner versus a policeman and that the miner was coming off worst.

'Oh.' Annie stroked her daughter's hair.

'It's not really appropriate for a seven-year-old.'

'No, it's not. You're quite right. We'll have a chat.' She smiled at Lizzie, who had a slightly panicked look on her face because she wasn't sure if she was in trouble or not.

The teacher's nostrils flared a little. 'Perhaps you and your husband could try to make sure Lizzie doesn't overhear adult conversations. She's been a little unsettled lately.'

Annie took hold of her daughter's hand. She felt the heat in her cheeks. 'Like I said, we'll talk to her,' she said. 'Come on now, pet.'

They climbed into the car. Lizzie strapped herself into the passenger seat and leaned forward to turn the radio on. The *Ghostbusters* theme song was playing. The little girl normally liked to sing along with this one, but today she was quiet. She watched as Annie turned the car not in the direction of home, but the opposite way.

'Where are we going?' she asked.

'Into Matlow.'

'Why?'

'I need to see Grandma and Grandad.'

'Why?'

'I just do.'

Lizzie had picked up the Barbie doll she'd left in the car that morning. She smoothed the doll's princess dress. Annie glanced at her.

'Lizzie, you mustn't worry about things.'

'I don't.' She made the doll sashay across her knees and pressed its face up against the window. 'What things?'

'Grown-up things. Me and Daddy and other people. We're all big enough and ugly enough to take care of ourselves.'

'I know.'

'This strike will be over soon and then everything will go back to normal. You'll see. People will have forgotten all about it in a few weeks. And Daddy will catch the bad man and we'll all live happily ever after.'

'And Uncle Paul.'

'Hmmm?'

'Uncle Paul will help catch the bad man too.' She jerked the doll forward so its head banged on the glass and then let it fall across her lap.

Annie eyed her. 'Has Ruthie Thorogood been on at you again?'

Elizabeth shook her head.

'Are you sure? She hasn't said anything?'

'No.'

'If you're worried about anything, you talk to me, OK?'

'OK.'

'Promise me?'

'I promise.'

'Good.'

Annie drove back into Matlow the same way she'd come, past groups of men drifting from the colliery. They looked exhausted. Some of their clothes were torn, some were shirtless. She saw one man holding a rag to a cut on his forehead and another whose head and shoulders were spattered with blood. She glanced at Elizabeth. The child was holding her toy dog Scooby up, making him wave at the miners, but nobody saw, or if they did they did not bother to wave back.

They reached Rotherham Road. Annie parked the car outside her parents' house and knocked on the door. Still nobody answered. She and Elizabeth walked through the alley at the back and across the common, which had been dug up to grow vegetables, to the Miners' Club. Children were playing on the swings outside. The interior was being used as a makeshift medical centre. Men sat on the chairs with their elbows on their knees and women cleaned up their wounds as best they could. Annie glanced down at Lizzie. 'There's nothing to worry about here, Lizzie, OK?'

'OK.'

They went tentatively forward.

'Excuse me?'

A man looked up at her. His face was bloody and bruised. He said, 'You're Den Jackson's girl, aren't you?'

Annie nodded. 'Have you seen him?'

The miner shook his head.

Gillian Up-the-road came over to Annie and took her arm. 'See what the police did to the men today? The bastards. Are you going to tell your husband about this? Are you?'

'Gill, I'm looking for my dad, that's all.'

'Well, he's not here. Look somewhere else.'

'Is that Den Jackson's lass?' somebody called.

'Aye!'

'Tell her they took him.'

'Who took him?'

'Who do you think? Put him in the back of a van and drove him off.'

'He'll be down the local nick.'

'Him and all the rest.'

'Thank you,' Annie said. 'Thank you, Gill. If you see my mum . . .'

'I'll tell her you were here.'

'Come on.' Annie took hold of Lizzie and hurried her away. They ran back to the car and clambered in. Annie locked the doors.

'Why is everyone upset?' asked Elizabeth.

'It's been a bad day,' said Annie. 'It'll soon be over.'

She drove towards Matlow police station, but couldn't get close. The road had been closed at both ends and hundreds of people were milling about outside. Some of them were shouting. A bottle flew through the air and a moment later there was the sound of breaking glass. Elizabeth was sitting up straight, gazing out of the car window and holding tight to her dog. The doll, forgotten now, lay in the footwell.

'Is Grandad here?' she asked.

'I don't know,' said Annie.

'Are we going to look?'

'No. I think we'd better go back to Everwell.'

'But what if he's waiting for us to come and get him?'

'We'll ask Daddy to look for him when he comes home.'

Annie put the car into reverse and turned it around. Crowds of people were walking down the road, men with their arms around each other's shoulders, women comforting one another. Annie's hands were trembling. She had trouble changing gear. She could not wait to be out of the town, away from all this, back at Everwell.

When they got there, there was no news.

Mrs Miller said nobody had called on the telephone all afternoon. Annie gave Lizzie a glass of squash and a sandwich, turned on the television in the living room and went through the motions of preparing dinner. She watched the first few minutes of the news but it was all about Princess Diana, who was pregnant again.

When the telephone rang, she ran to the hall and picked up the receiver: 'Hello? Mum?'

There was an embarrassed laugh at the other end of the line.

'No, it's Julia Thorogood. I just wanted to check that you weren't ill.'

'I'm not ill. But why are you asking?'

'Because you missed the meeting.'

'What meeting?'

'The planning meeting, for the well-dressing. It was this afternoon. I called you last week to remind you and you said you'd definitely be there. So when you didn't show up, we were worried.'

Annie exhaled shakily. 'Sorry, Julia, I completely forgot. I have a lot on my mind at the moment.'

'Perhaps I could come up to Everwell now?'

'Now's not really a good time.'

'But there are things that can't wait, Annie. We need to make some decisions. We were wondering if we should even have a well-dressing this year. It might look as if we were supporting the miners.'

'I don't see what the well-dressing has to do with the strike. And what's wrong with supporting the miners? Mining is what our community is all about.'

'But the strike's not legal, Annie. That awful man Scargill is manipulating those men and they don't have the brains to see it.'

'My father is one of those men.'

'Oh, of course.' There was a long silence. 'Well, let's not fall out over politics. Can I pop up to see you?'

'No,' said Annie, and she put the phone down. She turned to go back into the kitchen. Ethel and the nurse were coming the other way. Ethel gave Annie a filthy look.

'Who's that?' she asked the nurse. 'Who is that person and what are they doing in my house?'

Annie thought, *Give me strength.* She went back into the kitchen. The onions were burning in the butter at the bottom of the pan and the potatoes had boiled over. She put the onion pan under the cold tap in the sink, and started again. The phone rang for the second time at the same moment as William came through the front door. When Annie reached the hallway, drying her hands on a tea towel, he handed the receiver to her.

'It's your mother,' he said. 'She's in a phone box.'

Of course she's in a bloody phone box. 'Thanks,' said Annie. She took the telephone. 'Hello, Mum?'

'Your dad's been arrested,' Marie said. 'Along with a dozen others. He's locked up at least for the night.'

Annie glanced at William. He had picked up the mail on the hall table and was not looking at her.

'Are you coping, Mum?'

'What do you think? At least I know where Den is – it's not him I'm worried about. Johnnie was supposed to help out at the kitchens today but he never turned up. You haven't seen him, have you?'

'I saw him this morning. He said he was going straight to the Miners' Club.'

'Something must have happened. Johnnie's never let me down; never. If he says he's going to do something, he does it. Not like some.'

She was right. Annie knew she was right. Dread was growing inside her; it was like a rock in her stomach.

'I'm on my way, Mum,' said Annie. 'I'll be there as quick as I can. We'll look for him together.'

CHAPTER THIRTY-THREE

They found Johnnie in the South Yorkshire Infirmary in Sheffield. He had been brought there by ambulance, his injuries deemed too severe for the staff at Matlow General to deal with.

The hospital receptionist was middle-aged, bleached blonde, kindly. She was relieved when Annie and Marie turned up asking about a seventeen-year-old, red-headed lad because the one who had come in earlier had no identification on him. Marie described the St Christopher Johnnie always wore around his neck and the receptionist said it was definitely the right boy.

'We didn't know who he was, or who to contact,' the woman said. 'I'm a mother myself and I didn't like to think of the lad lying there on his own, with nobody knowing his name.'

'How is he?' Marie asked. 'Is he all right? What happened to him? Where is he?'

'Just wait here a moment and I'll find out for you,'

said the receptionist. She smiled. 'Try not to worry,' she added. 'He's in the best place.'

Marie turned away while the receptionist picked up the telephone and dialled. Annie followed her mother into a waiting area. An assortment of tired people were spread untidily about on battered chairs. Some were reading magazines or newspapers. Most were just waiting.

'I'll kill him,' Marie muttered. 'I'll kill your father. The only time his family bloody needs him and he has to go and get himself arrested.'

'He wasn't to know about Johnnie.'

'Selfish bastard, he is. Always acts first, thinks later.'

'Mrs Jackson?'

The receptionist was standing behind them. Annie didn't like the look on her face. It was supposed to be reassuring but there was a definite panic in her eyes.

'You can see Johnnie, but first I need you to have a little word with the consultant.'

Marie nodded.

'I'll take you to the private waiting room. It's nice in there. You can have a bit of peace and quiet.'

'Thank you,' said Marie.

They were shown into a hot little room with no windows but quasi-religious pictures of doves and clouds on the wall. The room made Annie more worried than ever. She suspected the lack of windows and the doves were clues that this was the room where relatives were brought to be told their loved ones had passed away. Marie sat on a chair with her hands on her lap and her back straight and she stared at the door, willing the doctor to hurry.

Eventually he came. He was brisk and explained Johnnie's injuries and their implications precisely and in detail. His words came and went in and out of Annie's mind like images in a dream. She glanced at Marie, who looked as dazed and lost as Annie felt.

'I don't understand,' Marie said. 'What are you saying? Is my son going to be all right or not?'

'We don't know yet,' said the doctor. 'It's too early to tell.'

'What happened to him?' Annie asked.

'The injuries are consistent with a motorcycle accident. I understand the people who found him said his helmet had come off. He's cracked his skull. The bleeding is putting pressure on his brain.'

Marie was white-faced; her lips were a scarlet line. 'The straps were broken on his helmet,' she said.

'That would explain it.'

'I told Den to fix that helmet. I told him a thousand times. I said: "Our lad's going to have an accident, Den." I told him, and he didn't listen.'

'What does that mean?' Annie asked. 'Is Johnnie's brain . . . is it damaged?'

'The honest answer is, we don't know. We'll have a much better idea of his condition in a few days.'

'How many days?'

'Four days. Five maybe. Perhaps a little longer.'

'Thank you,' said Marie. 'Thank you very much, Doctor.'

'There's one more thing. His left arm was partially severed. We've done our best but I can't promise we can save it.'

'Thank you,' repeated Marie. She was shaking. 'Severed,' she whispered to Annie. 'Severed!'

Annie put her arm around her mother. 'It'll be all right,' she said gently.

'You can go through, if you like,' said the doctor. 'Talk to him. His appearance will be a shock to you. Try not to be alarmed.'

Annie took hold of her mother's hand and held it tight. Marie squeezed back. The two women followed the doctor's white coat along a warren of corridors, through double doors, and into a brightly lit room. There was a bed in the centre of the room surrounded by machines.

'That's not our Johnnie,' Marie said.

'I'm afraid it is,' said the doctor.

Marie walked slowly towards the bed. Then she pulled up a chair and sat down beside her son. She took hold of Johnnie's right hand, lifted it, kissed his fingers. Annie went to the other side of the bed. Johnnie's left arm was bandaged from the shoulder and raised above his body by a hoist. He was covered to the waist by a sheet. Monitors were wired to his skinny boy chest. He lay flat on the bed. His head had been shaved and his skull looked bare and vulnerable. A plastic tube fed oxygen into his mouth, held in place by a bandage wrapped between his nose and his upper lip.

Marie talked to Johnnie, speaking quietly and slowly, as if addressing a much younger child. She told him a story about when he was seven and he fell off the yard wall and broke his collarbone, and how they had to wait in Casualty with all the Saturday drunks, and how one of them kept trying to feed Johnnie crusts of bread that he kept in his pocket for the pigeons. It was an old story, one she had not told for years. She kept forgetting details, correcting herself as she went along. Her voice was gritty, but gentle. Annie remembered that voice from when she was young. It was the voice Marie used for children, for old people, for the vulnerable.

After a while she looked up at Annie and said: 'It's important to keep talking to him.'

'Yes.'

'We could bring some music in tomorrow, couldn't we? We could pick out some of his favourite tapes and bring his cassette player in. The Specials. He likes The Specials.'

'That's a good idea.'

'Four days,' Marie said. She turned back to Johnnie and stroked the back of his hand very softly. 'The doctor said we've got four days of talking to you, love, until you come round. And we're going to make the most of it while you can't talk back.' She tweaked his finger to show she was teasing.

Annie glanced at her mother. 'He said in four days we'd know more about Johnnie's condition.'

Marie ignored her daughter. 'That means you'll be coming back to us on Saturday,' she said. 'You were born on a Saturday, Johnnie, it's always been your lucky day.'

CHAPTER THIRTY-FOUR

William was still up when Annie returned to Everwell. It was dark outside but the light was on in his office. He had not drawn the curtains and she could see him sitting at his desk with papers spread before him. His sleeves were rolled up to the elbows and he had undone the top buttons of his shirt. She could see his grey chest hair and knew from the way he slouched over the desk that he was listening to his music and that he had been drinking. William hardly ever drank.

She took off her boots and went inside. Opera came out of William's office – a female voice was singing a mournful solo. Annie went into the kitchen, shrugged off her coat and hitched it over the back of a chair. William came into the room after her, a whisky tumbler in his hand. The door to the study was wide open and the music was louder.

'Annie,' he said. 'How is Johnnie?'

'He's on life support.'

'Dear God.' William rubbed the thumb of his free hand against the fingertips. 'When you called me from the hospital you sounded optimistic.'

'I had to. Mum was with me.' Annie was tired to the bone. She felt desiccated, as if all the life had been drawn from her. 'Where's Lizzie?'

'In bed. She wouldn't settle. I had to be firm with her.'

'Oh, William.' Annie held on to the back of a chair and let her head fall forward. 'You have to be patient with her. She's only seven! It's all too much for her.'

'What is?'

'Everything. All this uncertainty.'

'I don't know what uncertainty you mean,' said William. 'The outside world might be in turmoil, but as far as I'm concerned our family life is as stable as it ever was. Unless you know different?'

'Are you angry about something, William?'

'No.'

'William.' She took a step towards him and held out her hand. He did not respond and so she turned the gesture into something else. She took a glass from the dresser and filled it at the sink tap. She drank some water and said, 'I wish I could wave a magic wand and put everything back to how it was.'

'How it was when?'

'Before the strike,' she said quietly, but she really meant before Mrs Wallace died. She meant before everything started going along the path that had led them all to where they were now. William watched her. He watched her as she rinsed the glass under the tap and put it, upturned, on the drainer.

'Do you know how Johnnie was injured?' he asked.

'Only that he came off his bike. His helmet came off.'

'It was on Crossmoor Lane. Two constables in a patrol car found him.'

'I didn't know.'

'They gave him first aid. Looked after him until the ambulance arrived. He was lucky.'

'Lucky . . .' Annie echoed. She pulled out a chair and sat down. She put her head in her hands. Still William made no move towards her.

'Was anyone else involved in the accident? Did anyone see it?' she asked.

'No. It's a remote spot.'

'Why was he up there?'

'The other roads were closed. I expect it was the only way he could get round.'

'I'm so tired,' said Annie. She rubbed her eyes with the heel of her hands.

William moved then. He took a bottle of wine from the compartment in the fridge door, opened it and filled a large glass, which he passed to Annie. She took a drink. She would have preferred something hot and soothing – tea or Horlicks – but did not want to seem ungrateful for his one act of kindness.

'There's something else,' she said. 'Dad was arrested today.'

William nodded.

'You knew?'

'Of course I did. He made sure the arresting officers knew exactly who he was. They found it highly amusing that he was my father-in-law.'

'Oh.' Part of Annie wanted to apologise on behalf of Den, but the stronger part wouldn't let her do this. 'I drove through town,' she said. 'It looked like a disaster zone. Everything is such a mess.'

'It's the law of increasing entropy. The natural tendency of things to turn to disorder.'

She stared at him. 'But you don't allow that, William. You keep things in order. That's what you do.'

'I try,' he said.

Annie drank the wine although it was cold and acid in her stomach. It made her feel dizzy and sick. She had not eaten for hours. She longed for bed, warmth, sleep.

She put her empty glass down on the table and stood up. 'I'm going up now,' she said. 'Are you coming?'

'In a while. I still have things to do.'

'Suit yourself.' She did not try to kiss him but made her way past him towards the door into the hall.

'One thing, Annie,' William said, as if a thought had just occurred to him.

'Yes?'

'Where were you today?'

'I told you. I was in town.'

'What were you doing?'

'Shopping.'

'What did you buy?'

'Nothing.'

'Mrs Miller said you were out the whole day.'

'Yes. I couldn't find what I wanted.' Annie stood perfectly still. She tried to breathe normally, but it was as if she had forgotten how, and her pulse was beating in her ears like a drum. William frowned. She held her breath and then he relaxed and she could not read his face; she could not tell if he was relieved or disappointed, if he believed her or not.

'Goodnight then,' he said.

'Goodnight. I'll see you in the morning.'

She went upstairs, wrapped herself in a dressing gown and crept barefoot, so as not to wake Elizabeth or Ethel, across the creaky landing to the bathroom. Filling the basin with water as hot as she could bear it, she washed away every trace of the day that had begun so well and ended so badly. She patted her face dry with a towel and watched the sudsy water spiralling down the drain. In the bedroom, she put on a nightie and burrowed down into her bed, pulling the quilt over her head to dull the sound of the sorrowful aria that crept up the stairs from William's study.

CHAPTER THIRTY-FIVE

Next morning, the moor was all light and shadow, the grassland buttery-green, the old bracken turning orange in the sun and the new growth beginning to show as a million baby ferns uncurled their fronds. The birds had set to singing their chorus and baby rabbits hopped at the field edges, the grown ones keeping an eye on the buzzard pair that circled the moor edge.

Two figures were coming down from the lower slopes with a large dog at their heels. As they emerged from the shadows into the sunlight Annie could see that one of the men was William in his camouflage jacket, with his gun slung over his shoulder. He was carrying a brace of pheasants. The other was Paul, in jeans and a jacket, trotting to keep up. Paul's dog was carrying his huge shaggy head low, following behind his master. Paul kept pushing his hair back out of his eyes, and every now and then he nodded as if he were agreeing with whatever it was William was saying. Annie watched as they came towards the house, their breath streaming behind them, and she wondered what it was they were discussing and why they had arranged to meet so early.

The men stopped when they reached Paul's car, parked beneath one of the beech trees at the side of the drive. They talked for another moment or two, and then they shook hands, and William patted Paul's shoulder. Paul looked up at William, and he smiled a broad smile. Then he opened the driver's door, held it while the dog jumped into the car, and then he too climbed in.

Annie dressed herself in jeans and a cheesecloth grandfather shirt with a green woollen cardigan over the top that her mother had knitted for her. Down in the kitchen, she emptied the big old twin-tub washing machine, tipped the wet washing into a plastic basket, and heaved it outside. The air was cold, shot through with sunbeams, a late frost sparkling in the grass. She dropped the washing-line prop and shook out the first sheet. It flapped damp about her legs as she pegged it out. Across the meadows she could hear Jim Friel calling his cows into the milking shed. The sheep on the moor were baa-ing to the lambs in their almost-human voices; the lambs were bleating back like babies. Perhaps everything would be better today, Annie thought. Perhaps there would be good news. She picked up a towel and pegged it to the line.

William came round the side of the house and stood outside the lobby door. He did not see her. He hooked the dead birds over the bracket he'd put up for that purpose and washed his hands in the cold water at the outside tap. Annie watched him from behind the washing. She watched him and she was sorry for everything she had done, and for everything she might do. She was sorry for the humiliation William had endured because of her father. She was sorry – and at the same time she was afraid.

When she'd finished with the washing, she went back into the kitchen. Elizabeth was up and had helped herself to the slice of cold chicken pie that had been on a plate in the fridge. Scooby the toy dog was nestled in the crook of her arm.

'Hello, you.' Annie leaned down and kissed her daughter, enjoying the sweet smell of her, the froth of messy hair. A kiss wasn't enough – she wrapped her arms around Elizabeth, feeling the bone and muscle of her; the heartbeat.

'What?' Elizabeth complained, wriggling away. 'Don't do that!' Her breath was rich with the flavours of leek and pastry. She continued eating, crumbs catching on her jumper and the stone floor.

'Where did Daddy go?' Annie asked. 'Is he in his study?'

Elizabeth shook her head. 'He went up for a shower.'

Annie switched on the kettle and rinsed out the coffee jug. 'Did you have a good sleep last night, Lizzie?'

'No,' she said. 'I dreamed about Johnnie. I dreamed he was dead and he was lying on the floor all stretched out and I was holding his face between my hands and kissing him and telling him please please please to wake up, but he didn't. And then Daddy went out with a spade and dug a big hole for him. You said we could plant a rose on top of him. I was crying.'

This was exactly what had happened when the family's pet Labrador, Martha, had died six months earlier.

'Oh, Lizzie.' Annie sat down beside her daughter and tidied her hair gently.

'Johnnie's not going to die, Mummy, is he?'

'I hope not, pet. I hope he's going to be fine.'

Elizabeth bit into the last of the pastry with her little white teeth.

'Good,' she said, 'because I made him a card and I need to give it to him.'

'He's in hospital, Lizzie.'

'I know he is. I can visit him.'

'I'm not sure children are allowed in the ward where he is.'

'Oh.' Elizabeth sucked the end of her fingers and considered this. 'You could give him the card though, couldn't you, Mummy?'

'Yes, I could.'

'And you'll tell him it's from me.'

'Yes.'

'Well, that will have to do then.'

Annie stepped back and looked at her daughter. 'When did you get so grown up?' she asked.

Lizzie grinned. 'While you were looking the other way.'

When Elizabeth went upstairs to get ready for school, Annie picked up the card from the table. It was a picture of Elizabeth holding the hand of a bigger lad with orange hair, sticking out from his head like flames from the sun. The boy's mouth was an inverted smile. Blood was dripping from a red-felt pen wound on his head and pooling gorily on the line drawn to represent the floor beneath. Elizabeth had written: *I love you Johnnie* above the picture and surrounded it with multi-coloured kisses and hearts.

Annie kissed both the faces on the card and then she put it in her handbag.

CHAPTER THIRTY-SIX

William came down, showered, shaved and dressed. Annie passed him a cup of coffee.

'I'll go into the station this morning, see what's happening about your father,' he said.

'Thank you.'

'Obviously I can't pull any strings.'

'Nobody has asked you to.'

'But perhaps your mother would regard it as disloyal if I don't.'

'How you conduct your professional life is none of her business,' Annie said flatly.

William glanced at her. 'I'm not sure she would see it like that.'

He stood in front of the little mirror on the kitchen wall and straightened his tie. Although he was groomed, he was as wan as Annie. She knew he had slept no better than she had. She had gone to the bathroom in the early hours and then come downstairs to make tea, and although he had said nothing, she had known from the lightness of his breathing that he had been awake when she got up and when she returned to bed.

'I spoke to the forensic team yesterday,' William said. 'I wanted to know how they were getting on with the results from the gamekeeper's cottage. It's taking a ridiculously long time.'

Annie looked up. 'I expect they're stretched the same as every other department.'

'I've asked them to prioritise our results. We need to know if anyone with any previous convictions has been in that cottage.'

'Of course.'

'They might want to come here and take your prints,' William continued.

'Why would they want to do that?'

'To exclude you. Although I told them that none of us had been in that cottage for years.'

'Is Mummy in trouble?' Elizabeth asked.

'No, I'm not, Big Ears,' said Annie, 'but you will be if you don't hurry up. Put your coat on quick now, and say goodbye to Daddy. It's time for school.'

'Bye bye, Daddy.'

William turned to his daughter and he looked at her with such love in his eyes that Annie had to turn away. She waited by the door while they embraced. That morning, William held on to Elizabeth as if he did not want to let her go, and she, surprised and pleased by this display of affection, hugged his neck and pressed her cheek up against his.

After she'd dropped Elizabeth at school, Annie drove to Occupation Road. She hid the car behind the rank of shops, and did her best to disguise herself with a headscarf and a pair of sunglasses. When she rang the bell to the flat, Tom came down straight away wearing a pair of tracksuit trousers with a towel wrapped around his neck. His hair was wet, hanging in dreadlocks down to his shoulders and there were specks of shaving foam on his throat.

'Annie!' He moved towards her and she took a small step backwards. 'Come in, come upstairs.'

She followed him up. There was an old carpet in the middle of the staircase that zigzagged up through the centre of the house to the three upper flats. The carpet was crumpled in some places and worn in others. The banister was old and shiny, the stairwell tatty, in need of plaster and paint, and the plant on the first-floor windowledge was dead, its leaves folded over the edge of the pot.

Annie had not noticed these things the day before. She supposed she had been too eager to get inside, to be alone with Tom. That day, she followed him up to the flat and she noticed all the details. Inside, she did not sit down but hovered by the door. He embraced her but she was awkward in his arms. She pushed him away, made a barrier with her arm.

'Have you heard what happened to our Johnnie?' she asked.

'Yes. Yes, I have. How is he?'

'He's in a bad way.'

'Jesus, I'm sorry.'

'He's going to take up all my time now, Tom. Him and my family. I won't be able to see you, not while he's this poorly.'

'Let me help you.'

'You're a doctor now are you? A brain surgeon? No? Then you can't do anything to help me.'

'I can look after you.'

'No, you can't. You can't, Tom. You're not . . . You aren't . . .'

'I'm not your husband.'

'No.'

'I would do anything for you. You know that.'

'Stop it, Tom. Don't say things like that, not now. It's just – it would feel even worse, even more wrong to see you while Johnnie . . .' she tailed off. 'I can't help thinking that this is a kind of punishment.'

'It's not.'

'It feels like it is.'

'Crossmoor Lane is a terrible track, full of pot-holes, and the camber's diabolical. It wasn't fate, Annie, or karma or anything like that. It was an accident waiting to happen, that's all.'

Tom reached out and smoothed the hair at the side of her face. She made no move to stop him. She sighed.

'They're going to find out we were together in the

cottage,' she said heavily. 'William is going to find out about us.'

'It'll be all right.'

'No, Tom, it won't be all right.'

'Then perhaps we should tell him first, before he finds out.'

Annie caught her breath. 'Tell William that I've been seeing you, now, while my brother's in hospital half-dead and likely to lose an arm? While my dad's locked up, and there's Lizzie already out of sorts with all the troubles? Are you mad, Tom? Have you completely lost your mind?'

'All right,' he said, 'all right.'

'I'm so scared.'

'I know.' Then: 'Is Johnnie's bike still up there on the lane?'

'I don't know. I hadn't thought about it. I suppose it must be.'

'I'll go up in the truck and fetch it back. I'll leave it in the alley at the back at your mum's.'

'You can't go there, Tom. If anyone sees you . . .'

'I'll be careful.'

'No, really you mustn't.'

'It'll be OK.' He took hold of her hand, lifted it to his lips and kissed the back of her fingers. 'Never mind me, you need to take care of yourself, Annie Jackson.'

'Howarth,' she said. 'I'm Annie Howarth now.'

'Come and see me whenever you want. You know where I am.'

'Yes.'

'Annie . . .'

'No,' she said, 'don't say anything soft, not now. I don't think I could bear it.'

She picked up her bag and left the flat. As she ran down the stairs, Annie passed a girl coming up. It was the same one who'd been playing guitar in the bar at the Haddington Hotel. She smiled at Annie.

'Hi! Is Tom in?'

'Yes, he's up there.'

'Oh good. I need a lift.'

She carried on up the stairs, leaving behind a draught and the scent of pear. Annie went down. In the hallway she put on her sunglasses and pulled the scarf up over her hair. She opened the door cautiously, and looked out. The florist, Sally Smith, was standing outside her shop, talking to a woman with a push-chair. The woman was Janine Fleming. She looked over when she saw Annie come out of the house. Ignoring her, Annie pulled the scarf tight around her chin and hurried away back to her car.

She drove to Rotherham Road and let herself in. Gillian Up-the-road was sitting in the kitchen with Marie. The skin around Marie's eyes was puffy and mascara-stained, and her hair was sticking up madly so all her dark roots showed against the blonde curls. She looked as if she'd been awake all night but the back of her hairdo was completely flat, so she must have lain on it. Annie crossed the room and hugged her. Marie fished a tissue from the cuff of her cardigan and wrung it between her fingers.

'I don't know what to do with myself,' she said shakily.

Gillian reached out and put her hand over Marie's. 'All right, lass,' she said. 'Settle down now.'

'Is there any news?' Annie asked.

'They've charged your dad with unlawful assembly.'

'I meant about Johnnie.'

Gillian shook her head. 'We called the hospital just now and they said he was the same, didn't they, Marie? But no news is good news.'

'The doctor said to expect this,' Annie said. 'He said nothing would happen for a few days.'

'What's that you've got there?' Gillian asked, nodding towards Annie's bags.

'I brought a few bits and pieces from home.'

Gillian picked up one of the bags and peered into it. 'Lamb chops,' she said. 'I haven't seen a chop in weeks.'

'There's a bit of neck end too. Three rabbits and a pigeon.'

'You take some, Gillian,' said Marie. 'Give her some, Annie.'

'Won't Mr Howarth wonder where it's gone?'

'He doesn't know what's in the freezer,' said Annie. 'If you saw how much is in there . . .' She tailed off. The contents of the Howarths' freezer would, like as not, remain a mystery to Gillian and Marie. She began to unpack the bag, putting tins into the cupboard, bread into the tin.

'I didn't sleep a wink last night,' Marie said. 'That's the first night since we were married that I really needed Den, and the first night in thirty years I've been in that bed without him.'

'You should've made the most of the peace and quiet, Mum.'

'I should've been more careful what I wished for.'

'I'll drive you up the hospital when you're ready,' Annie said.

She pulled up a chair and sat down. Her knees knocked against her mother's under the table. She reached across and took hold of Marie's hands.

'Don't worry, Mum. It'll sort itself out in the end.'

Marie snorted. 'My son's in a coma, my husband's locked up and my daughter . . .' She glanced at Annie and then at Gillian and did not finish. The despair in her eyes cut through Annie like a knife.

'Your daughter's here with you, where she should be,' said Gillian.

'Makes a bloody change,' sniffed Marie.

CHAPTER THIRTY-SEVEN

Annie sat alone in the living room at Everwell turning down the hems on Elizabeth's school pinafores. Anxiety had settled on her shoulders; it was heavy, wrapped around her like a shawl. The lamp on the table beside her cast an oval light. She was nervous as a kitten, jumping at the spit of wood-sap in the logs in the fireplace, the wind rattling the windows in their frames and the whispers in the shadows of the old house. The water was settling in the pipes, making them creak and tick; the trees outside were bowing and blowing, making moon-shadows through the windows. She listened out for William, she wanted to know what he knew, what had happened today at the police station, why her father had still not been released.

When she heard the creak of the back door, she laid her sewing down on the arm of the chair, crossed the hall and pushed open the kitchen door. The room was in darkness, but she could see her husband silhouetted against the window behind. The palms of William's hands were flat on the kitchen table. His shoulders were hunched, his head hanging low. Beyond, through the window, Annie saw a pair of headlights jolting down the farm track, the beams bumping up and down, distancing themselves, heading for the road. One of the lights was slightly out of kilter.

'William?' She took a step forward. There was something about his posture, a sadness that alarmed her. 'What's going on? Why didn't you put the light on?'

He stood up. She could not see his face.

'I thought you'd be asleep by now,' he said. 'I didn't want to disturb you.'

'Why are you so late?'

'There were things to sort out.'

Annie watched the lights reach the junction of the track and the lane and, instead of turning left towards the town, the vehicle turned right up towards the moor. Perhaps a cow, or more likely a calf, had died and Jim was towing it away in the trailer to dispose of it somewhere remote.

'Would you like something to eat?' she asked. 'I saved you some dinner.' She gestured towards the covered plate of food on the counter. 'It's not much, only a bit of ham and some potatoes. I could warm it up.'

'No, I'm all right, thank you,' said William.

She could tell that he wanted to be alone. He would like to go into his study, shut the door and put some operatic music on the record player. He would like to drink a glass of whisky, sit back in his chair, close his eyes and listen to the music until it had cleared his mind of whatever it was that was troubling him. It was very late.

'Did you find out about Dad?' she asked.

'I'm terribly tired. Can we talk in the morning?'

'Of course, but—'

'Your father's fine. He should come up before the magistrates tomorrow.'

'Thank you, William.' She stepped back, put her hand on the door handle. 'Goodnight then.'

She washed, undressed and lay in bed. William's music wound up the stairs; she recognised Sibelius, though not the piece – it was mournful music. Every so often, she heard the chink of the stopper being replaced in the whisky decanter. She could not sleep. She wondered if she would ever sleep again. She heard the grandmother clock in the hall chime the quarters up to two o'clock, and then the double ring of the hour. Some time after this, the farm dogs set to barking. A fox had trotted across the yard maybe, or else Jim had returned from wherever he had been. She pulled the quilt up to her chin, moved down into the old bed, her feet seeking the warmer, softer patches of sheet and blanket.

She was hovering around the edge of a dream, all lost in darkness and Johnnie's accident and the scenes from the picket line and the dead woman's face and her own guilt swirling around her mind like water, when William came into the bedroom. He left the door ajar, and undressed by the light spilling in from the landing. There was little point in Annie pretending to be asleep. She knew he knew she was watching.

William hung his trousers carefully on a hanger that he replaced in the wardrobe. He put on his pyjamas, picked up the soiled clothes and took them into the bathroom to put in the laundry basket. Annie heard the water gurgling down the drain as he washed his face and brushed his teeth.

When he got into bed, smelling of carbolic soap, she turned towards him. She reached out her hand for his, but he did not take it. He lay on his back and stared up at the ceiling.

'William?' she whispered. He did not answer. She turned away from him again, curled herself into a comma, pressed her cheek into the pillow and longed for the morning.

CHAPTER THIRTY-EIGHT

Elizabeth propped Scooby against the sugar bowl and stood on a chair to spoon the cake mix into the paper cases, while Annie prepared the vanilla butter-cream filling. They were listening to the music charts on the radio and it made a pleasant change, Annie thought, from opera. Even so, the volume was turned low so as not to annoy William.

Mrs Miller came into the kitchen and set about making up a tray for Ethel. Elizabeth wiped the mixing bowl with her finger and put the cake mix into her mouth.

'I saw that,' Annie said. Elizabeth giggled and the doorbell rang.

'I'll get it,' William called from the study. 'Stay where you are.'

Annie went to the kitchen door and looked through the gap into the hall. Paul Fleming was standing at the front door. He and William exchanged a few hurried words, and then William picked up his coat from the rack and the two men went outside.

'Who is it, Mummy?' Elizabeth asked, turning from her work. A blob of batter dropped from the spoon on to the floor.

'Uncle Paul.'

'What does he want?'

'I don't know.'

'Can I go and see baby Chloe?'

'We'll ask Auntie Jan next time we see her.'

'When will that be?'

'I don't know. For God's sake, Lizzie, I can't see into the bloody future.'

'Don't swear, Mummy.'

'I'm sorry.'

'It's rude to say "bloody".'

Annie narrowed her eyes. 'That was no excuse for you to say it. Don't mither me, Lizzie, I'm not in the mood.'

The phone rang in the hall.

'Oh, what now!'

Annie went through, picked up the phone. There was silence at the other end.

'Is there anyone there?'

'Annie?'

'Tom?' She held the receiver close to her mouth and turned away from the open kitchen door. 'What are you doing calling here?'

'Can you speak?'

'If you're quick.'

'Johnnie's bike,' Tom said. 'It wasn't on the lane. It had been taken away.'

'The police?'

'No. I spoke to a woman out walking her dog and she said she'd seen two men loading it onto a trailer.'

'You mean it's been stolen?' Annie sighed and ran her fingers through her hair.

'It looks that way.'

'Mummy!' Elizabeth called from the kitchen.

'I'd better go,' Annie said. 'Thank you for trying, Tom.'

'When can I see you?'

'I don't know, I—'

'Mummy! I need you *now*!'

'I've got to go. I'll call you when I can.'

She put down the receiver and went back to the kitchen. Elizabeth stood on the chair, imperious, batter spattered around her like the remnants of an explosion. Annie stared at the mess.

'Are those cakes ready for the oven?' she asked.

'I don't know! That's why I was calling you!'

Annie crossed the room, picked up the metal baking tray and put it in the oven. She lifted Elizabeth down from the chair, brushing sugar from her hair with her fingers. The granules sprinkled on the floor and were gritty beneath the soles of Annie's shoes. She would have to wash the floor now or they would end up sticking to it. Out in the hall, she heard the front door open and close again, and, a few minutes later, the sound of music from the study. It was Sibelius again.

When she looked through the window she saw Paul Fleming driving away. It struck her as odd that he had not come in to say hello.

CHAPTER THIRTY-NINE

It was the fourth day after the accident, the fourth day Annie had spent in the intensive care unit, with her mother, standing beside Johnnie's bed. They had run out of things to say to Johnnie and to each other a long time ago.

'Turn off that bloody cassette recorder,' Marie said. 'I'm sick of that music. I've heard it that many times I'm reciting the bloody lyrics in my dreams.'

Annie reached over and pressed the stop button. She stood up and walked around the room.

'How's Dad?'

'Like a bear with a sore head.'

'I thought he'd have come here today.'

'He doesn't do hospitals. You know what he's like. I told him to go and make an appointment with the Union officer to get himself some legal advice. He's going to need it.'

'He certainly is.'

'That was good of your William to stand bail for him.'

Annie nodded. She sensed the subtext of this comment, the implication that the cuckolded husband was the one who was helping out the family in its time of need. To avoid any more conversation, she moved closer to Johnnie, looked at his face. The bruises grew more vivid every day and the scabs become blacker and thicker, but perhaps the swelling was subsiding a little. The skin around his eye no longer looked as if it were about to split.

Marie and Annie were doing their best, but they were getting on each other's nerves now. Marie was losing weight, becoming a shadow of the woman she was, and as she grew smaller and more gaunt, so she also seemed to age. Annie kept exhorting her mother to rest, eat a proper meal, knit, read, laugh, sleep, get drunk – anything but hover over Johnnie – but Marie refused. It was as if she feared he would sense any tiny aberration in the constancy of her love and her vigilance, slip through the smallest tear in its fabric, and be lost to her forever.

The door to the room opened and a young man came tentatively forward. It was Johnnie's best friend.

'Sam!' Marie cried, genuinely delighted. 'Oh love, how nice to see you, how good of you to come.'

'I caught the bus.'

'He caught the bus to Sheffield, Annie, all the way from Matlow. That must have cost an arm and a leg and you're on strike too, aren't you, Sam? You and your brothers?'

'We are,' said Sam. He took a step closer to the bed.

'You mustn't be scared. He looks worse today because the bruises are coming out,' Marie said. 'That's a good thing. It shows his body's healing.'

'I weren't expecting . . . I knew it were bad . . . It doesn't look like Johnnie.'

'It's still him though, Sam, it's still our Johnnie.'

Sam stood at the end of the bed, fidgeting. He shifted his weight from foot to foot, he glanced at his feet, at the walls, at Annie – anywhere but at his friend.

'It would be good if you talked to him, Sam,' Annie said. 'He must be sick to death of my voice and Mum's by now.'

'What should I say?'

'It doesn't matter.'

Sam looked awkward. Then he seemed to brighten.

'Come on, Johnnie,' he said. He glanced at Annie, who nodded encouragingly. 'We need you to get better. The football team needs you. We were crap without you on Saturday – beg pardon, Mrs Jackson.'

He pushed the bottom of Johnnie's undamaged right leg gently, with his fist.

'You can do it,' he said more quietly. 'You can get over this. It's only a bloody bump on the head, Johnnie. I've seen worse than that on the football pitch.'

Johnnie lay on the bed and the oxygen pump inflated and deflated and the machine made its soft, whooshing noise, its artificial breath.

Sam wiped his nose with the back of his hand and

scratched behind one leg with the foot of the other; Marie held her wrist against Johnnie's forehead as if to check his temperature.

Annie turned away.

'I'm going to get us some tea,' she mumbled. She walked through the hospital corridors until she reached the Ladies, and then she locked herself in a cubicle, put her face in her hands and for the first time, she cried.

CHAPTER FORTY

While she was in Sheffield, where there was still a good selection of food in the shops, Annie had bought prawns, smoked haddock, sweetcorn and cream. When she came home, she followed a complicated recipe for fish chowder. The soup was bubbling in the pan and there was rhubarb fool in the fridge for pudding.

Elizabeth was spending the night with a friend and Ethel and Mrs Miller had already eaten so it was just the two of them, Annie and William. She put a cloth on the circular patio table that was normally in the conservatory and took it outside, with two chairs. She lit a candle, laid the table properly, made it look pretty. She knocked on the study door and pushed it open. William was reading some papers. He put them face down on the desk when Annie came into the room. His skin was grey with tiredness, puffy at the jowls. The whites of his eyes were bloodshot. His colours were so cloudy, all greys and beiges, so different to Tom.

Stop it! Stop comparing William to Tom. It's not his fault he's old. None of it is his fault.

'Dinner's ready,' she said.

'Right.' He put a cardboard file on top of the papers, covering them up so she could not see.

'What's that, William?'

'It's nothing.'

'It's not nothing. Why don't you want me to see it?' She reached out playfully, as if to grab the papers, but he caught her arm, held her wrist tight, and then pushed it away.

'Don't do that,' he said. 'You know my work is confidential.'

'And I'm your wife. You ought to trust me.' Annie recognised the irony of those words at once, and turned away, rubbing her wrist. 'I'll put the food on the table,' she said. 'I made chowder. I know you like the way I make it.'

He did not respond but a few moments later he followed her outside and sat down at the table. The air was still balmy, there was a hint of summer in the air. William broke a piece of bread from the loaf in the bread-basket, buttered it, and began to eat his soup, pushing the spoon away from the side of the dish, sipping at it in his normal pernickety way. Annie tasted hers. It was smoky, strong-flavoured, too fishy for her taste.

'Do you like it?' she asked.

'It's good.'

'It's a Keith Floyd recipe.'

'Who?'

'The chef – you know, the one who always drinks while he's cooking.'

'No,' said William. 'I don't know.'

Well, no, you wouldn't know, you don't watch television, do you? You aren't interested in that kind of thing.

'I'm sorry if I overreacted just then,' William said. 'I apologise.'

'Look, there's no need to be so formal. I'm your wife.'

He dabbed at his lips with his napkin. He wasn't looking at her. Was she imagining it, or had something changed in him? Had *he* changed?

'I was upset,' said William.

Annie paused, her soup spoon halfway to her lips. 'Why?' she asked.

'We know who she is,' he said, and then corrected himself. 'Who she *was*.'

'The woman on the moor?'

'Yes.'

'Oh.' Annie put the spoon down.

'She was called Jennifer Dunnock – Jenny. Aged twenty-two. She was a working girl.'

'A prostitute?'

'Yes.'

'God.' Annie sighed and leaned back in the chair. She watched a blackbird collecting grubs from the grass and felt the breeze on her skin. She thought of all the living that poor girl would miss.

'Was she local?'

'She was from Sheffield. She had a son who lives with her sister in Bacup. No boyfriend, or partner. No father's name on the child's birth certificate. She used to split her time between Bacup and Sheffield. That's why nobody realised she was missing. Everyone just assumed she was somewhere else.'

'Poor thing. Does this help with finding out who killed her?'

'It's always difficult when it's someone like her.'

'Because she was on the streets?'

'Because she had a chaotic life.' He took another spoonful of the soup, swallowed, dabbed at his lips. 'She must have come into contact with a good many undesirable characters.'

'I suppose,' Annie said casually, 'that means we don't have to worry about the cottage any more.'

'Why not?' William put his spoon down. The chowder was finished.

'Because whoever killed her obviously picked her up in town – in a pub, probably.'

'There's no "obviously" about it. They could have met anywhere.'

Annie looked at him. She wanted to say: *It wouldn't have been in our gamekeeper's cottage though, would it?* but she didn't.

'What are you going to do now?' she asked instead. 'Are you going to warn the other working girls? Are you going to talk to them?'

'It's more complicated than that. We're dealing with a shifting population at the moment. So many people are moving around – police, miners, pickets, supporters.' He sighed deeply. 'The prostitutes follow them around like a bad smell.'

'They've got to earn their money where they can. I suppose it makes getting to the truth more difficult.'

'True. There are more layers of confusion than usual.'

He stood up, picked up his wine. 'I need to get back to work. I want to read through the interviews to make sure there's nothing we've missed.'

'Can't it wait until tomorrow?'

'No, it can't.'

Annie watched him go and then she sat alone with the detritus of the meal and wondered if there was any civilised way to unpick the lacework of a marriage. She thought of all the little habits and customs, all the ways she and William had learned to live together, the things they knew not to say, not to notice, the irritations they tolerated and also the small kindnesses they carried out for each other. She had learned so much about him in the past years; it was a delicate knowledge, fragile as spun sugar, and the only way to dismantle it would be to crush it underfoot and trample all over it. It made her sad to think of what she might be about to do.

CHAPTER FORTY-ONE

Annie wanted to be with Tom. It was all she wanted. She left her car in the usual place and rang the bell to his flat; he did not look out of the window, but a moment later the door opened. It was the Indian lady from the ground-floor flat. She held the door open for Annie, and Annie thanked her and went in, squeezed past the bicycles, the pram and other paraphernalia in the dark shared hallway, and ran up the stairs.

At the top, outside Tom's flat, she paused for a moment to catch her breath. She knocked gently on his door and it swung open.

She realised at once that the flat was empty. He had not known she was coming, of course. There was no reason why he should have been there; it was a weekday and he was probably working. She decided to go in and wait for a while.

She walked through the living room into the narrow little kitchen. The red plastic bowl in the sink was half-full with dirty dishes. The water was still warm, the suds still foamy. Tom's damp washing was hung over a foldable wooden clothes rack beside the radiator. Annie ran her fingers along the crease in a grey T-shirt. She turned on the radio and sang along to the words of 'Tainted Love'. She walked around the flat. The original large rooms had been partitioned to divide them into smaller ones, and the proportions weren't right. The rooms were long and narrow. They had high ceilings and were papered in wood-chip painted a burnt orange colour that had been fashionable a few years earlier. Tom had stuck up posters and his records were stacked on shelves that were only planks of wood balanced on upturned bricks. There were no curtains, only blinds at the windows. Tom had made hardly any effort to turn the flat into a home; it was just somewhere to be until he was somewhere else. Annie had not noticed this before, but now she did and it unsettled her. This would be an easy place to leave.

She wandered from room to room. Tom had left little ghosts of himself behind, a damp green towel dropped on the bedroom floor, a dented pillow on the bed; the sheets still held his shape. She opened the wardrobe doors and looked inside. It was almost empty; just three hangers, two shirts, a jacket, a tie looped around a hook nailed to the back wall. She saw her own reflection in the mirror on the inside of the wardrobe door and thought she glimpsed someone behind her – but she turned and there was nobody there. It was only the movement of the door distorting the reflection.

She pulled open the drawers in the tallboy. Underwear was rolled up in one, T-shirts folded in the second. The third was full of papers; invoices made out from Greenaway Garden Services, receipts, bills and letters. She recognised an envelope. It was the letter she had written, the one she'd given to Jim Friel to give to Tom. Beneath it was a postcard. She took the postcard out of the drawer. On the front was a painting of a woman writing at a table. On the back, the writing was loopy, a woman's writing. It said: *I hope you find what you're looking for. I hope she makes you happy. Regards S.*

Annie put the postcard back in the drawer and pushed it shut. She opened the fourth drawer. This was full of papers too – letters and newspaper cuttings and official forms and documents, but these were neatly organised. She took out a file and opened it. It was correspondence between Tom and his lawyer. Annie started reading at the back of the file and worked her way forwards. Tom had started writing the letters immediately after his conviction. He was desperate to clear his name.

Annie sat on the bed and read. At first the letters were scrawled, desperate, full of wild accusations; Tom sounded paranoid. He accused the police, and William in particular, of planting evidence, of distorting his words, of framing him. The lawyer wrote back in a sympathetic but unhelpful fashion. She said an appeal would only be permitted if new evidence were produced. There *was* no new evidence. Tom asked if a private investigator could be commissioned to look into the police enquiry. The lawyer replied that private investigators were expensive and she doubted she could find one prepared to work for nothing. The letters went backwards and forwards, but nothing changed. The last letter was dated the week before Annie had married William.

Annie climbed into the bed. She lay with her cheek on Tom's pillow, inhaling the smell of him. She rolled over onto her back and looked up at the ceiling, the texture of the plaster, the little dents and protrusions, and she watched the play of light on the ceiling. After a while she gave in to her tiredness, pulled Tom's duvet over her and went to sleep.

She awoke later, much later, with a start. She was still alone in the room, and the light had moved over to the far wall and she could hear traffic on the road outside. She checked the time on her watch. It was late. She slipped out of the bed, put on her shoes, drank a quick glass of water in the kitchen. She had intended to leave a note but now there was no time. She left the flat, closing the door quietly behind her, then trotted down the stairs, out of the front door and down the steps.

As she turned into the car park behind the shops, she walked past the phone box. A thick-set, bald-headed man was inside hunched over the receiver. He was wearing a scarf, even though it was a warm afternoon. Her eyes were drawn to him. There was something about him that did not feel right, but she could not tell what it was. He was holding the receiver close to his mouth but the pose was artificial, like somebody acting at talking on the telephone. Annie caught his eye, and the man turned his back and she knew. She was certain he had not been talking to anyone. He had been pretending. But why would he do that?

Annie walked past. The hairs on the back of her neck were prickling; she felt cold and frightened. At her car, she turned again and the man was still there, in the phone box, and he was still holding the receiver, but his lips weren't moving now. He was no longer pretending to make a phone call; he was watching Annie. The feeling of something malevolent creeping up on her returned.

It's nothing, she told herself, and she gave a little shake to shrug off the bad feeling. She opened the car door and got inside, and she locked the door shut again. She fumbled with the key, dropped it into the footwell and had to scrabble for it, and when she found it and looked over her shoulder, the telephone box was empty.

She turned the radio on to a pop music channel and sang along to Kate Bush. Her voice was shaky but by the time she reached Elizabeth's school she felt a little better. She picked up her daughter and stopped at the ice-cream van parked at the top of the hill to buy her a lollipop as a treat before they went back to Everwell.

Mrs Miller had been looking out for them. She opened the front door before they were out of the car.

'Your mother called, love,' she told Annie. 'She's been trying to get hold of you all day. I didn't know where you'd gone. She said you need to get yourself down to the hospital as quick as you can.'

CHAPTER FORTY-TWO

Denis and Marie Jackson and Annie walked through the park. They walked past couples going the other way smiling and holding hands, children on scooters and bicycles and old people moving slowly. The big trees were just coming into leaf and there were tulips in the flowerbeds. Marie had said she needed a breath of fresh air and the park, with its ice-cream kiosk and the dogs chasing squirrels and the children feeding the ducks and swans, was just a short walk from the hospital.

May had arrived, properly, suddenly, in the last few days. May had always been Annie's favourite month yet it did not feel like May this year, and she knew her parents could not feel it either. She could see it in the set of her father's face, her mother's held-high head.

She tried not to look about herself, tried not to smell the air or notice the drifting clouds, or the colour of the afternoon light on the black stone of the town's walls and buildings – how, behind it, all the moors had turned from peat-brown to green. She didn't want to remember this. She didn't want similar days, in the future, to remind her of this happiness and sadness all mixed up together like two different paints poured into the same pot.

'It won't take long,' the doctor had said, as he took the forms from Denis and Marie, as if he were afraid they would change their minds at the last moment.

There had been a strange, initial euphoria in the consent, a sense of joy in the fact that Johnnie would survive, but that he must lose his left arm. It had seemed a small price to pay, somehow, a reasonable trade-off: a life for an arm, but the euphoria had worn away quickly.

'We've done the right thing, haven't we?' Marie asked now.

'It's the only thing we could do, love.'

'When he comes round and finds out . . .'

'We'll be there for him.'

'We've looked after him, Den, all this time. Patched up his bumps and scrapes, kept him in one piece. And now he's going to lose his arm on our say-so.'

'He'll understand. He'll be OK. He's stronger than you think.'

'He's only a kid,' Marie said. 'He's just starting out on his life. He doesn't deserve this.' Denis put his arm around her and pulled her close.

They reached the end of the path. They went through

the gate and out onto the pavement that followed the road. They walked a little further and came to a pub. Denis looked at the light shining through the top half of the door and he hesitated. He looked at Marie. Their heads rested against one another. They needed one another. They didn't need Annie.

'You two go and have a drink,' she said. 'I'll see you tomorrow.'

'Annie . . .'

'I'll be all right, Mum,' she said. 'I'll pick you up from home, tomorrow at the usual time,' and she kissed Marie's cheek.

Marie held on to her. 'You are going home now, aren't you, Annie? Back to your husband and daughter?'

'Yes, of course.'

'You're not going to . . .'

'No!' Annie shook off her mother's hand. 'No, I'm not.'

Marie frowned and Annie frowned back. *Not now*, she mouthed. *Don't start having a go at me now*.

'Come on, Marie,' said Denis. 'I'm gasping.'

Annie waited until the pub door had closed behind her parents and then she turned and headed back towards the place where she had left the car, walking quickly, with purpose.

She stopped at the phone box, fumbled to find the right coins in her purse, and then called Everwell. Mrs Miller answered. Annie explained about Johnnie, and Mrs Miller said it was a crying shame but that Johnnie would manage. She said everything was fine at her end, that Elizabeth and Ethel had had their tea and were watching *Coronation Street*.

'William's not back then?'

'No, lovey. He called to say he's staying away tonight. He'll be back tomorrow.'

'Did you tell him where I was?'

'I told him you were at the hospital.'

'Was there any message from him to me?'

Mrs Miller hesitated. 'Only that he'd be back tomorrow.'

The pips sounded on the phone. 'I'll see you soon,' Annie called over them and Mrs Miller told her to take care.

Annie held the receiver to her chin. She had another 10p piece.

She dialled Tom's number. He picked up on the second ring.

'Where are you?' he asked. 'What's happened?'

She told him, quickly, and he said: 'Can you come to the flat?'

'No,' Annie said. 'I have to get home, Mrs Miller's waiting for me. William's away again.'

'Then I'll come to you.'

'You can't.'

'I can. I'll wait for you in the garden. By the well.'

'Tom . . .'

'I have to see you, Annie. I have to know you're all right.'

'Then be careful.'

'Don't worry. I will.'

She hurried back to the car. As she drove away from the hospital, she thought she saw the bald-headed man going into a tobacconist's shop, but she wasn't sure. She told herself she was being paranoid, and she started to think about the night ahead and soon she forgot about the man; he was the last thing on her mind.

CHAPTER FORTY-THREE

'Hello!' Annie called.

Mrs Miller's head appeared around the kitchen door. 'Hello, love, come through here. I've made you a bite to eat.'

Annie went into the kitchen. The table had been laid for one. There was bread, cheese, pickle and a portion of Bird's trifle in a bowl.

'Thank you,' Annie said. 'That's so kind.'

'It's nothing,' said Mrs Miller. 'You look worn out. Well, you would do, wouldn't you, after the day you've had. Poor thing.'

Annie smiled at the woman. 'Is Lizzie in bed?'

'Yes, her and Mrs Howarth.'

'Was Lizzie good this afternoon?'

'She was no trouble. She sat at the table and did some colouring.'

Annie crossed to the sink to wash her hands. Mrs Miller took her coat from the hook by the door and slipped it over her arms.

'I'll be off now then. I reckon you should have a nice bath and a glass of wine and then get yourself to bed early. You look like you could do with a good night's sleep.'

'Yes,' Annie said. 'Yes, I'll do that.'

After Mrs Miller had left, Annie went upstairs and looked in on her mother-in-law and her daughter. They were both sound asleep. She changed and went downstairs. She made sure all the doors and windows were closed and then left the house via the French windows in the conservatory, closing them carefully behind her. It was a dark, moonless night, but she could see, from the back door, the glow of a small fire close to the hedge. Tom was sitting on his haunches beside it, cradling his knees in his arms, fading into the night. When he saw Annie he stood, stretched out the muscles in his legs and walked towards her.

'Hello,' he said.

'Hi.'

'Are you OK?'

She nodded, but she was not OK. The sense of dread that had been shadowing her for weeks was growing stronger by the moment. She felt it all the time now, like something looming behind her, something she knew would engulf her at some point, only she did not know when.

'Did you park the truck somewhere where nobody can see?' she asked.

'I left it in Matlow. I walked up the moor.'

'Good.' She crossed her arms and looked around her. 'Are you sure nobody saw you?'

'Yes, I'm sure.' He took her face in his hands. He soothed her temples with his thumbs. Said: 'You're so cold.'

'I'm fine,' she said. Then: 'I know you didn't hurt Mrs Wallace. I'm sorry I ever doubted you.'

'Leave your husband,' said Tom. 'He set me up; he sent me away.'

Annie shook her head. 'No, it wasn't him. He believes you are guilty. He always has. The ring was found in your room.'

'The police put it there.'

'Why must it have been the police?'

'The door was always locked. I was careful.'

'It was a room in a lodging house, Tom. There must have been dozens of spare keys. It could have been anyone.'

Tom crouched by the fire. He poked at it with a stick.

'Nobody else had any reason to set me up.'

'William had no reason either.'

'He wanted me out of the way so he could have you.'

'He wouldn't do that.'

'It should have been me, Annie. I should have been the one you married. You should have had *my* child, *our* children. It should have been us.'

'Yes, I know.'

She sat beside him by the fire and watched the

flames. Beyond she could see the house, the lights in the windows.

'I ought to check on Ethel and Lizzie,' she said.

'Can't we go inside?'

'No.' She shook her head. 'It's William's house.'

She ran inside, softly up the stairs, and checked that all was well. She locked the door to Ethel's room, just in case, and left the light on for Lizzie. She took blankets and pillows from the wardrobe in the spare room, and went back outside. Tom was waiting for her.

They made love in the firelight and afterwards they sat, wrapped in blankets, feeding the fire, drinking wine. Annie looked up to the star-filled sky, the smoke winding up from the little fire and fading into the black.

'What's in your mind?' Tom asked.

'Johnnie.'

Tom pulled her to him and held her tight. He told her she was the most beautiful, precious thing in the world to him. He kissed her head and he whispered endearments and reassurances. He waited for her to finish with her tears for her brother and when she had, he still held her close.

And perhaps it was just that she was so tired, perhaps it was that the fire had burned down and the night had become so cold, but Annie's sadness turned to fear.

She sensed a movement behind her and she turned, but she couldn't see anything in the black of the night garden.

'Somebody's watching us,' she whispered.

Tom stood up to look but she grabbed hold of his arm and begged him not to leave her alone. He called out: 'Is anyone there?' and there was nothing, no movement, no sound, no intake of breath. He sat down again. He put his arm around Annie.

'There's nobody there,' he said.

'You think I'm imagining things?'

'I think it was probably just a fox.'

'It wasn't a fox, Tom. It's not the first time I've felt someone watching. I feel it all the time.'

'Shhh,' he said. And he kissed her.

CHAPTER FORTY-FOUR

Annie stayed with Tom in the garden that night. She tried to relax but sleep evaded her and she was cold to her bones and afraid, afraid that if she closed her eyes she would open them to see William standing over her. As soon as the first fingers of a watercolour dawn streaked the sky, she dressed. She kissed Tom's cheek, and whispered to him that she must go. She picked up as much as she could carry and ran across the lawn, her feet leaving dark prints in the silvery dew.

She let herself in to Everwell through the kitchen door, put the blankets into the washing machine and hurried upstairs to check on Ethel and Elizabeth, who were both still sleeping almost exactly as she had left them the night before. She came down again, filled the kettle and turned up the heat on the stove. She sat close to it, pressed up to the doors where she could absorb some of its warmth. Her head ached, but at the same time it felt empty. She knew she should bathe, she should change, there were a million things she should do, but she let time go by while she sat by the stove and drank hot tea and did nothing until Mrs Miller arrived.

The nurse said: 'My goodness, dear, is something the matter? You look terrible,' and Annie wished she had at least washed her face and shampooed the woodsmoke from her hair. She was dizzy with lack of rest and sex and fear. She didn't know if she wanted to sleep like a stone for a week, or shatter into myriad fragments of energy. She caught sight of her face reflected in the window and pulled a small brown leaf from her hair.

'I didn't sleep well,' she said and Mrs Miller replied: 'No. I can see that.'

The morning took its normal course. It was Elizabeth's day for ballet at school and, as usual, she complained about it over her breakfast.

'You're lucky you have the chance to learn to dance,' Annie said.

'I'm not lucky! And anyway, ballet's not dancing, it's doing stupid stuff with your arms and legs.' Lizzie pulled an ugly pose to demonstrate. 'Who cares which way your toes are pointing? Who cares if it's quarter to three or half past six?'

'That's a good point,' Annie said. She folded her daughter's cardigan into the ballet bag. 'Who does care?'

Just then, the telephone rang in the hall.

'I'll get it!' Elizabeth cried. She jumped off her chair and rushed to answer it. Annie put the bag on the drainer, wiped her hands on a tea towel and walked through to the hall. Elizabeth was standing on one leg, holding the other behind her back and telling her father a long and complicated story involving two girls in her class who had fallen out over the alleged theft of a purple felt pen.

She finished, at last, said: 'I love you, Daddy,' blew elaborate kisses into the receiver and handed it to Annie.

Annie took a deep breath, and said: 'Hello, William.'

'Hello, Annie. How are you?'

'I'm fine.'

'How is your brother?'

'He's going to live, but his arm has been amputated.'

She heard William take a sharp breath at the bluntness with which she delivered that news.

'Has he regained consciousness?'

'Yes. He's a bit dazed still, but he's OK.'

'Is there any brain damage?'

'Why do you ask that, William?'

'Because often, after a severe head trauma . . .'

'He's lost his short-term memory, but apart from that he seems all right. As far as anyone can tell at the moment.'

'I see.'

There was a silence. Annie could feel an anger growing inside her. Couldn't William just for once show some emotion? Some passion? She thought of Tom in the garden the night before, how he had encouraged her to talk, how he had held her, how he had made her feel safe. Already she ached with missing him. Tom was like the after-image of the sun in her eyes, like an echo calling. Almost there; not quite.

'I'm sorry I didn't make it home last night,' said William. 'You heard what happened in Nottingham?'

'No, I didn't.'

'There was another clash – worse this time. Some serious injuries. The government is pressing us to clamp down on the troublemakers.'

I don't care. I don't care about the pickets and the police, I don't care about the government, I don't care about your stupid policies and your stupid strategies and your stupid work.

'There was a press conference.'

'Really?'

'It went quite well. I thought you might have seen it on the news.'

'I had other things on my mind yesterday.'

He cleared his throat. *Stop doing that!* 'Of course.'

'Will you be back tonight?' she asked.

'God willing.'

'I'll see you later then.'

Elizabeth came into the hall and skated across the polished floor in her socks, parodying the ballet moves she would have to do later. Her hair was already coming loose from its pigtails, her socks were around her ankles. She grinned at Annie, and there was a gap where one of her top front teeth was missing.

'Annie?' It was William again.

'Yes?'

'Oh, nothing.'

CHAPTER FORTY-FIVE

Annie took a deep breath. She looked across at her mother. Marie was cleaning the kitchen table at 122 Rotherham Road with a rag made from a pair of Den's old underpants.

'Mum,' Annie said, 'could I bring Lizzie and come and stay here for a bit?'

'What do you mean "for a bit"?'

'For a few days. A week maybe. That way, I'd be here whenever you needed me to take you to the hospital or to run errands.'

'No,' said Marie. 'No, that's not a good idea.'

Annie finished unpacking the food she'd brought. Not that she ever got any thanks for it.

'It would make life easier for you,' she said. 'I'd be able to drive you around. I'd come and help at the Miners' Club if you wanted me to.'

'No, Annie. I don't want you living under my roof while you're still carrying on with that man.

I won't collude with your dirty little affair.'

Annie inhaled deeply.

'Don't sigh like a teenager, Annie Howarth. It might feel like *romance* to you, but to the rest of the world it's just sex. You made your sacred marriage vows in church, in front of your family and in front of your husband and in front of God, and now you're acting as if none of that matters.'

'You don't understand, Mum.'

Marie laughed. 'Oh, I think I do!'

'William never talks to me.'

'Many women would regard that as a bonus.'

'I feel so lonely in my marriage.'

'And does William beat you, Annie? Has he ever laid a finger on you? Huh? Or Lizzie? Is he cruel to his old mother, does he withhold money from you, does he abuse you in any way?'

Annie shook her head. 'No.'

'Does he stay out all night drinking? Does he lie and cheat? Does he break the law or see other women? Is he a layabout? A gambler? Is he lazy? Is he a slob?'

'You know he isn't.'

'Then you have nothing to complain about, do you hear me? *Nothing!*'

'I don't love him.'

'He still loves you.'

'How would you know? He never says he does.'

'He doesn't have to say it. You know that he does. You're just trying to shift responsibility and that's disgraceful, Annie. You're the one at fault here, not William. At least have the decency to admit that.'

Annie twisted her wedding ring around her finger.

Marie lowered her voice and hissed: 'What you're doing is wrong, and I won't be a party to it any more than I already am.'

'I'm not asking you to do anything.'

Marie gave a bitter laugh. 'I'm having to keep the truth from my own husband, aren't I? From my friends? From Johnnie? Because of you, *I'm* a liar now. I'm deceiving people I love to protect you and that waste of space, that *murderer* you're screwing.'

'He's not a murderer! I know he's not!'

'And the Pope's not a Catholic.'

Annie said: 'I'm sorry you feel like this.'

'Not sorry enough to give him up though?'

'No,' said Annie. 'No.'

'Come and talk to me when it's over. Come and talk to me then, but don't expect any sympathy because you won't get any.'

There was a knock on the kitchen window. They both jumped. From the other side of the glass Gillian Up-the-road held up a pie dish in front of her face. Steam was still escaping from between the rim of the lid and the base.

'Come in,' Marie called. 'The door's open.'

Gillian came in and put the pie on the table. 'It was on the doorstep,' she said. 'Smells like minced beef and onion.'

'I'll take some to the hospital for our Johnnie later,' Marie said. 'He'll appreciate that.'

Annie stood up. 'I'll be off then,' she said.

'Don't go yet, love, I've hardly seen you. Stay and have a brew with me,' said Gillian. Annie scowled at Marie and Marie scowled back. 'Oh,' said Gillian, 'have you two been having words again?'

Marie and Annie turned from one another.

'You're worse than a pair of kids,' said Gillian. 'Annie, put the kettle on and Marie, you can tell me all about your Johnnie.'

Marie was still frowning, but she said: 'They've moved him out of intensive care and into a room at the end of a ward. He's looking more like his old self, isn't he, Annie?'

'Yes.' Annie picked a mug off the drainer and wiped it dry with a threadbare tea towel.

'Although it's hard to get used to the arm not being there when it's been there all his life. I don't like to think about it, what they've done with it.'

'I'd try not to think about it if I were you.'

'They're ever so good at the hospital. They're already giving him physiotherapy, teaching him to do things with just one hand. Even things like looking at the newspaper are difficult when you're missing an arm like that.'

'How will he tie his laces?'

'I don't know, but they'll show him. They think of everything, really they do.'

'I'm glad to hear it.'

'Say what you like about our country, but you can't beat the NHS.'

'And it's not like an amputation's the end of the world these days, is it, Marie? Remember Dougie Gray?'

'Him as lost the arm in the winding accident?'

Gillian crossed her arms, a sign she had a good story to tell. 'That's the one. He still plays golf, you know. My Stu reckons he's one of the best in the club.'

'He married that girl, didn't he? The runner-up in the Miss Yorkshire competition?'

'He always was a good-looking lad. Always had the girls after him. Talking of which, there was an article in the paper today about that lass they found up on the moor. She was a working girl, by all accounts, but her family didn't know. It must have broken her mother's heart when she found out.'

Marie gave Annie a meaningful look. Annie looked away.

'We all have our crosses to bear,' said Marie, 'especially when it comes to our daughters.'

Annie rolled her eyes and banged a mug of tea on the table in front of her mother.

'They said the police ought to be doing more,' Gillian continued. 'They've been so caught up in the strike that they've forgotten all about finding her murderer.'

'That's not true,' Annie said. 'They're doing what they can. It's difficult at the moment because of all the comings and goings.'

'Well, you'd know about that, wouldn't you?' said Marie.

'It's enough to give you nightmares, isn't it,' said Gillian. She opened her handbag and produced a quarter of gin. 'How do you fancy a little pick-me-up in your tea, Marie?'

Marie pushed her cup towards her friend. 'Thank you, Gill,' she said. 'I don't mind if I do.'

CHAPTER FORTY-SIX

The next Sunday was glorious.

The Howarths went to church as usual and afterwards they and the Flemings returned to Everwell to eat. The Thorogoods did not join them.

After lunch, Janine helped Annie clear away. Little Chloe was asleep in her Moses basket on the kitchen floor and Lizzie sat beside her 'babysitting'.

'How are you feeling now?' Annie asked Janine.

'A bit better. I'm getting used to being a single mother.'

Annie gave her a sympathetic glance. Janine laughed a little bitterly. 'I might as well be one for the time I spend on my own with the baby. It was my own fault, I suppose, having her at exactly the same time as the miners' strike. I should have planned it better.'

'Paul will regret it later,' Annie said. 'That he didn't spend time with the baby when she was small.'

'Oh, I doubt it. His work is a million times more

interesting. I can see his eyes glazing over when I try to talk to him. I expect I would be the same. Just because every little thing about Chloe is fascinating to me, I can't really expect anyone else to care.'

Annie smiled. 'It passes very quickly, this infant stage.'

'So people tell me. Anyway,' Janine picked up a handful of wet cutlery and dried it with the tea towel, 'I can't imagine William was a particularly hands-on father.'

'No, he wasn't.' Annie rinsed a serving dish under the tap. 'He was keen for us to have a child quickly, before he was any older, but after Elizabeth was born . . .' she glanced towards her daughter in the corner. 'Well, no, he didn't do much. It seems to be the way with policemen.'

'What does?'

Annie turned. Paul had come into the room. He came up behind his wife and put his hands around her waist. Janine stiffened a little. 'Get off,' she said, 'I'm busy.'

'William and I were thinking about taking a drive out into the countryside,' Paul said. 'We could stop and have a drink at the pub.'

'That would be nice.'

'William suggested that?' Annie asked.

'No, I suggested it but he agrees it's a good idea. We've been working like the devil for weeks now. We deserve to spend a little time with our girls.' He nuzzled Janine's neck. She flushed and pulled away.

'OK,' said Annie. 'Why not?'

She helped Ethel change into a comfortable dress

that buttoned up the front and Elizabeth was allowed to put on her dungaree shorts and a pair of plastic sunglasses. Annie stood in front of the mirror and brushed her daughter's hair. She could not look into her own eyes. She hardly recognised herself.

There were too many people to fit comfortably into the Howarths' Jaguar, so Paul took his car too, and the Flemings followed behind. From the back seat of the Jaguar, Annie turned to wave to Janine but Janine wasn't looking. She was sitting beside Paul, but her head was turned away from him, gazing out of the passenger window, watching the countryside. William drove across the moor, along the lane where Johnnie had fallen from his bike and out across the countryside far away from Matlow and the colliery and all that had happened, to a pub by the river called the Millhouse.

It was a popular place; the car park was full, children were playing around the benches in the garden and there was a queue at the bar. The group found a table with a sunshade and ordered their drinks. Elizabeth took off her shoes and socks and went to paddle at the river's edge with the other children. William stretched out his long legs and loosened his collar. Paul bounced Chloe on his lap and Janine leaned back and let the sun shine on her face.

'It's been a long time since we did anything like this,' Janine said.

'It's been mental,' Paul said. 'I hope I never have to go through anything as stressful as this again.'

'Think of the overtime, Paul,' said Annie. 'You'll be a wealthy man.'

'That's not the point,' said William. 'None of us is doing this for the money. It's not our choice to work so many hours.' Janine looked up then and caught Annie's eye. Annie had to hide a smile. William didn't mean it, but he could be so pompous sometimes; so self-important. He hadn't finished yet. 'The country would have descended into chaos by now if it weren't for those policemen and women who have made personal sacrifices to protect society. It's a responsibility and the responsibility is reflected in our salaries. You can't have one without the other.'

'I think you do an amazing job, William,' Janine said.

'What about me?' Paul asked. Chloe had grabbed hold of a handful of his hair and was trying to make it reach to her mouth. Janine gently unprised her daughter's fat little fingers.

'You too,' she said.

'She's only saying that because you're here,' Paul said to Annie. 'At home all Jan ever does is moan.'

'That's not fair.'

Paul pulled a mardy face and mimicked a woman's whine. '"Oh Paul, I'm so bored! It's so hard being alone with the baby all day! You don't know what it's like for me!"' He took a drink of his beer. 'You were the one who wanted a baby, sweetheart.'

'I didn't produce her on my own.'

'No, but you're the one lounging around at home

while I'm out all hours dealing with the scumbags and pondlife and criminals. You think you have it hard? You don't know you're born! Women like you don't know how lucky you are.'

Janine's cheeks had coloured. She looked furious but she didn't respond to this.

William cleared his throat. 'Well,' he said, 'it's good to get away from it all, isn't it? The strike feels a long way away from this place.'

'I don't like to watch the news on television,' said Ethel.

'No,' said Annie. 'I know you don't.'

'All you ever see these days is people being angry with one another.'

'Yes.'

'I don't know where it will end.'

Annie helped Ethel with her drink and tried to look interested as William launched into a monologue about a radio documentary about the evolution of the Conservative Party. Paul had turned his back to Janine and was listening intently. He was interested. He was trying to better himself. He hadn't had the privilege of an education like William's, but he wanted to learn. Annie fought back a sudden sadness, an ache for Tom and a sympathy for William, Janine and Paul. *None of us is the person we want to be,* she thought. *We're all striving after something we can't have.*

'How is your brother?' Janine asked Annie. 'Is he on the mend?'

'He's being stoic. He's doing his best.'

'It must be difficult for him.'

'Yes. He's trying to make a joke of it, but it's hard. I'm so proud of him.'

'Do you see him every day?'

Annie nodded. 'William hasn't been yet.'

William heard this. He paused, for the briefest moment, and then continued his conversation with Paul.

Elizabeth came running over to the table, laughing. Her hair was hanging over her face and the legs of her shorts were spattered with water. She reached up and took a long drink of lemonade through a straw.

'Are you having fun?' William asked. She nodded and ran off again.

'I expect she's looking forward to the well-dressing,' said Janine.

William put his pint down. 'That reminds me, Annie. I was talking to Julia Thorogood at the church earlier. She said you'd been a little . . . difficult with her.'

'I've had a lot on my plate, William.'

'That's not the point. As the mistress of Everwell—'

'I'm not the mistress of Everwell, for God's sake! You make me sound like a character in a period drama.'

She had spoken too sharply. Paul and Janine were both looking at her in surprise and William was silently making a fist of his hand and then stretching out his fingers again.

'I'm sorry,' she said. 'I didn't mean to snap. I just don't like Julia talking about me behind my back. Can't she sort the well-dressing out herself? She doesn't need me to get involved. She always ends up doing exactly what she wants anyway.'

'It's our house, Annie, our garden. You can hardly expect Julia to manage the whole thing.'

'All right.'

'I think it would be politic if you called her.'

'I said "all right". Where's Elizabeth?'

The four adults looked around them. Annie stood up. She shielded her eyes with her hand and gazed around the garden but she could not see the child. She walked away from the table, towards the river. A small group of children were playing there, floating objects down towards the weir.

'Elizabeth! Lizzie Howarth!' Annie called, but she could not see the yellow of her daughter's T-shirt. She took off her sandals and hooked them over her thumb, then hurried down the grassy bank, stepping around young couples who were sitting on the grass drinking beer and walked carefully along the river's edge. She had almost reached the weir when she spotted Elizabeth feeding crisps to a large, old dog who looked just like Martha. Annie smiled and walked forward. She almost tripped over a young girl sitting cross-legged on the grass and wearing a straw hat. The girl looked up and Annie recognised her. It was the girl who lived in the flat below Tom's, the one who had sung in the bar at the Haddington Hotel the evening of the police dinner dance.

'Hi,' she said, and the girl shielded her eyes and said, 'Hello,' and the next moment, Annie's eyes were drawn to a man in jeans and a shabby green shirt walking towards her with a glass in each hand. The man had long dark hair and a beard.

It was Tom.

CHAPTER FORTY-SEVEN

Annie took Elizabeth back to the table.

'Sit down and eat your crisps,' she said, pushing the child down into her seat.

'What's the matter?' William asked.

'She was down by the weir. I *told* her – I told you, didn't I, Elizabeth, that you weren't to go out of my sight? You frightened me half to death. You could have fallen in the water and drowned.'

Elizabeth scowled and rested her cheek on her fist.

'Eat your crisps.'

'I hate you!'

'Talk to me like that, young lady, and you'll feel the back of my hand!'

'Annie.' Janine's voice was gentle. 'She's safe. She wasn't so far away and she's here now.'

Ethel looked up anxiously. 'Is everybody all right?'

Annie wiped her hair back from her forehead.

'Yes,' she said. 'Everybody's fine,' and she sat back

down on the bench. She didn't want her wine now, she just wanted to be out of the place. She had her back to where Tom and the girl were sitting, but they must still be there, looking out at the sunlight on the river, the swans.

Tom had been as surprised to see her as she had been to see him. She'd seen the shock in his face and they'd been forced to act out a polite little conversation for the benefit of the girl. Tom had introduced her to Annie as *my friend Selina* and Annie to the girl simply as *Annie.* She knew she had no right to feel upset by this – he could hardly have said *the married woman I'm sleeping with,* or even *the woman who was my first love,* but even so it had felt awful for Annie to be so officially insignificant. Selina had been very young close up, slight, pretty, with freckles on her nose and cheeks, dark eyelashes and a friendly smile. Her hair was hidden beneath the hat, but tiny black curls had come down onto her skinny shoulders, the black top she was wearing with her bra straps showing. She had said: 'Thanks, babe,' when Tom passed her the drink. She had smiled up at him and her teeth were white and slightly crooked. She had a soft, Scottish accent. Annie had stood there with a rictus smile on her face.

Thanks, babe. *Thanks, babe.*

'Darling?'

She looked at William. For the briefest moment she did not even recognise her husband, she had forgotten he was there. She looked at his long, intelligent face, his pale grey eyes, the wrinkled throat inside the collar of the pale blue shirt, and she tried to pull herself back to the present.

'Sorry, I was miles away.'

'Mother needs the lavatory.'

'Oh Ethel, I'm sorry. Let me help you up. Do you need to come too, Lizzie?'

Elizabeth shook her head. She was still wearing the mutinous expression.

Annie helped Ethel to her feet, and took hold of her arm. They walked very slowly up the path and into the pub. When the old woman was settled in the cubicle, Annie stood beside the door, holding it shut.

She knew there was no reason why Tom should not come to a country pub with a friend on a day when he knew Annie was unavailable. She had no right to dictate to him how he lived his life. And she hoped he wasn't, she really hoped he wasn't – but if he was having sex with Selina, it was nothing to do with Annie. She still shared a bed with William, so was it fair to expect Tom to sleep alone every night? But how many hours had it been since he had lain with her beside the fire in the night? How many more days and nights could she bear to be without him? How much longer could she carry on like this before something gave, something broke, something happened?

Ethel rattled the handle to let Annie know she was done, and Annie helped the old lady straighten her underwear and wash her hands. They went back out through the pub. Annie stopped to buy an ice-pop for Elizabeth to make up for snapping at her earlier. As they emerged from the gloom of the interior to the brightness of outside, Ethel squeezed Annie's arm and said, 'Look, dear, there's our driver.'

'Oh yes,' Annie said.

'He's with someone. Look, Annie, don't they make a lovely couple.'

CHAPTER FORTY-EIGHT

Annie had fallen into a mire of jealousy, of hurt and guilt and confusion. She felt as if she were losing her mind. While William was outside in the garden at Everwell with Elizabeth, she had picked up the telephone to call Tom but she'd put it down again, too afraid of the words that might come out of her mouth. She would not be able to be casual about the girl, she would not be able to laugh off the encounter in the pub garden, the collision of their two worlds.

For the rest of that day, she went through the motions. She attended to her daughter and her mother-in-law, she made sandwiches for their tea, she smiled at her husband and was relieved when he disappeared into his study rather than spend the evening with his family. She didn't even complain when Julia Thorogood and one of her boring sidekicks turned up and she had to spend an hour listening to them drone on about the well-dressing and agree an action plan. She even promised to type the plan up, she being the only one of the three with secretarial experience.

That night, in bed, she lay on her side while William worked on downstairs with his music turned down low and she tried not to think about what Tom might be doing with the girl. She tried not to think of his body, his arms, his lips, his hair. Her jealousy was like a pain; it would not go away and it would not let her sleep.

She was busy the next day. Johnnie had been transferred to Matlow General and Marie could not go in to see him because she was going on a protest march with the Matlow Miners' Wives Action Group. So Annie spent the morning at the hospital, talking to Johnnie, to the physiotherapist and the doctor. After that, she had to pick up Julia and go with her to look at the designs for the panels for the well-dressing. The theme was The Earth Belongs To Everyone and the artist had done an excellent job on the sketches. Annie couldn't get rid of Julia until it was time to go and meet Elizabeth from school. She was almost certain she saw the bald-headed man again, sitting in the driver's seat of a small, black car parked outside Julia's house, but she couldn't be sure it was the same man and when she looked again, the car was gone.

Elizabeth was one of the last girls out of the grand double doors at the front of the school and again she was accompanied by a teacher. Elizabeth's head was held low and she was scuffing her feet. Annie took a deep breath, got out of the car and walked forward to meet the two of them. A squally wind had come up, and the first drops of rain were falling from a huge cloud-bank overhead.

Annie put a confident smile on her face. 'Hello,' she said. All around her conversations dried up as the other mothers and the au pairs strained to hear.

'We have a problem, Mrs Howarth,' said the teacher.

'Oh?' Annie's hair blew across her mouth, and she shook it back. Beside her, the grand trees at the school entrance bowed and tossed their branches. The other women were creeping closer, forming a semi-circle around her so they would miss nothing.

The teacher huffed a little. She clasped her hands in front of her. 'Elizabeth slapped another child,' she announced, 'in ballet class.'

Annie caught her daughter's eye and gave her a wink of reassurance. She put her hands to her face to keep the hair out of her eyes. The wind was tugging at the hem of her coat.

'I'm sure there must have been a good reason,' Annie said. 'Elizabeth doesn't make a habit of slapping other children for no reason. She and I will have a talk about it.'

'She will need to apologise to Philippa and she will be punished.'

'No,' Annie said. 'There won't be any punishment. Elizabeth and I will sort this out between us.' She reached out her hand and Elizabeth took hold of it.

'Thank you for bringing this to my attention,' Annie said, and she was pleased with the tone of her voice. She sounded like William. She walked back towards her car with her head held high and Elizabeth scurrying along beside her. The other mothers grabbed hold of their daughters and turned away, back to their cars. There was an outbreak of chatter.

They drove back to Everwell in silence. William's car was outside. Annie could not face going inside, not yet. Even though the moor was wrapped in cloud, she felt its pull.

'Come on,' she said to Elizabeth, 'we're going for a walk.'

'But it's raining.'

'So? We'll get wet. It won't hurt us.'

They walked across the garden. Elizabeth's grey felt hat blew off and cartwheeled along the drive. It would end up in a hedge somewhere, ruined, but Annie did not care. They reached the stile into the home meadow and she helped the little girl over.

'Where are we going, Mummy?'

'We're going to climb the moor. I used to love going up there to watch the sky when there was a storm. It's the best place to be.'

'But we're not allowed on the moor. There's a murderer hiding in the caves.'

'Elizabeth, we've been through this.'

'Everybody knows he's there! He kills people. He puts his hands around their throats and he kills them and then he lays them down on rocks and—'

'Sshhh,' Annie said. 'There's no murderer up on the moor today.'

Elizabeth looked doubtful. Annie took her hand. She couldn't turn back now or it would look as if there really were something to fear.

'See that big rock sticking out from the side of the moor up there? The one shaped a bit like a dog's head? I used to sit on top of that and watch the clouds roll over the valley. Come on.'

They found a little path and followed it uphill. Annie walked quickly, taking deep breaths. Raindrops fell cold on her forehead and cheeks, and she felt herself unwinding and becoming a little more like herself.

'That rock, the dog one, it's called Martha's Stone,' Annie continued. 'Did I ever tell you the story?'

Elizabeth shook her head.

'It's very sad. Hundreds of years ago, there was a noble warrior. I can't remember his name, but Martha was his dog and his best friend, his loyal companion and—'

'Philippa Ede said Johnnie had his arm sawed off and the doctors put it in the rubbish bin.'

'Oh.'

'I said she was a liar and she said she wasn't. She said it again and again and I hit her to make her stop saying it.'

They had reached a little beck. The water was clear as glass rushing over black and green stones, a little dam of caught twigs. Annie jumped over, and helped Elizabeth as she followed. She led her to a crumbling drystone wall where an old hazel tree, warped and bent by the wind, offered some protection from the rain. Annie sat on the mossy stones beneath the tree and she pulled Elizabeth gently down beside her. She smoothed the damp hair from her daughter's angry little face.

'It's not true, is it?' Elizabeth said. 'She's a dirty liar, that girl.'

Annie took a deep breath. 'It is true, love. The doctors had to do an operation to take off Johnnie's arm to save the rest of him.'

'Why didn't you tell me?'

Annie thought about this. 'I didn't want to,' she said.

'Why not?'

'Because it's so sad.'

'You still should have told me.'

'Yes. I should have.'

'Now you've made me look stupid. Now everyone will think *I'm* the liar.'

'I didn't mean to, love, I—'

'And everyone laughs at me already because of Grandad being in prison and you're always somewhere else and Daddy's always in his study and now Johnnie only has one arm and everything's gone wrong!'

'Not everything. Oh Lizzie . . .'

'Get off me! I hate you!'

Elizabeth pushed herself to her feet and ran away from her mother, jumping the tussocky ground, scrambling uphill. The rain softened her outline and the colour of her grey school coat until she was no more than a smudge against the green of the grass and the brown of the bracken.

Annie sat on the rock and waited. She watched as Elizabeth picked up stones and threw them into the beck, and after a while, she went to join her. She picked up a large grey pebble and passed it to Elizabeth. The girl smashed it into the water. It cracked against a rock and ricocheted away. Annie passed another. Elizabeth's hair was wet now, dark and clinging to her skull. Water ran down her forehead, and she had to blink to keep it out of her eyes. The shoulders of her coat were soaked.

Annie picked up some more pebbles. She said, 'I am sorry, Lizzie. I was thinking about myself too much and not enough about you.'

Elizabeth threw another stone.

'Is Johnnie getting better now they've taken his arm off?'

'Yes, he is. He's much better than he was. He's got the card you made him pinned up next to his bed in the hospital.'

'Can I go and see him?'

'Yes.'

Elizabeth let her hands fall to her side. She stood there in the rain, bedraggled but proud in her school coat with the badge embroidered on the front with its Latin motto, and the rain fell all around and the beck bubbled and ran. Annie put her arms around the child and held her close.

'I am sorry, Lizzie,' she said. 'Really I am.'

'It's OK,' Elizabeth replied. And they stood together and watched the rain sweeping across the valley, a curtain falling from the clouds above.

CHAPTER FORTY-NINE

William had come in, put his briefcase in his study, and gone straight upstairs to shower. When she heard the boiler firing up to heat the water, Annie went into the hall, picked up the telephone receiver and dialled Tom's number. It seemed to take forever for the dial to turn back to its original place after each digit, and it seemed to be making an inordinate amount of noise. As she held the mouthpiece close to her mouth, Annie watched the staircase, listened for any movement.

Please, she thought, *oh Tom, please be there. Please pick up the phone*. It connected. She heard the bell ringing out into Tom's flat. It rang four, five, six times. She was on the point of losing her nerve and putting the phone down when he picked up.

'Hello?'

He sounded tired. Perhaps he had fallen asleep on the settee; perhaps she had woken him. Perhaps somebody was with him – the girl Selina – cross-legged on the floor curled over Tom's guitar with her pretty face and her pretty hair and her pretty voice. And once that thought was in Annie's mind, she found she could not speak, she did not know what to say.

'Hello?' he said again. 'Who's there?'

She heard the bathroom door open, then footsteps on the landing. Very carefully she replaced the telephone in its cradle.

After school, she took Elizabeth to visit Johnnie. The girl sat very still in the passenger seat, clutching her toy dog Scooby on her lap, together with the box of Ferrero Rocher she had insisted Annie buy for Johnnie because she said they were his favourites.

'They're your favourites, Lizzie. That's not quite the same,' Annie had said.

'Johnnie loves them too, I know he does.'

She became even quieter when they arrived at Matlow General, went up two floors in the lift, then walked along a series of windowless corridors. Elizabeth stared at the people who were attached to drips, the hobbling, shuffling, coughing people, the decrepit old people snoring on trolleys lined up in the corridors.

'Is that man dead?' she whispered as they passed one particularly pale and emaciated man. The patient opened one eye and said: 'No, he's bloody not!' Elizabeth squeaked in alarm.

'Are you allowed to say "bloody" in hospital, Mummy?' she asked.

'Only if you're very old or very ill,' Annie said.

'What if somebody is very bloody because they've hurt themselves?'

'Well, yes, I suppose, then too.'

Johnnie was in a semi-private cubicle at the end of one of the men's wards. Elizabeth and Annie walked down the middle of the ward, and the men in the beds watched them over their newspapers and their puzzle books. Annie heard Marie's rough laughter before they reached the end of the ward and Lizzie ran on ahead, although she stopped when she saw Johnnie. He was sitting up, half-propped on pillows. The bruising on his face had subsided and his hair was beginning to grow back over his skull, a velvety orange fuzz. A big, absorbent pad was taped over the place where his arm used to be. He was drinking lemon barley water through a straw and he grinned when he saw Elizabeth.

'Hello, Ugly Mug,' he said.

Elizabeth looked at him shyly. She did not speak.

'It's all right, pet,' Marie told her. 'He looks a bit worse than usual, but it's still the same Johnnie, still daft as a brush.'

'Thanks, Ma.'

Annie smiled and perched on the side of the bed. She tweaked her brother's knee.

'How are you doing?'

'Mustn't grumble,' said Johnnie. 'Are you going to share those chocolates, Lizzie, or are you going to guzzle them all yourself?'

Elizabeth pushed the chocolates towards Johnnie. 'They're for you. They're Ferrero Rocher.'

'My favourites!' he said.

'Told you,' Elizabeth whispered to Annie.

'You'll have to unwrap one for me, Lizzie,' Johnnie said. 'While you're at it, unwrap all of them so I can eat them when you're not here.'

'Are you all right to keep an eye on Lizzie while me and Annie go and get a cup of tea?' Marie asked.

'I don't want tea, Mum,' Annie said.

'You can keep me company while I get one.'

Annie pulled a face over her shoulder at Johnnie and Johnnie pulled one back. A few other visitors were arriving now and there was a buzz of conversation in the ward as they walked back through it. Marie held her head high and nodded greetings to the people she recognised. Annie trailed behind like a shamed child.

The moment they were through the double doors at the end of the ward Marie said: 'Well then?'

'Mum, please, will you stop talking to me as if I'm five years old.'

'I'll talk to you how I like. Have you finished your dirty little affair? Have you told Tom Greenaway to leave you alone?'

'I don't have to listen to this,' Annie said and she turned, but Marie grabbed her elbow.

'It won't go away, you know,' she said. 'This situation won't magically resolve itself. If you don't sort it out now, there'll be a tragedy and you'll be the one who gets hurt. You mark my words.'

Annie shook her arm free.

'You've got yourself into a mess – a dangerous mess – and you need to get yourself out of it.'

'I know what I'm doing.'

'You know what you're doing? That's a laugh! Risking your marriage, your family, your whole life, for sex with a murderer.'

'Oh stop it, Mum!'

'You need to end it,' Marie said. 'End it now before it's too late.'

'Excuse me.' Annie and Marie looked up to see a porter coming along the corridor pushing a man in a wheelchair. They stepped to the side of the corridor.

'Annie . . .' Marie said.

'I heard you,' said Annie. 'Now leave me alone.'

She could feel her mother's eyes on her as she marched back through the ward doors and over to Johnnie's bed, where she sat herself down on the side. Elizabeth was making a den underneath the bed with Johnnie's pillows and the chocolates. Annie took hold of her brother's hand and examined it, the long, knuckly fingers, the bitten-down nails, the prominent veins.

Johnnie turned his head towards her and smiled. She smiled back although she was smarting inside, as if she had been slapped.

'I won't be much good for owt now, will I?' he asked.

'There are loads of things you can do with one hand.'

'Brain surgery's out of the question as a career.'

'You never wanted to do that anyway.'

'No.'

'Nor rocket science, as I recall.'

He sighed. 'Do you think anyone'll fancy me with one arm missing?'

Annie squeezed his hand. 'You're still Johnnie Jackson, aren't you? Everything else still works, doesn't it?'

He smiled. 'Yep.'

'Is there anything I can get you?' Annie asked. 'Anything you want?'

'Not really. They look after me all right in here.' He grinned at the peach-faced nurse who was checking the chart at the foot of his bed and she beamed back.

'There is one thing, our Annie,' he said, 'I've been wondering what's happened to my bike.'

'Somebody took it from the lane.'

'Stole it, you mean?'

She nodded.

'That's a bugger.'

She kissed the ends of her fingers, and planted the kiss on her brother's cheek.

'Leave it with me,' she said. 'I'll ask William. I'll see if there's anything we can do to track it down.'

CHAPTER FIFTY

'Daddy!' Elizabeth ran into the hall as they arrived home and launched herself at her father. William caught her and held her close as she wrapped herself around him like a starfish.

'So did you see Johnnie?' William asked.

'Yes!' Elizabeth said. 'And do you know, Daddy, even though he doesn't have his arm any more, he can still feel his fingers. And sometimes he thinks he's got pins and needles, but when he goes to stretch, he realises his hand's not there!'

'That's because his central nervous system is still trying to communicate with the amputated extremities,' said William.

'No, it's because his brain thinks his hand is still there. I can't wait to tell Philippa, she'll be so jealous.'

William put his daughter down and she ran off to find Mrs Miller to tell her the news. Annie, at the doorway, picked up the mail from the hall table.

'How are things?' asked William.

'Fine, thank you. Johnnie's improving every day.'

'Good.'

'William, before you go back into the study, Johnnie was asking about his bike.'

'What about it?'

'After he crashed, somebody took it away.'

'And?'

'Johnnie would like it back. He'd like to see if it can be repaired.'

William gave a small laugh. 'He can hardly ride a motorbike with one arm, Annie.'

'That's not the point. He built that bike himself, more or less, and he wants it back. Could the police help trace it?'

William shook his head slowly. 'Do you really think we have the resources to search for a badly damaged Yamaha that was worth very little in the first place, when we're dealing with . . .'

'A strike and a murder. I know. I shouldn't have asked.'

'Talk Johnnie out of it,' William advised her. 'It's a ridiculous idea. Cars can be adapted for disabled drivers. Perhaps he should consider that instead.'

He went back into his study and closed the door. Annie stared at the closed door for a moment or two, then she picked up her keys and went back out again.

Annie drove along Crossmoor Lane. She drove very slowly, since she was not sure exactly where Johnnie had fallen off his bike, but when she came to the place she recognised it by the scrape marks on the tarmac. She bumped her little car onto the grass verge and turned off the engine. She looked left and right, up and down the lane, but there were no houses, no landmarks, only the rough countryside. The spot was isolated, remote and lonely. Annie did not really want to get out of the car in this place where her brother had almost died.

Telling herself not to be stupid, she climbed out of the car. She stretched her arms and looked around her, but nobody was there, nobody was watching. She walked slowly up the lane following the marks on the road. She didn't know what she was looking for, but she was afraid of what she might find. She didn't think there'd be any blood, since anything like that would have been washed away by now by the rain, and the tyres of other vehicles – but what if it hadn't been? What if it was still there?

A strip of grass grew Mohican-like down the centre of the lane, which was badly maintained, hardly used and more pothole than tarmac. It was narrow, winding, hunch-backed. In winter it was often impassable, the surface iced over for weeks at a time.

Loose pebbles moved beneath the soles of Annie's feet, the grit and soil and mud washed down off the moor by the rain. She crouched down at the spot where the scratches in the tarmac began and put her fingers in the gouges, as if they were a wound, and she felt the shape of them. The tarmac was cold and damp and hard. Tiny pieces of aggregate crumbled into her fingers.

She imagined Johnnie's soft cheek lying against the rough road. She imagined his blood.

Something caught her eye, something glinting in the sunlight. It looked like a tiny fragment of glass, no larger than a fingernail. She bent down to pick it up and behind her somebody said: 'What are you looking for?'

Annie turned. Behind her was an old woman hunched over a walking stick with an ancient-looking dog that could hardly lift its head from the ground.

'My brother fell off his bike here,' Annie said.

'Oh aye,' said the old woman. 'The ginger-headed lad.'

'You saw him come off?'

'I saw the police car. I came over to have a look, me and my Jack here.' She reached down and touched the wiry head of the little dog. The dog sighed and its chin dropped even closer to the ground. 'How is the boy? Did he make it?'

'He's all right,' said Annie. 'He lost his arm though.'

'Aye well. It's no wonder, the speed they were going.'

'The speed who was going?'

'The police.'

'Oh. The ones who found him, you mean? In the patrol car?'

The old woman snorted. 'We thought he was a goner, didn't we, Jack?' She hawked and spat at the verge. The dog shuddered. Annie brushed her hands on her skirt. 'Anyway, you're not the first,' the woman said. 'There's been others up here asking questions before you. Man with long hair. Bloody hippie.'

'That was my friend,' Annie said. 'He came up in his truck to fetch the bike but it had already gone.'

'Pikeys,' the old woman told her. 'They was pikeys as took it, with a pikey dog. Loaded it into a trailer and drove off, they did.'

'There's no hope of finding it then,' Annie said.

'If I was you, I'd try the scrapyard.'

Annie had no better ideas.

'Thank you,' she said. She reached her hand down to pet the dog.

'Oh I wouldn't do that,' warned the old woman. 'He'll have your finger off.'

There was no scrapyard in Matlow. The closest was in Burnley. Annie had been there with her father once or twice when he was looking for parts for whatever clapped-out old banger he was trying to do up at the time. Burnley was the neighbouring town, bigger than Matlow and with a steelworks but no colliery. It took Annie less than half an hour to get there. She drove through Burnley's tangle of narrow roads lined with the kind of shop she never went to any more, second-hand furniture shops, pawn shops and dusty-windowed shops with hand-drawn signs advertising fabrics and lampshades and children's clothes. The pavements were busy with old men wearing flat caps and women pushing prams.

She drove on, past the King's Arms, the pub that had been burned down, supposedly for the insurance, two years earlier. The flames had risen so high into the night that Annie had been able to point them out to Elizabeth from the upstairs window of Everwell, and the undersides of the clouds on the far side of the moor had glowed in the blaze. The pub had, by all accounts, been glorious that night; now it was a boarded-up, burnt-out shell, shards of wood sticking bleakly into a mardy sky. Beyond that were the arches, which the railway line followed on its way out towards Matlow.

Annie drove slowly past the first three arches and slowed when she saw the metal sign propped up against the black brick wall of the fourth. The sign said: *Rossiters Scrapyard*.

She turned the car into the narrow gap beneath the arch. Beyond was a wall of cars, the vehicles piled on top of one another; some were upside down, none had its wheels, some were just shells. She parked her own car close to the wall of the arch and stepped out. A battle-scarred Rottweiler on a chain set to barking and snarling, and a man with a huge stomach and a rock-star moustache came out of a cabin with a half-eaten sandwich in one hand.

'Yes?' he said.

Annie smiled her best smile. 'I'm sorry to bother you. I'm trying to track down a bike. It might have ended up here.'

'What kind of bike?'

'A Yamaha 125. It would have been pretty smashed up.'

'And you want it back?'

'Yes.'

The man jerked his head to indicate that Annie should follow him back into the cabin, and she did so, walking carefully around the dog. The interior was hot and cramped and smelled of egg and dust and kerosene. The man sat down behind a desk and flipped through the pages of a diary.

'What day did you say?'

'I'm not sure, but recently.'

The man ran his fingers down a page full of notes, took a bite of his sandwich and said with his mouth full. 'Nope. Only bike that came in was a Honda.'

'Oh.'

'Stolen, was it?' he asked, swallowing.

'Yes.'

'Whoever took it will have broken it up for parts by now,' he said. 'You won't see that again, love.'

'If I give you my number and the registration, if it does come in, would you call me?'

'It's a lot of trouble for something that's worth bugger-all.'

'It's for my brother,' Annie said. 'It's important.'

'In that case, love, you'd best let me know how I can get hold of you,' the man said, burping behind his hand.

She wrote Everwell's phone number on the back page of his notebook, offered him £20 which he refused to accept, thanked him for his trouble and left.

CHAPTER FIFTY-ONE

Annie wandered through the garden at Everwell. Dusk was falling and it was full of shadows, its colours dulled by the fading light. A breeze drifted across the lawns and over the flowerbeds. Annie walked slowly past the shrubs and trees, the pools of darkness. She walked to the well, slid down and rested her back against the inscribed plinth at the well-head. She wrapped her arms around her knees and looked up at the moor. She saw the songbirds in the sky, heard them singing. Puddles and pools had formed in the grassy dips and hollows of the hillside and they reflected the sky and its watery evening gold. The scrubby little trees were green now and the drystone walls criss-crossed the lower slopes like garlands. Annie imagined walking away from Everwell, walking up the moor, up to the ridge and then across the backbone of the hills, where barely anything grew and no one went, only the foxes and the rabbits skittering down the scree slopes. She imagined what it would be like to be dead – the quiet of it, the peace; the loneliness.

She threw pebbles into the small clearwater pool which collected the well-water. It was channelled down to the old stone horse trough at the farm. Leaves blown down by the wind were floating on the black surface of the pool, spinning slowly. The house loomed tall and grey behind, the light from the windows shining brightly. From beyond, Annie could hear the cows calling, a cacophany of their voices. Jim Friel must be late for milking. *Poor things*, thought Annie, and she rested her elbows on her knees and her chin in her hands and she stayed there until the sun had gone down.

She felt hollow, husk-like, drained – but she had come to a decision. She hadn't seen Tom since the time at the pub, and not seeing him had helped clear her mind. She knew now what she must do. She would not – could not – risk losing Elizabeth or causing further damage to her daughter, and the only way to protect her was to finish the affair. Still, the thought of losing Tom made her feel raw inside and out. Without him, she knew her life would not be a life lived completely. It would be a life of convention, a life standing beside her husband, a life faking a love she did not feel. She looked at the patch of ground still singed black by the fire Tom had lit the night he had come to the garden, and she was doubled over by pain, by grief, by the memory of him and his love.

Stop it, she told herself. *Stop*.

Annie stood up. She had not cried a single tear. Perhaps she was becoming like William. He could not be doing with the messiness of love, the chaos of emotion. He understood what an excess of love could do; he knew the destructive power of jealousy, the viciousness of grief. It was his job to understand. Perhaps that was why he shunned intimacy, why he always held a part of himself back. Perhaps he was right.

She walked back towards the house, away from the well, from the fire, from the past.

If she chose William, then love would be behind her, the kind of love she wanted. It would be over. She did not want to give it up for ever, but it was what she had to do.

Annie heard a car coming up the drive. She went around to the front of the house. A Panda car had pulled up. A young policewoman climbed out holding a large envelope in her hand.

'Hello,' Annie called.

'Hello! I was looking for Detective Inspector Howarth.'

'He's not in,' Annie said. 'Can I help?'

'Would you give him this? It's a forensic report he's been waiting for. He wanted to see it as soon as possible.'

'I'll give it to him,' Annie said. 'Leave it with me.'

'Thanks,' said the policewoman. 'It saves us making another journey.'

Annie waited until the police car was gone and then

she went back inside the house. She took the envelope into the downstairs cloakroom and locked the door. She stood for a moment, looking at it. A label had been stuck to the front with William's name and address printed on it. Somebody had scrawled URGENT across the top in blue ink. The envelope was sealed. Annie slid her thumb beneath the seal and opened it.

Inside were a few pieces of paper clipped together. There was a handwritten covering letter from somebody called Amanda. Under the heading *Subject,* Amanda had written: *Forensic report, Everwell Gamekeeper's Cottage.* The letter went on to apologise for the scruffy nature of the report but Amanda explained she had rushed it through as fast as possible, as requested. Annie flicked on to the next page. There was a lot of technical jargon that meant nothing to her. She turned to the third page. Human hair had been retrieved from the blanket removed from the cottage but it did not match any existing records. At least two different sets of fingerprints had been found but there were few good examples. However, at least one of the prints identified a person known to the police, one Thomas Logan Greenaway.

Annie tore out the page. She tore it into little pieces and dropped the pieces into the toilet bowl. She flushed it to get rid of them. She hid the rest of the report in the small cupboard where the toilet paper, towels and cleaning supplies were kept, pushed the door shut, leaned against it. She'd get rid of it later.

Her hands were shaking. She washed them at the basin, dried them on a towel.

She was going to finish it with Tom. What was the point of causing more trouble with the forensic report? It didn't matter now. It didn't mean anything.

CHAPTER FIFTY-TWO

Annie sat on a bench in the sunlight in the park outside Matlow General. She watched an old woman with a gaggle of little children feeding bread to the ducks in the pond. When the shadow fell over her, she looked up. It was Tom. He was wearing jeans and working boots, a fluorescent jacket, and was holding a safety helmet. Tiny flecks of wood were caught in his hair. A harness was fastened around his upper body. He took off his gauntlets, held them in one hand and patted them against his thigh. She squinted into the sunlight. She had not been expecting to see him here.

'Hello,' he said.

She smiled. 'Hi.'

'I was up a tree attending to some overgrown and potentially dangerous branches and I looked down and saw this incredibly beautiful woman walk into the park,' he said.

'Where did she go?'

'She's sitting right here.'

'You need your eyes testing.'

'Ha ha. Is it OK if I sit down?'

She shrugged.

Tom sat beside her with his knees apart and his arms resting on his thighs. He slotted his fingers together, twiddled them. 'You've been avoiding me,' he said.

'I've been so busy with Johnnie and the well-dressing and everything.'

'You didn't have a moment to call me?'

She looked down at her knees.

'Annie?'

'I tried. You were never in when I called.'

'You could have put a note through the door. You could have sent a postcard.'

'I don't think I can do this any longer,' she said quietly.

'What?'

'You heard me.'

'What's changed?' he asked, also very quietly.

'Johnnie. Lizzie. William. Me. I've changed.'

'Come on,' he said, 'let's go and get a coffee.'

They walked to the café on the corner of Bridge Street. It was full of men, and they turned to look at Annie when she walked in. She did not look at them. She stood at Tom's side while he ordered two mugs of coffee then they sat together at a table by the window. Annie stared at the steam wisping up from the surface of the coffee. Part of her wanted to take hold of Tom's hand and say: *Let's not waste this time we have together. Let's find somewhere and make love. Let's go to a pub, have a laugh, be happy while we have the chance.* But she said nothing. She sat beside him silently and looked out of the window behind Tom, looked at the wall opposite that was covered in strike graffiti and fly-posters, and she felt bone-tired.

Tom said: 'Do you remember we used to come in here before?'

She shook her head.

'I used to wait for you outside the Town Hall and we'd come here when it was cold. You always had the hot chocolate.'

'I remember the hot chocolate.'

'I remember everything. I remember how you used to have your hair held back in a band. I remember how I used to light your cigarettes for you and you used to cup your hands around mine as I struck the match. You used to close your eyes when you inhaled. You used to sip the chocolate froth off the spoon. I could never have enough of you. You were perfect.'

And I thought you were perfect too.

Annie poured sugar into her coffee from the dispenser on the table, and stirred.

'You still are perfect,' Tom said.

'Let's stop now,' she said, 'before anyone is hurt.'

'If we stop, then we will be hurt.'

'We don't matter.'

'Is that what you really want?'

'Yes.'

'I don't believe you.' He reached across the table and took hold of her hands. 'I love you and I know you feel the same. We belong together, Annie. I can make you happy – I'll do whatever it takes to make you happy. Look at me!' She looked. She saw herself reflected in his eyes. 'Annie,' he said, 'my love, I'd give you the world if I could, I—'

'Look,' she said suddenly. 'Quick – look behind you!'

'What?'

'See that man, that one there, walking quickly with his hands in his pockets?'

'Which one?'

'The bald one! Turning the corner by the old electrical shop. Did you see him?'

'No. Who is he? What about him?'

'Everywhere I go, he's there too. I think he's following me.'

Tom frowned. 'Are you sure?'

'Yes.'

'I've had a couple of weird things happen too. Phone calls when nobody's been there, that kind of thing.'

'That might have been me. Sorry.'

Annie sipped at her coffee, but she kept an eye on the street outside, over Tom's shoulder.

'Let's just come clean,' Tom said earnestly. He leaned in close to her. 'You tell your husband that your marriage is over and we'll move away, make a new start. You don't need to take anything from him. He'll understand.'

'It's so easy for you to say, Tom. So easy to say.'

'But if we don't do that, what are we going to do?'

'It's no use, Tom,' she said. 'I can't go away with you and we can't carry on like this, sneaking around, worrying all the time, risking ruining everything for everyone. I'm sorry for all you've been through and sorry to let you down again. But I have to, I don't have any choice.'

'Annie, no!' She pushed back her chair and stood up. 'Where are you going?'

'School. It's time to pick up Elizabeth.'

'But we haven't finished talking.'

'I've said all I can say, Tom. There's nothing else.'

'You can't just end it like this. You can't! When will I see you again?'

'I don't know,' Annie said, and she walked away.

CHAPTER FIFTY-THREE

Mrs Miller and Ethel were watching television in the living room. Annie put her head round the door.

'I'm going up for a shower,' she said.

'All right, love,' said Mrs Miller.

'The photographer's coming tomorrow, from the paper. They're doing an article about the well-dressing.'

'Oh yes?'

'Julia Thorogood organised it. She thinks it will help raise more money for charity.'

'That's good.'

'Although I don't see how having our photograph in the *Chronicle* will make a blind bit of difference to anything.'

'You go on then,' said Mrs Miller. 'We'll finish watching our programme.'

Annie pulled back the curtain and stepped out of the shower. She reached out to the radiator and picked up a large towel, which she wrapped around herself, tucking it in beneath her arms. She made a turban of a second, smaller towel around her head. She was relieved that the day was almost over and that soon she would be able to sleep.

She wiped the steam from the bathroom mirror and looked at her reflection, smeared and distorted. She could see the tiredness in the purple bloom around her eyes, the unhappiness in the downturn of her lips. Annie dipped her fingers in a jar of Pond's cold cream and smoothed it into the skin of her neck and chin, rubbing it in gently.

Back in the bedroom, she crossed to the window to draw the curtains before she switched on the light and felt a draught.

She turned.

It was William.

'You made me jump,' she said. 'Why don't you turn on the light?'

William put one hand out to steady himself against the wall. From the other side of the room Annie could smell the whisky on his breath. He was swaying slightly.

'Where have you been?' she asked.

'I've been to the pub with my friend.' *But you don't have any friends.* As if he had heard her thoughts, he corrected himself. 'With Paul.'

'What did you talk about?'

'We talked about you. Did you know, Annie, that your name means "favour" or "grace"?'

'No. I didn't know that.'

'There's a Saint Anne too. She was the mother of the Virgin Mary.'

'I wasn't named for any saint. I was named for my mother's cousin, who died of whooping cough.'

William gave a cold little laugh. 'That's my Annie. Always prosaic. Where's the poetry in your heart, Annie?'

'Please, William, put the light on.'

'Did anyone drop off a package for me this week?'

'No.'

'Are you sure? It should have been here by now.'

'No, nothing came. Put the light on.'

William reached out and pressed down the switch and the light half-blinded Annie. She covered her eyes with her hand to protect them, and when she took it away, William was standing right in front of her, so close that she backed away and fell onto the bed.

She bounced awkwardly on her elbows, and the towel that had been wrapped around her gaped open. She saw him look at the flash of her bare skin, saw him staring at her nakedness and she panicked. She tried to grab the towel and stand up, but he pushed her back again and this time the towel came off altogether and slipped onto the carpet. She reached for it, but she wasn't quick enough. William snatched it away and pushed her down a third time and she lay there, on her back, on the bed, with him standing above her, looking down at her. She tried to cover herself with her hands but that felt ridiculous. She had never felt more bare, or more vulnerable. William never looked at her naked, ever. He always looked away. He never came into the bathroom when she was bathing, he kept his back to her while she was changing. They had never made love with the lights on, never above the covers, never naked. But that evening he stared at her and his gaze ate into her. She lay there and she waited. She did not know what would happen next; there was no precedent.

Nothing happened. He didn't do anything. He stared at her and his face was flushed and his breathing was quick, but he didn't touch her.

After a moment he dropped the towel onto her stomach. She took it and covered herself.

'Goodnight, Annie,' said William, and he walked away.

CHAPTER FIFTY-FOUR

'That's perfect – perfect – just lift your arm a little higher, Annie – no, your *other* arm . . . that's it . . . and turn your face a tiny bit more towards me – and *smile*! Smile, my lovely – that's it!'

The camera flashes went off, *pff pff pff*, and Annie blinked to clear the dazzle from her eyes. She was standing by the well with her left arm linked through Julia Thorogood's. In her right hand she was holding a bucket to which a homemade poster had been glued. The poster was advertising Matlow's hospice, which was where funds from the well-dressing celebrations would be directed. Annie had been through a similar ritual every year since her marriage, but it had never seemed such an ordeal before. Julia was giggling like a schoolgirl, flirting with the photographer and being obsequious with the journalist, and Annie's cheeks ached with smiling. She could not forget what had happened in the bedroom with William. She could not get the sensation of being naked and exposed out of her head. And she could not come to terms with her own hypocrisy, posing as a happily married woman, a pillar of the community, when she was mired in so much deceit and confusion.

Mrs Miller and Ethel were standing to one side watching while the photographs were taken. Ethel was smiling and clapping her hands.

'What a lovely wedding!' she said. 'Isn't this perfect!'

The photographer lifted the camera so the strap came free of his neck and put it carefully down on the stone steps. The journalist, who had introduced herself as Georgina 'call me Georgie' Segger, stepped forward and made a note of everyone's names in her notepad. She told them the picture would be in the paper the next day. She asked if she could give away any clues as to the theme of the well-dressing and Julia said all she would say was that it was *not 1984* or anything at all to do with George Orwell.

'Any reference to the miners?' the journalist asked.

'Oh, my goodness me, no!'

As they walked back to the house, Georgie – a pretty, blonde-haired woman about the same age as Annie – said: 'You're married to the detective superintendent, aren't you?'

Annie nodded. She wrapped her arms about herself. She was wearing as many clothes as possible and still she did not feel covered up enough.

'I saw him last week at a news conference,' the

journalist said. 'He implied there was going to be some big news this week about the murder on the moor.'

'You know more than I do then.'

'Look, I don't mean to be intrusive, but are you feeling unwell? You're very pale.'

She laid a cool hand on Annie's arm. Julia Thorogood and the photographer were ahead of them, Julia's wide bottom swaying alongside the photographer's narrow one. Ethel and Mrs Miller were back inside the house. There was nobody else around. William had always told Annie not to trust journalists, but she was so lonely. She needed to talk.

'Would you like to stay and have a coffee with me?' she asked and Georgie Segger smiled and said she'd love to.

They went into the kitchen. The door was open and birdsong came in with the sunshine, the moor beautiful through the windows beyond. The journalist had a good look around, making no attempt to disguise or temper her curiosity.

'I love this room,' said Georgie. She sat down at the table. 'I love this house, I love these gardens, I love your life.'

Annie pulled up a chair opposite the journalist and passed a packet of biscuits to her.

'I'm very lucky,' she said.

'So what's it like being married to South Yorkshire's most charismatic policeman? It must be terribly interesting. Does he tell you everything? All the gory details – all the little snippets that we're not party to?'

'No.' Annie shook her head. 'No, he doesn't. He rarely tells me anything.'

'How perfectly true to character!'

Georgie prised a biscuit from the top of the packet with her thumb. She dipped it into her coffee mug and then bit into it.

'Everyone's fascinated by your husband, you know. His nickname at our office is Mr Enigma.'

'Really?'

Georgie glanced at Annie and her cheeks coloured a little. Annie thought: *She has a crush on him. She wants to sleep with my husband.* And she wondered if it was just this woman, or if there were others. She had never considered William in that way; it had not occurred to her that anyone else would be attracted to him. She remembered the way he had looked at her the night before and she shuddered.

'It's not as romantic as you'd imagine, being married to William,' she told the other woman. 'He's very involved with his work.'

'Of course he is. He has to be. He has so much responsibility.'

Annie felt tired. She wasn't enjoying this gush of admiration for her husband and regretted inviting the woman in now.

'I thought you'd be older,' Georgie went on. 'I imagined Old Grey Eyes married to someone terribly posh and thin, a fading society beauty or an ex-model or something.' She put the rest of the biscuit in her mouth. 'Not that you're overweight or anything – and you're very attractive, obviously, but not in the way I imagined.'

'It's all right,' Annie said. 'I know exactly what you mean.'

Georgie picked up one of Elizabeth's crayons lying on the table and began to sketch on the back of an unopened envelope. 'So how did you and Mr Enigma get together? I'm only being nosy. I'm not going to write about your marriage or anything, but I simply find people so *fascinating*.'

'I used to work in the Town Hall, next to the police station. The police and the council shared the secretarial pool. William used to dictate his letters to me.' She had a good look at Georgie. It was likely she knew about Mrs Wallace and Tom, and her involvement with him. She thought back to the immediate aftermath of the court case, a time when she'd been hurting even more than she was now, and for the same reason, more or less. William had been the calm after the storm. He had picked her up, dusted her down, and set her on her feet again. She felt a strong compulsion to say this, but knew she must be careful. 'William was very kind to me,' she said. 'He seemed to understand me. It was a quick courtship. We were married within a few months of our first dinner together.'

'Did he take you somewhere nice that first night?'

'The Beachcomber in Scarborough.'

Georgie raised an eyebrow and made a little whistling sound. 'And was it terribly romantic?'

'It felt very grown-up.'

'How do you mean?'

'I mean . . .' She had been used to Tom, to having no money, to making a half of cider and black last all evening, to eating chips, to running around on the moor and swimming in the river. She had never been to a proper restaurant before, never had waiters light candles for her or shake out her napkin for her, never had wine poured for her into a glass with a stem so thin she was afraid it would splinter each time she picked it up, never eaten food so dainty or so pretty or so delicately flavoured. She had not been used to fast cars with powerful engines that hardly made a sound as they sped around the country lanes, nor the smell of expensive cologne, the touch of silk on a man, the politeness, the deference, the quiet. 'I mean the kind of life that William showed me was not the kind of life I knew. I wasn't used to being treated like a lady.'

Georgie drew a swirly pattern around the edge of the envelope. 'I can imagine,' she said. 'Is it true that he is completely honest?'

'As far as I know. I don't think he's ever lied to me.'

'They say he's the only incorruptible copper in England.'

'Do they?' Annie smiled.

'Yep. A stickler for the rules. He also has a reputation for ruthlessness, you know.'

'William?'

'Yes. He's a man who should never be crossed.'

Annie sipped her coffee. A picture flashed into her mind, of her and Tom lying on the grass beside the well and the feeling that someone else was there, that they were being watched. But it couldn't have been William. He had been away and he would never in a million years sneak around in the dark; he would never watch her like that, he would not.

'So what do *you* know about the murder of the woman on the moor?' Annie asked. 'Is there more than has been put in the papers?'

'Mmmm. Well, apparently the Sheffield girls have been worried about one particular punter for a while. Some guy who's a bit of a weirdo. I mean, if you ask me, any bloke who gets a kick out of paying for sex is not quite right, but this one – they were worried about him.'

'Is it someone local?'

Georgie shrugged. 'Don't know. He doesn't talk much, according to the girls. They call him the Quiet Man. What's worrying the police is that there are a lot of prostitutes in South Yorkshire at the moment who don't belong here so it's hard to know if anyone else is missing.'

'That's what I'd heard too.'

Georgie drew a big orange flower. 'Whenever things go wrong, it's always the working girls who seem to end up being murdered.' She put the crayon down. 'Anyway,' she said, 'let's hope they find whoever it was who killed

Jennifer Dunnock soon. Maybe they're close. Maybe that's what this *big news* is.'

'I hope so,' said Annie.

Georgie stood up. 'Well, thanks for the coffee. I expect I'll be back for the well-dressing in a fortnight.'

'I'll see you there then.'

Annie took her through the hall to the front door and watched her walk away, swinging her bag over her shoulder, and she felt sad. Sad for Jennifer Dunnock and sad for herself. She picked up her book and went to sit in the sunshine, hoping to lose herself for an hour or two in the story of somebody else's life.

CHAPTER FIFTY-FIVE

Without Tom, without any prospect of ever being with him again, Annie felt empty. She grieved in silence and hid her loneliness. When her mother telephoned to tell her that Johnnie would soon be discharged from hospital, Annie wanted to talk to her; to tell her how she was feeling. She wanted Marie to acknowledge that Annie had done as she'd been told, and that her obedience had brought her nothing but unhappiness. She wanted some sympathy.

Marie talked at length about Johnnie and how Den was making adjustments to the house to accommodate his disability. Then she said: 'We haven't seen you in a while.'

'I've finished it with Tom,' Annie said. 'I've done what you wanted.'

Marie was silenced for a moment. 'Oh,' she said. 'Well, that's good.'

'It doesn't feel good.'

'You've done the right thing.'

'But Mum, I miss him so badly.'

'That's as may be. You brought this on yourself, Annie.'

'I know.' Annie tried to keep herself from crying out loud.

'It's for the best,' Marie's voice was gentler now. 'You'll see. In a few weeks you'll have forgotten all about this.'

'I'll never forget.'

'Try not to think about him. Try not to dwell on it. It's over. Everything will be better soon.'

Annie heard the pips from the call box, and she put the phone down before Marie could put another coin in the slot.

In all that time Annie did not talk to Tom. He wrote her letters. He left flowers for her, silent messages of love in places where only she would find them, little bunches of wildflowers bound together with tiny pieces of garden twine. He left them at the end of the drive, on the front doorstep, tucked into the handle of her car door. She did not talk to him but she saw him twice. Both times she was in her car. The first time, he was working on the hedgerows, pollarding trees outside the Haddington Hotel, and the second he was walking up Occupation Road with his hands in his pockets and his shoulders hunched, and Annie had to fight herself not to stop the car, not to call him to her, not to press her mouth against his and beg to be consumed by him. She had to cut off the blood supply to her heart. It would only function for so long without love. Soon enough it would become desiccated and dead and there would be no more hurt. It was the only way.

In June, there was a battle at the Orgreave coking works. It was a long way from Matlow, but after that the mood in the town changed. People were angry, sullen, dejected. Thatcher was not backing down. This time she'd been prepared for the strike. Coal had been stock-piled to keep the power stations burning. She had also made changes to the welfare benefit rules. Dependants of strikers could no longer receive urgent needs payments. Marie was worried about how the family would manage with Johnnie incapacitated. The strike was turning into a battle of wills. It was a question of who would hold out longest, the government or the miners and, for the time being at least, neither side was showing the least inclination to back down.

After the trauma of Orgreave, William had a few days' leave. He looked gaunt and was still distracted, lost in thought, keeping away from his wife and making barriers with his music, his study door, his shooting. Annie asked about the well-dressing, if he would be there, if they were to follow the usual routines and he said: *Yes, of course. Why should things be any different this year?* And after that he had gone back into his study and closed the door again.

She walked. Summer was coming in. The verges were

lush with wildflowers – the countryside around Matlow as joyful as the town was depressed. She went back to the place where Jennifer Dunnock's body had been found. She was drawn to it. She sat on the rocks and dropped flowers over the edge. She thought back to the night Jennifer had died, the night of the dinner dance, and she remembered that it had been a cold night, but clear in the evening, before the mist set in. She wondered if Jennifer had seen the lights of Everwell when she came up the moor with whoever it was who brought her there. Had she been afraid? Had she known what was coming? Had she screamed out, hoping the residents of Everwell might hear her, come to find her and save her? Had she wondered why nobody came?

Annie sat on the rock and tilted back her head so the sun warmed her throat. She remembered how Tom kissed her throat, how he started in the hollow at its base and kissed his way up her neck. She bit her lip as hard as she could to take away the longing. Without Tom, the joyful sex she'd known with him was over too. All that remained were decades of occasional, lights-off intercourse on high days and holidays, and memories. She would always have memories but they were too intense, too close to revisit now.

Annie pushed herself up to her feet. She was hot and thirsty. She followed the path the honeymooners should have taken the day they found the body, away from Everwell, until she forked left along a dusty bridlepath, overhung by the branches of birch trees, that took her back to the lane. She walked down the hill, through the dappled shade. The lane became narrower and rougher the closer she came to the farm turning. Even the verge was steeper, stonier and pitted and clodded with mud that had come loose from the tyres of the tractor. She reached the cattle grid at the entrance to the farm. Flies were buzzing and she could smell the stink of cow-shit, hear the dogs barking.

Annie rarely walked this way, she had no reason to. She looked across the farmyard, beyond the barns, to Jim and Seth Friels' cottage. It was a witchy little house with a steeply sloping roof and small windows. It looked dirty, unkempt and unwelcoming. There would be nothing pretty inside, she thought, no table lamps or curtains, no flowers or cushions on the chairs. Outside was a badly tended vegetable patch but no real garden. Scrawny brown and black hens pecked amongst abandoned tyres, rolls of chicken-wire and odd pieces of machinery. A washing line was strung from one wall to the gatepost, and three pairs of overalls puffed and waved in the breeze, dancing weirdly, as if they were alive.

As she looked at the cottage, the feeling of being watched returned to Annie. She glanced around her, but there was nobody else there – at least, nobody she could see. The calves had been moved out of the stable and into the open-sided barn; they were poking their wet noses through the metal bars, banging against the railings. A filthy collie dog was tied up outside the barn, its eyes on her, its chin on its paws. Perhaps that was what was bothering her. Perhaps that was all.

CHAPTER FIFTY-SIX

The evening before the well-dressing, Annie turned the dining room into something beautiful. The table was set with the best silver, the best crockery and the antique heirloom candlesticks. She filled a vase with tiny bud roses and baby's breath, and placed it in the centre of the table. Wine was cooling or coming to room temperature on the sideboard, and the best crystal glasses twinkled in the candlelight. Starched linen table napkins were folded at each place.

Annie stood back and surveyed the table, and knew she had done well. William might not say anything, but he would be pleased.

The guests – the vicar and Julia Thorogood, the Lord Mayor and Lady Mayoress and Paul and Janine Fleming – were enjoying pre-dinner drinks with William in the conservatory. The French doors were open so they could look out across the gardens – walk outside, if they so wished. The well had been prepared to receive the panels for the morning's ceremony. The branches of the trees had been strung with lanterns and bunting, and a marquee had been erected for refreshments and entertaining.

Annie carefully filled the water glasses on the table. The door opened and Janine came in, carrying her sherry schooner. She was wearing make-up, for a change, and she had pinned her hair up. It suited her olive-green dress and she looked better than Annie had seen her look for a while.

'Hi,' she said. 'Is there anything I can do to help?'

'It's all in hand, thanks,' said Annie. 'How are you?'

Janine trailed her fingers over the back of a chair. 'This is the first time I've been anywhere without Chloe since she was born. Do you mind if I stay here with you? It's so hard talking to those other women.' She lowered her voice. 'That Lady Mayoress is a funny one, isn't she?'

'Funny peculiar, you mean?'

'God, yes. I know everything there is to know about her fibroids.'

Annie put her hand over her mouth. 'She didn't tell you about the time she . . .'

'In Hull Town Hall? Yes!'

Both women covered their mouths to contain their laughter.

'At least her heart's in the right place,' said Annie.

'Unlike Julia Thorogood's.'

'Oh, don't get me going on *her*.'

'Does William enjoy this kind of thing?'

Annie smoothed a wrinkle in the tablecloth. 'He has to entertain these people. It's important for his career so he doesn't have much choice. It'll be the same for Paul, if he follows in William's footsteps.'

'Oh, Paul loves all this. He loves how the older people treat him like some kind of pet protégé.' Janine took a drink and wrinkled her nose. 'He tries so *hard* to be like William. Sometimes, you know, I hear him recounting anecdotes that William has told him, as if they were his own. Do you think that's odd?'

'Not really. Everyone does that, don't they? Everyone pretends to be the person they wish they really were.' Annie put the water jug on a coaster on the sideboard and drew the curtains. 'Light the candles for me, would you, Janine? The matches are on the sideboard.'

Janine persisted. 'But Paul tries so hard to please William, it's almost embarrassing. He stays up all night trying to figure out a problem and then I hear him on the phone: "Good morning, sir, I just happened to notice . . ." as if he hadn't spent hours and hours on it. The moment William asks him to do something, he's: "Oh yes, sir; of course, sir; right away, sir; three bags full, sir".' She sighed.

'Perhaps you should be pleased he's ambitious,' said Annie, and she hated herself for saying it – she who understood that ambition was a fruitless pursuit, that it was like chasing rainbows, that it could never lead to fulfilment.

'He doesn't think he's good enough. That's the real problem. Every day he has to prove himself all over again. It will never end.'

'Maybe it will when he reaches William's rank and he has someone like himself to mentor.'

'Maybe.'

Janine followed Annie into the kitchen. Ethel was standing by the window. She had dressed and made herself up, and she looked such a state that Janine cried out.

'It's all right,' said Annie. 'It's William's mother. Stay there so you don't alarm her.'

Ethel was wearing a white satin dress that Annie had never seen before over her slippers. Lipstick had been smeared around her mouth and there were blotches of blue eyeshadow on her forehead. She was holding a champagne flute full of red wine. Mrs Miller had left a couple of hours earlier, having informed Annie that Ethel was in bed, asleep. The old lady must have left her bed, dressed, come downstairs and helped herself to a drink. Some of the wine had spilled down the dress, staining the silk blood-red.

'Hello, Ethel,' Annie said, gently, reaching out and taking the glass from her. 'How are you?'

'I'm feeling a little sad,' Ethel said.

'What is it? What's wrong?'

'I'm missing my husband. When he was alive I used to find these kinds of dinner parties tiresome. Without Gerry, they are simply an ordeal. I feel, my dear, that I am an embarrassment to you all.'

Annie put an arm tenderly around her mother-in-law's shoulder.

'Of course you aren't,' she said. 'I thought you enjoyed entertaining. William has told me you used to throw the greatest parties.'

'I was acting.' Ethel patted at her hair. 'That's what women have to do, Annie, women like us. We don't have to be happy. We don't even have to try to be happy. We just have to be good actresses.'

Janine kept an eye on the dinner while Annie took Ethel back upstairs, washed her and settled her back into bed. She gave her an extra half a sedative tablet with a sip of water.

'You'll be all right now,' she whispered. 'You'll sleep like a baby now.'

'But I'm so lonely,' Ethel replied, and there was nothing Annie could say to that, to make her feel any better.

After that, the dinner went much as Annie had expected. She drank enough to feel anaesthetised but not enough to make her incapable of taking good care of her guests and her husband. She caught sight of herself in the large mirror on the dining-room wall each time she stood up to clear the plates, or fetch something from the kitchen, and it was like looking at a stranger with her hair in curls and wearing her blue dress, with the pearls her husband had given her for their last wedding anniversary. She drifted through the evening and the hours went by, and afterwards, after their guests had left, Annie kicked off her heels and stood barefoot in the kitchen washing up while William sat in his study and did whatever it was he did in there. Annie felt that the chasm between them had never been wider or more deep. She thought of what she had given up for him and her resentment swelled.

She missed Tom every moment. It was worse than it had been before, the missing. It was the kind of missing she did not think she would be able to bear, yet she knew she *would* have to bear it – for the rest of her life.

CHAPTER FIFTY-SEVEN

The next morning was the occasion of the well-dressing. Annie heard the telephone ring while she was still in bed. William answered and there was a brief, terse conversation. Then he came upstairs.

'There's been a fatality,' he said. 'On the picket line. I have to go.'

'But William, it's the well-dressing!'

'I'll be back as soon as I can.'

It was no use, he was already on his way out.

Soon after, the well-dressing committee and their helpers arrived to set up the garden ready for the festivities. Mrs Miller came early too and was so long upstairs with Ethel that Annie took a tray of tea up to them both.

'How's it going?' she asked the nurse.

Mrs Miller pulled a face. 'Frail,' she mouthed. 'Shaky.'

Ethel was sitting by the window, hunched and wrapped up warm. The room was dark, the heavy curtains only open a fraction and she was peeping through the gap at the garden.

'She doesn't like seeing all the strangers in the garden,' Mrs Miller whispered.

Ethel looked up. 'Who are they all?' she asked. 'What are they doing here?'

'It's the well-dressing,' Annie said. 'Do you remember, Ethel, they come every year?'

'Oh no,' the old lady fretted. 'No, this has never happened before. They're tramping all over the gardens, ruining the flowerbeds and I don't know what they want, I don't know who they are.'

Annie crossed to the window, drew back the curtain a little and looked out. Grey clouds were forming around the moor and the sunlight was gauzy and fragile. 'I'm not sure the weather will hold,' she said.

Ethel tugged gently at her sleeve. 'What about the people?' she asked. 'Can you make them go away? Please make them go away.'

Annie looked at Mrs Miller for help.

'Perhaps you should sit away from the window, dear,' Mrs Miller suggested. 'Come and sit over here and we'll listen to the radio and I'll read you some of the stories from the newspaper. We could see what's on television tonight. Perhaps *Bergerac* will be on. That will be something to look forward to, won't it?'

Back downstairs, Elizabeth was skipping in and out of the house enjoying all the fuss and the people. Annie went outside. The committee had set up a small stage and roped off an area for the band and the schoolchildren to one side of the well. The WI were heating tea urns in the marquee and a hog was slowly turning on a spit, filling the air with the salty scent of cooked meat. Annie looked up to the moor. Nobody was up there. Everyone was down in the town today.

She turned and was walking back towards the house when she saw the truck coming up the drive. She was not sure, for a moment, if it was Tom's – but then she saw his name painted on the front of the cab and her first instinct was to run towards it. Then she remembered where she was and who she was, and she held herself back. She walked demurely over to meet Tom as he jumped down from the driver's seat. Two other men were in the truck with him. They got out from the other side.

'Tom,' she said quietly, and she felt she could not keep the joy from her face, she was so happy to see him. He looked terrible, grey and wan, and he had lost weight in the days since she had seen him; but then so had she.

'Hello,' he said, and he reached out his hand and touched her gently on the arm.

'What are you doing here?'

'I've brought the panels for the well-dressing.' He turned to indicate over his shoulder. The other two men had already climbed up into the back of the truck and were untying the knots in the plastic rope that was securing the panels in place.

From the corner of her eye, Annie could see the committee members hurrying across the lawn to receive the panels. Any minute now they would reach the truck and the moment would be gone; she would lose him again and in that moment she knew she could not bear it.

'I was wrong to think I could live without you,' she whispered urgently. 'Please, can I see you again? Can we find a way to be together? Will you help me get out of this marriage?'

'Annie!' Julia Thorogood was waddling across the lawn as fast as her peep-toe shoes would take her. 'Don't let them move the panels until we're ready!'

'Where?' Tom asked. 'Where can I see you?'

'I don't know. Come to me. Find me. Come soon.'

He nodded.

'Thank goodness you're here,' Julia said bossily to Tom, and she pushed past Annie and took over, telling the men in which order to bring the panels so they would be correctly assembled. Annie drifted away again but she knew Tom was watching; she knew he was keeping her in his line of sight.

'That looks spectacular, doesn't it, Annie?' Julia Thorogood said.

'It looks fantastic,' Annie agreed. The well did look good. The panels were colourful and cheerful, butterflies and ladybirds scattered amongst fish and flowers, lions and rabbits.

Julia was puffed up with pleasure. 'I don't think I've ever seen such a beautiful well. And the sun's come out. God is smiling on us.'

Annie looked over Julia's shoulder. She couldn't see Tom. Julia put her head close to Annie's. 'I was just talking to the head of the Women's Institute and she said everyone is saying the well-dressing committee has done an excellent job with the arrangements this year. We should all be very pleased with ourselves.'

'Good,' Annie said distractedly.

'They're thrilled with the marquee. Thrilled! Have you been in yet? You should go in, dear. They've laid on a fantastic spread of refreshments.'

'That's great,' Annie said. And then, because she wanted to get away, 'Of course, it's all down to you, Julia. It simply wouldn't have happened without you.'

She walked away from the well. The conservatory French doors were open and she could see the band inside the house, putting on their jackets and getting their instruments out of their cases. Children from Matlow Primary School were being disgorged from three coaches that had lined up on the drive and were forming a disorderly crocodile at the side of the house.

Elizabeth sidled up to walk beside Annie and took hold of her hand.

'I used to do that,' Annie said to her. 'I used to come up here on a coach and be made to stand in a line like that.'

Elizabeth grinned. She was shy around the Matlow

children, unsure of them and their broad accents. All her friends went to the private school, as she did, and they weren't used to mixing with the town kids.

Annie gave a little laugh as she remembered. 'There was always someone who was coach-sick, even though we were only on it for about ten minutes. And always someone who needed to go to the toilet.' She smiled down at her daughter. 'We were a right load of ragamuffins. I never thought any of us would end up living at Everwell, not in a million billion years, especially not me.'

'What about Daddy? Did he come on the coach too?'

'No. This was before Daddy lived here and he's not from Matlow.'

Elizabeth scratched her thigh. Annie had allowed her to wear her stripey tights today. It was warm and she had a feeling Elizabeth was regretting her choice.

'Is Grandma Marie coming to see the well-dressing?' Elizabeth asked. 'Is Grandad Den?'

'Not this year, Lizzie. They've gone to bring Johnnie home from hospital.'

'Back to Grandma's house?'

'Yes.'

'Is he better then?'

'Better enough to go home.'

It took a long time for the two of them to make their way through all the visitors in the gardens because they had to stop and say: *Hello, how are you?* to everyone they met, including some people they didn't recognise, and Elizabeth had to tolerate being clucked over and told how she had grown since this time last year. All the while Annie's eyes were searching for Tom. She couldn't see him. When she had a chance, she looked on the drive. His truck was gone, and William's car was back on the drive. She felt her heart fall.

They went back to the well. The brass band was warming up, the musicians – a jolly bunch of men in royal-blue jackets with gold braiding – were tooting and parping their instruments, and the vicar and his wife and the Lord Mayor and his wife had taken their places. The children were lined up, fidgeting and chattering. As she drew closer, Annie saw William standing behind the stage. His left arm was folded across his waist, his right bent at the elbow and he was holding his chin in his right hand and listening intently to a uniformed officer beside him. In front of them, on the stage, a young man, all dressed in black and with mullet hair, was tapping the microphone.

'Daddy!' Elizabeth called, and she ran across the field towards her father. William looked up when he saw his daughter and he smiled. Then he caught sight of Annie behind her and the smile faded. Annie felt the ground shift slightly beneath her feet. William returned his attention to the police officer beside him.

Bang on noon, the brass band struck up the tune of the 'Floral Dance' to signal the beginning of proceedings. The vicar blessed the well and a little boy in a suit far too big for him came on to the stage and shyly read the Psalm for the day. The schoolchildren sang a hymn and the watching adults all smiled at each other and touched their hearts with their fingers and whispered about how sweet the children looked. The same photographer from the *Chronicle* was back and he took lots of pictures, and the journalist, Georgina Segger, spoke to some of the children and some of the teachers before interviewing the committee, the vicar and the dignitaries. She wrote what they said into her notebook in shorthand. At one point she looked up and caught Annie's eye; she waved and Annie waved back.

When the formalities were over, the band played some happy tunes and the Lord Mayor did a little dance with Julia Thorogood. The children were free to sit cross-legged on the lawn and eat their sandwiches and their crisps.

Annie looked for William but he had disappeared again. Elizabeth was playing tag with a group of the village children. Annie took a glass of Pimm's that someone offered her and stood in the shade of the walnut tree.

'Hiya,' said a friendly voice. She turned and there was Georgie Segger standing beside her clutching her notebook and biro.

'Did you speak to everyone you wanted to?' Annie asked.

Georgie nodded. She put her notepad away in her bag. 'I was hoping for a quick word with your husband but I can't find him.'

'Did you want him to say something about the well-dressing? Only he hasn't really been involved.'

Georgie looked at her. 'No-o-o. That wasn't what I wanted him for. You have heard, haven't you?'

'Heard what?'

'Oh Christ.' Georgie took a packet of Camel cigarettes out of her bag and offered one to Annie. Annie shook her head. 'I probably shouldn't say anything, it's not my place.'

'Please tell me,' Annie said. 'What is it? What's happened?'

Georgie put a cigarette between her lips and searched for her lighter.

'It's happened again,' she said. 'There's been another murder. And this time it's not a prostitute and it's somebody local.'

Annie felt her heart slide.

'Is it another young woman?'

'Yep.'

'Where?' she whispered.

Georgie flicked her eyes upwards and to the left. 'Up there again,' she said. 'On the moor.' She lit her cigarette with an orange plastic disposable lighter and blew out smoke. 'The police are going to be in all kinds of trouble for not doing more to prevent it.'

'What could they have done?'

Georgie drew on the cigarette again. 'They could have caught the killer.'

CHAPTER FIFTY-EIGHT

At last the day was drawing to a close. The children had been packed back into their coaches and driven away, the brass band was gone. The well-dressing committee had tidied up as best they could. The panels would stay in their place over the well for the next week and the gardens would be open to anyone who wanted to come and take photographs.

Annie drank tea and watched the lights of the cars winding their way back down the lane. Then she put her head around the living-room door. Ethel was sitting on the settee with Mrs Miller beside her, holding her hand on her lap, and Elizabeth was lying on her tummy on the floor. The child smiled up at her mother.

'We're watching *'Allo 'Allo.*'

'I can see.'

'Do you want to watch it with us?'

'Later,' Annie said. 'I'll be back soon.'

She went outside and walked over to the marquee.

Inside, trestle tables were still lined up along one side and a temporary wooden floor had been laid to protect the grass. She heard footsteps and turned, and there was William. She went towards him. He was rigid with tension.

'I heard what happened,' she said. 'I heard there was another murder.'

He breathed in through his teeth. 'We're trying to keep it quiet.'

'I heard it was another young woman, and that she was found on the moor. I suppose . . .' she looked at him '. . . I suppose this means it's the same person who killed them both?'

'We're working on that assumption.' William sighed. 'This time we know who the victim is. This time we'll get whoever did it. I came to tell you that I'll be out for a couple of hours.'

Annie looked at her husband and she took a deep breath. 'William, we need to talk.'

'Not tonight,' he said. 'If we need to talk, we can talk tomorrow. I'm hoping that by tomorrow this will be cleared up.'

'You know who it is then?'

'We have a good idea.' He cleared his throat. 'I'll be back before midnight.'

'All right,' she said. 'I'll save you some supper.'

He left. She made a light meal for Elizabeth and Ethel and settled them both in bed. After that she went outside again and she lit the candles in the lanterns that hung from the branches of the trees and she sat by the well and she drank some wine and watched the stars come out in the night sky.

She knew he would come. She did not doubt it for a moment. She looked out towards the moor and after a while she made out the shape of him, a dark figure crossing the home meadow. She jumped up then and climbed the stile to run to meet him. They kissed in the long grass, amongst the gentle cows, and bats darted above them and the little night moths were all around. Annie knew at once that something had changed; it was in his voice, in his arms, in the way he pressed her to him. He kissed her so hard that in the end she could not bear it and had to pull away.

'What's wrong?' she asked.

'Without you, everything is wrong,' he said. 'I didn't see the point of anything. If I couldn't be with you, nothing mattered.'

'Oh Tom.'

'And then this afternoon . . .' He paused and took in a gulp of air. 'This afternoon, Annie, after I'd come here I drove back to the flat and it was chaos there. I parked at the top of the road. There was a line of police cars in front of the houses and our house was taped off; there was a sergeant standing at the door. Nobody knew what was going on.'

'What did you do?'

'I went to the café and I had a drink and I listened to what people were saying. It was speculation. They were saying someone else had died, and I wondered if the police were after me, Annie. I wondered if they were trying to stitch me up again. I walked around for a bit and when I went back they were still there, inside the house. So I went to pick up the truck and they were towing it away. The police were towing my truck away! Christ! Why would they do that? Do *you* think they're trying to frame me?'

'There's been another murder,' Annie said, 'on the moor.'

'Oh Jesus Christ. Oh no. Do you know who it was?'

'No.' She put her hand up to his face. She stroked his beard. 'It's a woman, a young woman, that's all I know.'

She thought of the forensic report she'd flushed down the toilet. She thought of the paperwork still hidden in the cupboard. 'Try not to worry,' she said.

'But why were they taking my truck?'

'I don't know, love. I have no idea.'

'Don't you feel – doesn't it seem that everything's going weird, Annie? That the world is turning at the wrong speed? Everything is out of sync. People who ought to be working together are fighting one another, and bodies are being left on the moor like sacrificial victims, and you and me are apart when we should be together.'

'We're together now.'

'I feel as if I'm losing my mind. I feel as if everything's wrong.' He leaned down to kiss her. 'Oh God,' he said.

'My God, you're so beautiful. You taste so sweet. I've missed you.'

'I've made up my mind,' Annie told him. 'I'm going to leave William. I tried to live without you, and I can't. It's you who makes my life worth living, Tom.'

'Oh my love, my Annie . . .'

'It will be terrible. My mother won't speak to me and it will destroy William and Elizabeth and Ethel, and I shall feel guilty for the rest of my life. But you said that people get over these things; they survive, don't they? There are worse things that can happen to people, aren't there?'

'If you're sure. *Are* you sure, Annie?'

'William knows something already, or suspects. The way he looks at me, the way he's been with me . . . I've been afraid to talk to him. I thought it would be all right when I tried to finish with you, but it wasn't all right. If anything, it was worse.' She paused. She bit at her nail. 'There's no good way, is there, to tell him I love you more than I've ever loved him. There's no good way to end a marriage.'

'You don't need to say anything. Just leave him. Talking won't make it any easier. Just come away – quickly, now, before anything else goes wrong.'

'And Elizabeth?'

'Bring her with you. We'll sort it out. We'll manage. It won't matter where we are, as long as we're together.'

He kissed her again. Her face, her jaw, her neck.

'And all the police are here,' he said. 'They're all in

South Yorkshire. They've taken the men from the ports, from everywhere. If we go quickly, before they start to look for us, we could catch a ferry, go to Ireland, rent a cottage somewhere.'

'Could we do that?'

'We can do whatever we want. Whatever *you* want. We'll be so happy, Annie. I'll make you happy. I promise I will. I'll make you happy every day for the rest of your life.'

'Oh God,' she said and she pictured, in her mind, a little house in the countryside, green fields and hedges lined with cow parsley and she and Tom and Elizabeth together and everything wonderful.

Tom sold the dream to her and at the same time he began to undo the buttons on her dress. 'It's lovely there, Annie. I shared a cell with a man from Donegal. He described it to me, he said it's like heaven. You'll love it, I know you will. And we can live properly there. We can grow our own vegetables, have more babies . . . you can have all the books you want, your own library.' He slipped the dress from her shoulders, kissed her neck.

'Tom, if anyone comes . . .'

'They won't.'

'What was that?'

'I didn't hear anything.'

'I'm sure I heard something.'

'No, no,' he said, 'it's only the cows, it's nothing.'

They listened for a moment and Annie heard nothing but the cows tugging at the grass in the dark.

'All right?' he whispered and she nodded.

'Yes, but be quick.'

He shrugged off his coat, fought the belt off his trousers, pulled the shirt over his head. She put her hand flat on his chest, and she felt his heartbeat through her hand, felt it inside her and he put his arms around her and lifted her, so that she was clinging to him and she thought: *Oh thank God*. And there was no need for talking any more. No need for anything but sex. She didn't care about anything but Tom now, because he had told her what their future would be and she was certain it was what she wanted; she was certain he would give it to her.

It was quick and cold and breathless. It was over in moments. Afterwards they held on to each other. She was exhausted and dizzy, lying in the damp green grass when the flashlight beamed across the field beside them, an arc of dazzling white light.

'What's that?' she cried, and then she clamped her hand over her mouth. She tried to scramble to her feet but she was half-naked, and then she heard her husband's voice calling her name. 'Oh God, dear God!' She fumbled with her dress.

Tom tried to help but she pushed him away.

'You have to go,' she whispered. 'Go now! Go quickly!'

'I can't leave you like this.'

'Tom, please,' she cried, 'just get away from here. He might have his gun!'

'Annie!' William's voice rang out through the darkness.

'I'll come back for you,' Tom whispered. 'I'll be back soon.'

'Oh be careful, Tom.'

'I will be. And, Annie?'

'Yes?'

'I love you.'

'I know you do,' she said, 'I know.'

Annie stumbled to her feet and made her way back to William, wading through the long grass, hoping he would not see her in the meadow, scrambling over the stile and grazing the palms of her hands, going towards him furtively as he called her name and searched for her in the garden, and then he found her in the beam. The light blinded her. She stood still with her hands over her eyes while he ran towards her, and she knew what a mess she was, how dishevelled and muddy, as if she had been dragged through a bush backwards. He grabbed her arm.

'What's happened to you?' he cried. 'Are you hurt? Did someone attack you?'

And she realised what it looked like to him – it looked as if she had been taken against her will up towards the moor, and that she had escaped and run back towards the house, and she was appalled at herself for frightening him so.

'I'm all right,' she said. 'I'm fine. I went for a walk, that's all.'

'To the moor?'

'Through the meadow.'

'You know someone's out there killing women on the moor and still you went out on your own in the dark!' he cried. He shook her. 'How could you do that? How could you be so foolish? What the hell is wrong with you?'

She had no defence, no excuses.

'I needed some air,' she said lamely. 'It's been a long day.'

'You could have stayed in the garden.'

'I felt safe amongst the cows,' she said and then she had to stifle a laugh; she wanted to bend over and roar with laughter at the ridiculousness of it all – this dance of deception, these crazy, stupid lies.

In the kitchen, she busied herself tidying up. The room was full of boxes, tangled bunting and black plastic bin bags full of litter, crisp packets, paper plates and plastic cups. She poured herself a large glass of wine and William drank whisky and watched her. She felt as if his eyes could see right through her clothes, see through to her skin still flushed from Tom's kisses, see to the sex between her legs. She felt like an exhibit in a museum, a laboratory rat. William had studied criminal psychology and he knew how to recognise the behaviour and body language of a liar; she did not know how to disguise it so she said little and kept herself busy with the bags, a cloth, a bottle of bleach.

When the kitchen was tidy, she made a pot of tea and

went upstairs to bathe. She lay in the water until it went cold, and when she returned to the bedroom William was already asleep. He must have been exhausted, as he had fallen asleep on top of the bed, with his clothes on. Annie carefully took off his shoes and covered him over with the eiderdown. He was lying on his back snoring gently through his open mouth and his breath smelled of Laphroaig. He looked old and tired and vulnerable. He was growing older every day, fading in front of her. *Old Grey Eyes*, the journalist had called him. *Mr Enigma. The only incorruptible copper in England*. Annie felt a stab of pity for the man. She climbed carefully into the bed beside him and lay there awake, wondering how she would tell him that she was leaving, and how much it would hurt her to watch his face as she tore his life apart.

CHAPTER FIFTY-NINE

The next morning they went to church as usual and, as usual, the Thorogood family came back for lunch. Annie was exhausted by her own deception, shocked at the risks she had taken, terrified of what she was going to do. She messed everything up that day. The lunch was awful – the meat tough and overcooked, the roast potatoes still hard in the middle and the cabbage burned where the water had boiled out of the pan. Annie could not join in the conversation, she could not keep up with it. She did not understand it; it was as if the others were speaking a different language. She kept thinking: 'Perhaps this will be the last time I do this.'

William disappeared during dessert to answer the telephone and he was gone for a while. He had shut the dining-room door behind him but Annie could still hear his voice: *Yes*, he said, *of course, do what you must*. There was a pause. *I don't care what it takes*, he said, *make sure you find him, and quickly*. He came back into the dining room and sat down. He wiped his hands on his serviette.

'Any news?' Reverend Thorogood asked and William nodded.

'But I don't want to discuss murder at the dining table,' he said.

After lunch, Julia suggested a walk. Nobody wanted to climb the moor but the woods were full of new leaves and they lasted for such a short time, Julia said, it would be a sin not to enjoy them. Her husband agreed and said it would do the children good to have some fresh air. Ethel was having one of her better days. She said she would be happy to stay behind and have a nap, so Annie settled her in her bedroom and made sure she had everything she needed before closing the door.

'We won't be long,' she promised.

'Be as long as you like,' said her mother-in-law. 'It makes no difference to me.'

'I'm sorry you can't come with us.'

'It's all right, dear. I've had my time for walking on the moors. Off you go now, don't worry about me.'

Still Annie hesitated. 'Ethel . . .'

'Yes?'

Annie wanted to say something about love. She wanted to warn Ethel about what she was going to do, she wanted her understanding and her forgiveness. She thought that Ethel, who had loved her own husband to the ends of the earth, who loved him still, would understand why she had to be with Tom. But there was too much to say, too much to explain. And Ethel's heart, her loyalty, belonged by rights to William – not Annie.

'I'll see you later,' was all that Annie said.

'You'd better lock the door,' said Ethel, 'in case I've forgotten who I am when I wake up. You don't want to come back and find I've wandered off again.'

Annie smiled. She wanted to say: *I wish I'd known you when you were young and healthy*, but she felt that would be too cruel. 'Are you sure you want me to lock the door?' she asked and Ethel said: 'I'm senile, dear, not stupid,' so Annie had locked the door.

The two families, the Howarths and the Thorogoods, walked across the home meadow, past the very spot where Annie had met her lover the previous evening, past the cows with their slippery jaws and their attendant flies, their swishing tails, and through the gate at the far end. They climbed the path up to the woods and it was beautiful up there. Annie took off her cardigan and looped the arms around her shoulders. William was wearing a golf shirt. He was breathing hard and there was colour to his cheeks. Elizabeth swung from his hand.

'It's a shame we don't have a dog,' William said suddenly. 'I miss Martha. Especially when we're out.'

'I miss her all the time,' said Elizabeth.

'We should get a puppy.'

It was such an un-William thing to say that Annie stopped in her tracks. Elizabeth stared up at her father.

'Really?' she asked and then, realising that she had better wrestle a guarantee from him before he changed his mind, she began a barrage of questions and demands for promises, confirmation that a new puppy would come. Annie smiled at Julia as if she too thought a puppy would be a good idea, when really, in her heart she was thinking how difficult it would be to leave a puppy behind with William when she and Elizabeth fled to Ireland, and how cruel to take it from him; that it would be one more life to consider, one more future for which she would be responsible.

'I think we should think about it before we decide,' she said to William.

He smiled. 'My wife spends half her life telling me I should be more spontaneous,' he said to Julia, 'and then when I am, she reins me in.'

'That's women for you,' said the vicar. Even Julia frowned at that comment.

That evening, Annie bathed Elizabeth and then brought her downstairs, flushed and powdered and ready for bed, for a snack. The television was on in the living room and Annie heard the theme for the local news. She went into the room to watch.

A young woman was being interviewed on screen. She must have been standing at the top of the road that led out of Matlow, with the moor and the colliery in the background behind her. Annie thought she looked familiar, but she did not have a local accent. Her eyes were red and teary and she had to stop speaking to dab her nose with a tissue.

'She was lovely,' the woman said. 'She was beautiful and popular and talented. But,' she paused and took a gulp of air, 'but most of all she was my sister and I loved her.' She started to sob and Annie held tight to Elizabeth and tried to turn her from the television so she would not see the woman's distress. She reached down to turn the channels over to something less terrible, only as she did so she paused. A photograph of the second murder victim had appeared on the screen and this time Annie did recognise her. She even knew her name.

It was Selina Maddox, the girl who had played guitar in the bar at the Haddington Hotel, the girl who had been with Tom at the pub by the river; the girl who lived in the flat beneath his, the girl who had called him *babe*.

Annie waited until William was asleep and then she crept from the bedroom. She walked carefully down the stairs, treading softly so as not to make the boards creak. She checked her watch in a shaft of moonlight; it was gone 3 a.m.

She knew she would not sleep again. She was twisted by anxiety. Where was Tom now? What was he doing? Had he found a safe place to sleep? Did he know that Selina was dead?

She went into the kitchen and filled a glass with water from the tap. She stood at the window to drink it.

Outside, the moon was casting shadows in the garden and on the moor. She didn't like to think of Tom out there in all that darkness, on his own.

It would be better, she thought, safer for him if he were to go right away; leave Yorkshire, leave the country. But how would she ever find him then?

She jumped as the light went on, spilling water down her nightgown. William was standing at the kitchen door. Her mind was so full of Tom that it took a moment for her to recognise her husband.

'What are you doing?' he asked.

'I came down for a drink.'

'You're always wandering about in the dark these days, Annie.'

'I couldn't sleep. I didn't mean to disturb you.'

Annie tipped what was left in the glass into the sink, rinsed it and put it on the drainer. William stood, watching. She dried her hands on a tea towel.

'Excuse me,' she said, squeezing past him at the door. She went back upstairs, not waiting to see if he was following, and tucked herself back into the bed, wishing she were anywhere but where she was.

In the morning she returned to Occupation Road, hiding her face behind sunglasses and a scarf. She walked up to the door and she rang the bell to Tom's flat. Nothing happened. She pressed the other buttons, the bells to the other flats, her palm flat against the buzzers ringing them all at once. At last the door opened. It was the Indian woman, she was holding a little boy's hand.

'Yes?' she said. 'What is it?'

'I'm looking for Tom Greenaway. The tenant in the second-floor flat.'

'He's not here,' the woman said. 'He won't show his face round here again. And if he does, the police will have him.' She nodded in the direction of a saloon car parked on the other side of the road with two men inside. 'It's been a nightmare,' the woman hissed. 'That poor girl murdered, him gone, the police and press all over the place. We don't want him back here. We hope he never comes back, the bastard. And if you know what's good for you, you'd better stay away too.'

She closed the door with a bang.

CHAPTER SIXTY

Annie felt as if she might implode with anxiety but there was nobody she could speak to, nobody she could call, nobody she could ask for reassurance.

She had to stay calm, she had to try and behave as if nothing was wrong.

That night she knew she would not sleep, but for the second night running William went to bed early. Annie, dry-mouthed and light-headed, stayed downstairs, pretending to read a book in the conservatory while thoughts churned in her mind.

Tom had no truck, no home, no family. He had nowhere to go and nobody to ask for help. He might try to reach her. If he came to Everwell, she reasoned, he would be able to see her through the windows. He would know she was waiting up for him and he would find a way to let her know he was there.

But deep down, Annie knew he would not come, not yet. How could he risk coming to the house with

William there, and the patrol car still driving up and down the lane, and he having no way of knowing where Annie was, or even if she was awake. Eventually Annie dozed off and when she woke in the morning she was cold and her neck hurt and she was sick with nerves.

That morning, the telephone rang early. Annie answered.

'Hello, Annie, love. It's Paul. Is your husband about?' He sounded cheerful.

'I'll call him,' Annie said. She turned and William was already there, standing behind her. She passed the receiver to him and returned to the kitchen. Elizabeth was dressed in her school uniform, sitting at the table eating scrambled egg on toast and swinging her legs. The toy dog was on the table, propped up against the milk jug. Annie went to stand behind her daughter, plaiting her hair. She looked up when William came into the room.

'You look like the cat who's had the cream,' she said.

William stood behind her. He put one hand in the small of her back. 'It's nearly over,' he said. 'We know who killed those two women. The whole force is looking for him. We'll have him soon.'

'That's a relief,' Annie said. She continued to work on Elizabeth's hair, twisting it between her fingers.

'Don't you want to know who it is?' asked William.

Annie dropped the hairpins she'd been holding and they scattered on the floor.

'I don't think we should talk about this in front of Lizzie.'

'It's someone you know, Annie. We're working with other forces to track his movements. It's possible he's been involved in other incidents elsewhere. These people often move around to hide their tracks.'

'These people?' Annie asked. She was trying to ignore the noise in her head, a kind of low-pitched buzzing sound, like a wasp trapped in a jam-jar. She rolled the elastic band down her wrist and fastened it to the bottom of Elizabeth's plait.

'Murderers. Men addicted to murder. Sexual sadists.'

Annie looked up and William's face seemed to be coming close to her and then moving away; it was like looking into a distorting mirror. She waited for him to tell her what she already knew, but instead he picked up Lizzie's moth-eaten toy dog and looked at it quizzically.

'What's this thing doing on the table?' he asked.

Elizabeth paused, the fork halfway to her mouth.

'That's Scooby,' she said. 'He always has his breakfast with me. You know that, Daddy.'

'You're too old for baby toys like that now, Elizabeth. You're almost eight.'

Annie rested her hands on the back of her daughter's chair. She was trying to breathe; it felt as if her body had forgotten how to do it.

'Eight is still little,' she said. 'It's not doing any harm, William.'

'What does your mother know?' William asked his

daughter. 'What does silly Mummy know? I was at boarding school when I was eight. We certainly weren't allowed toys at the table.'

Elizabeth crunched her toast. She looked from her father to her mother and back again.

'What's boarding school?'

'Is it Tom?' Annie asked. 'Is Tom the man you're after?'

'Daddy?'

'It's where children are sent to learn manners and values. It's where they go to learn how to follow the rules.'

'Tell me, William! Is the man you're looking for Tom Greenaway?'

William put the toy back on the table. He could not hide the satisfaction in his eyes. 'Yes,' he said. 'It is.'

CHAPTER SIXTY-ONE

The next morning, a patrol car drove up to Everwell and parked outside. Nobody got out.

'What's that car doing there?' Annie asked.

'There's going to be a police presence here round the clock,' William said.

Annie stared at her husband. He did not look at her.

'You're not to go anywhere on your own, Annie,' he continued. 'You're not to leave Everwell. If you need to go into town, an officer will take you.'

'You make it sound as if I'm under house arrest.'

'It's a temporary measure. It's for your own good.'

Annie hid her panic behind a sudden briskness. She picked up Elizabeth's bag. 'Come on, Lizzie, it's time we were off,' she said. She looked at her husband. 'I really do not need an escort for the school run.'

'Weren't you listening to me?' William said. 'I told you, you can't go anywhere alone. Not to the school, or to the shops; nowhere. Not on your own.'

'That's ridiculous.'

'It's a necessary precaution.'

You don't trust me, Annie thought. *You want to control me completely.*

She threw the car keys down onto the counter. 'No,' she said. 'If I can't drive my daughter to school like I always do, then I'm not going.'

'Suit yourself,' said William.

William took Lizzie to school that morning. Annie sat in the garden by the well. She knew she was being watched. One of the policemen had followed her into the garden, was standing at a distance casually smoking a cigarette but keeping an eye on her. She wondered what would happen if she were to make a run for the moor. Would the officers chase after her? Would they wrestle her to the ground? Arrest her? Put her in handcuffs?

This is madness, she thought. She looked at all the space around her and she realised that if she were not free, it meant nothing. She might as well be in a prison.

Was Tom watching? she wondered. Did he know what was happening? Did he realise how dangerous the situation was?

Mrs Miller came across the lawn with a mug of coffee in her hands. She passed it to Annie and nodded to the police officer. He did not respond in kind.

'Miserable so-and-so isn't he?' said Mrs Miller.

'I'm hoping if I sit here long enough he'll get bored

and go away,' said Annie. Mrs Miller leaned against the well head.

'I shouldn't count on it, pet,' she said. 'Anyway I came to tell you that your mother called. She only had 10p so I said I'd take a message. Your brother's been asking after you. He misses you. You haven't been down to see him lately.'

'No, I haven't.' Annie felt a pang of regret. She'd been so wrapped up in herself she had neglected her brother.

'Your mum says he's on his own today. Perhaps you could ask your friend over there to drive you down to Matlow. If you're stuck with a police guard, you might as well make use of it.'

Annie drank the coffee and then walked back to the house. She took food from the bread-bin, the pantry and the fridge, packed it into carriers, picked up her keys and her handbag, and went outside. The police officer from the patrol car took his hat off and she told him what she wanted to do. They both got into her car and the officer drove down to Matlow. They didn't say a word to each other. The pickets and the police were still grouped outside the mine but some of the energy had gone from the protest; the men were subdued. Annie wondered if it were possible the mine really would close, and she thought: *No, of course it won't.* Without the mine, the town would have no purpose. The colliery had always defined the shape of the town and the way it worked. It was all Matlow had going for it.

The officer took the direct route down Occupation

Road. Everything looked the same as always. There was nothing to mark out the building where Tom lived. The geraniums in the window boxes of the ground-floor flat were beginning to flower and somebody had strung an NUM banner between the windows on the top floor but there was no police tape, nothing out of the ordinary. Nothing to suggest a murder victim had lived in one flat and the man accused of killing her in the one above it.

Where was Tom? Where had he gone?

At Rotherham Road the officer parked up and told Annie he'd wait in the car. A ska beat was thumping from the house. The front door was unlocked so Annie pushed it open and went inside. Johnnie was sitting at the kitchen table playing clock solitaire and listening to his cassette recorder. He was wearing his favourite hooded tracksuit and he looked so normal that at first Annie forgot about his arm. She ruffled the short hair on his head and he said: 'Get off, Shitface,' and she said: 'Shitface yourself.' She turned down the music and leaned against the sink.

'How are you?' she asked.

'Bloody brilliant,' Johnnie said. 'Never been better. How d'you bloody think?'

'Don't be so mardy. You're such a whinger.'

'Did you come here just to moan at me?'

'Yes. Shall I make you something to eat?' she asked. 'Bacon sandwich?'

'We haven't got any bread. Or bacon. Or marge for that matter.'

Annie held up the bags. 'You have now.'

Johnnie beamed. 'Well done, Sis,' he said.

Annie found the packet of bacon she'd brought with her, opened it, and laid the rashers under the grill. She buttered some bread. 'Where's Mum?'

'Up at the Miners' Club with her cronies. They're making a magazine.'

'Oh yeah?'

'It's called *WAG the DOG*. For Women's Action Group. Mum's packed in the cleaning. She says she can do better than that now.'

'It's funny, isn't it, how the strike has changed things.'

Johnnie looked at his arm.

'Oh Jesus, sorry,' Annie said. She pulled up a chair and sat opposite her brother. 'Black five on red six.'

'I know, I know.'

'Well, move it then.'

'You're always bloody interfering.'

'Tosser.'

'Cow.'

Annie stood up, moved to the grill and turned the bacon. 'Shall I fry you a couple of eggs too?'

'Did you bring some brown sauce?'

'Yes.'

'You're an angel, Annie.'

She laughed.

'So what do you want to do today, Johnnie?' she asked. 'We can go wherever you want to go. We've got our very own police driver to look after us.'

'Oh, give over.'

'We have! Go and look out the front-room window. He'll be in the driver's seat of my car or standing next to it trying not to look conspicuous. Quick, while I make your buttie.'

Johnnie went through to the front room and Annie heard his whoop of delight. He came back into the kitchen with a wide grin on his face.

'I don't know about you, Annie,' he said, 'but I fancy a trip to the seaside.'

When he had finished his breakfast, Johnnie and Annie went outside and told the police officer they wanted to go to Bridlington. He looked dubious.

'It's OK,' Annie said, 'if you don't want to come, we'll go on our own.'

'No,' said the officer. 'I'll take you.'

Johnnie sat in the front next to the officer and after some initial awkwardness, the two soon got chatting about football and Annie was free to sit in the back quietly with her thoughts.

When they reached the town, and had parked up, Annie and Johnnie bought some food and sat on the beach wall and he ate vinegary chips and after that they went onto the sand and lay in the sun until their skin was hot and pink. They paddled in the icy sea and splashed one another. They both drank tea and Johnnie ate a pasty in a café. She bought him a punnet of winkles, and then an ice-cream. The officer stood at a respectful distance and watched.

Annie imagined booking into a bed and breakfast. She imagined having a little room to herself, a bed, a window, a basin. She imagined sitting alone, staring out of the window at the people on the seafront, watching them walk by, looking out for Tom. Sooner or later she would see him. She imagined sleeping on her own, and going down to breakfast alone with nobody knowing her name or who she was. She tried to imagine how it would be, not to have to think, or lie, or worry for the rest of her life, only wait for Tom. She could not imagine such peace.

Annie was a little late at the school that afternoon. William was there already. The Jaguar was parked conspicuously amongst the other cars, standing out from the women's little runarounds. William was conspicuous too amongst the women and children waiting outside. He stood with his back straight, as always, head and shoulders above the mothers, facing the school door.

Annie left the officer in her car and walked towards her husband. The distance between them seemed to become no smaller; if anything, it expanded. In Annie's mind William was on one side of the universe and she was on the other. He was wearing his casual clothes – an open-necked shirt, chinos, a belt; he appeared relaxed. He had something in his arms, an old towel.

'Why are you here?' she asked. 'You never meet Lizzie from school.'

'I've brought her a present.' He lifted an edge of the towel, and beneath it was a puppy.

'Oh!' said Annie. She took it from him. It was black and white, silky-haired, soft-nosed. It had the dogmeat smell of a farm puppy, a tiny tail, baby eyes. Annie held it close. 'Oh,' she said again, and for the first time in weeks William smiled at her, a natural smile, a smile like the ones he used to give her. The puppy sucked at the collar of her shirt.

Inside the school, the bell rang and a moment later the door opened and the first little girls emerged into the early summer afternoon. They were followed by others, gaggles of girls, running and skipping, chattering like parrots. Elizabeth came out on her own, caught sight of her father, and her face broke into a wide smile. She came running over. Annie held the puppy close. Some of the children had spotted it and were coming to look. William went forward to meet Elizabeth, took her hand, said something to her. They walked towards Annie. Annie crouched down so that Elizabeth could see the puppy properly.

'Is it for me?' she asked, wide-eyed, incredulous.

'He's all yours. Do you want to hold him?'

Elizabeth nodded.

Annie passed the puppy gently to her daughter. He seemed much bigger in the child's arms. He looked up at her and Elizabeth looked back.

'Hello,' she said. 'What's his name?'

'You can call him whatever you like.'

'His name's Martha.'

William crouched down so that his head was close to Elizabeth's.

'Will he do?' he asked.

'He's the best present ever,' Elizabeth replied. She kissed the puppy's forehead. William smiled and put his arm around Annie's waist. She felt the warmth of it, the strength. She remembered how safe she used to feel with William, how protected and secure after the chaos of her time with Tom. She knew the police officer was watching this show of solidarity and she thought how easy it would be simply to keep that arm around her and play Happy Families until the end of her days.

'We're going to be fine now,' William said, as if he had read her thoughts. He pulled her closer. 'Everything will go back to how it was. You don't have to worry about anything, Annie, ever again.'

CHAPTER SIXTY-TWO

The Matlow murders and the suspect on the run made the national newspapers the next weekend. William had them delivered to Everwell so he could read what was being said. He sat in the conservatory, drinking coffee and pulling out the pages that made mention of the South Yorkshire police.

Annie watched William through the open door of the conservatory. She could see by the slight puff of him, the brightness of his eyes, that he was buoyed by the attention that was being heaped upon his team. There was some criticism that the prime suspect had not yet been apprehended, but the police had covered all bases. It would only be a matter of time.

She must have made a noise, or else her husband sensed her presence because he laid the papers down, took off his reading glasses and turned towards her. He held out his hand to draw her into the room.

'Are you feeling better?' he asked.

'Hmm?'

'You said you were going for a lie-down.'

'Oh yes. Yes.' She went over to the window and looked out into the garden. Lizzie was playing with the puppy on the lawn. Ethel and Mrs Miller were sitting on fold-down chairs watching them.

'You're still up to going out this evening?'

'Out?'

'The hospice dinner. We need to present the cheque from the money raised at the well-dressing.'

'Oh yes, of course.'

William brought her hand to his lips. He kissed it. Annie pulled it away. She wrapped her arms about herself, pressed the hand into her side.

'Right, then,' said William. 'I have a little work to finish. I'll see you shortly.'

He picked up all the newspaper pages he'd selected but one, and left the room. A few moments later Annie heard the click of the key in the lock to the study door. She sat in the chair he'd left, it was still warm, and looked at the page he had left for her to read. It was from the *Telegraph*. There was a photograph of Tom and an article, written by a psychiatrist. The article was headlined: WHAT TURNS A MAN INTO A MONSTER.

Annie did not want to read it, but she was compelled to do so. The psychiatrist began by describing Tom's underprivileged childhood, the death of his mother and the abuse he'd suffered at the hands of his father. She explained how his father's constant criticism would have eaten away at Tom's sense of self-worth and self-esteem.

Tom was incapable of overcoming his claustrophobia. No matter how often his father punished him, he could not 'cure' himself. In order to deal with the ensuing self-hatred, the young man was forced to develop an emotional veneer. Perhaps the only person he trusted was Edna Wallace, the octogenarian widow whose garden he tended and with whom he discussed his plans for the future.

Unfortunately, the relationship with Mrs Wallace came to an end with her death. Greenaway always maintained he did not deliberately set out to harm Mrs Wallace and went on to convince himself – and anyone else who would listen – that he was innocent. It is, of course, the nature of the psychopath to be convincing and plausible. It is why such people are so successful.

There were some quotes from the lawyer with whom Tom had corresponded from prison. Annie winced as she came to the next part of the article. It described how Tom, on his release from prison, had returned to his home town:

to try to pick up with his former girlfriend, a local woman who had rejected him after his conviction. When he discovered she was married, he went into town and met up with a prostitute who closely resembled the girlfriend. It was a chance meeting. Greenaway must have picked Jennifer

Dunnock from the dozens of working girls who were congregating at strike locations. She was in the wrong place at the wrong time. Greenaway probably did not set out to kill that night either, but Dunnock's availability gave him the chance to dissipate the humiliation he felt after the girl-friend's rejection. He left the body on the moor, at a place where he and the former girlfriend used to go courting – the symbolism is too strong to be accidental.

Annie put the article down. She could not bear to read any further. She had not been named, but everyone in Matlow would know who she was. The psychiatrist was implying it was her fault Jenny Dunnock had been murdered. It was all coming out again, all her dirty laundry. She would be the talk of the town again. *Oh God.*

It all made sense. Everything that had happened was connected to Tom, everything tied in – and yet she knew that everything was wrong. She opened the French doors and went out into the garden. The puppy was lolloping around and Lizzie was chasing it. She lay down on the grass and let the puppy and Lizzie crawl over her. She felt the sun on her skin. She wondered where Tom might have gone, where he might be. Was he hiding up on the moor – and if so was he watching her now?

CHAPTER SIXTY-THREE

The charitable dinner was a dull affair, held in the reception room at Matlow's Town Hall, a gloomy building with few redeeming features. The food was mediocre, the wine corked and the company boring. The photographer from the *Chronicle* was there, but Annie could not see the journalist, Georgie Segger. William played his part. He listened with interest to the speeches and talked to the people who spoke to him. Annie sat on the other side of the table between two middle-aged men who battled like cockerels for her attention, all puff and preen, the one spitting food over her plate in his garrulousness, the other so obscenely attentive that Annie knew, from his glances, that William could sense her revulsion from twenty feet away.

As the company broke for cigarettes between the main course and the dessert, William excused himself and walked round the table to where Annie was sitting.

He offered her his arm and they walked outside together. The night air was cool and fresh; the street lamps glowed yellow, an undernourished dog tugged at the contents of a spilled bin bag.

They leaned on the railings and looked out over the town.

'Why did you bring me out here?' Annie asked.

'I wanted to have you to myself for a while. I wanted you to remember.' William looked at her fondly. 'This was where it all started for us, Annie, here in the Town Hall.'

'I suppose it was.'

'The first time I ever saw you was in this building. I knew at once that you would be my wife.'

'How could you have known that?'

'Because you were always the only one for me.' William gave a self-conscious little laugh, the sort that invariably preceded some self-deprecatory anecdote that he considered amusing. 'I was like a lovestruck teenager. Paul used to tease me about it. I was forever coming to the typing pool under the flimsiest pretexts so that I could talk to you. Do you remember how I used to ask you to type up even the most insignificant memos? How I'd get you to redo the same letter time and again?'

'You were always finding fault.'

'No, it wasn't that! Didn't you realise I was finding excuses to be close to you?'

Annie looked at her hands holding on to the railings.

She had not realised, no. Her head had been so full of Tom.

'I was afraid of you at first,' she said quietly.

'Afraid of me? Why?'

'You were so important; so senior. I was just a typist.'

'You didn't say anything.'

'I didn't want to let on how I was feeling.'

Annie remembered how kind William had been to her after Tom's arrest. How he had looked after her, protected her with his authority and how necessary that had seemed to her at the time.

'I never thought somebody like you would be interested in someone like me,' she said more gently.

'I will never stop being interested in you,' William said, 'never.'

He stiffened his back.

'We'll have Greenaway soon,' he said. 'There are officers all over Yorkshire looking for him. And when we have him locked up, then our life can get back to normal.'

'I can hardly remember what "normal" feels like,' said Annie.

They were silent for a while.

'What if Tom didn't do it?' she asked quietly. 'What if it wasn't him?'

'He *did* do it,' said William. 'He murdered both those women. There is no doubt at all that he is responsible for their deaths. He's mentally unbalanced. Psychopathic. He's not the man you think you know.' William rubbed his chin. 'This has been a difficult time for you,' he said. 'I haven't been around, I've been distracted.' *Don't,* she thought, *don't apologise for your behaviour.* 'And it was . . . difficult for me too. I've been so worried about you, Annie. I've been so, so worried.'

'There was no need.'

'Wasn't there?' He cleared his throat and she tried not to hear him. 'I think we should have a holiday,' he said. 'We've all been through a lot these last weeks. We could take Elizabeth out of school for a fortnight; with what we're paying, they couldn't possibly object.' Annie opened her mouth but he hushed her. 'We'll go away and by the time we return, Greenaway will have been apprehended and the fuss will be over. And while we're away, perhaps we could try for another baby?'

For a moment Annie was speechless. Then she said: 'William, what makes you think I'd want another baby?'

'You told me the happiest time of your life was when Elizabeth was little. You haven't been happy lately. I'm not the most sensitive man, but even I can see you haven't been happy. I'd like to see you smile again. And in any case, don't you think it would be good to have another child? Good for us, I mean, as a couple and as a family.'

'I . . .' Annie looked around, searching for the words. 'You think a baby would make things better between us?'

'Yes.'

'Where has all this come from, William?' Annie

asked. 'Why are you saying all this to me now?'

'Because I know we've had a few problems lately. No, don't say anything. I know we have.' He cleared his throat. 'But I also know that things will be better from now on.'

'How can you know that?'

'Because I'm going to make it happen,' he said.

CHAPTER SIXTY-FOUR

Annie got through the next day. Somehow she got through it. She made herself do the things she had to do; she put on a brave face. She would not fall apart, not this time, no.

She played with the puppy, she cleaned up his messes, she chatted to Mrs Miller, she marinated some fish, she peeled some potatoes and put them in a pan of water, she separated six eggs to make a lemon meringue pie and only broke the yolk of two of them. She laughed with Mrs Miller at the comedy programme on the radio, she read to Ethel for an hour to give the nurse a break, she watered the plants in the pots in the conservatory, she hung out a load of washing and brought a different load in, she ironed a pile of shirts and sheets, she made sandwiches for the policemen outside, she boiled some chicken and rice for the puppy's supper, she made herself up and went to parents' evening at the school. The officer waited in the car outside. Annie smiled at the teachers when they praised Elizabeth, she frowned when they criticised her behaviour, she nodded when they suggested ways that she could help her daughter curb her imagination and improve her concentration, she made small talk with another mother. She did not start drinking until she had cooked the fish and the potatoes, made a salad, laid the table and William had come home.

And then Mrs Miller came into the living room and she was holding something in her hands – an envelope. She said: 'Excuse me, Mr Howarth, but I found this in the cloakroom. I don't know how it got there. It's addressed to you and it says it's urgent.'

William took the envelope and opened it. He looked at the forensic report with the page missing and then he put it back into the envelope and he tore the envelope into several pieces and he put them into the rubbish bin.

He never said a word.

Annie held herself together all the way through the dinner, even when the filling had not set in the lemon meringue pie and it spilled out all over the tablecloth when she sliced into the pastry. It wouldn't stop running out and she burned her hands trying to stop it because it had taken so long to make it, so long to squeeze all those lemons and scrape off the zest and separate all those eggs – and there it was, all that lovely lemony syrupy filling making a sticky puddle on the tablecloth and the pie was ruined and she couldn't catch it in her fingers, she couldn't stop the flow.

'Annie, leave it!' William said and she looked at him. He had hold of her by the shoulders and his face was close to hers, and behind him she could see Elizabeth looking startled and anxious, and she held up her hands and all the lemon goo dripped from her fingers onto the carpet and her fingers were burned and she began to cry.

William washed her hands under the cold tap and then he took her up to bed. He made her sit on the side of the bed and he undressed her like a child. He helped her into her nightclothes, he passed her a warm flannel to wipe her face and a toothbrush to clean her teeth. He gave her a glass of water and two pills.

'What are they?' she asked and he said: 'They're Mother's sedatives. Take them. They will help.'

She swallowed the tablets and almost at once she felt an exquisite numbness. It crept through her tiniest capillaries and then it spread to her fingers and her toes, her face, her hands. She lay down and the pillows were soft and welcoming and cool.

'Sleep,' William said quietly. 'You'll feel better in the morning.' And he kissed her forehead and she knew he would take care of her because William always took care of her, that was what he did.

'I'm sorry,' she mumbled. 'I'm sorry for everything.'

'Let's not talk of it,' he said, and she sighed: 'All right. Let's not.'

William went noiselessly from the room and she waited for sleep to overtake her. It was a black sleep, a deep-black velvet sleep that came over her as if someone had covered her completely beneath a soft blanket; a sleep like drowning. When she woke she heard Elizabeth's voice and William's somewhere, distant and close all at once. She did not hear what they said but she knew she did not have to get up so she let herself fall again, slip back into the blackness and it was better than being awake. And then she woke again, a second time – something woke her and she recognised the sound of the vacuum cleaner on the landing, going backwards and forwards. She tried to lift her head but did not have the strength. She knew that she needed to think, but her head was a mess; she could remember odd flashes from the previous evening but everything was disjointed. She was confused. So she gave up trying to think and went back to sleep and the noise of the vacuum cleaner was her lullaby.

When she opened her eyes for the third time, the blackness was less intense but Annie thought she must be dreaming. Because there was Marie in the bedroom at Everwell. Marie was wearing denim overalls and a pink T-shirt, and her hair was held back by a pink band and she was standing by the window. The curtains had been opened and the light was flooding in and Marie was now grunting and trying to lift the sash window. Annie thought she was dreaming and closed her eyes again.

And then, a while later, maybe a minute or maybe an hour, there was Marie again, her face much closer now, so close that the hoops of her earrings were tapping against Annie's cheek. She shuffled a little further beneath the covers and Marie said: 'That's enough of that now. Sit up. I've brought you some coffee.'

It took another few minutes, but Annie managed to open her eyes. She managed to prop herself up on her elbows. She was almost certain that she was not dreaming. She could smell the coffee and Marie's hairspray, and there was a dent in the mattress where Marie was sitting watching her with an exasperated expression.

'What are you doing here?' Annie asked.

'I've come to tell you to stop feeling sorry for yourself.'

'Mum . . .'

'I told you it wouldn't end well.'

'God.' Annie closed her eyes. 'Mum, please don't start.'

'Somebody's got to sort you out.' Marie passed the mug to Annie. 'I made it strong,' she said, 'with sugar.'

'Why did you come?' Annie asked.

'William fetched me. Mrs Miller's taken old Mrs Howarth out. He said you'd taken some pills and he didn't think you should be left alone.'

'He gave me the pills. He made me take them.'

'Hmm,' said Marie. Her arms were crossed. 'Drink your coffee. I'm going to run you a bath and then you can come downstairs and have something to eat.'

Later, when she was bathed and dressed, Annie sat at the kitchen table while Marie fried bacon, tomatoes and eggs, commenting all the time on the quantity and quality of food in Annie's fridge. She put a plate in front of Annie and sat down too. She looked at Annie for a moment, then reached out her hand and cupped her daughter's cheek.

'Oh love,' she said, 'I hate to see you like this.'

'Please don't say that you told me this would happen, Mum. Please don't.'

'Annie,' Marie said, 'listen to me. Listen. I know you think you love Tom Greenaway. I know how you feel about him, but it's not real love. It's a lie. It's like a poison in your system and I know it hurts now but soon it will stop. It will stop because it's not real, it never *was* real. It was no more real than his lies. You weren't loving the real person, the murderer; you were loving a false Tom Greenaway, the version that he presented to you. It was a shadow, that was all. A reflection. It wasn't real.'

'No.'

'Now eat your breakfast. I won't have you wasting good food.'

'I can't.'

'I'll have it then. Does William know? About you and Tom, I mean.'

'He knows something but he's pretending he doesn't.'

'He is such a wise man. If only there were more like him.'

'You think that's good? Sweeping everything that's wrong under the carpet?'

'I think it's a damn sight better than the alternative.'

Annie watched as her mother ate the food she had cooked.

After a few minutes, she said quietly: 'I can't stay with him, Mum. Not after all that's happened.'

Marie banged her knife and fork down on the table. 'Oh Sweet Jesus Holy Mary Mother of God! Have you lost your mind?'

'How can I stay when I don't love him?'

'Annie, listen to me.' Marie's voice was urgent. 'You leave your husband now and what is there for you? Nothing! You have no job, no money – nothing. Your dad would kill you if he knew what you'd done. You'll be pilloried in town. If people find out you were screwing a murderer behind your husband's back . . . Dear God, can you imagine what it would be like for you? You have to make this marriage work, Annie, you have to.'

'But I don't love William.'

'It's not about love, Annie! For God's sake, how many times must I tell you!'

Marie sighed and ran her fingers through her hair. She gazed at Annie in anger and frustration and Annie gazed back.

The telephone rang. 'You'd better get that,' Marie said. 'It might be your husband. He might be calling to find out how you are.'

Annie went into the hall and picked up the receiver. 'Hello?' she said.

'Hello, Mrs Howarth?'

'Yes.'

'It's Rossiters scrapyard. You asked us to call you if anyone brought in a Yamaha 125 registration GN 87V?'

'Yes.'

'Well, they just did. It's here now.'

CHAPTER SIXTY-FIVE

Marie and Annie went outside. The police officer walked over to them.

'Who's this then?' Marie asked.

'He's my minder. He's supposed to accompany me wherever I go,' Annie said, 'to keep an eye on me.'

'Oh,' said Marie. She looked the officer up and down. 'Well, you can stand down now, young man, because I'm with Madam here and I'm not going to let her out of my sight.'

The officer protested and Marie leaned in closer.

'Listen, Sonny Jim, Mr Howarth fetched me himself to look after my daughter. He entrusted her into my care. He knows she's with me and he's perfectly happy with that arrangement. Call him if you don't believe me. Go on, call him on your radio!'

The officer looked uncomfortable but he backed away and while his back was turned Marie grabbed Annie's arm and pulled her into her car.

'Bloody cheek,' she muttered. 'Him still wet behind the ears thinking he can tell me what's what.'

As they drove away from Everwell, Annie watched the officer and his colleague arguing from her wing mirror. She reached out her hand and touched her mother's arm.

'What?' said Marie.

'You,' said Annie. 'Sometimes you're just amazing.'

'Don't be soft.'

They picked up Johnnie from Rotherham Road and then drove to Burnley, Johnnie sitting next to Annie in the front of the car and Marie in the back. Annie still felt woozy so she drove very slowly and carefully; Marie kept up a constant stream of criticism about her driving from the back seat until Annie told her to shut up or get out.

At the scrapyard they piled out and gave the dog on the chain a wide berth as they walked around to the cabin. The same man with the huge belly and the rock-star moustache came out and he nodded when he saw Annie.

'Brought the family this time, have you?' he asked.

'It was my bike,' said Johnnie, and the man looked at him, looked at the place where his arm used to be and said: 'Sorry, mate. It's over here.'

They followed him round the back of the cabin, and there was Johnnie's bike, propped up against the side of an old campervan.

'It's in a bit of a state,' said the man.

'You can say that again,' said Marie. 'What happened to it?'

'The lads who brought it in said they'd found it dumped on the moor at the back of the colliery. It was hidden in undergrowth off the path.'

Johnnie dusted the mud from the exhaust pipe with his hand. 'It doesn't look too bad,' he said. 'I mean, it doesn't look much worse than it did before.'

'Oh Johnnie,' said Marie. 'Is this what happened when you fell off? All this damage?'

'The front's had it. The forks are wrecked. And there's a huge dent in the fuel tank.'

'Did the lads who brought it here want money for it?' Annie asked the man.

'I gave them the scrap value. I'm getting all sorts brought in these days – garden railings, copper tubing – you name it. If it's metal, people will bring it in. They need cash. You're welcome to buy it back off me if you want.'

Annie looked at her brother. He was crouched down, smoothing the rear wheel lovingly.

'Let's have a word with your dad first,' Marie said. 'Thank you,' she said to the man. 'We'll let you know.'

'Aye, well don't take too long about it. It's fit for nowt but the crusher, that one.'

Marie, Johnnie and Annie got back into the car and Annie reversed it carefully back out through the archway.

'It doesn't make sense,' she said. 'I know that two men

took the bike from the lane on a trailer the same day Johnnie crashed. Why would they do that if they were just going to dump it?'

'Perhaps they thought they could fix it and then found they couldn't.'

'They were trying to hide it,' said Marie.

Annie stopped the car. Then she took it out of reverse and drove forward again.

'Let's have another look at it,' she said to Johnnie.

In the scrapyard she got out, waved to the man, and they all trooped round again to where the bike was parked.

'That front fork, see how it's twisted,' Annie said.

'It must have been when it was pushed into the undergrowth.'

'Would that have happened? They'd have had to push it pretty hard to bend it like that. And that dent in the fuel tank . . .'

The scrapyard man bent down. He ran his fingers down the metal.

'That was a vehicle as did that,' he said. 'I've seen plenty of these in my time. This bike has been under a car or summat.'

'I don't understand,' said Johnnie.

'You crashed your bike into a car, didn't you? Or a car crashed into you? Or a van, maybe? A truck?'

'No. I skidded on the lane and came off. There was no other vehicle involved.'

'You remember this, do you?'

'I don't remember anything.'

'Maybe something ran into the bike after Johnnie was in the ambulance,' Marie said.

'No, the police got there first. They moved the bike onto the verge.'

'Can you tell us owt else?' Marie asked the man.

'It looks like white paint on the bike. Can't really say more than that.'

'A white car then?'

'Maybe.'

'If it was a car as hit our Johnnie, would the car have been damaged too?'

'I'd say so. Look at the state of the bike. The bike would have come off worse, but you'd know the car had been in the wars too.'

Annie felt a rush of adrenalin. She could tell the others felt it too. 'Will you keep the bike here for us for a few days? I need to have a word with my husband. He's a policeman.'

The man stood up and dusted down his hands. 'No problem,' he said.

'You reckon someone knocked me off the bike?' Johnnie asked slowly.

'Yes.' Annie's voice was grim. 'And then they tried to hide the evidence.'

Annie dropped Johnnie and Marie back in Matlow and then she drove to the police station. The female officer at the desk welcomed her.

'How are you, Mrs Howarth?' she asked.

'Fine, thanks. Is my husband here? I need to talk to him,' said Annie.

'He's around somewhere. Would you like to come into the office to wait?'

'Thank you,' said Annie.

She followed the woman along a carpeted corridor. She could see, up ahead, the main office, hear the ringing of telephones and the buzz of talk, but she didn't go that far. Instead, she was shown into an empty interview room.

While she waited, Annie paced the room. It was grubby, with just one small, barred window, was painted an ugly green colour and had an institutional smell. Apart from a table, two wooden chairs and a clock on the wall, the room was empty. Annie wondered if Tom had been in this room when he was arrested the first time, if he had been questioned here. It was a small room, no more than three paces square. If he'd been locked in here, Tom would have panicked. Annie began to feel anxious herself. She went to the door, tried the handle, thought for a moment it was locked and tugged at it. The door opened suddenly and she stumbled out into the corridor and almost bumped into a man hurrying past.

'Sorry,' she said, and he muttered: 'No harm done,' and carried on walking. Annie stared after him. She was looking at his back, but she was almost certain that it was the same man she'd seen in the telephone box, the bald-headed, thickset man who had, at one time, seemed to be shadowing her every movement. His shirt-sleeves were rolled up and he had a tattoo on his forearm. He went out of a door marked FIRE EXIT and the door slammed shut behind him. Annie leaned against the wall. Hung on the wall opposite was a pin-board covered with notices: rotas and lists, a map of the area, the telephone numbers for the site managers of different collieries. She looked more closely at the map. Everwell was marked out. Somebody had circled it in red marker.

The door to the offices opened and the female officer came back out. She looked apologetic.

'Detective Superintendent Howarth's in a meeting,' she said. 'He might be a while. You're welcome to wait. It's up to you.'

'I'll give him five more minutes,' said Annie.

She went back into the room and sat on a chair with her head in her arms on the table. A few moments later she heard a door slam shut and from the room next door came the sound of raised voices. One she did not recognise, the other belonged to Paul Fleming.

'I can't give him these!' Paul cried. 'Look at them, they're a shambles. Are your officers illiterate? Don't they know how to write reports?'

The other man mumbled something.

'It's not good enough! I told you before that the statements have to be clear and concise, and they have to tell the same story about what happened. For fuck's sake, don't you think we've got enough problems as it is? Bloody press breathing down our necks, miners making accusations left, right and centre. And you think it's acceptable to present a load of contradictory reports?'

'What do you want me to do then?'

'I want you to have a word with your officers and get them to write their statements again. Go through the confrontation minute by minute. Get your story straight.'

'You're asking us to falsify the statements?'

'No!' There was a bang, like the sound of a fist hitting a table. 'I'm telling you to decide what happened and make sure everyone agrees on what happened, and then make sure all the accounts agree. I'm trying to protect you, don't you realise? I'm trying to bloody help!'

Annie pushed back the chair and stood up. She walked quietly down the corridor, and back into the front reception.

'I have to go,' she said to the policewoman.

'Very well,' said the woman. 'Do you want me to give Mr Howarth a message?'

'No,' said Annie. 'No, you're all right.'

CHAPTER SIXTY-SIX

She was exhausted. She waited until midnight but William still wasn't home, so she left a meal out for him and went to bed. The police car was still outside on the drive and she found its presence threatening, rather than reassuring. She wondered if the officers inside were making notes of movements inside the house. Were they watching her now, recording the time she went upstairs and the drawing of the master bedroom curtains?

When William arrived home, she heard him talking to his colleagues outside, and then his key in the lock and his footsteps on the stairs. He came into the bedroom and Annie pretended she was asleep. He stood beside the bed looking down at her, and although he said nothing, she knew he was not fooled. He stood beside her for what felt like an age, then he turned and went back downstairs. Annie rolled over and curled herself into a ball and she ached with the missing of Tom Greenaway; she ached with loneliness.

The next morning, she waited until William had left before she came downstairs. Mrs Miller was outside with the puppy, and Ethel was in her usual spot in the conservatory.

Annie was desperate to talk to somebody. She called Janine Fleming and they arranged to meet at lunchtime.

Annie then made tea and went to sit beside Ethel in the conservatory. The old woman's hands were trembling in her lap. She turned to her daughter-in-law and looked at her with rheumy eyes.

'Look at you,' she said, 'pale as a ghost and all out of sorts. It's him, isn't it?'

'Who?'

'The driver. He doesn't come any more. You're missing him.' Ethel turned her head towards the window and, in the light, Annie noticed that her cheeks were wet with tears.

She took her hand and said: 'Oh Ethel, what is it? What's the matter?'

'I miss my husband,' the old lady said. 'I miss him so much, every day and especially now. Sometimes I can't remember who I am or why I'm here and it's so frightening, dear, to feel like that. If Gerry was here, if only he was here, then I wouldn't mind so much. I'm so lonely without him, you see. So lonely.' She gazed out into the garden. 'You have to take your happiness where you find it, dear,' she said quietly. 'Don't waste it, don't waste a single drop of it because one day it will be gone and you'll never get it back, no matter how much you want it.'

Annie kissed Ethel's cheek, and she went outside. She stood on the lawn and she stretched her arms and she looked at the moor. *Are you up there, Tom? Are you watching?* She wandered over to the vegetable patch and picked some rhubarb stems, long and pink and satiny. Rhubarb was Ethel's favourite. In the kitchen she cut the stems into sections and put them in a pan with sugar and water. She took butter from the fridge and flour from the pantry and started rubbing them together to make pastry.

She had to find a way to get through these days. She had to take one step at a time. She would start by making rhubarb pie for Ethel. That would be the first step. And then she'd drive over to the Flemings' house, and after that she'd find something else to do, and after that something else. And before she knew it, time would have gone by and things would be clearer in her mind. One thing at a time. First the rhubarb pie.

Just then, Mrs Miller came into the kitchen with the puppy in her arms.

'I'm worried about this little chap,' she said. 'He doesn't look right to me.'

Annie brushed the flour from her hands and took him.

'What's up, Martha?' she asked. 'What's the matter?'

'He doesn't want to play,' Mrs Miller said. 'I'm sure

pups are supposed to be more energetic than this.' She washed her hands at the sink. 'My Barry once brought home a lurcher he'd found tied to a lamp-post and it had the same given-up look about it. The vet said the kindest thing was to put it to sleep.'

'Oh no!'

'I felt terrible for weeks after. It upsets me even now to think of it.'

Annie held the puppy close. 'We can't have you being sick,' she said. 'Not a dear little thing like you.' The puppy closed his eyes and snuggled up closer, as if he wanted to be right beside her heartbeat.

'Do you think he's just missing his mum and his brothers and sisters?' she asked.

'I don't know. You could go and ask Jim Friel,' Mrs Miller said. 'He'll know.'

Annie nodded. She turned off the heat under the rhubarb, covered the bowl with a tea towel, put on her jacket and wrapped it around the puppy. She decided to follow the lane up to the farm, rather than trying to climb the stiles and carry the puppy at the same time. She told the police officers where she was going and that she'd soon be back. Even so, one of them followed her up the track.

As she approached the farm, she could hear from the commotion that the cows were in the yard. The animals trundled together, their bony backs bumping into one another, swinging their haunches against the metal gate, making it clang, a moving blanket of black and white, green-brown shit stains on their rumps and huge heads with glassy, knowing eyes as big as plums.

Seth was standing on the fence making strange, calling sounds from his throat, guiding one cow at a time into a narrow metal cow-sized cage. Once it was in, he pulled down a trap door behind it and the cow could not move. A man in a flat cap and brown overalls, the agricultural vet, was standing with Jim on the other side of the cage, vaccinating the cows. It only took a few seconds. When they were done, Jim opened the trap at the front end and the cow meandered out and followed its sisters down the track beyond towards the field.

Annie walked around the yard wall until she was close to Jim Friel and then the farm dogs saw her and rushed up to her barking. The puppy cowered in her arms. Jim quieted the dogs with a whistle, said something to the vet and walked round to meet her.

'Aye up,' he said.

'Hello, Jim. The puppy's a bit off-colour. Would you have a look at him? See what you think?'

Jim hawked and spat into the grass verge.

'Oi, Seth!' he called. 'Can you manage on your own for a bit?'

Seth, sitting astride the fence, his back hunched, scowled at Annie but he gave the thumbs-up.

'Come on,' Jim said. 'We'll look at the little bugger indoors.'

He walked up the scrubby path that led to his cottage, the dogs at his heels, and Annie followed. Jim opened the door and then stepped back so Annie could go inside first. He told the dogs to wait and they lay in the shade, their chins on their paws, whining.

It took a while for Annie's eyes to become accustomed to the darkness in the cottage, but when they did, she saw they were in a tiny room, with an electric cooker that must have dated back to the 1950s, a small wooden table with two chairs, an open fireplace and a settee covered with faded cushions and tatty crocheted rugs. A large, modern television set dominated the room. Apart from the TV, everything was very old, but it was clean. Breakfast dishes had been washed up and stacked on the drainer. A fridge rattled in the corner.

'Sit down,' said Jim, and Annie perched on the settee. It sagged beneath her weight, the seat pulling away from the backrest. She unwrapped the puppy from her jacket and put it on the sofa beside her.

Jim shucked off his overalls and hung them on the peg at the back of the door. He washed his hands at the sink and dried them on a threadbare towel. 'Right then,' he said, 'let's have a look at the little fella.'

Annie handed the puppy to him. Jim held him in his big hands. He stretched the puppy out carefully, ran his fingers over its pink tummy.

'Worms,' he said.

'Worms?'

'Aye. See how his belly's swollen? He's full of them, aren't you, boy? Full of the buggers.' He held the puppy up to his face. 'Wild garlic and wormwood. That's what you want, isn't it, my lovely? That'll get rid of those bastards!'

'What's wormwood?'

'It's a herb,' Jim said, 'but you're not counting the pennies, are you? Take him to the vet's in town and get some proper tablets. They'll sort him out in no time.'

Jim held out his hand to pull her to her feet and then passed the puppy back to Annie. She wrapped him back in the jacket.

'Thank you so much, Jim.'

'Oh, you're welcome,' he said. 'Any time I can do owt for you, you know where I am.'

Mrs Miller had finished making the pastry for the rhubarb pie and was putting it into the oven when Annie returned to Everwell.

'Mr Howarth called – you just missed him,' she said.

Annie kissed the puppy's nose and put him back in his bed. 'He has worms, apparently.'

'Oh. How disgusting.'

'Yes, but easily sorted. I'm going to pop into town and pick up some tablets from the vet's. Do you want anything?'

'No, you're all right.'

Annie picked up her jacket and patted the pockets. Her purse had been in there, she knew it had.

'Mrs Miller,' she called, 'I must have dropped my

purse at Jim's. I'm going to run back and fetch it. I won't be long.'

The yard was empty by the time she returned to the farm. The cows were all back in the field and there was no sign of Jim or Seth Friel, or the vet. Annie called out, but there was no answer; even the dogs didn't bark a response.

She followed the path to the door of the cottage and knocked but there was no answer. She turned the door handle and pushed it open.

'Hello!' she called, but her voice soaked into the darkness of the downstairs room and she could tell that the cottage was empty.

She only had to go inside, pick up the purse from the settee and leave again. She'd be in and out in two minutes.

'Hello!' she called, louder this time but the only response was silence.

If you don't get the purse now, you won't make it to the vet's and back in time to meet Janine. That poor puppy will have hours more pain.

She stepped into the gloom, leaving the door open, walked straight to the settee and patted amongst the cushions. The settee sagged and her arm sank in almost to the elbow. Her fingers touched grit, coins, a comb and the sharp end of a spring. There was so much give in the cushions you could have lost a brick down the gap. Her fingers tiptoed across the debris until she felt the beading of her purse. Next to it was a key. She took hold of both items and pulled them out, intending to leave the key on the cushion where Jim would find it – but when she could see it, she recognised the fob. It was a plastic fob in the shape of the A-Team van. It was Johnnie's key, the key to his bike.

CHAPTER SIXTY-SEVEN

Annie sat in the waiting room at the vet's surgery with the puppy warm on her lap. She turned the key between her fingers. Every now and then the puppy tried to bite it. A woman with alopecia sat opposite and a honey-coloured rat twined itself around the woman's neck. It had tiny, hand-like paws, tiny white nails, and it balanced itself with a muscular, naked pink tail that was both revolting and fascinating.

Annie was called in to see the vet before the rat lady and she put the key in her pocket and forgot about it while the puppy was examined and Jim's diagnosis of a severe worm infestation was confirmed. The vet gave the puppy a tablet. He and Annie had a chat about puppy-care and she returned to the car.

Her escort drove her from the vet's straight to the Flemings' house. Janine said Annie could put the puppy in the shed. She found a blanket for him and Annie settled him. The Flemings' huge German Shepherd, the failed police dog, Souness, was in his run at the back of the house.

Annie washed her hands and waited in the living room with baby Chloe while Janine assembled some lunch in the kitchen. The Flemings lived in a new house on a new estate to the east of Matlow. It was a redbrick house, spotlessly neat and clean inside and out, with double-glazed windows, and it smelled of new carpets and Mr Sheen. Annie sat on a cream leather settee decorated with Laura Ashley cushions. Chloe was propped up on a mat on the floor, surrounded by her toys.

Annie called: 'Are you sure there's nothing I can do to help?'

'No, you're fine,' Janine called back. Annie looked at the framed photographs on the fireplace. Taking pride of place on the wall was a large, framed picture of Janine and Paul on their wedding day, in soft focus. The couple were holding hands, so that Janine's rings were on display, and they were staring into each other's eyes. Both of them had permed hair. On the mantelpiece were a range of smaller pictures. Most were of Chloe, but there was also one of Paul shaking hands with William at some police function. Both men were in uniform. There was another picture of William with Paul and Seth Friel at a cricket match. They were standing together at the edge of the pitch, and the cricketers were playing behind them.

Janine pushed open the door with her foot and came in with a tray.

'That was last summer,' she said. 'Do you remember that day you took me shopping, just before Chloe was born? The boys had gone to Headingley and we bought up half of Mothercare.'

'Oh yes.' Annie smiled. 'I didn't know Seth Friel was at the cricket with them too.'

'They bumped into him.' Janine put the tray on the coffee table. 'Paul told me Seth was another of your husband's pet projects.'

'He helped him out once. Seth was caught breaking and entering. William managed to get him on one of those programmes that's supposed to help turn around young people's lives.'

'Do I detect a note of cynicism, Mrs Howarth?'

'No, not really. As far as I know, Seth's not been in trouble again. It's just he . . . well . . .'

'He gives you the creeps?'

'Yes, exactly. How did you guess?'

'He's been round here once or twice, doing jobs for Paul. I don't like him much. I won't have him anywhere near Chloe.'

Annie took a plate, and a slice of quiche from Janine. She could feel the key fob in her pocket pressing into the side of her thigh.

'Does Paul ever talk to you about his work?' she asked.

'Mmm.' Janine nodded. 'Sometimes. He goes on about the strike an awful lot. Really I'm sick to death of hearing about it now.'

'Has he talked much about the moor murders?'

Janine flushed at once, her pale skin glowing almost painfully red. She nodded and let her hair fall forward to hide her face. Annie said: 'It's all right. I know they think it was Tom.'

'But it must be so terrible for you,' Janine said. 'I can't imagine what it must feel like knowing that someone you once . . . Someone who you . . . Someone you know is a murderer.'

Annie broke off a bit of quiche and put it in her mouth. It was unpleasantly eggy.

'And of course he's on the run now, isn't he?' Janine continued. 'He could be anywhere. Paul thinks—'

'What?'

Janine shrugged. 'It's not very nice but I don't suppose you'll mind me saying it. He thinks Tom Greenaway might have killed himself.'

Annie's heart turned over. She felt a searing pain in her chest. 'Why would he think that?'

'Just that he has no options left now. He's claustrophobic, isn't he? He won't want to spend the rest of his life in prison.'

'What if he's not guilty?'

Janine looked at Annie with a surprised expression. 'I don't think there's any doubt about the fact that he *is* guilty, Annie.'

Annie put the plate back down on the coffee table. She had no appetite any more.

'Janine, I'm sorry but I don't feel very well. I'll fetch the puppy and go home.'

'Oh God, I've upset you, haven't I? I'm so sorry. I'm always saying things I shouldn't and . . .'

'No, no.' Annie tried to smile. 'Really,' she said, 'it's nothing you've done or said. I've just had a terrible week.'

'Are you sure? Is there anything I can do?'

'No, no. I'm fine. I'll be fine.'

Annie stood up. She picked up her bag. 'Can I just ask you something, Janine. Does Paul know a police officer with a bald head? A thickset man with tattoos on his left forearm.'

'Oh, you mean Alan Gunnarson?'

'Probably. Does Paul know him well?'

'Yes, they're good friends. They play squash sometimes.'

'Thanks,' Annie said. 'Thanks for everything.'

CHAPTER SIXTY-EIGHT

Sleep eluded Annie again that night. In the early hours, she took another of her mother-in-law's sleeping pills to give her some peace from the images that kept rolling through her mind, a loop of Tom in desperation throwing himself from the top of a cliff or ending his life in other ways. The artificial sleep was a respite but as soon as she awoke the thoughts were back in her mind, that he was dead, or dying, or planning his death.

It was almost midday now and she'd only just got up. She came down into the kitchen, holding the key in her hand, in her pocket.

William was washing his hands at the kitchen sink. He was lathered up to the elbows.

'I thought you'd gone to work,' Annie said.

'I've been out shooting. It's such a beautiful morning. I didn't want to wake you.'

'But shouldn't you be at the station?'

'I'm not going into the station today. I'm going to take you out for lunch instead.'

Annie turned her face away so that he should not see her expression. She turned the key fob over in her pocket.

'I can't go out for lunch,' she said. 'I need to keep an eye on the puppy. He's still poorly.'

'I'll keep an eye on him,' Mrs Miller intervened. 'Go on, go and have a few hours with your husband. Heaven knows he works hard enough and you deserve a treat too every now and then.'

'I don't feel like going out,' Annie said.

'It will do you good,' said William. 'I won't take no for an answer.'

Later, when they set out for lunch, Annie saw that William had put the top down on the Jaguar for the first time that summer. The guard police officer was admiring the car, looking at his own reflection in the paintwork, probably imagining how it would feel to drive a car like that through the countryside.

It used to amuse Annie how William liked to pose in that car. He liked the thought of himself driving the Jaguar, open-topped, around Matlow. He liked wearing sunglasses. He liked the way people looked at him as he drove, one elbow resting casually on the door and his young wife at his side, her hair blowing in the wind. That day, she could hardly bring herself to climb into the seat, but she did and William smiled at her, saluted his colleague and started the engine.

'Where are we going?' Annie asked.

'It's a surprise.'

Summer had settled in by now. The countryside was soft and green, the wildflowers white and yellow and the hedgerows bright with their new summer leaves. Annie had her sunglasses on and her hair streamed behind her as she glanced at William. His face was set in its normal expression of concentration and she felt a pang of affection for him, for his little conceits, and at the same time a sadness. She was sorry that she had never loved him and never would love him as she had loved Tom; sorry for both of them, sorry for whatever it was that would happen between them.

The wind buffeted her face. It was impossible to talk and she had to look straight ahead to stop the wind blowing dust into her eyes, so she sat next to her husband, stiff and still as a mannequin and all the while her fingers played with the key fob in her pocket.

William took her to a small pub, one she had not heard of before, tucked away on the far side of the moor. There was a garden, a sun-trap, a wooden gazebo entwined with honeysuckle that was just beginning to flower. Annie sat on the bench and warmed herself while she waited for William to fetch drinks and order food, and she watched sparrows flapping their wings in the dust and swallowed back thoughts of Tom.

William returned and he put a large glass of chilled wine on the table in front of her.

'I asked for bitter lemon,' said Annie.

'I think you deserve wine.'

She pushed her sunglasses onto the top of her head. William was staring at her. 'What?' she asked. 'What are you looking at?'

'You. You're beautiful.'

'No.' She did not feel beautiful.

'Here.' William took a small paper bag out of his pocket and pushed it across the table towards her. 'It's for you.'

'No, William, I don't want presents.'

'Don't argue. Open it.'

Annie opened the bag. Inside was a jewellery case. Inside the case was a silver chain with a charm on the end, three little silver forget-me-not flowers.

She took it out of the box, let the chain slip through her fingers. 'It's lovely,' she said.

William cleared his throat. He drank the top two inches of beer from his glass.

'I wanted to say sorry,' he said.

'You have nothing to be sorry for.'

'I have everything to be sorry for. I haven't been paying attention.'

'William, I—'

'No, Annie, let me speak. I know I have come very close to losing you. The thought of that, it's unacceptable; inconceivable. So I hope you'll accept the necklace along with my sincere apology and agree that we can start again, from today, on a new and better foot.'

He took the chain from her, undid the clasp and

fastened it around her neck. She felt his fingers warm on her nape, felt his breath. She did not know what to do, so she did nothing. She drank her wine, and when their lunch was served she picked at her ploughman's and William ate his and the two of them hardly exchanged a word.

When she had drunk her second glass of wine, she told William about Johnnie's bike; that it had been taken away from the lane and had turned up at the scrapyard.

'The worst of it is, Johnnie didn't just fall off his bike,' she said. 'Someone ran into him.'

'What makes you think that?'

'The scrapyard man knows about these things. He's seen bikes that look like that before and they've always been involved in collisions.'

William raised an eyebrow and took a drink of his beer.

'That's impossible,' he said. 'It must be a different bike.'

'It's definitely Johnnie's bike. And why would it be impossible?'

'Because I spoke to the two police officers who found him myself. I know exactly what happened. Annie, do we have to talk about this now?'

'I think you should have a look at the bike. I'd *like* you to look at it.'

'If it means that much to you, I could get someone to look into it. Although to be honest, there's not much we could do about it after all this time.'

'The thing is, if someone did run into him, that's an offence, isn't it? Johnnie would be liable for compensation, wouldn't he?'

'Eligible.'

'Sorry?'

'He'd be eligible, not liable.'

He could not help being pedantic. He couldn't help it. She took a breath. 'If he could get some money, that would help him get his life back on track. It's important to him, William.'

'I'll see what I can do. It's possible, of course, that someone ran over the bike after he'd come off.'

'But you told me the two policemen who found Johnnie had moved it off the road. That's what you said. Anyway, there's something else.' The key was in her pocket. She reached down and touched it with her fingers. 'The Friels are involved somehow.'

'The Friels? Oh come on, Annie, how could the Friels be involved?'

'Not Jim, maybe, but Seth. That night, remember that night when you came back late, when you'd been in London – well, I saw somebody drive out of the farm and go up the track towards the moor. It might have been Seth Friel, taking the bike up there to dump it. And then this morning,' she took the key out of her pocket and held it in the open palm of her hand, 'I found this in their house. It's Johnnie's.'

William looked at the key.

'You've been busy,' he said.

'I want to help Johnnie. He's my brother.'

William cleared his throat. He rubbed his chin. 'Annie, have you talked about this with anyone else?'

'No.' She shook her head.

'Good. Leave it with me. What's the name of the scrapyard?'

'Rossiters. It's in Burnley.'

'I'll look into it.'

'Thank you,' Annie said. 'Thank you, William. And you'll tell me what you find there?'

'Yes, of course I will.'

CHAPTER SIXTY-NINE

Back at home, Annie changed into some old clothes and wiped off her make-up. She took the puppy out into the garden while William went to collect Elizabeth in the Jaguar. When he came back he sent the guard away. He said there was no need for an extra police presence while he was at Everwell. Annie looked up to the moor, hoping to catch sight of Tom, hoping for a signal, but there was nothing. She lay in the sun, drowsy with wine, and fell asleep for a few moments, but was woken by Elizabeth's voice.

'Martha! Martha!'

Annie pushed herself up and held out her arms to her daughter. Elizabeth ran to her and she held her tight. 'Are you going to keep calling that dog Martha?' she asked. 'Only really he should have a name of his own.'

Elizabeth stood on one leg. Her socks were round her ankles and her knees were grass-stained. 'Everything I think of doesn't suit him,' she said.

'It's OK. He can be called Martha. At least for now.'

William called out: 'I'm going inside to make some phone calls, Annie.'

'All right,' she called back.

The afternoon went by and time moved on and the afternoon became evening. When William had finished on the telephone, he went into his office. Mrs Miller gave Ethel a bath and Annie served the rhubarb pie at dinner. She congratulated herself on getting through another day – but as soon as she thought that, she thought of Tom, and even thinking his name, even saying it in her head, was enough to bring back the fear, the thought of a lifetime without him, the awful not knowing if he was even still alive.

There was a chill in the air that night: it didn't feel as if it were almost July. Annie lit the fire in the living room and the family sat together. Ethel was closest to the fire. A crocheted blanket lay over her knees and the puppy, comfortable now, was curled up asleep on top of the blanket. Ethel's fingers trembled on his back. Annie sat on the settee, a glass of wine on a coaster on the small, polished table beside her and an open book face-down on the floor. Elizabeth lay beside her with her head on her lap. They were watching a quiz show on television. William sat on the other chair. He had a book on his lap, a political history of Germany, but he was not reading. He drummed his fingers together, he fidgeted; he did not seem to know how to relax. It was obvious that he would rather be in the study with his papers and his music.

William snorted as one of the contestants got an answer to a question wrong.

'It was Churchill,' he said. 'Every imbecile knows that.' Annie glanced at him. 'Honestly, are these people so uneducated?' he asked. 'Do they never read? Aren't they interested in the history of their own country?'

'If you'd rather not watch it . . .'

'No, no, it's all right. Mother's enjoying it,' William said.

'Not everyone had the benefit of your education, William,' Ethel said.

'I know, Mother.'

'It's not necessarily their fault.'

William rolled his eyes and Annie smiled. The programme finished and another one started. Ethel fell asleep and began to snore quietly. Annie felt tired too. *Another five minutes,* she thought, *and I must take Lizzie up.*

It was some time after that when she heard a car approaching the house, the scrunch of tyres on the gravel drive outside. Annie looked out through the window and saw a pair of headlights approaching through the half-light of the dusk. The car came up to the house and parked parallel to the window.

'It's Paul,' Annie said. 'Whatever does he want at this time of night? Why didn't he ring you?'

She opened the front door. Paul looked terrible, as if he'd been in a fight. He was wearing a suit but it was torn and dirty; the skin on his face was grazed and there was mud in his hair. He was wet, and shivering with cold.

'Oh Paul!' she cried. 'What on earth's happened?'

Paul glanced over her shoulder at William. 'I need to talk to you, sir.'

William frowned.

'In private.'

'Go and sit in the living room,' Annie said. 'Paul, sit next to the fire and warm yourself up a bit. Only keep your voices down so you don't disturb Ethel.'

She and Elizabeth went into the kitchen and heated some milk. They had just poured hot chocolate into mugs when Annie heard the men's voices in the hall again.

William was putting on his jacket. His face was grim. Paul stood behind him. His shoulders were hunched and his eyes were downcast. He looked like an angry child. He had taken off his filthy jacket and was wearing one of William's sweaters.

'Surely you're not going out now, at this time?' Annie asked.

'We have to,' William said.

'William, what's going on?'

'I'll see you later.'

They left without another word, William taking the steering wheel of Paul's car and accelerating down the drive. Annie watched until the rear lights had disappeared around the corner, she heard the tyres skidding on the lane, then she closed the door and fastened the lock. She went back into the living room. Ethel was still sleeping. Elizabeth was curled up back on the settee, her eyes half-closed, her head on a cushion and her arms wrapped around the puppy.

Annie pulled the living-room door to and she crossed the hall to the study. In his hurry to leave, William had left the door open. She went inside and switched on the desk lamp, which cast an oval of light on the surface of the desk. William had left four files out on top. The largest was a box file with the word STRIKE written on the top in black marker pen. Beside it, lined up square, were two clip files labelled *Jennifer Dunnock* and *Selina Maddox*, and at the back of the desk, behind these three files, was a buff cardboard envelope-file with nothing written on it at all.

Annie pulled up her husband's desk-chair and sat down. She opened Selina's file and flicked through sheets of paper – witness statements and information about the girl. There was a photograph of Selina's bedroom in the flat below Tom's. She slept in a single bed covered with a home-made patchwork quilt. The walls were covered in posters of Debbie Harry, Bob Marley, Tracy Chapman. On the windowledge was a pile of books – romantic novels – and a teddy bear was perched on top of the books.

Annie read a witness statement from a friend of Selina's.

She was really friendly, really sweet. She pretended to be streetwise but she wasn't. She didn't have a steady boyfriend, but there was someone she liked a lot. He was a gardener. He was interested in her music.

Annie played with her hair. She thought of Tom's smile, his easy way, how he had walked towards Selina the day she'd seen him at the pub. The girl was young and lonely. Tom had looked after her. He'd fetched her from the cinema. He'd driven her to the Haddington. It didn't make sense that he would hurt her.

She read on: *Selina liked him but he was already involved with someone else, a married woman. She was upset about this. As a Christian, Selina thought it was wrong for someone who was married to be unfaithful. She tried to persuade him to give up this other woman but he wouldn't.*

Annie sat back in the chair. The file was on William's desk. He must have read it. He must have known, or at the very least suspected that she was the married woman Tom Greenaway was seeing. She closed the file and pushed it back. Her hands were trembling.

'Mummy?'

'Oh God! Don't creep up on me like that, Lizzie – you scared me!'

Elizabeth stood in the doorway, sleepy-eyed. She rubbed her eyes with her fists.

'What are you doing?'

'Nothing.'

'Why are you in Daddy's office?'

'I was looking for something.'

'What were you looking for?'

'Come on,' said Annie, 'I'll take you upstairs.'

She carried Elizabeth up the stairs, helped her into her nightclothes and tucked her into bed. It was dark outside now, the night had come in quickly. Elizabeth lay back and her eyelids slowly closed.

'I heard Daddy tell Grandmother that we might have another baby,' she said sleepily.

'You shouldn't have been listening.'

'Are we going to have another baby, Mummy?'

'I don't think so. We've got Martha now.'

'Do you like puppies better than babies?'

'At least puppies don't talk.'

Downstairs, in the hall, the phone began to ring.

'I'd better get that,' she said.

'Night night, Mummy,' yawned Elizabeth.

'Night, lovely. Sleep tight.'

CHAPTER SEVENTY

She ran down the stairs in her socks to pick up the telephone. Nobody ever called with good news after nine o'clock at night. She grabbed the receiver.

'Hello?'

'Hi, is that Annie Howarth?'

'Yes.'

'It's Georgie, Georgie Segger. From the *Chronicle*.'

'Oh hello, Georgie. How are you?'

'I'm fine. I know it's late, and I'm sorry to disturb you, but is your husband about?'

'No. Why do you want him?'

'It's a bit awkward. It's to do with the strike. Some accusations have been made against the police. They've been accused of falsifying witness statements. I'm sure it's nothing, but . . .'

'William wouldn't have anything to do with that.'

'I'm not saying he does, but obviously he's in charge and—'

'No. You've got this all wrong. It's not William you should be talking to.'

'Could you tell me where your husband is?'

'No,' said Annie. 'I couldn't.'

She put the phone down and then picked it up again and dialled Matlow police station. Somebody picked up, a man whose voice she did not recognise.

'I'm trying to get hold of my husband,' Annie said. 'William Howarth.'

'He's not here, love.'

'Do you know where he is?'

'I haven't seen him.'

'If he comes in, please would you get him to call me?'

The man said that he would.

Annie paced around the ground floor of Everwell. She went into the living room. Ethel was sound asleep in her chair, her head tipped to one side. The fire had died down. Annie picked up the puppy and held him close. She stood in front of the television. She listened to the news, another report about the strike. There were new accusations of corruption against the South Yorkshire police. She saw the miners who were lining up to testify that the police reports were wrong. That things hadn't been how they said they were. And she knew that the miners' version would not be believed but that the truth would, eventually, out. And she also knew that William had had nothing to do with this.

Annie turned off the television. She carried the puppy around the house with her, checking that the windows were locked. Now that the patrol car was gone, she felt vulnerable. She turned on the outside light and took the puppy onto the lawn, waited while he turned circles and sniffed about the undergrowth before he finally did his business, and then she scooped him up and brought him back inside.

By now it was almost eleven. She was settling the puppy into his bed when the telephone rang again. Annie answered: 'William?'

'No, it's me.' Janine sounded fragile, nervy. Annie could hear the baby crying in the background.

'What is it?' Annie asked a little sharply.

'Oh God, I'm sorry, I didn't know whether to call you or not and I know it's late, but is Paul there?'

'No, why—?'

'Your husband was here earlier. They were talking for ages and then they had a terrible argument, him and Paul. William hit Paul. I think he might have broken his nose, there was blood all over the carpet, and then they both stormed off separately and I don't know what's going on, Annie. I'm scared.'

'All right, Janine, all right,' Annie said. 'There's some trouble brewing about witness statements being tampered with, that's probably all it is.'

'*No!*' Janine wailed. 'No, it's not that. They were talking about the murders – the murderer. I think someone else might have died . . . I'm so frightened I just don't know what to do with myself.'

'Janine, listen to me. You have to stay calm. Go and

settle your baby and then have a glass of wine or something, have a bath. I'll call you if I hear anything and if I don't hear anything tonight, I'll call you in the morning.'

She put the phone down and paced the hall again. She tried to slow down her own thoughts, to put them in order, but she could not. *Is Tom dead? Is that what this is all about?*

The house was growing cold now as the night closed in. Annie went into the living room. Ethel was still sleeping so Annie fetched a second blanket and covered her over. She turned off the television but then she could hear noises outside and although they were only the usual sounds of the countryside they assumed a sinister significance: footsteps on the gravel, the sound of somebody trying to suppress a cough. She went into the kitchen to fetch a drink but the wine bottle was empty so she returned to the study to help herself to some of William's Laphroaig.

The desk lamp was still switched on. Annie sat down once again in the chair and poured herself a generous measure of whisky. She lifted the buff cardboard file and opened the sleeve. Inside were mostly loose papers, household paperwork, nothing of interest. She pushed the papers back inside and tried to close the file but one sheet of paper slipped out and fell to the floor. She picked it up and looked at it. It was a record sheet. The paper had been divided into columns and each column was headed: *Date, Location, Arrival, Departure, Comments.*

Annie looked at it. It took her a few moments to work out what it was, and when she did, she cried out in distress. It was a record of her meetings with Tom. Every time, almost every time she had seen him, somebody had been watching. There were other numbers next to the entries, reference numbers, ticks and crosses. Somebody had scrawled the letters 'pic' next to some of the entries; photographs. So William had known about Tom and Annie, he'd known everything. She thought back to when his attitude towards her had changed, when he had become withdrawn and cold. It was after he'd discovered the break-in at the gamekeeper's cottage. That was when he became suspicious, that's when he must have asked his colleague, the bald-headed Alan Gunnarson, to follow Annie, to get proof of her infidelity, of her affair, of the extent of her deception.

She touched the forget-me-not necklace at her throat. What had William meant by giving her the gift? That he believed Tom was out of the picture? That he wanted them both to put the affair behind them? That he wanted to start again?

Feeling shaky and nauseous, she tipped everything out of the buff file, scattering papers on the floor and the desk. She riffled through them. She didn't know what she was searching for, but knew she would know when she found it. There was an envelope, an ordinary white envelope. She opened it. Inside was a thin, transparent paper sleeve and inside that were strips of photographic negatives. Annie's hands were shaking as she pulled the first strip from the sleeve and held it up to the desk light. She knew what to expect, but even so it was a shock. The blacks and whites were all reversed so the images were ghostly, ghastly, but there she was standing outside the door to Tom's flat, badly disguised and obviously recognisable. Five or six pictures had been taken in rapid succession, Tom opening the door, her stepping inside into the darkness beyond. And on the next strip there they were together on the moor, she and Tom, and then back at his house again and in the park. There were photographs of the two of them in the garden at Everwell in the dark, the light of the fire now turned to darkness, the black of the night turned to light. They were kissing, there was a close-up of Tom's hand, of her thigh, dear God.

She took out the last strip and held it up to the light. She was not sure what it was she was looking at – she couldn't make sense of it at first, and as she turned it over, wondering if it would be clearer in reverse, she felt the draught as the door behind her opened and she turned and looked up into the eyes of her husband.

CHAPTER SEVENTY-ONE

He stood there and took in the scene – Annie in his chair, the opened file, the negatives on the floor, the scattered papers – and he exhaled very slowly.

'You found the pictures,' he said calmly.

'How could you?' she asked.

He cleared his throat and pulled at the collar of his shirt. He looked exhausted and dishevelled. The knuckles of his right hand were bruised and bloody.

'How could you get someone to spy on me? How could you do that to me?'

William turned away. He went to the LP records lined up alphabetically in the shelves above the stereo and he ran his fingers along the spines.

'With all due respect, Annie, you were the one who was being unfaithful. I think having you followed was the lesser crime.'

'If you wanted to know, you could have asked me. You could have confronted me. I would not have lied. We could at least have preserved our dignity.'

'I think our dignity disappeared when you began sleeping with that man.'

'Tom,' Annie said. 'His name is Tom.'

William sighed. He pulled a record from the shelf and held it square in his hands.

'Where is Tom now?' Annie asked. 'What's happened to him?'

William ignored her question. He shook the record out of the sleeve, held it carefully between the palms of his hands, so that his skin was only touching the outer rim of the disc, blew across its surface. 'You could have been more careful, Annie,' William said. 'If you really cared about me, then you could have tried a little harder to be discreet. I saw you with him, with Tom Greenaway. The day of Johnnie's accident.'

'You were in Sheffield.'

'No. The meeting was cancelled and I was driving back through Matlow.'

He held the record up to his eyes to check it had not distorted. Annie sank down into the chair and covered her face with her hands.

'I stopped at the florist's on Occupation Road to buy you some flowers,' William said. 'I bought yellow roses, the scented ones, the kind you love. I bought a dozen roses with dark green leaves and I had the florist wrap them in cellophane and tie the bunch with a ribbon. I was imagining the look on your face when I gave them to you. I wanted to show you that I knew you, that

I knew what you liked. I wanted to make you happy.'

'William . . .'

'And I came out of the florist's and there you were. You were standing on the other side of the road, and you were smiling. You looked beautiful. I'd never seen you look more beautiful. And I called your name, Annie, I called you but you didn't hear. The door opened and there he was, that man; there he was, on the doorstep, and you put your arms around his neck and you kissed him. You kissed him, and then he took your hand and he led you inside and the door closed and I was standing there, with the flowers in my hand. I was standing there . . .'

'What did you do?' she whispered.

'I went back to work. Paul said there'd been an accident on Crossmoor Lane.'

'Johnnie's accident?'

William lifted the lid of the stereo system and dropped the record onto the spindle. He spun it a couple of times with the flat of his hand.

'I didn't know it was Johnnie. All I knew was what Paul told me: that a young lad had been knocked off his bike by two officers in a patrol car.'

Annie pushed herself up in the chair. 'That's not right, William. You told me the officers *found* Johnnie. You never said they caused the accident.'

'They ran into the bike on a blind bend. They weren't local, they didn't know the road. There was nothing they could have done to avoid it.'

As he spoke, it was as if the world was shifting beneath Annie, sliding away from her. She frowned as she pieced this new version of events together in her mind, replayed the story.

'If what you're saying now is true—'

'It is.'

'Then you lied before. You, William.' Annie stood up now. She reached out for her husband but he shook her off. He lifted the arm of the record player and moved it back to set the mechanism that spun the turntable in motion. 'Why?' she asked. 'Why would you do that?'

William was leaning over the record player, with his back to her. She could see the wrinkles and folds of skin on his neck, the mole on his jawline, the stubbly grey hair, shaved very short, at the nape. He did not turn to face her.

'Imagine, Annie, what would have happened if word got out that a miner's son had been injured by police brought in on overtime. That he'd been hit by a car driven by two officers who'd done a twenty-four-hour shift, who were perhaps going a little too fast on a road they didn't know. Think what the newspapers would have said about that. The NUM. Scargill. The political capital they'd have made from it? Whichever version was made public, it wouldn't make any difference to the lad. The officers gave him first aid and saved his life. Paul persuaded me that they didn't deserve to lose their careers over an accident.'

'My brother lost his arm!' Annie cried. 'He almost

died and you let Paul *persuade* you to cover it up?'

She pulled at his arm to make him face her but again he pulled away. She dropped back down into the chair and sat there numb with confusion.

William placed the arm of the record player carefully on to the edge of the record and watched it revolve. The arm bumped up and down. There were a few whispery crackles, like the sound of shallow breaths, and then the first, very quiet, strains of music began to play. It was a violin concerto.

Annie tried to grasp hold of something that she knew, for certain.

'You don't cover things up, William,' she said. 'You don't tell lies or bend the rules about anything, ever. I can't believe you would do that.'

The music was mournful. William closed his eyes to listen.

'Put yourself in my shoes,' he said. 'Your father was stirring things up at the colliery. The men were laughing at me, talking about me behind my back. I was losing control. I knew it and they knew it. And you, you were with Greenaway.' He grimaced. 'I was lost, Annie. I didn't know which way to turn. The only person I could trust was Paul. He stood by me. He showed me how I could win back the respect of my men. All we did was alter the details of the story to save the lads in the patrol car. Paul paid Seth Friel to dispose of the bike. It was easy.'

'And none of your colleagues objected to this? Nobody tried to stop you?'

'They patted me on the back, Annie. They bought drinks for me. I'd nailed my colours to the mast, I was one of them again. They showed me that loyalty is sometimes more important than truth. I persuaded myself that it didn't matter; it didn't change anything.'

'It changed you.'

'Yes,' William acknowledged. 'Perhaps it did.'

Annie tried to think back to that day, that time. She remembered how things had been different afterwards. She had not seen what was happening; she'd been so tied up in her own thoughts, her concern for Johnnie, her longing for Tom. She could not bear to look at her husband. The music waxed and waned, the violins like ghostly, whispering voices.

'Did you talk to Paul about me?' she asked.

'He already knew. He'd seen you with Greenaway, put two and two together. He said he had it all in hand, that he'd sort it out, like he had the first time.'

'What does that mean? "Like he had the first time"?'

William rubbed his forehead with his fingers. 'I didn't know until tonight. I didn't fully understand the strength of his loyalty to me.'

Annie had felt dread before, but not like this; not on this level. She looked at William's hand, swollen now and raw about the knuckles. He had hit Paul – Paul, who he loved like a son. He'd hit him hard enough to break his nose. She made herself look at his face and she saw how grim and old it had become. It was not the face of the man she had married, but the face of someone she hardly recognised. She saw something in his eyes that she had not seen before; it was shame.

She knew then what William had meant.

'Paul framed Tom, didn't he? He framed him for Mrs Wallace's death?'

William said nothing but she knew it was the truth by the blankness in his eyes and she realised, too, that it was not the worst of it.

'What else has he done? *What else?*'

William hunched over. He seemed to lose a little more of his dignity.

'The murders,' he said.

She did not understand, not at once. 'He's covered up the murders?' she asked, stupid with fear, and William shook his head.

'He killed the women. He killed them for me.'

'Oh God!' Annie doubled over as if she had been punched. It seemed impossible, and yet there was a terrible logic to what William had told her, if it was the truth.

'So that Tom would be blamed?' she asked in a whisper.

'Yes.'

'Both of them?'

'In Paul's mind everything was all right while Tom Greenaway was in prison. Paul was the only person who knew the truth. And then Tom came back.'

'So Paul killed Jennifer Dunnock?'

'She looked like you. He knew Tom would be

blamed. But that didn't work, so he killed someone else to make sure.'

Annie looked at William and saw the despair in his eyes, and she knew it was true.

'Oh God, he's mad!' Annie gasped. 'He's completely mad. He's sick in the head.'

'Yes.' William closed his eyes. He rubbed his temples with his fingers. 'But in his skewed mind it all made sense. It was the most straightforward route to putting things right.' He gave a sardonic little laugh. 'He's so utterly corrupt, Annie, that he doesn't see that he's done anything particularly wrong. He said he was only trying to protect me. He did it for me, for Christ's sake, he wanted to *please* me.'

Annie felt light-headed. It was the music and the horror of all this, the brightness of the room, the darkness of the night outside, William so close, so different now in her eyes, and trying to rethink all that had happened in a different way, and still she did not know what had happened to her lover.

'Where is Tom?' she asked again. 'What's happened to Tom? Tell me, William.' She didn't care any more if William saw the depth of her love for Tom, all she cared about was knowing where he was, if he was still alive. 'What has Paul done to him?'

'You know we've had men looking out for Tom since he went missing,' William said. 'Today Gunnarson spotted him on the edge of the moor. He called Paul and Paul joined him and together they followed Tom up the moor. At last they'd got him exactly where they wanted him.'

'What do you mean?'

'Keep up, Annie. They needed him to be somewhere remote before they attacked him because it was supposed to look like suicide. In Paul's mind that tied everything up nicely. Greenaway would be gone and the murders would stop. There'd be no need for a trial, no picking over the details. You and I would go off on holiday and have another baby. Everyone would be happy.'

'What have they done to Tom?'

'Paul thought it would be easy,' William said. 'He had Gunnarson with him. They jumped Greenaway on the moor. It was supposed to be all over in seconds. They hadn't counted on a couple of local lads hiding up there in the dark. They were out lamping.'

Annie imagined it, the darkness, the desolation of the moor at night, and Tom all alone. She imagined the footsteps behind him, the fear, him running over the bracken, tripping maybe, stumbling, his heart beating too fast, the cold air in his lungs; then the thump of a fist in his belly, shouts and then what? Other voices, other fists and feet and shoulders; dogs, lights, the two police officers realising the only way to save their skins was to run before they were recognised.

She remembered Paul earlier, the state of him; the panic.

'What did they to do Tom?' she asked again.

'"Tom this, Tom that," you're like a stuck record, Annie,' William said. 'Is he all you care about? Is he all that matters to you?'

'Please, William, tell me.'

He rubbed his temples. 'They left him there; wounded but alive. He's with the lampers. I imagine they'll have taken him to a hospital by now.'

'Oh thank God,' she whispered.

'And what of us now, Annie?' William asked. 'What do we do now?'

Behind William the study door slowly swung open.

He felt the movement and turned. Ethel stood framed in the doorway with the light of the hall behind her. She was wearing her nightgown, long and white, buttoned up at the neck, and her dressing gown trailed behind her. She looked like a ghost-bride, a stooped old bride with her white hair framing her tired face, her pale blue eyes, her skin soft as powder and the yellow nails of her toes peeping out from the lacy hem of her gown.

'Mother.' William straightened himself. He cleared his throat, made an effort to compose himself. 'What are you doing? You should be in bed.' He covered his damaged hand with the one that was still intact as if he didn't want his mother to know he'd been fighting.

She looked at them both, William and then Annie.

'What's going on?' she asked.

'It's nothing, Mother,' said William.

'But it's not nothing. You used to be so happy together, but these last weeks everything's gone sour.

You think I'm too doolally to understand, but I can see what's going on.' She held out one shaky hand and touched her son on the shoulder. 'I heard you talking earlier. I heard what you said to Paul, that he will go to prison and that baby of his will grow up without a father. It's so sad. And what about you, William? What will happen to you?'

Annie thought of Georgie Segger, her eagerness to chase a story, and of all the other journalists, how they would hold the events in Matlow up as an example of corruption, of bad management, of everything that was morally wrong with the police. She thought of the miners and their supporters and how they would use every opportunity to stick their political knives into William. She thought of the re-written police statements that he didn't even know about yet. *The only incorruptible copper in England.* She thought of how the people of Matlow would jeer at him, how they'd relish his downfall, how they would laugh at him, pity him, despise him. And the man he had trusted most, the man he had loved like a son, was the one who had destroyed everything.

The music was softening now. It wreathed around her husband like smoke. He could not hold her eyes.

'Oh William,' she said softly.

Ethel groaned then, as if she were in pain. 'Will somebody take me upstairs?' she asked. 'I'm so tired. I've had enough of all this.'

'I'll come with you,' Annie said. She put her arm

around Ethel. She could feel her ribs through her nightgown, could feel how frail she was and Ethel leaned against her and she was as light as a bird. 'Oh you poor thing, you're freezing,' Annie said. 'Let's get you tucked up into a nice, warm bed.'

'Annie?'

'Yes?' She turned to look at William. He was standing with his arms at his side and his eyes were bloodshot. There was the air of a man completely defeated about him; a man who knew he was finished. His shoulders slumped and his face had become slack. His left hand was bruised and swollen, there were blood spatters on his shirt. The integrity that had held him upright had been broken. He was ruined. 'What is it?' she asked.

'It's over, isn't it?' he said. 'You and me. Whatever happens next, we are over.'

'Yes,' she said very quietly.

'Are you going to leave me?'

'I'm going to find Tom and I'm going to be with him.'

'Is there anything I can say, or do, to stop you?'

'No, William,' said Annie. 'I don't think there is.'

Ethel trembled beside Annie. Every step was an effort. Going up the stairs was taking forever and Annie was worried about the old woman. She was so cold. She rubbed the hand that she was holding, but the hand was like ice.

'Gerry will be wondering what's happened to me,'

Ethel said. 'He'll be looking out of the window, watching out for me.'

'I know,' Annie said. 'I know.'

'He hates to be apart from me. He says he needs me to be close so that he knows where I am.'

'Do you want to stop here for a little rest? That's right. Catch your breath, Ethel.'

'Don't be too hard on William, will you, dear. In his own way, he loves you very much.'

'I know he does.'

'He was never very good at showing his emotions. But then some men are like that, aren't they? I'm all right now, Annie, I can go a little further.'

They reached the top of the stairs and stepped onto the landing. Annie heard William go into the kitchen; she heard the click of the lobby door. 'Do you need the bathroom, Ethel?' she asked.

'No, thank you. I just want to see Gerry. He's waiting for me. I miss him so much.'

'I know you do. This way. I'll put on the light. Wait here a moment, Ethel, let me turn down the bed for you.'

From downstairs she heard the strains of the concerto winding up from William's study. She heard the study door close.

'Isn't it cold,' Ethel said. 'Hasn't it turned cold all of a sudden.'

'You'd never know it was summer.'

'But that's England for you. Always lulling you into a false sense of security.'

Annie reached down to switch on Ethel's electric blanket. As she smoothed the undersheet, the music followed her into the room and wrapped itself around her. It pulled and pushed at her, it tugged and strained as if it were trying to tell her something. William had the volume up loud – too loud, Annie thought. It would wake Elizabeth. Annie felt the music vibrate through her; she felt it in her heart, she felt it was becoming part of her.

'Here you are, Ethel,' she said. 'You sit on the bed, gently now. Is that all right? I'll lift up your legs . . . there, you make yourself comfortable. Now I'll cover you over.'

And the music grew louder and louder. Annie looked at Ethel, but the old lady seemed oblivious as she lay back on the pillow dreaming she was in the arms of her dead husband. Annie reached across her to turn on the bedside light and the music billowed up; it was drowning her – and suddenly she knew what was going to happen.

'No!' she cried, and she leaped up, raced out onto the landing. '*No!*' she screamed. 'William! *NO! NO! NO!*' but the shot rang out before she had reached the top of the stairs.

ACKNOWLEDGEMENTS

With heartfelt thanks and love to Marianne Gunn O'Connor, Vicki Satlow and Pat Lynch. Thank you to the team at Transworld whose patience, good humour, professionalism and expertise saw this book through its various drafts. In particular, thank you to Harriet Bourton, Vivien Thompson, Bella Whittington and Joan Deitch. You are all wonderful and I feel so privileged to work with you. Cat Cobain read this first – thank you Cat and love to you and your beautiful family.

I'm writing this in Lacock village hall on a rainy Friday morning at a writers' session arranged by the lovely Rachel Brimble on behalf of the Romantic Novelists' Association's West Country chapter. The friendship of the writers in this group means a great deal to me. Also thanks to my Facebook and Twitter friends whose unending wit, support and animal videos are a godsend.

Love and thanks as always to my dear friends and to my amazing family. I love you all more than I can say.

In Her Shadow

Louise Douglas

Hannah Brown never thought she'd have a best friend like Ellen Brecht. Ellen is everything she isn't – beautiful, daring, glamorous and fierce. Growing up together in rural Cornwall, life seems perfect. But their idyllic childhood is shattered by obsession, betrayal and, ultimately, tragedy.

Hannah has tried for twenty years to forget what happened during that terrible summer. Then, one ordinary morning at work, she glimpses a woman who is identical to Ellen. Can it *really* be her? And has Ellen returned to forgive her – or to punish her?

'Enthralling and unnervingly absorbing . . . Our top holiday recommendation so far this year'
HEAT MAGAZINE

The Secrets Between Us

Louise Douglas

A chance encounter

When Sarah meets dark, brooding Alex, she grasps his offer of a new life miles away from her own. They've both recently escaped broken relationships, and need to start again. Why not do it together?

A perfect life

But when Sarah gets to the tiny village of Burrington Stoke, something doesn't add up. Alex's beautiful wife Genevieve was charming, talented, and adored by all who knew her. And apparently, she and Alex had a successful marriage complete with a gorgeous son, Jamie. Why would Genevieve walk out on her perfect life? And why has no one heard from her since she did so?

A web of lies

Genevieve's family and all her friends think that Alex knows more about her disappearance than he's letting on. But Sarah's fallen in love with him and just knows he couldn't have anything to hide. Or could he?

A mesmerising novel reminiscent of Daphne du Maurier's *Rebecca* – a passionate love story and a haunting page-turner that will keep you gripped to the very last chapter.